THE................
PALACE
GROUNDS
PRESS

TM

The Man Who Walked Backward Down the Na Pali Coast

Stephen McMillin

This story came wholly from my imagination and although many threads of acquaintance, experience, and situation have raveled there, the final output is entirely fictional. Any resemblance of the characters in this book to real people is purely coincidental.

THE PALACE GROUNDS PRESS
To order this book please visit:
www.themanwhowalkedbackward.com
or
www.thepalacegrounds.com

ISBN 978-0-9790615-4-7
ISBN 0-9790615-4-7

First Printing   November 2006
Cover Layout By: PrintmediaBooks.com
♻ Inside pages printed on recycled paper

Photo credits:
Cover photo of trail used with permission of HawaiiWeb.com
Photo: ©1999 – 2006 HawaiiWeb.com
Sunset photo on front cover used with permission: Vincent K. Tyler
Hawaiin LandMark Images http://www.hawaiianphotos.net/VKTylor.htm
Back cover Kalalau Sunset used with permission: Scott Tylor

Acknowledgements:
Thanks go out to my editors, Vidya Frazier (petal), Beth Bruno (stem), and Sabrina Dalla Valle (seed). Also thanks to Peter Coleman at PrintMedia Books for keeping the ball rolling. Thanks to my brother Michael for being there, always. And to the others, who have come and gone but who never leave.

In memory of my mother,

Mary

Prologue

Looking back, I see now, I have spent too much time looking back. Memories bear fruit among the vines of those yesterdays. There also blossoms a peculiar truth on that plant; its harvest is measured most honestly, from petal, to stem, to seed.

As with all recollections, this story belongs to the past. Never before had I followed a trail so treacherous. Always, I had thought twice and in that second thought found solace. To have traveled with The Man Who Walked Backward Down The Na Pali Coast, it wrestles within me now, in a tenor vision, like that jagged green shoreline pounded by waves beneath a winter sunset. I allude to pinks and purples under a hibiscus sky; a lovely impeachment of reality.

Looking Back

the opening

The weather had changed overnight and I was at home watching clouds the day the letter arrived. Without warning, autumn had come to Venice Beach and the temperature had fallen with the season. It was not warm enough to go down to the water; even the Westside regulars were staying away, fearing rain from a suspicious, coal-grey sky. The boardwalk was empty, the tourists were gone, and the bums were trapped inside their cardboard hovels, muttering lines from Dylan.

When there is no work and all that is left is time, killing a little each day becomes a very important ritual. One weapon I used was to go to the row of mailboxes in the foyer of my apartment building to meet the mail carrier. From the window of my first floor apartment, I could hear her pushing her cart along the sidewalk, whistling a song under her breath. After its many years of service, the melody had been rubbed smooth but I could still make out the tune within the improvised bars. As I approached the boxes, the carrier looked in my direction with her whistling lips puckered but now silent. She acknowledged me with an imperceptible nod.

"How's it going?" That was the question I asked each day.

Cocking her head, she looked over the top of her four-dollar sunglasses. Her brow was deeply furrowed below the flat plain of a forehead that was the color of Nigerian topsoil. We read from a play. Always the same question, always the same reply.

"No complaints." It was a simple drama and the carrier read well. Her voice was blue and husky; the words floated out from her thick and rounded lips like helium mixed with honey.

Sticking to the script, I delivered my next line. "Got anything for me?"

Picking through the bundles the carrier sorted my mail out of turn. "Think I do." She handed it to me with a simple commentary. "Got some bills here—"

"Yeah." I responded without emotion. This was my character, forever brooding.

"—and— let's see— looks like I got a letter for you."

"A letter?" I asked. Something was wrong. These words were not in this scene. Perhaps she had missed her cue. "Yeah," I repeated, hoping she would pick up her line.

"Yep. Got a letter for you. Postmark is Hawaii." She smiled at me and raised her eyebrows. "Looks like a girl's writing. You got a girl in Hawaii?"

The carrier scrutinized me as she handed over my mail. The play had been disrupted by the invention of the letter; the script was useless. Snatching the letter from her hand, I retreated down the hallway. Over my shoulder I improvised an answer to her question. "Not that I can think of, but if I do, you'll be the first person to know."

Inside my apartment, I threw the deadbolt into place. Scouting the room, I looked into the red-eyed glow of my answering machine; the steady shimmer told me that no one had called looking for a photographer while I was out.

The awards that grace my wall reveal the fact that I am not just any photographer. The pictures I have taken memorialize with troubling certainty the existence of demons. Mine is a history snapped frame by frame with a mystic finger that does not belong to me as far as I know. The truth told by the film was witnessed through a viewfinder an instant before, by an eye that I would like to think of as my own. My photographs have brought me acclaim, so although my phone never rings, I am certain, my best work is yet to come.

Without undue ceremony, I dumped the daily harvest of junk mail into a brown paper sack and walked into my living room. Sitting in my broken recliner, I held the letter up to the light but nothing could be seen through the paper.

The envelope was wrinkled and with slight curve, as if it had been carried in the back pocket of someone's jeans. Grabbing a letter opener that was sticking out of a pencil caddy on the TV stand, I opened the envelope and looked inside. There was a sheet of paper lying in the crib. Grasping the edge of the paper, I pulled it from its harbor and unfolded the first overlay and then the second. In slow motion, a great flock of presidential parrots fluttered to the floor. Stapled to the paper were a cashier's check and a plane ticket.

The details of the letter were easy to digest. In large scrawling handwriting was an address, a date, and a time. The address was written below the name of a restaurant in Hanalei, Island of Kauai. The date was one week away. My redemption had arrived in the U.S. mail and miracles were beginning to happen in a simple format. After seventeen months of unemployment, I was going back to work, at my trade and in the tropics.

Placing the paper with the ticket and the check on the TV stand, I started to collect up the litter of hundred dollar bills. One by one, I laid the notes down, making a mark in my mind for every hundred and then each accumulated thousand. Reading the figure on the cashier's check, I settled back in my chair and took a deep breath.

On the table was five thousand dollars in a stack of one-hundred-dollar bills. The cashier's check was for ten thousand more. The ticket was round trip to Kauai on the day after Thanksgiving. Five days pay in advance for my standard rate of twenty-five hundred dollars a day plus five hundred a day for expenses. Expenses and first day's pay, all cash. Everything was in order.

Retrieving the envelope, I turned it over in my hands. On the back flap was the only hint of who had given me this commission and what the job would entail. In very neat writing that looked like a woman's cursive script were these words: **The Man Who Walked Backward Down the Na Pali Coast.** That was it. A Honolulu postmark and no return address. I put the envelope down and tried to think.

One thing was clear, whoever sent this letter knew something about me; I am one of those lame suckers who lives by his word and prays at a comic book altar of integrity. Some men in my situation would simply pocket the money and pretend it had never arrived. After all, the letter was not registered.

Whoever sent this letter, if they knew my financial straits, had great faith in my character. Whoever sent this letter lived with great faith, indeed.

walking backward

At a restaurant in Hanalei, I found the darkest corner of the bar and I sat there as still as a clown in a doctor's office. The quick descent out of the clouds onto the runway at Lihue had left my head reeling.

It must have been the third drink that did the trick. The liquor had brought on a dead glow and I was smiling mechanically, staring up at an electric fan that was spinning above my head. From the exposed rafters hung a fishing net that would never see water. The net was buoyed at its edges by several green, softball-sized glass balls, and draped down so that its webbed bellies rode just above the heads of the tallest customers. Within the net was some common sea life painted in bright colors to match the island decor.

Hanging from the walls, Polynesian masks stared straight ahead at nothing. Spears and surfboards rode side by side on a shelf behind the bartender but I didn't look that way. I was staring at the ceiling, thinking about the past.

I had been to Hawaii once before on a commission. I had gone with my wife, who is my ex-wife now; we had called it a honeymoon. The honeymoon ended early one morning at the top of the Haleakala crater.

Viewing the sunrise from the summit of this volcano had become a tradition on Maui, a spiritual requisite for the new-age crowd who vacationed there. For some reason, my photographic agent thought that I above all others could capture the true essence of this tropical satori.

My job was to snap a few large format shots of the evolving sunrise from the upper rim of the crater and for that purpose I had brought a camera that morning. After a few minutes standing in the darkness, my wife excused herself and headed back to the car. "Stay outside as long as you want," she said, seemingly unaware that guilt is like a twin brother to me. As dawn began to light the sky, I set up my camera, but I couldn't stop thinking about my bride sitting in the gloom, watching me through the fogged window of the tiny Japanese rental car.

Numbed by the cold wind that blew across the lava plain and up the crumbling ramp of the cinder cone my hands rested on my camera. Above the hollow black summit, wispy clouds tore off in cottony shrouds; they rose angelic and folded into themselves like cool meringue. Footpaths traced the floor of the cone and disappeared like pieces of thread strung over the spouts and spills of the ancient eruption. Suddenly, somewhere on that plain of glassy black rubble I saw my life passing by in a world without my beloved.

Driven by this hellish vision, I broke down my equipment, stowed it into its cases and rushed back to the car. Inside the vehicle, I received a warm hug and then a kiss. My nose was too cold though and pushing me off she ordered me to drive.

It's a little hazy now but I think when we returned to our room we rubbed tanning lotion onto each other and made love for an hour on the flowered bedspread until we slid ourselves unstuck. We spent the remainder of the trip lying on the warm sand of the hotel beach. The equatorial breeze was delicate on our skin but that is all I remember of the trip, except for a pineapple that was perfectly ripened.

Before long it was time to go home but I still hadn't taken the pictures. Amid the tropical bliss was a gnawing concern that I could not pack away. At three-thirty in the afternoon on the day before our departure, I rolled off my beach towel, mumbled some excuse to my wife, and drove back to the top of Haleakala.

The air was cool and pleasant on the upper slopes of the volcano. Driving with my windows open, I watched as the island shrank below me; the far shorelines stretched into the blue-eyed ocean. At the parking lot on top of the extinct crater, I turned off the engine and waited.

It was a perfect afternoon for my task. Clouds surrounded the entire volcano like the brim of a hat shoved down hard over its pointy head. At five o'clock the sun started to fall toward the horizon and I began to take pictures. The colors were miraculous, pink backdrops fell across the sky while spears of sunlight shot out from the sun at graduating angles. As twilight fell, the island was wrapped in the golden, fleece collar of King

Dusk. In awe, I snapped two hundred frames.

And so began the paradox.

When I delivered the photos, my agent was ecstatic. The product was masterful. He would have no trouble selling the pictures. He got on the phone and he raved. And the pictures sold. One photo became the cover of the March issue of *Far Travels Magazine.* In a stationery store I picked up a greeting card and there was one of my pictures with a poem across the afternoon sky telling of the wonder of the morning sunrise and the magic of the new day dawning. I won top prize in a national photo contest. For a moment, my new career stumbled forward, but when my marriage fell apart I began to drink and heavily. Soon, there was no trace of my former life to examine or latent talent left to speculate upon.

What I learned from this experience is that the past represented in my photographs holds reference only in how I allow the subject to be defined. If I take a picture of the sunset and say it is a sunrise, decorum protects my honor and allows my dishonesty to retain its validity. Let's say for instance, I take a picture of a fallow field somewhere in the Central Valley of California, near Sacramento. Unless you are the farmer who tills that ground and sows its furrows, you would not know the difference if I told you that the photo was of a field in Nebraska near Lincoln. The green hills of Kauai look much like the green hills of Southeast Asia. And to the static eye of a single reflex camera, a man walking backward down the Na Pali Coast was going to look just like a man walking down the Na Pali Coast frontward.

Somewhere in my recollections, a chapter either long or short came to a close and I motioned for the waitress to bring me another drink. She took a drag off her cigarette and headed my way. Looking around I saw one of the carved tribal masks staring at me angrily so I glared back at it real tough. That's when I saw him at the rail of the bar. There wasn't one thing in particular that made him stand out but I was certain he was my contact. Studying him closely, I searched for clues.

The man was small and his stature was handicapped even further by a bend in his shoulders. His bones were wrapped in wiry muscles that stuck out of his shirtsleeves. His pant cuffs were rolled up almost to his knees. Leaning against the bar, his nipples hit the molding and kept him from sliding down to the floor. He was wearing worn out sandals on wide callused feet. His blue jeans were tied up with a piece of rope and his plaid shirt was white where his bony shoulders had rubbed through the weave of the fabric. To me, he looked like a sea hobo who had fallen on bad times.

A rough sailor's beard hung down in a half moon below his chin. The hair on his head and his beard were reddish with grey brindle. Both his manes were wild and uncombed. He had a crazy look to his face and he did not smile. He stared at the barkeep with his crooked lips tucked over protruding teeth.

Since it took less energy to sit, I stayed that way and watched the old sea dog in a mirror on the wall behind the bar where the liquor was lined up. Finally, the waitress sidled up to the little man and spoke close to his ear. She motioned with her nose in my direction. Standing, I swished the last of the Blue Hawaiian around the bottom of my glass and throwing my head back, I finished the drink. Pulling a pair of Ray-bans from my shirt pocket, I strapped them onto my face and weaved forward.

a cuf a coppee

Reaching the bar, I hung on without shame. My mind was flooded like an estuary. It was full of storks and pipers and all sorts of other long-legged, stalking birds. There were clams shut up in their stony shells in the black muck of the bottom and brine stains on the high banks of the shore. The tides flowed in and out in spastic pulses. Behind the sunglasses, my eyes were twitching involuntarily. Only speech could break a spell cast this deep but the first sentence was straddling my throat with a vowel dug into each side of my esophagus. My only chance was to keep it simple.

"Hi. I'm McDonald." I burped and my head jerked back.

The little man studied me maliciously until the silence became excruciating.

"Marlie," he finally responded. "Buy me a cup of coffee, would ya?"

The request caught me off guard.

"Sure, Marlie. Not a problem."

The little man stared at me through eyes that swam in pools of past defeats. His face betrayed a time worn fear, that long drawn out fear that turns very easily into anger and bitterness.

"So where is my client?" I inquired.

Again he waited until the pause was tortuous.

"He's at the end of the road with the others. He doesn't come to town anymore. Hasn't been here in three years."

"The others?" I asked, trying to turn the conversation in my direction.

"Yeah the others." He leaned on the counter and watched me in the mirror between the rows of bottles.

"How many others are there?"

He talked to my reflection and ignored the question.

"He wants to be back in the valley tomorrow. Did you bring a good pair of walking shoes?"

Using a different tactic, I kicked off my courtesy and answered him without a ribbon.

"Sure. Hi-Techs. They're in my bag." I motioned with my head at the two bags parked at my feet. "What am I expected to furnish as far as supplies?"

"Nothing. Everything you need is in the Valley. And I'll carry your bags. All you do is take the pictures. You got that?"

"I can handle that."

Catching the waitress' attention, the little man ordered two cups of coffee. He was one of those look over the rim and take a sip kind of coffee drinkers. When he lowered the cup from his lips, tiny drops of the liquid were stranded on the branches of his bushy mustache.

"Kona." He said without emphasis. "There's no other coffee like it in the world. You can taste the wind blowing down the slopes of Mauna Kea."

I took a big gulp and swished it around in my mouth. He glanced at me with his eyebrows creased.

"You in a hurry?"

"No. We're in Hawaii, right? It's lay back time."

"Kauai, sport. Hawaii is the Big Island. This is Kauai. And over there is the wettest spot on the face of the earth." He pointed with his chin in the direction of the front door and the lush green mountains beyond.

"See that ridge over there, chief?" He was quickly relegating me into the realm of the unfamiliar noun.

"Uh-huh."

"Back of that ridge is a swamp that is nothing but a dishrag."

"Dishrag?"

Marlie glared at me.

"Yeah, brother. Just a big green sponge stuck in a valley up there at the mouths of seventy flash flood rivers. When that sponge has sucked up all the water that it can drink, what you'll see on that ridge is eleven waterfalls jumping like lemmings onto the plain where the poi fields are. When it rains like that the big creeks overflow. That closes the bridges on the main road. You getting the idea, mister? Changes the entire feeling of the place, just like that." He snapped his fingers sharply.

Whether it was the coffee working me over or whether it was his omen and the deliberate crack of his fingers, I felt a change coming over me. The world, which had receded into a low fog inside my head, suddenly grew very clear. When I removed my dark glasses, bright sunshine as sharp as a pencil point stuck me in the eyes. The distant mountains shone with an emerald green brilliance while beside me, Marlie stood like a cartoon whipping me right and left with his piss. I forced myself to think. Only danger made me feel this way and I wondered where this spontaneous pinch of fear was coming from.

"I'll take you up there after you finish the job if you want, junior. It ain't no place to go without a guide."

Knowing that he had me, Marlie continued his monologue.

"Don't worry. I don't charge nothin'. I don't care what anyone else gets to do their job. That's my home up there in those swamps. I can't go out on boats anymore except as a cook but stirring grub on a ship is the one thing that makes me seasick. That's the truth. The more it rains in that swamp the closer I get to my element. Is that hard to understand?"

"No, it's not. But what about Na Pali?"

The little man looked into the depths of his coffee cup. His demeanor seemed to be connected to the subject at hand and when he looked at me his mood had softened.

"Na Pali is a kitten, McDonald. Kalalau is a roller coaster and those cliffs are nothing but an amusement park." Changing the subject, he hardened again. "You still gotta be careful though. And remember, you just take the pictures and then you're out of here safe and sound. You got that?"

"You're making it pretty clear."

"Good."

"So?"

"So The Man walks backward down that trail just like a baby coming out of its mother's belly. All you do is watch him through your glass. When the Fates talk, you listen and you push the button on your camera." He took another sip and put the cup on the counter. "But I don't have to tell you your business, do I? You get the picture."

"That's what I do, Marlie. I get the picture."

"So listen to me, then. Do what I tell you and you'll stay out of the quicksand."

"Aye-aye, captain."

The little man stopped cold. "Around here, that's a strong climbing vine. Watch what you're saying when you talk. *Kanaka* don't give grace to *haoles* even if they're too dumb to know they're being stupid. Keep your mouth a step behind your brain and you'll stay around long enough to spend all that money you're getting paid. Am I making sense to you?" The little guy had dressed me down for all occasions.

"Yeah, I guess so. Makes sense to me." It was impossible to hold my composure under this onslaught.

"Don't stutter either, son. That and a shell necklace are nothing but a sucker's badge on this rock. You catch my drift."

"Yeah, I caught it." I finished the last of my coffee and set my cup on the counter next to his.

"Let's go, then."

As we stood, I pulled the folded envelope from my back pocket. I wanted to gauge Marlie's reaction when he saw it and I was not disappointed. A subtle change came across his face. The worry lines around his eyes deepened and his mouth tightened into a valve that cut off any comment.

In his taut facial muscles there was a hint of sorrow hanging breathless on a thought of something lost. It did not appear that the money was the object of his concern. It was something that the money represented. But that was as far as I could take it. Extracting the shattered remains of a twenty, I set down a five for the two cups and a dollar for the tip.

"Leave her another dollar there, brother. She's a hemophiliac. Costs her seventy-five a bottle for the coagulant. I stole her a case once but that's long gone. They lock it up tighter now and I can't get to it."

I picked up the five and the one and put a ten in its place.

"Do you have money for a taxi or do you want to walk the three miles to the end of the road? It's your call, jack." He had already picked up my bags and slung them over his shoulder. The waitress was watching from the side of the bar.

"I don't care, mac. I don't mind walking."

"There's a cab waiting out front. And listen, mate. Don't call me Mac. The name is Marlie. You got it?"

I nodded.

And looking back, that is how the past began.

Walking Backward
Down The Na Pali Coast

the end of the road

The taxi pulled up on a circle of asphalt, and I stepped out of the car and looked around. The cul-de-sac was clotted with the tiny, red Japanese sedans that are so popular with the rental car agencies on the islands.

Beyond the bumpers of the encroaching cars and past the line of picture snapping tourists, there was a lovely beach. The ridge above the beach was lined with coconut palms, their fronds flag-poled on trunks that leaned windward. Above the tops of the trees, black, terraced cliffs, stair-cased into the lush green forest and disappeared into a powder blue sky. The beach wrapped around a promontory and vanished beyond the point.

The swell of the ocean was broken by a black coral reef sunken under a foot of water twenty yards off shore. The rippling waves came over this reef and tiptoed onto the beach in foam-armored ranks, twelve divisions strong. The reef had created a natural bay for swimmers and a perfect harbor for the fleets of Polynesian canoes, which had moored here in the past.

"What's the name of this beach, Marlie?"

Looking over my shoulder to see if he had heard me, I saw that my guide was still at the door of the taxi getting the change right with the driver.

"Key Beach," answered a tourist who had a cheap, digital camera hanging from his wrist. He walked right up to me but forgot that his belly had advanced before him and I had to step back to avoid being bumped.

"Isn't that right, honey?" he asked a woman who was evidently the other half of the bloated couple. "Key Beach." Although it was spelled *Ke'e,* the tourist pronounced it like Key West.

The woman walked toward us. "That's right, honey. Isn't it romantic?" They included me in their discussion as if I were a member of their pod.

"Who can tell though? There isn't a sign." The husband took off his baseball cap, which had HAWAII stitched across its crown. He wiped his forehead and squinted into the sun. "Do you see a sign?"

"No, dear. But it says right here on the map that this is Ke'e Beach." She still pronounced it Key.

By now, Marlie had finished with the cab driver and he was standing at the edge of the pavement. When I looked over at him, he shook his head and glared at me. Shrugging my shoulders, I stepped away from the tourists.

"Hell of a place. All these people and no sign. How are you supposed to know where you are if there isn't a sign in the picture?"

Not having received any input, the tourist couple maneuvered away from me and walked back toward their car.

Then I noticed, so close that I might have fallen into it in my next step, a broken bank of dirt where the sign had stood. Probably the last storm had washed it away, although it was hard to believe that the waves could come this high. Near the fissure, the bank fell nearly five feet down to the beach.

"What are you doing talking to the tourists, conch-head?"

Glancing around I tried to locate my guide. Looking down, I found him standing at my side, staring up at me. The swamp in my head was evaporating and I almost laughed when I looked at the little man. Outside the darkness of the bar, Marlie looked unusually silly. His pants were falling off his assless hips and the frayed ends of a rope that belted his trousers dangled almost to his knees. He had slipped on an old blue stocking cap and he looked out from under its brim trying to intimidate me. I smiled but did not answer.

"Come on, chief. The Man is waiting."

Stepping around the landslide where the sign had stood, Marlie hopped down a cut in the bank and shuffled onto the beach. He walked ahead, a crusty old sailor whose ship would never come in.

at first glance

Out in front, Marlie increased the distance between us. Taking slow steps across the sand, I waded through filtered light that slipped in through the jungle above me. From my position twenty yards behind him, I could see exactly where Marlie was headed.

On the west side of the beach, where the sand came to a point, a jetty built of black lava rose out of the water. It was a stew of large and small boulders, a six-foot breakwater planted at the wedge. On top of the bank, in the moraine of rocks, a clump of palm trees was growing in the thin soil.

Under the shade of these trees, a group of motley sunbathers were gathered. In front of the sunbathers, a tall, thin man with long straight hair to the middle of his back stood with his legs apart and his neck slightly bent. His gaze was fixed on a point twelve inches in front of his eyes where he was juggling three anorexic bowling pins.

Several yards behind the juggler three young women were sitting on a mat. As I closed the gap between us, the woman closest to me turned her head and offered up a smile that you would see in an insane asylum. Her mouth was open too wide, her eyes floated in glossy pools of uncried tears; her face, a perfect circle, was surrounded by thick kinky hair down to the nape of her neck.

The woman in the middle was a broad-shouldered blonde who was nearly invisible in the bright sunshine. Held up by her shoulders was a pair of large, flawless breasts. It was a comic strip chest impossible to cover even in the one-piece swimsuit she was wearing. This girl glanced at me quickly but did not smile. When she looked away, I knew I had been cased.

The third girl on the mat was a common looking brunette who was more attractive than her face might allow. She had the aura of the girl next door, that special someone your mother would love to see you standing next to in a wedding album. She didn't bother to look at me. She was concentrating on the juggler.

At that moment, as I was stepping up to the mat where the women were sitting, I saw The Man Who Would Walk Backward Down The Na Pali Coast. He was standing near the jetty about twenty feet from the group with his back to everyone.

Beside my client, wearing a tiny Speedo was a short man with a round stomach who had a bamboo flute in his hands. When I looked in his direction, the round man raised the flute to his lips with a reflex that was conspicuous. His eyes were cocked to the side so he could spy on me. The man puffed up his chest with a large gulp of air and began blowing into the instrument. Out of the pipe came a screaming arpeggio of notes. As the flute player blew his discordant melody, I saw that he was signaling The Man by raising and lowering his eyebrows and rolling his eyes in my direction.

Having reached the mat where the women were sitting, I remained aloof. I knew that I would fare better in future bargaining if I let my client come to me. The Man stood with his back to us. When it was clear that I would not pursue his audience, the flutist gave another signal with his eyebrows, this time with a more intense message.

As I watched, The Man took a step toward me, backward. Once he got going, he approached at full stride with his back facing me. He was tall and broad shouldered. His black hair fell onto his neck in thick locks, which bobbed gently as he walked. He was wearing a grey muslin robe that went to his ankles. Watching him walk, I was taken by the poise with which he moved. His legs were hidden beneath the robe so it was impossible to see the mechanics of his gait. However, I did notice that he was wearing sandals, which were visible at the hem of his outfit. His stride was so graceful that instead of walking on the ground he seemed to be floating through air. As he approached his head fell back and he laughed good-naturedly.

"McDonald," he called out with the pomp of a party host. Taking three more backward steps, The Man stood in front of me. He did not turn around, however, and his back remained facing me, so to speak.

With the last of the tidal bore sloshing around inside my head, I was pushed into action. Standing in front of him, I addressed his back, which seemed logical at the time although thinking about it later I am not sure why.

"McDonald here." It was trite and I wished that I could take back the words even as I was saying them." You must be The— Um— my— uh—."

"You can call me anything you like, McDonald. You can call me heaven or earth. Call me the four winds of tomorrow. Call me the straight one. Call me reason or rhyme. My name is unsaid. My name is unchanged. The word means power. The letters are TMWWBDTNC. Anyhow, I am the one you seek."

I had to listen carefully since his voice came from around the edge of his body. But even listening carefully it was hard to translate the madness of his pronouncement.

"Glad to meet you." I stuck out my hand but since he was standing with his back to me he didn't see the offer.

All of this was a little strange. But of course it was only a job. Brought up in California at the end of the sixties, I was familiar with this type of turn-key spirituality and it did not put me back one inch. Stepping around The Man, I positioned myself so that he had to look at me. Our eyes met across a sympathetic chasm. My paw hung in mid-air like an hors d'oeuvres tray. He gazed at me with a mildly quizzical expression, one eyebrow slightly suspended in a dark brushy arch.

"You can call me John." The Man had spoken.

One of the women coughed loudly and I could feel surprise emanating from the followers. On the mat, the girl's nudged shoulders unconsciously. Out in front, the juggler dropped a pin. He reached down and grabbed it but when he resumed juggling, his pace had quickened.

Next to John, the flutist dove into a series of high-pitched musical lines, his face lifted to the sky. In the trees, the screaming melody was answered by calls from the Amakihi, Omao, and creepers that flew deeper into the jungle.

"John. All right." I grabbed his hand and clutched it lovingly. "I'm Peter. Peter McDonald."

"Glad to meet you, Peter," he said and pulled his hand away.

I continued to plow forward.

"It's going to be great working with you, John. I have forty rolls of slide film and four thousand frames of black and white." Falling into my shtick felt good but my client did not seem interested in my spiel.

As I chattered, The Man looked beyond me toward the water. Where the surf petted the shore, a man and a woman sat in a small rubber kayak. Tied to the kayak with a thin nylon rope was a child's inflatable pool that was decorated with tiny stone-age children who walked toward each other from all directions.

The Man had his own navy and this was his fleet. The admiral of the flotilla was a tough but sweet-looking surfer type who didn't smile but appeared friendly. He was not tall and he was young. I guessed that he was from Florida, since he was too thin to be from the West Coast. His sun-bleached hair rode down to his shoulders in thin strands that framed a handsome face. His reddish beard nearly matched Marlie's in shape and color except for the old sea dog's brindle. The girl who sat beside the surfer was cute with a wholesome countenance. She was thin-bodied and small-chested. Brown locks curled to the sides of her cheeks so that her face appeared to be floating below thick brown clouds.

The captain of the kayak kept an eye on us with an expression that barely alluded to attention. His girl sat in the craft fully disinterested, which showed that she knew what it took to be a good first mate. I made a mental note to befriend them at my first opportunity. After all, one thing is certain, allies are mandatory when dealing with men like The Man.

introductions

"Rick, can you handle his bag?"

The Man had called out to his admiral from across the sand. Moving slowly, the surfer stood from his skiff and ambled up to where we were standing. Facing John's back, Rick looked at me and nodded a greeting. His expression did not change.

"No problem. But the tide is starting to change so we need to get going."

"Will you make it to the valley tonight?" asked The Man.

"Before you even get close to Honokoa."

"Four hours?"

"About three and a half."

"Are you prepared for the worst?"

"Sure. Lynn got us some chili. Two cans of that good O'Malley's with red beans."

"Play it safe then and pull your own weight."

"Will do."

The sailor walked back across the sand carrying my duffel bag and my shaving kit. Loading my gear into the child's pool, Rick prepared to sail. With Marlie's help, the rubber kayak was pulled into the surf with the plastic pool in tow. The woman picked up a small metal paddle that she used to steady the craft. When he was up to his hips in water, Rick heaved his legs over the edge of the kayak, grabbed a second paddle and began to cut the water with great strokes.

As we watched, the boat and its aquatic trailer left the safety of the bay. It slid along the shoreline, and into open water. Within minutes they were far enough out that we could no longer see the bobbing of the craft in the swells. There was only the silhouette of the kayak and the two bodies rowing easily with the current.

"Bon voyage," The Man said under his breath.

"How far do they have to go?" I asked. The Man turned toward me but when he realized he was facing me he seemed uncomfortable.

"As the crow flies it's about eight miles. But Rick is clear, and when you are clear to your purpose every distance is the same." This pronouncement was made with great vigor as if he were attempting to speak above his unease.

"I suppose so."

The Man kept his back to his followers and I kept an eye on his face.

"Well, Peter. I think that introductions are in order."

The Man began by stretching out his arms as if he were presenting the world to me.

"Brothers and sisters, I want you to meet Peter McDonald. He is our photographer and he comes highly recommended. He is to be considered one of the family from now on."

The six followers stood stiffly listening to The Man but they seemed embarrassed.

"First, I want you to meet Joe. He's our resident juggler and sleight of hand specialist. He's also an expert carpenter and can build mazes that are nearly impossible to escape."

Joe smiled at me warmly outside of his juggler's trance. His face held all of the innocence of a farm boy. Reaching out with his thin arm, he offered his hand.

"Hi, Peter." This was as complicated as Joe would ever get.

Nodding toward the flutist, The Man continued, "This is Ron. He makes flutes out of valley bamboo and he can play up a storm." Ron smiled a crazy-eyed grin but he did not look at me directly and did not offer his hand or any word of greeting. I was happy when John moved on.

"Now for the girls. Oops. I mean the women." The women smiled when John corrected himself. They walked toward me in a line.

"This is Judy."

Judy was the one with the asylum shining in her glassy eyes. Her joy was so pronounced that I suspected her of harboring some deep-seated pain. She looked at me with a wide grin that was hard to examine because it exposed her entire soul. I smiled back but I felt intimidated by the depth of her presence.

"This is Caren. She's a newcomer. She's only been in the valley a short time. You two should get to know each other."

Caren was the invisible blonde. When I looked at her I felt my male instincts take a deep breath. She was a knock out, with the face of a South Dakota Swede and the animated body of a celluloid sex queen. When she winked at me my libido broke into a trot. John continued.

"This is Shannon. She just got out of a Thai prison for smuggling gold into Bangkok for a Chinese businessman. We're glad she is back with us."

Shannon gave me an odd look as she was introduced—a smooth, sad expression. She was prettier than I initially thought but I recognized in her downcast face and upward glance a begging for sympathy. With her pout, she was coming on to me, inviting seduction, demanding attention, and wagering that I would fall for her act.

I told myself to watch out for this one and said a quick hello in a matter-of-fact manner. She scowled coquettishly as I looked back at my host.

"You met Marlie already, so that's it."

Like a bizarre family portrait the followers looked at me, each with their unique expression. Ron, of the rolling eyed smile. Marlie flatly disgusted by the courtesy that was being wasted on me. Joe smiling like the last of the corn had been harvested just before the rains; Judy riding cross-town with her beaming, over ripe smile. Caren winking again as I began to fall for her like rain, spattering over her ankles, up her legs and points north. Shannon gave me her sultry stare, which made me wonder how long she had been in jail. Off to the side stood The Man, gazing at the ocean, his back to his flock.

The feeling of this place, magnificent yet tinged with peril, and the curious mood of these people, had created a strange sensation inside me. As I examined this clan of oddities I could not help but wonder, just how much trouble was I going to get myself into this time?

setting out

The day was moving on and when Marlie went in the direction of my camera bags I assumed that it was time to begin the journey. Stepping forward, I jostled the old sea dog with a low elbow and beat him to my gear by two steps.

"You want me to carry your bags or not, skipper?" Marlie stopped abruptly and dug in with his voice.

"Is it time to go?"

"That's right, champ. If we don't get out of here soon we won't make camp before nightfall. You don't want to get stuck on that trail in the dark, I'll tell you straight."

Stooping, I reached into one of my bags and took out a pair of Nikons. Holding one in each hand, I looped their straps over my neck and twisted a wide-angle lens onto each of the boxes. One of the cameras was loaded with color slide film; in the other I had vaulted a roll of Tri-X black and white.

Shoving my finger down on the triggers, I checked the motors to make sure they were operating correctly. By the time I was satisfied, the rest of the group was milling around waiting for a sign. The signal came from Marlie.

"Let's move out, troops. Everyone goes ahead of The Man except for me and McDonald. It's six miles to Honokoa and we have to get there before dark. So we gotta keep a good steady pace and no stopping for nothing."

Ignoring the growing tension between Marlie and me, The Man turned and walked away backward. The followers went ahead of him and I walked off to the side. As we marched ahead, John veered in my direction and moving in close he spoke into my ear.

"Caren wants to help carry your cameras. It's a bright idea, wouldn't you say?" He smiled and walked past me.

Caren was the invisible blonde with the muscle man back. When I glanced at her she caught me at it and smiled. I returned the smile with a nod of appreciation but I held onto my cameras for the time being.

The group made its way to the cul-de-sac where the trail officially began. At the edge of the asphalt a new contingent of tourists had replaced the old. These newcomers were lined up in the same well-formed ranks as the last pack, taking pictures of the beach, then returning to their cars without stepping onto the sand.

At the head of the trail, there was a painted plywood sign mounted between two brick pillars that were covered by a small gabled roof. This sign was the starting point of the 11-mile, Kalalau Trail. A crooked, green line painted on a map of the northwest coast of Kauai was the route we would take and Honokoa, a red dot situated halfway to the Kalalau Valley, was our first destination.

The Kalalau Trail was the favored trail for hardcore hikers in Hawaii and the most traveled by backpackers. The Sierra Club rated it a nine on a scale of ten, which meant that it was tough. The Trail had the added attraction of being entirely unpredictable. Because of the rainstorms that battered this leeward coast, it was impossible to guarantee a fair weather trip. The cliffs along the trail had a tendency of falling away in the middle of a squall, leaving hikers stranded in the valley until the rain stopped and the forestry crews could come in and make repairs. There was no reasoning with this strip of earth. If you decided to hike the trail, you did so by a set of rules that was not your own.

As I studied the sign, John began to speak with his back to his audience.

"Thank you all for being here today," he said, sounding very formal. A quiet murmur of 'you're welcomes' was an invitation for him to continue. "We have a long row to hoe this afternoon so I will make this short and sweet." A murmur of acceptance rose up from the group. John cleared his throat before he began to speak again.

"We live in troubled times. But a spirit guides us, so we will be safe. There are people in the world who would like to pull the wool over our eyes. But the spirit allows us to see beyond the illusion. There is no reason to believe that the spirit is different today than it has always been. Behind us is the future. That is as it should be. You are witnesses to this day. The magic of the journey will remain with you forever. Keep this in mind, and to this moment, say good-bye, forever."

When the speech was finished I half expected an 'amen' but instead Marlie simply waved his hands forward to get us moving. The followers went first, all except the little sea urchin, who stayed in the back eyeing everyone menacingly.

As we started down the trail, it suddenly occurred to me just how strange this trip was going to be. What would it be like when The Man squared his shoulders and looking back took his first step down the Na Pali Coast? Slowly the wheels began to turn and reality became unreal. The Man stared straight ahead, behind him, and stepping forward, backward, with his arms swinging at his sides, he began to Walk Backward Down The Na Pali Coast.

ancient walls

Swallowed into the gullet of the jungle we walked through a world of shadows and half-light. Amid the filtered cry of small birds we took a path that ran parallel with a wall that was constructed of black lava rock stacked three feet high and two feet thick. The contrast between the dark green of the jungle and the ebony rock made each of the colors more vivid. The trail ran straight but the wall took a turn and disappeared into the trees. Twenty yards farther ahead, it reappeared and crossed the path at a right angle. We topped the wall and followed the path up an easy slope.

Since he was walking backward and I was behind him, John and I faced each other, which took some of the oddness out of his strange mode of travel. When he wanted to talk, all he had to do was lift his face and we could converse. This was the one advantage I had found in his backward approach. Even as I considered this, John raised his head.

"Peter, this is an ancient native wall. It was built by Polynesians over a thousand years ago."

It was a firm wall but I doubted that it was a thousand years old. On the point, barely visible through the trees, were the gables of a small modern house. I suspected that the wall led to its door.

"The people who lived here were very wise. They existed within laws. If they broke those laws, they were punished."

I remained silent which allowed him to continue.

"Look closely, McDonald. See how they built protective enclosures around those trees. The natives knew that if the trees died they were doomed."

The Man looked at me with a righteous expression. The trees were no more than fifty years old I guessed, but I did not convey my reservations to him.

"These are drainage channels they built to take the water off the hill."

Indeed, running into the grass from out of the foliage, were shallow troughs paved with black lava flagstones. These culverts drained over the path, down the bank, and toward the ocean. Again, I guessed the work to be no more than fifty years old.

On a long bend in the trail, we took a path that led up a steep hill. The jungle thickened and I came to a large outcropping of black pumice buried in the ground. I had been walking with my eyes down, watching the trail so that I did not fall. When I raised my head, The Man was nowhere to be seen. Backtracking, I returned to the place where I had lost him. I stood there looking around stupidly, feeling bewildered.

"McDonald! Hey, Peter. Up here."

Looking up, I saw John standing a dozen yards ahead of me on another trail that cut toward the tall cliffs.

"Did you lose your way?" he called out.

"I didn't see where you went," I answered as I started up the hill.

"Better stay close to me. It's easy to get lost."

He waited until I had caught up before he resumed his backward stride.

"Come on," he said, "I'm going to show you the *heiau*."

"Hey Yow?"

"Hey E Ow. Ancient Hawaiian altar."

Even though he was walking backward it was hard for me to equal his pace. Running forward, I closed the distance between us by three steps.

"How far is it?"

"Not far. Follow me."

He continued to march backward.

"Is this the beginning of the trail?" It was everything I could do to keep up. "Maybe I should get some more film."

The Man stopped dead in his tracks so that I almost ran into him. We were face to face. His eyes were opened wide and he was staring at me with great intensity.

"Listen close, McDonald, I am only going to say this once. We are going to an altar and that means spirits. I know you've done some portraits; I've seen your work. But you can't take a picture of something that is all around you. Now, get a hold of yourself, Peter. This is serious business."

There was nothing I could say so I clamped my mouth shut. The liquor had worn off and I could feel my face tingling beneath the skin of my cheeks. When John walked away backward, I followed, still trying to keep up.

ti for two

At the top of a steep hill we entered a clearing where the crumbling tiers of a naturally formed pyramid rose sixty feet above us in twelve black-skirted terraces. Looking up the slope, I knew immediately that this was the real thing—an ancient and primitive place of worship.

Using the terraces as switchbacks we climbed the pyramid until our progress was halted by a low cliff wall. In the face of this wall was a large cleft that was pockmarked by a multitude of small, natural indentures. Standing beside the cleft, John reached down and pulled two broad leaves off a short bush.

As he worked, I looked over the roof of the jungle toward the beach. From this vantage point, I could trace where a village had once thrived with vibrant life. When I turned back, John was facing the altar holding the leaves that he had gathered.

"What are those leaves, John?" I asked and stepped in closer to see what he was doing.

"*Ti* leaves," he said. "Very powerful medicine."

At the time, I had taken it as another of The Man's eccentricities. Only later would I find out the correct spelling of the word.

"Here, pick up a rock and wrap it with this." He handed me one of the leaves. "You will need protection to walk into the Valley."

Many of the pocks in the face of the cleft were filled with these leaves and their stony parcels. The shrouds were in different stages of decomposition. Some of the rocks sported crisp leaves stained with fresh plant blood. Other rocks were swathed in the brown hides of dried leaves. Someone must have recently passed this way because at the base of the cleft were several incense sticks with smoke curling off their tips. Taking the leaf, I chose a rock from the ground, folded the leaf around it, and looked for a hole. The Man set his dressed stone on a fist-sized shelf near the center of the niche. I set mine down among the others. His chore complete, John turned around so that his back was to the altar. When he spoke, his voice was clear and quiet.

"Do you want to know why I walk backward, McDonald? And why I want you to photograph me walking backward down the Na Pali Coast?"

The smoke from the incense curled over The Man's shoulders and rose in twisting fingers around his face.

"Should it make a difference to me, John?"

"It might later, Peter."

"Then maybe you should tell me."

"It's simple. Take a guess."

The pungent smell of jasmine filled my nose. I did not like this game but I did not know how to remove myself. Speaking slowly, I tried to stay in control.

"Well, I would say that you want to walk the trail backward like you are coming out of your mother's belly."

The Man laughed.

"I told that one to Marlie. He is such a copycat."

"So, why did you hire me, John?" It was a question that I actually wanted answered. "Fifteen thousand dollars is a lot of money to pay for pictures of you walking down a trail backward."

"Do you think I'm blowing this out of proportion, then?"

"My job is not to think, John. My job is to take pictures. But tell me what you have in mind and I'll tell you if I think it's a waste of time."

"It's not a waste of my time, Peter." The Man paused and then continued. "If I tell you why I walk backward will you promise not to tell another soul?"

"I give you my word."

The Man looked out across the ocean, his eyes focused on a place far away. His back was to the altar and to the rocks, which lay in their niches, serving their aspirants the only way they knew how. Somewhere below us the followers were on the trail waiting. The trees of the jungle spread their arms around us. In a soft voice, The Man spoke.

"I walk backward because I do not want to forget."

A smile curled up at the edges of my mouth.

"You gave your word, McDonald. This is between you and me and the others."

"Not a problem, John. I won't tell a soul."

"You understand, then?" he asked in the same quiet voice. "There is nothing a person can do these days to be remembered. There are no new mountains to climb. No new oceans to sail. No virgin lands to discover. Every city has its name and every street has a sign. All we can hope for is the strength to never forget. That is why I walk backward. The others are like children. I teach them to find meaning in life. And how never to forget."

"That's considerate of you, John. But what exactly are you trying to remember?"

"I am not trying to remember anything, McDonald. I am trying not to forget. Do you understand the difference?"

"I guess." I am not sure if I shrugged my shoulders but I should have if I didn't. The Man continued.

"Do you see where you fit in, then? How you will help me?"

"Not really, John."

"You take the pictures."

"O.K. I take the pictures."

"That prove that I did it. That I walked backward and that I did not forget."

"Look, if that's all you need from me, then our relationship is solid."

"There is one other thing."

"What is that, John?"

"I want you to pray with me."

"You want me to pray?"

"Yeah, you know. For a safe trip, sunny days, anxious lovers."

"Listen, John. I might as well tell you right now, I am not a religious person. In fact, I'm an atheist. Is that going to get in the way of us working together?"

"No. Absolutely not. But pray with me, McDonald. It will help us form a bond."

"But there's no one for me to pray to, John. As far as I am concerned, it's just you and me here. "

"Try this, McDonald. Pretend there's a spirit at the edge of the forest and it is dying to hear from you. The lines are open. The spirit is waiting for your call. "

"Is this one of those 976 numbers?"

"No," he laughed, "it's toll free. There is a call center staffed by a million service reps. They want to hear from you but you have to call right away. It's like one of those television commercials where there is always an operator waiting."

It was obvious that the only way to end this conversation was to accede to his request.

"Alright. But the only thing I would pray for right now is a helicopter to take some aerial shots of that beach." I pointed back toward the gorgeous Hawaiian shoreline that lay at the foot of the hill.

"Let's try this prayer, McDonald. I made it up especially for you."

As I stood beside him, John fell to his knees on the rough ground, his back to the altar. Grabbing my wrist, he pulled me down beside him. Closing his eyes, he clasped his hands in front of his face. He was silent for a moment and then he began an incantation that I found impossible to follow. It went like this:

"Almighty vision, save us from calamity. On this day deliver us news that will make headlines. Allow us to edit freely and when our words have no meaning, give us their definition—."

In front of my eyes the world went flat. I turned my head to look at the beach while John continued to pray. In the distance I could see where the village had stood. On the spit of land behind the barrier reef the canoes would pull up and the sweet Polynesian women would come to meet their men returning from the sea. Out of palm trees coconuts would fall and after cracking them open the children would drink the milk from their shells. Now, a thousand years later, I was kneeling on their altar and praying to different gods. The ancients were gone and their spirits were forgotten.

The hike down from the altar was made without discussion. This gave me time to consider my next move. A creeping intuition was taking hold of me and I wondered if I had gone wrong accepting this job. The decision had been made based on a courage retained from my fearless youth. In those days, I had been resilient and jacked-up for the fight. The residue of that courage was no more than a delusion of fantastic powers which I could no longer assemble. This hubris clung to me like a shrunken sweater but there was nothing left to judge my current faculty except the memory of imaginary medals, rattling like tin cans against my sunken chest.

The more I thought about it, the more my intuition pounded in my ears as if angels were playing billiards inside my head for a buck a ball. My client, who had so regally lined the pockets of my favorite 501's, who had rallied me from the depths of my depression to help him in his quest to never forget but not necessarily remember, who carried in his spirit the lives of his disciples—my redeemer, The Man, was one hundred and fifteen percent crazy.

the trail

Back on the main trail, we reunited with the followers and resumed our hike. On the way down to the lower elevation, I had turned on an irrigation of shame, which brought back my fighting spirit. Walking made me feel better and my mind began to clear as I started taking pictures.

The trail was wet with run-off from a spring somewhere up the hill that used the path as a channel. The water pooled in low areas, turning the trail into a muddy bog which we simply had to slog through. Twice I nearly fell while running ahead trying to capture The Man in the chambers of my Nikons.

In order to take the pictures, I had to run ahead several steps—stop, focus, and shoot. Keeping ahead of John was not easy, especially since I was now trotting backward, looking over my shoulder at the trail in front of me, trying not to trip over rocks or step into puddles. He, on the other hand, never once looked back to see where he was going. He climbed confidently, feeling along the trail with his sandals, always aware of obstacles behind him, laying down his feet from toe to heel.

Immediately, Caren became a big help. When I was having trouble balancing on the mud-slicked rocks, she would put her hand under my armpit to steady me. When I needed to switch cameras she was there handing it to me when I reached out. Our relationship had become professional and there were no more winks. This allowed me to focus on my work, although as we ran and shot and slipped and repositioned, I couldn't help but peek. Her body was athletic, her chiseled hips the very definition of the feminine.

Half a mile up the trail, a clear view of Ke'e Beach was revealed through the trees. Up to this point John had continued to march backward without pause. The rigor of staying in front of him was costing me enormous energy. By the time we reached this opening in the jungle, I was winded. I looked at Marlie to see if we were going to rest. His scowl told me that he was reading my thoughts and that we would go on. Knowing that I was about tapped, I called for John to slow his pace so I could get a picture with the beach behind him and Hanalei in the distance. I pushed down the trigger of my camera and shot frame after frame until John had passed through the clearing. Finally, I had to stop to catch my breath. From this vantage, I could see the followers walking in the lead. In my mind these disciples were half the story. Clicking random shots of them added to my study.

Ahead of the pack, Judy was hiking barefoot. She caught me looking without my camera to my eye and smiled broadly from that crazy asylum which was firmly established inside her mind. Ron, the flutist, looked very serious, his short legs working the trail, his hands at his sides, his rainbow skirt billowing about his calves. His belly protruded over his belt line, which balanced him on the uphill grade.

Joe the juggler glided up the trail on his long legs with Shannon in front of him. They walked silently while Joe studied everything around him: the trees, the birds, and the sky. When we got to a rough part of the trail, Joe cut the leaves off an agave and laid them in a puddle. Shannon joined in, picking up a long stemmed papaya branch to sweep the path clear of any debris. When she saw a rock that might trip The Man, she reached down and rolled the rock off the trail or nudged it off with one of her feet. Aided by their effort, John walked backward with an air of accomplishment. They did not let him know that his trek was made easier because of their activity and he could not see them work because he was looking back at the place from where we had come.

After two miles, I could find no new angles so I let both of my cameras dangle around my neck. The trail dove beneath a towering magnolia and hugged a black and green cliff that rose skyward. Small waterfalls dashed onto the rocks above us and ran in rapids down the slopes. Relaxing, I let myself enjoy the run of the trail. When the group saw me surrender my vigil, they let down their guard. For the first time since I had joined them, I began to feel at ease. The sense of this place was heavenly, with its blue lyceum, lobelia, and wild gardenia. The air below the canopy was cool and fresh. Behind me, The Man walked backward. I could hear him coming over the trail as my mind went on vacation.

aloha honokoa

The sky above the jungle was growing dark by the time we reached the Honokoa Valley. At a clearing on a ridge above the final descent, I stopped and looked up at a sheer cliff wall. Tumbling off the moss-covered black lava at the mouth of the gorge was a waterfall, a hundred and fifty feet high. It shot out of a narrow slit in the cliff and spread conically. Six miles of hiking had made my legs tight and sore.

At Honokoa, I had expected to camp on a white sand beach where I could listen to the ocean striking the shore. Instead, we arrived at a soggy patch of ground with a fast moving stream running through it. At the first available plot of grass, I sprawled out to rest. Out of the gloom, Caren appeared with an armload of banana branches that she laid out for me and which I gladly crawled onto. She sat at my feet and unlaced my boots. Pulling them off, she massaged my feet, digging into my soles with the tips of her fingers.

"Lomilomi," she said quietly.

I lay back on the banana leaves and relaxed.

"Sounds like a member of the bologna family."

"It's a native word that means massage to relieve the fatigue of the trail."

I sighed and closed my eyes. Within moments, I was asleep.

"Hey, McDonald! Get up and bring your cameras."

I awoke with a start. Marlie was stooped over me, scowling into my face. Caren was gone.

"You don't get paid to sleep, do you?"

Rolling onto my stomach, I stretched out my cramped legs.

"My contract clearly stipulates that I get three R.E.M. periods in every twenty-four hours." My voice was muffled but Marlie was not interested in the fine print.

"Catch 'em later, lightweight. Let's move."

Slipping on my boots without lacing them, I reached into my bag and extracted a camera that contained black and white film. Reaching deeper into the bag, I pulled out a flash unit and a low light lens, both of which I attached to the camera. Feeling stiff and ill-tempered I stood and followed Marlie toward an open air building that was situated at one end of the camp ground.

The building was a government specs affair similar to what you would find in any state park, a basic twelve by eight-foot open rafter shed held up by six four by fours. The roof consisted of sheets of green corrugated plastic, which allowed light to come through during the day. The ground under the building was packed smooth from use.

An orange glow from a campfire coaxed a perimeter out of the surrounding jungle. Beside the fire was a tent, and in front of the tent was John, sitting and talking to a man and a woman who appeared to be together. John had his back to them but they were smiling at his back.

With Marlie behind me, I stepped into the light of the fire. The male component of the couple stood and offered me his hand in greeting. John remained seated.

"Hi. Dennis Fitzpatrick. This is my wife, Michelle." He motioned with his hand toward his female companion. The woman smiled, her face shining orange in the firelight.

"I'm—"

"This is McDonald," John finished for me. "He's my photographer." John made these two statements with all the effort it takes to fart after eating a Mexican TV dinner.

In most cases, I am not an overtly belligerent person but if John was going to treat me like an employee, I was going to be a menace. Besides, I was tired, my head was throbbing, and my throat was scratching around the desert floor of my brain searching for fluid. I was in no mood to take crap from a half rate holy man even if he would never forget my indiscretions. Digging in with my heels, I pumped up my wrath and let it loose.

"Yes, my name is McDonald. But you can call me captain, you can call me scout, you can call me flypaper baby. I am the hairy eyeball. I am—"

From the corner of my eye, I saw John looking at me with mild disgust from the corner of his eye. I could not help but smile. The couple stared at me with their chins slack, struggling to hide their confusion.

"Just call him McDonald. Sit down, McDonald. I was filling Dennis in on the details of my trek."

I sat and rested my head in my hands. My eyelids felt heavy and I fought to stay awake as the conversation continued.

"What a feat. Walking this god-awful trail backward. Michelle and I had trouble doing it frontward." Dennis laughed.

"Are you going to be in a record book of some sort?" Michelle asked.

"As a matter of fact I am," John replied. "Writers from several newspapers have contacted me about a syndicated piece on the trip. That's where McDonald comes in. His pictures will help me break the ice."

John looked at me with a benevolent smile.

"By the way, McDonald, Dennis went to school at USC."

I turned toward the couple.

"You went to USC, huh?"

"Yeah, I got my MBA there."

"I went to UCLA. You know, the University of Cons, Liars, and Anarchists."

Dennis laughed just enough but did not overdo it. That is the practice they teach business majors, how to steal everything in sight with perfect manners. There was no sense looking deeper, I had this guy pegged.

"That's a good one," he offered.

"Yeah, I thought so too. USC is a swell school. Great people, if you can afford to pay forty bucks for ecstasy."

From his seat, John watched me carefully, painfully aware that nothing could be done to stop me.

"You know what we call USC?" I continued.

Michelle was catching on and she sat back to defend herself. Dennis was intent on finding out the hard way.

"What's that, Peter?"

"The University of Spoiled Children."

Dennis had studied well. He laughed and slapped his knee.

"That's a good one."

I knew he had heard it before.

Beside him, Michelle tried to replicate his good humor but her face was turning into a grimace. John sat silently waiting for the foray to end.

"I just made it up." I chuckled for effect but I had used up all the energy I cared to expend on this diversion.

Any jerk with an MBA from USC was no friend of mine. These people would sell anything that did not explode in their faces and the public was nothing but a large basket of laboratory rats. I could see it already. By Christmas, the shelves of toy stores would be lined with The Man Who Walked Backward Down The Na Pali Coast dolls, their silly grins of rapture on plasti-formed faces, their backs to the tots teaching them to be righteous and how never to forget. There would be Big John bubble gum, a revelation in every stick. And books based on the life story of The Man as told to the author by a convert who knew an original follower who was actually on the journey into the Promised Land. The further removed from live witnesses, the easier it would be to embellish. It was a marketing opportunity of biblical proportions.

And here I was to take the pictures. Did I say that there was no God? Stupid of me. There has to be someone up there holding on to the joystick. Nothing as pointless as life could happen by accident.

Figuring I was squared away for Marlie waking me up, I decided to turn the conversation around and see if I could make amends.

"What do you do now, Dennis?" I asked.

"Michelle and I have an organic grocery store in Berkeley."

"Then you must be a Green grocer?"

I had to go easy. Dennis laughed but I didn't pretend for one moment that it was anything but a hopeless situation.

"Yes, in fact I am."

Dennis continued to smile as he looked over at John. "This guy's got a twisted sense of humor."

"As I said, McDonald is only the photographer. He joined us today from the mainland. He's freelance."

"I can tell."

Sensing my waning interest, John cut in and stole back the conversation. I retreated willingly.

"Would you like McDonald to take a picture of us as long as he's here?"

"You bet I would. This stunt is going to make you famous. I can always tell when someone has that special something."

As Dennis spoke, John stood, turned around, and grabbed Dennis's hand to help him up. Michelle was still looking at me with a beleaguered smile. Dennis reached down and pulled Michelle from her seat. Surprisingly, The Man did not turn his back to me. He stood next to Michelle and Dennis, facing the camera.

On my feet, I put my eye to the viewfinder and tried to locate my subjects in the gloom. Once I found them I moved them toward the fire so its light would glow in their features. It was the best shot I could get in the dark, on legs that tingled with spider flesh and a head full of sobriety. Taking my time, I focused carefully and spoke over the top of my camera. "Dennis, move a little closer to Michelle. That's better." As I gave direction, John looked into the lens with great anticipation, an immaculate grin spread across his face while I played him like a fugue.

"I want everyone to slide to the right. John, get on the other side of Michelle." I acted very serious and put my hand out to wave them from left to right. "Uhm. John, go back to where you were. No, not there. To Dennis' left. And Michelle, switch places. O.K." Fully satisfied with their positions, I changed my mind again and shifted John to the other side, put him back in the middle, and then changed Dennis from right to left. This entire process was done without snapping a shot. John held his smile determinedly while Michelle fought off that awful grimace and Dennis laughed in restless spasms each step of the way.

Finally when I could not play the game any longer without drawing a foul, I pushed my finger down on the trigger of the camera— "Hold it!" —and let it go into its mechanical drama— "Good." Every one point three seconds, the motor drive placed a frame in front of the shutter and every one sixtieth of a second, the mirror inside the viewfinder fell back into place so that I could briefly see my subjects.

To this day I keep a set of these photos in my portfolio as one of my most perfect character studies. As I watched and when I processed them later, something unique was revealed. In the fifty-two drawn out seconds that I held down the trigger, the facial expression of The Man began to twitch involuntarily. By the end of the roll, John was looking back at the strobing spots of the flash with such absolute rage that it was nearly impossible to recognize him from the first frame to the last. I lowered the camera and smiled.

"Should be a good one in there somewhere."

"Thanks, McDonald." John's voice was hissing out from between his lips. "You are a true artist."

"Can I go back to sleep now, John?"

"Yes."

Sometimes revenge can rot the teeth with its sweetness. I turned away from the fire with Dennis and Michelle thanking me graciously and walked back toward my banana leaf berth, giddy with victory but too tired to enjoy it.

When I returned to the site where I had been sleeping, I was surprised to find a tent in the space. For a moment I thought I would have to find a different place to spend the night. As I came closer though, I saw Caren sitting on a rock at the mouth of the tent. She smiled serenely as if she had been waiting there forever.

"Hello, Peter." Her voice was as sweet as the smell of the jungle flowers that permeated the night.

"Hi, Caren." I was tired and I did not feel like talking. She sensed my thoughts and opened the flap of the tent. Climbing inside, she motioned for me to follow. We sat together inside the nylon room, our heads touching the roof.

"More *lomilomi?*" Caren put a hand on my shoulder and rubbed my muscles with a delicate hand.

"Yeah, *lomilomi* me."

Before I lay down Caren slipped my shirt off, rolled it up, and put it under my head as a pillow and then began to knead my back. She had long, strong fingers and knew just where to throttle me to disperse the pain that ran the length of my body. As she worked my shoulders and down my back, my hips, and my legs, she leaned over me and I felt the brush of her nipple against my skin. As she pressed the front of her body against mine, I realized that Caren had removed her shirt.

Continuing to work on me, her touch penetrated each layer of my weariness and the press of her breasts on my skin excited me. Within this wonderful relaxation I pulled together enough energy to sit up, turn my head, and move my lips in the direction of her face. She let me kiss her without backing off but when I sat up with a more deliberate aim, she put her hand on my chest and gently stopped my advance.

"No, Peter."

That was all she needed to say. I lay back on my stomach and she resumed the massage. Leaning down, she whispered in my ear.

"Not so soon."

"You had me going."

"Peter, if you want me, that's easy enough, but nothing special is that simple. Relax now. There's always tomorrow."

Taking her advice and tucking away her promise, I let her touch disperse my aggravation. I didn't remember falling asleep, but when I awoke in the middle of the night, Caren was lying beside me and we were sharing a blanket. There was a flask of Vodka in my camera bag and since I was already awake, I decided to spike my sleep. Strangely, my mouth didn't respond to the liquor the way I thought it would.

Lying down, I reached out with one hand and laid it on Caren's breast. I tried to make out her face in the dark. Her features, framed in straight blond hair, shined in a patch of moonlight that came through the unzipped window. My touch did not disturb her and she continued to breathe, soft and feathery. In a moment I was back asleep and I did not wake up again until the morning filled the tent with a quiet glow.

When I awoke, Caren's arms were twined around me. Lying in the warmth of her embrace, I stared at the crisscross lines that ran through the nylon of the tent. In the waxing dawn, I felt more satisfied and content than I had in years. And I thought about what it was like to fall in love, when two people love together, not heartbroken or desperate or just plain beat.

And I wondered, what exactly was in store for me on this trip? Was I here just to take a few pictures of a Man walking backward down the coast of cliffs and crags of Na Pali or had I truly entered a realm of spirit that had no form but that would shape my future and fill my past?

red hill

We walked out of Honokoa in a damp fog. Up to our ankles in water, we crossed a narrow river that bisected the trail. It seemed like a bad omen to start the day with wet shoes and I cursed my luck. Although I had stolen a drink out of the flask before we broke camp, Marlie had rushed us forward, and my mood had become fractured and irritable. Seeming distant, Caren walked with the followers and we did not speak.

On the other side of Honokoa, the trail broke out of the jungle, onto a series of dry mesas where the trees were shorter; their limbs covered with blossoms the size of a woman's fist. Lining the trail were bushes with purple leaves and red flowers and giant grass with six-foot blades erupting from the dirt.

An hour into our hike we made our way onto the blunt boxer's noses that are the Na Pali coast. The trail followed the *palis* over headlands that were bare of trees. At times, as narrow as the width of a human body, the trail cut into the pitch of the hill. Here, the slope fell nearly six hundred feet of rocky decline into a foaming ocean that smashed relentlessly against the black lava shore.

In the distance were the towering walls we would soon traverse. Beyond these abutments, in the haze of the distance, I caught my first glimpse of the Kalalau Valley. A chasm opened to the sea, and judging by its size, I determined that there must be a generous beach there.

This morning Marlie was in the lead, but Judy was running point somewhere far ahead of the group. The followers were in good spirits. They walked together, talking amongst themselves. The farther we got from civilization, the more at ease they became. Or perhaps it was the closer we proceeded toward the valley. Snapping shot after breathtaking shot of The Man and the scenery around us, I relaxed in the sound of their laughter.

Out ahead, a cry rose through the noon air.

"Red Hill!"·

Around the next corner Marlie stood on a promontory, his hand shading his eyes. He was pointing with his other arm at the last hill before the great bowl of Kalalau. In front of us the ridges looked like the folds of a theatre curtain draped from the sky to the floor of the valley. When I looked again, the ridges appeared more like giant Polynesian statues.

"Are we there?" I asked Caren. It was nice to have an excuse to talk to her.

She smiled. "Almost."

At that moment, with Caren standing beside me, I felt myself looking forward to the time I would be spending in this paradise.

With their valley in sight, the group became electric. They stopped on the top of the ridge and mingled in a circle, celebrating their accomplishment. The women laughed and smiled while I snapped pictures. In the middle of the group, Ron played his pipe in a flurry of notes, Joe juggled five small rocks in his two big hands, and for the first time, I caught Marlie smiling.

Off to the side, The Man stood with his back to us and gazed at the trail from where we had come. I took several shots of him but I stopped when he turned his head toward me, letting me know he was aware of the camera. When we resumed our hike, John remained somber and kept his distance, as he walked backward toward his destination.

In high spirits, the followers navigated the last black cliffs.

From the top of Red Hill, a series of switchbacks led to the floor of the valley. From this vista, we could see the beach stretching in front of us. The waves came to shore from a half mile out; the ocean ran like quicksilver into the mouth of the valley.

The trail down Red Hill was paved with orange-red dirt packed down by the endless migration of hiking boots that had passed this way. At the top of the hill was a pasture covered with short grass that had been chewed to the roots by the feral goats that inhabit the island. Where the goats had eaten too deep, there were red gouges in the earth. Against these broken banks, a herd of the felonious critters scampered over a ridge and out of sight, bleating miserably as they retreated. Farther down the ridge the goats reappeared from behind a hill, bounding up the cliffs where more goats looked at us from the rocky ledges.

Taking a position near the edge of the meadow, John began to mumble and then speak out loud. The group looked on contentedly with the sun in their smiles and the blue sky all around them.

"We have arrived at our home where life is always ready to help us. The road is long but the light at the end of the tunnel shines bright. It is good to be here."

A resounding whoop went up from the followers. The Man allowed the celebration to die down before he continued.

"As I have walked, many thoughts have come to me."

The group sucked in their breath and became as silent as cloth.

"I have decided that the first thing we do when we reach home is to kill a goat for the feast tonight. Remember, by eating goat, we eat grass. So tonight, we eat goat."

Another cheer went up, this one even louder. Stepping in front to take pictures with the valley behind him, I saw that The Man was smiling broadly. Circling him, I pushed down the trigger of the Nikon. The Man loved it. He hammed without moving, the great panoramic valley at his back. As I shot, The Man began to walk backward down the trail.

Bolting forward, I jumped several bounds down the hill to get in position and stayed ahead of the others by only a fractured second. Turning, I shot, ran, turned and shot, and hustled several more bounds to refocus. Out in front, Marlie was showing off. Standing as tall as his little body would allow, he stared into the lens and played to the camera. He stayed a few steps ahead of the others, in the center of the action, his face prominent in every picture.

At the halfway point, the followers allowed John to move out front, although Marlie remained in the lead. In front of them, John swung his arms and walked backward down the red hill.

Seeing that we were close to the final decline, I decided to get a shot of

John leading his disciples into the valley. Taking a quick survey, I calculated where to station myself for the shot. On the axis of a switchback a high lump of grass rose two feet above the trail. From this position, I would be level with The Man when he was eight feet in front of me. Running ahead, I covered twenty yards with my cameras banging against my chest. The pad of grass was just big enough for me to stand on. It was perfectly situated so I could take a series of shots as The Man proceeded toward me backward. From my vantage, I could shoot as he passed and pivot as he made the turn.

Arriving at my grassy station, I climbed on top of the mound and dug my feet in. With my knees bent to steady myself, I put the camera to my eye. There was Marlie ahead of the pack. Judging quickly, I got an idea when Marlie would reach my position and pass out of frame. I dug in deeper.

Down the trail came The Man, his flock following behind. Of course, The Man had his back to the camera.

Peering through the lens, I saw Marlie growing larger in the frame. In ten more steps he was going to pass me. Marlie came on quickly with his head and shoulders now filling the entire frame. His eyes looked right at me through the glass of the lens. Suddenly, I felt his hand on my stomach, pushing me sideways off my perch, shoving me hard in the gut, attempting to dislodge me. With my free hand, I tried to brush Marlie away while keeping The Man in frame. The shutter of my camera was clicking but there was movement at the edges. My instincts took hold and fought to get the picture.

With a great sweep of my arm, which to this day I swear was only reflex, I swatted Marlie away from me with all of my strength. Shoving my eye into the cup of the viewfinder, I steadied myself. Here came The Man and his followers. Through the glass the composition began to shift. The followers looked at the place where the hill sloped toward the valley. Their expressions went from elation to shock. Pulling my eye out of the cup, I turned my head in time to watch Marlie rolling down the hill in a ball the size of a pile of dirty laundry.

Marlie tumbled through the sedge grass and the black brush. He kept on rolling until he came to a stop where the trail petered out. There he lay still. The followers were frozen. Everyone was silent. Except for me.

"Hey! Marlie. Are you all right?" I yelled down to him.

The little bundle didn't budge. It didn't attempt to untangle itself. After the seconds had become a minute, Marlie stirred. I could see his head because his mouth came open and he began to scream.

"McDonald. You crumb. You speck. What in the hell are you doing shoving me off the trail? When I pass, you allow. That's the deal."

"Marlie! I was trying to get a close-up. "

"You get out of my way when I tell you to. That's how the contract reads."

"Hey— Marlie— I'm just doing my job. That's what it comes down to."

"You twit, McDonald. I could call lightning down right now and burn you up."

Among the group of faithful, baited breath hung as heavy as a minnow on ten-pound test. The followers leaned forward balancing on their toes. All except John.

"What's going on down there?" John asked. He had not seen what had occurred because he had his back to the commotion.

"McDonald pushed me off the trail. The dwarf! I should roll him up and smoke him."

Marlie had stood and he was taking inventory of his body parts.

"Calm down, Marlie. This is our entrance into the Valley." John tried to soothe him.

"The shwank!!!"

Even I was becoming a little worried with this outburst.

Brushing himself off and without looking back, Marlie stormed down the trail. He disappeared into the brush at the base of the valley. He was out of sight before any of us moved.

Praising myself for holding my ground, I again dug in with my feet, pulled the camera up to my face, and fingered the trigger. Looking through the viewfinder, I picked out The Man as he stepped backward to continue his procession into the valley. Without thinking twice about what had just happened I picked my shots and depressed the button.

The Man was right where I wanted him with his followers a few paces behind. But when the entourage passed, as I got my well-earned close-ups, the dourness in the faces of the disciples was horrifying. As John came into focus, I saw the look of irritation in his face. Slowly, I lowered the camera from my eye and looked at Caren who had pulled in alongside me. I handed her the camera and stood silently on the mound.

Below me, The Man and his followers hiked onto the flat plain of the valley and disappeared into the brush. When they were gone, I stepped from my perch. Remembering to congratulate myself later, I finished the climb down Red Hill with a silent Caren. She did not give me a nod, a wink, or a whistle.

promised land

The bottom of Red Hill came none too soon. The altercation with Marlie had me feeling off-kilter. Into the valley I strode, my cameras around my neck, a gauzy film in my sobering mind. As I hiked, my eyes were drawn to a large snow white bird with a long, twin-speared tail that rode the air currents along the cliff walls. Several more of the birds appeared out of the green velveteen surface of the forest, disappeared into the trees, and reemerged again soaring.

"What kind of birds are those?" I asked Caren, pointing up to the heights of the pinnacled walls. It was my first attempt at breaking the ice and gauging the chill that had fallen between us. Shading her eyes with the flat of her hand, she peered into the depth of the valley. She apparently was not frozen solid.

"They call them Tropic Birds."

"That's original."

"You shouldn't have pushed Marlie like that." Caren looked at me with a serious gaze that was punctuated by a shallow furrow between her blonde brows.

"I didn't mean to hurt him."

"He's not hurt. Except for his pride."

"He has enough pride for two men his size."

"Be careful of Marlie. He can cause you problems. I'm serious."

"I'm only here for three more days," I said flippantly. "That's not long enough for Marlie to cause me any difficulties. This tribe or whatever you call them doesn't appeal to me."

"I'm just warning you."

She glanced at me with an air of resolve. My words had struck deep and I was sorry I had mentioned leaving. Her face was marked with an expression of pleading. Not with me, but with some thought that was crawling around inside her own mind.

"You never know, I may stay a little longer. It depends on what comes up," I offered, trying to redeem myself.

"You never know," she said.

Satisfied that the conversation had turned the corner, I maneuvered onto a different subject. "Let me ask you something. What are you doing here? These people don't seem like your type either."

"They're good people, Peter. They've dropped out of the mainstream for whatever reason and they're making a go of it. That's all. "

"What about John?"

"You'll have to figure that one out on your own."

"Alright," I said and then paused. "But you still haven't answered my first question."

"Which was?"

"What are you doing here?"

"The same as you, Peter. Just passing through."

"That's a little ambiguous."

"A little, yeah." She finally laughed, but I could still feel a distance between us.

The trail led into some low trees where water murmured in tiny streams hidden in the overgrowth. At a clearing, we reached the bank of the Kalalau River. Gentle ripples swirled over the surface of the clear stream. Using the largest rocks as stepping-stones, we crossed the narrow watercourse while hanging on to a yellow nylon rope tied between two trees on opposite shores. The rope was frayed from use and the stones that we stepped on were worn smooth by the thousands of feet that had traversed the river.

In the middle of the stream, trees grew on damp pads of dirt that had resisted the erosion of the current. At the back of the valley, a waterfall dove from the highest cliff, a shimmering exclamation point to the beauty that surrounded us.

"So where are you from?" I asked Caren as we reached the far bank.

Caren did not answer but I continued to prod.

"Let me guess. The answer is inside of you."

"You seem bitter."

"Alright then. You're from the Southside of Chicago and you came here to escape the crime and filth of the urban jungle."

"That's funny, Peter. I'm from South Dakota. I see why you and Marlie fight so hard."

"Another adversary?"

"Not me. I just tell it like it is. There, that's a hint for you." She smiled with closed lips.

We walked along the shaded trail, through the brush of the river bottom, and past a path that led both up and down stream. The main trail narrowed as we made our way up the bank of a dry streambed. To our right, waves crashed into the shore.

The ocean side of the path was covered with morning glory vines, their broad, heart shaped leaves crawling up any vertical object that was within their reach. Their petals were closed to the afternoon sun, twisty, pink fingers at the end of tendril hands. Against a low cliff, a thin column of smoke rose lazily and with as little interest, dispersed into the air. Indian summer rained down on us from Indian heaven and although it was November, the weather was warm and the day was gorgeous.

The beach was a perfect crescent of bleached, auburn sand. It stretched one quarter mile of perfection and ended at a gang of palis in the distance. At the close of the beach, was a short, thick waterfall where the forest met the sand. The beach followed the curve of the valley and we followed the curve of the beach toward the low fall.

At the back of the valley were three distinct canyons of two-thousand-foot cliffs. Inside this panorama, towering spires disconnected from the main wall shot straight into the sky. Curly green hair studded the lava chests of these conical spires.

Where the beach ended, sheer cliffs halted the Kalalau trail. This is where the small waterfall dropped into a rock basin. On a flat of land close to the fall, I could see tents of many colors and the slow movements of what I guessed to be happy campers.

dry cave

Halfway across the beach, between the river and the waterfall, a seven-foot bank led to a large pad of grass. Caren and I had caught up with the others and in single file we headed in that direction. When we reached the bank, the followers crawled up to the grass pad to rest. Marlie was nowhere in sight.

This was a heliport, Caren explained to me, used by the park service for emergencies. All activity and especially sunbathing, was forbidden. If someone was lying on the pad enjoying the day, the pilot would bring the chopper in low. The grinding air generated by the blades would negotiate a vacancy. If a tent was staked on the pad, the helicopter would flatten the tent to check its occupancy. If no one exited, the helicopter would descend, effectively blowing the obstacle out of existence.

The followers rested at the helipad only long enough to catch their breath. Moving again, we found our way to the main trail, walked through a camper's area, and trudged back into the forest. In the gut of a thicket, we passed a broken-down building that had a large rubbish pile in a ditch at its back wall. The garbage seemed out of place in this pristine setting. Further along, we passed a pair of portable toilets whose doors were jammed open with old cardboard boxes, tattered clothes, and broken camping gear. The debris rotted in the steam of the scat pit.

As we came over a rise, a short cliff appeared at the rear of the campground. We walked in that direction with John walking backward in front of us. The trail broke into a narrow clearing where a forty-foot wall of rock blocked our progress. The wall rose out of the forest floor nearly eighteen feet, then jutted another twelve feet forward before turning vertical again to continue its ascent. Inside the overhang was a large dry cave set up for housekeeping. The cave ran along the base of the cliff for a good thirty-five feet. The opening was in the shape of an eye, its lid round and high in the center. The eye's pupil, if it had one, would have been half buried in the ground. In the middle of the cave, smooth river stones charred black made a ring where a fire burned. A metal grill coated in black grease straddled the pit.

On the walls of the cave above the fire ring, natural ledges held the commodities of everyday life. On the low shelves close to the fire were bags of rice, spice bottles with faded labels, macaroni in a Bell jar, Lipton soup mix in foil packets, forks, cups and plates, and a shaker of salt set in a blue Chinese bowl.

In one of the crannies, a dog-eared calendar was opened to the previous month. This made me smile. There was a display of greeting cards unsent or spent, and postcards from all over the world. In one large nook were stamps, an incense holder with sticks of incense, and a small selection of books. There were beads and rings and prayers ripped out of bibles. Bits of string were tangled in with lengths of rope and sewing needles. Necklaces made from seeds were wrapped around boxes of tea. Clear plastic cups held pennies and nickels and dimes. More books sat on a long mantle, propped up with a square rock that looked like a piece of the cliff that had fallen down, been scooped up, and put in place. Empty first-aid boxes were filled with pencils and pens. There were sheets of unused paper and photographs of people who had come and gone. In the center of this mélange was a small, gold, laughing Buddha.

At the left side of the cave was an alcove big enough for a queen-size bed. Piled on the dirt floor of the alcove were sleeping bags and worn blankets. On top of this pile, a man was sleeping face-up with his mouth open, enjoying the last of the dwindling afternoon in his dreams.

While the followers took up positions inside, The Man stood, facing the ocean with his back to the cave and to his congregation. In order to assess the activity in the shelter, he had to turn around. He glanced over at his slumbering disciple. Betraying no emotion, John turned and was again looking at the ocean. After a moment, he sighed.

"Better wake Bill up if we are going to have that barbecue."

Walking to the alcove, Ron called in to the sleeper.

"Bill. Hey, Bill. Wake up. We're back. The photographer is with us. It's time to get the goat." This was the first time I had heard Ron speak and his accent flagged a New Jersey upbringing.

In his slumbers, Bill shivered. One of his eyes opened and he smiled at Ron. "Hey, man. What's going on?"

"John is back. It's time to get the goat."

Bill sat up and stretched. "Far out."

"Come on, Bill, I'll go with you to get 'im."

John stood with his back to everyone. The other followers remained silent.

Walking to the cave wall, Ron rummaged through a daypack that was lodged in a crevice. When he rejoined the group he held a small pistol. The barrel was thin and dark blue. It was probably a .22 caliber. Holding it at his hip, Ron looked over at Bill who was still sitting on his bed but smiling at everyone contentedly.

"Time to go get us a goat, Billy boy."

"A Bi-i-i-i-lly g-o-o-oat?"

My ears perked up as my hand instinctively reached for a camera. The followers smiled. Each sentence that Bill spoke he baahed out with the anthropomorphic voice of a goat. The high-pitched nasal sound was especially prevalent in words that had a vowel within their syllables. As it turned out, there were a lot of words in that category.

When Ron answered in this strange goat language, it became a contest. "A Bi-i-i-i--e-lly Go-o-o-o-oat, Bi-i-i-illly!"

"Bu-u-u-ut Ro-o-o-o-o-on. I-I-I-I-I ha-a-a-ve e-e-at-e-e-n soo-o-o-o-o mu-u-u-u-ch gooat, I h-a-a-ve ea-ea-ea-earned myyyy na-a-a-ame. And my-y-y-y n-a-a-ame i-i-is, Bi-i-ie-i-ie-i-ie-ie-ie--l-l-l-l-eeee-yyyy."

The final cry was shuddering, even for Bill. Shaking off the last of the comedy, he rose slowly and walked into the middle of the cave. He was shirtless and holding up his too-large-in-the-waist jeans with one hand. Stooping at the fire ring, he stirred the coals with a stick, pushed a teakettle onto the grill, and laid a few sticks in the embers. He did this in silence in one sweeping motion from nook to tinder, with a friendly smile plastered on his sleepy face. As he blew into the coals, Bill started laughing at something that none of us had heard, his eyes glowed at a cosmic joke. When the fire caught, Bill stood up with a cigarette dangling from his mouth, although I had not seen him light one or even pull out a pack. With a silly grin clutching the cigarette, he walked over and offered me his hand, which I gladly received.

"Hey. You must be the photographer."

"That's right."

"I'm Bill. You got a name?"

"Peter. Peter McDonald."

"Good deal, Peter. Welcome to Kalalau."

As quickly as he had spoken, without waiting for my response, Bill walked away from me, still holding his pants up. Cruising over to Ron, Bill took the pistol out of his hand with a curtness that made me smile. He wagged the little blaster around in the air and took a puff of his cigarette.

"This thing loaded?"

Ron held up two bullets in the palm of his hand.

"Two shots. That's all we need," said Bill snatching the cartridges from Ron.

While this scene unfolded, The Man fidgeted.

"Ron, Bill, come over here. The rest of you too."

Slowly, with the weariness of the trail reflected in our movements, we gathered around John. With that silly grin on his face and with the energy to do it, Bill was baiting John for a prank.

"John. What is happening, man?"

Bill beamed while John sucked air into one cheek and then the other.

"Bill?" John was staring limp-necked at his disciple although with his back to him. "Where in the hell is my goat?"

"Ah listen, John. We have a couple of bullets. It's more than enough for the job. I can shoot two goats with one bullet. I've done it before."

"That's true, Bill. But where is my goat?"

"The goat is out there somewhere, John. I just haven't killed it yet. It's up there on that hillside waiting for us to come and get him. I'm telling ya, he's just a waitin'."

It was clear Bill was delighted to have everyone returned to his company.

"How was the hike back in, John?" he asked.

"It was like the hike out rather than the hike in."

"Far out." Bill's face gleamed. "That means you aren't even here."

"Yes. That makes sense."

"Right. Far out. Hey look. I kept the fire going."

Bill chuckled again and smiled.

Everyone looked at Bill approvingly. John looked at me.

"Bill is the innkeeper here at the Aloha Hotel and Kitchen. That's his berth over there but feel free to rest there if you want. Make yourself at home."

"Yeah, really man, dig in. I got the bags all stacked on top of each other. That way I can watch them all at once." Bill smiled and wagged his head. Here was another ally. "Hey, have some tea. Or there's coffee. Anything. There's rice over there."

As he talked he swaggered back and forth, his chiseled grin mocking the sunny day to try harder, be brighter. He was not poking his good humor at anyone but he was not hiding that he was happy to be alive and living in Paradise. His face was thin and Nordic and decorated with a trim red beard. He was not tall, but he was lean and sturdy. He continued to smile as John addressed him.

"Anyway. Go get us a goat, would you? I promised Peter a feast to welcome him into the valley." John turned and pointed his long index finger at me as if I were a target. "If you bring back a nice fat one, he can take a picture of you with the kill."

"OK, John. I'm going after that goat right now. It'll be a goner in ten minutes." And turning to me. "We really have some goats out here. Damn feral critters are eating every blade of grass in sight."

John broke in. "By eating the goats we plant new grass and mix it with our mirth, which is boundless. In this way, we save the slopes so that our path into the Valley is not destroyed. We choose and what we choose is not to have choice." John once again spoke to Bill. "So go and get me a goat, Bill. Go with him, Ron."

With a final nod from The Man, the two hunters left the cave. They disappeared down a trail through the low scrub forest. At the same time, Judy left in the opposite direction with a day pack over her shoulder. Joe stood up and walked out of the cave with his juggling pins and Shannon right behind him. John looked toward the ocean, a forlorn expression on his face.

"I want to talk to you, Peter," he said, once everyone had gone.

"Sure." I accepted and took a step closer.

"I think this would be a good time for you to apologize to Marlie. You have a job to do but so does he."

A few minutes earlier, Marlie had entered the cave from the forest and he stood to the side measuring the situation.

Thinking quickly, I determined that my point had been made up on Red Hill. John was sanctioning a truce and there was nothing to be gained by keeping the feud going. Turning to Marlie, I saw that his little mouth had tightened and gone for cover under his beard. Taking a breath, I threw the words to him like a bone.

"I'm sorry about what happened out there" I said with as much earnestness as I could muster. "Sometimes it gets rough when I'm trying to get a shot. I did the same thing in Cambodia to a Khmer Rouge guerilla. He would have shot me except he got shot first."

Taking his time, Marlie relished the moment for all it was worth and when it was fully garnished he took the offensive.

"From now on when I pass, you fall out. That's the way the contract reads. If you have a problem with that, hire a lawyer."

"No problem, Marlie. But I don't think it will come to that."

"Alright then, captain, apology accepted."

Although I did not feel that I had done anything wrong, I gave in and let the little man have his say. I turned to John.

"That was easy," I offered with a slight shrug of my shoulders.

"As easy as pie," John offered as a way of finalizing the discussion.

"Right"

"Marlie, McDonald and I are going to the fall to have a talk. When Bill and Ron come back, get that goat skinned and soaked, would you?"

"Yeah, John, I've got a handle on it."

There was no doubt that Marlie could handle anything that came up. He was a tough one. Although I didn't care two licks about the little sea dog, I could see why John had picked him to be his protégé. Nothing got by Marlie. His eye was a sieve, picking out what could be used later. I had no choice. If I wanted these three days to pass in relative peace, I was going to have to play it low with Marlie. Although the jargon of power came from The Man, Marlie was running this outfit. Even after our reconciliation, he was eyeing me venomously.

With his final instructions delivered, John and I made our way out of the cave on one of the side trails. We walked face to face without speaking. He had walked out first, backward, and I was a step behind.

the fall

Under a canopy of oaks, we headed in the direction of the waterfall at the end of the beach. Inside the forest, I could hear the roar of the fall in the distance getting louder as we approached. At the foot of a cliff the fall landed in a bowl of rock that had been carved into a basin. From this pool a cloud of spray rose into the warm, blue sky of Na Pali.

Close to the waterfall, the path turned into a paved stone walkway. John and I broke out of the cover of the forest and onto a flat bank of ground that had several designated campsites for the tourists. In these sites was an array of two-person, domed tents that housed the initiates to the Kalalau Trail. The tents were the types that backpackers used, rip-stop nylon, red or blue being the most popular colors. The more seasoned trekkers had grey or buff green tents with maroon piping and ties. The drab tents were better constructed and showed a full dedication to the sport of hiking.

Milling about the sites, people were enjoying the day, each locked into their own particular diversion. The campers were sitting on blankets in front of their shelters reading books or writing in journals. Others were doing household chores such as sweeping their lots clean with papaya branch brooms or airing their sleeping bags on thin rope tied between trees. We passed the last camping space along the trail and stood at the base of the fall. John stepped down the bank and made his way toward some large rocks that bordered the pool.

The waterfall flowed through a trough that had been worn into the cliff and dove forty feet into the pool. Walking down the bank, I stood in the mist of the fall. At the front edge of the basin, the stream fell down a rocky stair to the beach where it became a wide and shallow delta that was sopped up by the sand and disappeared twenty feet from the waves. Stripping off my shoes and socks, I placed my feet into the water.

Under the stream of the fall, I could see a figure through the transparent slip of water. It was Judy, showering in the cascade, naked except for her jewelry, which consisted of bracelets, cloth anklets and rings on her fingers and toes. In her hand was a bar of soap and there was a bottle of shampoo set on a nook in the rock wall.

Her body was firm and tanned. Her breasts were large and full, with dark brown areolas. Her nipples were erect from the coolness of the water and stuck out of the horizontal surface creating tiny falls of their own.

Stepping out of the downpour, she poured shampoo into her hand, closed her eyes, and began to lather her scalp. She was smiling, listening to the symphony of the water over her skin. After stepping back under the fall to rinse her hair, Judy reappeared still smiling, her hair cleansed.

As usual, John was sitting with his back to everything in front of him but I was facing the fall, watching Judy taking her shower directly in front of me. Her feminine figure was holding my attention and reeling it in unconsciously.

John began to speak.

"So how do you like the valley so far, McDonald?"

Lost in my vision, I did not answer.

"Do you need more time to think?" he prodded.

"What was the question, John?" I said, distracted by the view.

"The question was: Do you need more time to think? We have all day."

"No, John. I don't need more time to think. Life is simple. I take it a day at a time. If something catches my interest, I go for it."

The wall behind the waterfall was covered with soft green moss. Judy was lathering herself with the bar of soap. She dipped back under the cascade and lay against the wall. When she popped out of the stream she wiped her hair back with her palms, her elbows in the air and all of her tight muscled beauty singing to my masculinity. Tiny beads of water fell from her nipples.

"But don't you want something in your life to last forever, Peter?'"

"Listen, John. I have child support payments that would choke a pig. That's as much forever as I want to participate in."

Judy was facing me with her eyes closed. Her body tapered down from her broad shoulders into the black delta hair of her pubis. Her muscular legs showed the strength she had gained walking the Na Pali trails.

"I can show you how to use your power to control of your destiny, Peter."

"Great. I'll try it quarterly when I have to send in my taxes. Sorry Sam, I am in control of my destiny and I have decided to withhold the two thousand dollars you requested. Will you settle for a briefcase full of Karma and a new issue of Dogma Bonds? The last time I checked, they were sky high."

"You're a funny man, Peter."

"It keeps my angst from showing."

Turning toward us, Judy grabbed a small towel and began drying herself. Leaning forward, her breasts drooped, pointing her nipples toward the ground.

"So you admit that you are not happy, then."

I turned to John in order to concentrate on what I was about to say.

"Look, John. I am as happy as I can be. Alright? So drop it."

I peeked out of the corner of my eye to watch as Judy stepped from the pool. She was standing in front of me almost touching John with her arm as she pushed back her hair. She smiled at me and I smiled back. Leaning over, Judy slipped her sandals onto her feet and retreated down a rocky bank that led to the beach. She reached the sand and walked away down the spit.

"Are you happy at this moment?"

Suddenly, from the blind side of the trail I heard a sound. Looking over John's shoulder, I saw Shannon coming over the rise and down the trail to the pool. As she reached the fall she stripped off her cloth skirt with one motion, removed her shirt and began to take the jewelry off her fingers. She laid the trinkets on the rock where Judy had last set the shampoo. Shannon stood naked, six feet from my eyes. She smiled at me and then plunged under the cascade of the waterfall.

"Yes. Basically."

I watched as Shannon bolted out of the downfall and wiped the water out of her face. When she opened her eyes she was looking at me and she smiled again.

"You are content with what you see around you?"

"Absolutely."

Shannon lathered herself slowly, starting with the calves of her well-formed legs and ending with her fingers cupping her small breasts with a circular motion. She disappeared under the water again and stayed there for a long moment.

"And you think there could be nothing better in the entire world than what you see right now?"

"No, John. This is it." I tried to pay attention to the conversation.

"So you feel that you are in heaven."

"Yes." Watching Shannon distracted me and I was not sure what I had said or how I had answered.

"And you never want to leave?"

"Not if I don't have to, John."

"But some day you will have to."

"Bummer."

"But if you follow what I say, you can have eternal life here in the Valley."

I remained silent and watched Shannon closely. I wanted to use all of my focus to narrow in on the skin and structure of her beautifully formed body. John was looking toward the ocean so I pretended to stare in front of me as if in deep thought. It appeared to be working because John retained a sober and studied expression.

"Listen, John. All I want out of life is to see the Giants win the series."

"You are a simple man aren't you, Peter?"

"My needs are very basic."

As Judy had done before, Shannon stepped out of the pool and stood directly behind John, who had his back to her. She smiled at me as she slipped her rings and bracelets back on. Naked as the Venus de Milo, she grabbed her towel and walked down the path that led to the beach. Once on the sand she stepped with grace, her hips shifting from side to side, pivoting just below her spine.

"But someday you will be judged." John would not let up.

"I was already judged, my friend. I lost my condominium, my furniture, and my car. I got the stocks and bonds and then the market collapsed. I only get to see my daughter on weekends and my lawyer's bill was more than I gross in a year."

"The trouble with you, McDonald, is that you live in the material world. Do you think I have all those problems? No way. I have streamlined my life. I am in control of my fate."

"I told you from the beginning that I wasn't interested in your preaching. If you want me to stay on through this commission then you are going to have to lay off."

"But we can move to the center of the universe, Peter. Life is what you make of it."

"Look, John, if you don't like living on earth, when the boys get back, why don't you take that goat popper they have and blow yourself onto a higher plane."

"You're a hard sell."

"I'm a no sale. You should save your breath and leave me off your roster. It will make us both—well, happier."

John stood and looked at the beach and the ocean in front of him. He did not appear to be disappointed with me although I knew he had to be frustrated.

"Distance lends enchantment to the view, McDonald. Eternity is a long time."

"Not to my dry cleaner."

John started to walk away backward but he stopped a few steps away from me. Looking up, I saw that he had a smirk on his face.

"I just hope that you don't find the Valley too comfortable, my friend. I would hate to see you wind up in heaven, which you dread so fully."

I was not given a chance to answer. When he finished his admonishment, John walked backward up the trail that we had come down and in an instant he was gone. I watched his face as he receded from sight. On my rock, I seethed at John's righteousness.

This feeling of anger did not last long. My mind was taken from its indignant roost by the most unbelievable sight yet. As I sat there fuming, Caren walked over the rise of the bank. She casually stripped her hiking clothes from her body and waded into the pool, her radiance an aura around her.

"Take your clothes off and let me wash your back, Peter," she said.

The statement came out with such simplicity that I did not bother to answer. In a mechanical motion, I removed my shirt and stepped from my pants. Sliding my underwear off, I entered the pool.

The water was cool, but in the heat of the day, it was a perfect temperature. Taking my arm, Caren helped me to balance. Gently, using both hands to grip my shoulders, she laid me back into a baptism of water.

Underneath the falling stream, I felt the mossy wall receive my back as I laid against the solid, slippery surface. The fall pounded down on my head, and the sound of thunder filled my ears while the pulsing water massaged my muscles. Lowering my chin to my chest, I found that I could breathe in the space that opened in front of my face. It was nearly a minute before I resurfaced.

"That's something else," I exclaimed as I burst out of the water.

"Great, isn't it? Liquid lomilomi."

"It's almost as good as the real thing." I stressed the word almost.

Darting under the water, Caren came out brushing her blonde hair out of her face. She smiled at me and grabbed a bar of soap. Her hands became slippery with suds. Lathering her breasts she took my hands and placed them onto their fullness. She held my wrists and made swirling movements with my hands.

"You do me first, Peter," she said and I did not argue.

"Boy, that John is something else." It surprised me that I spoke of John at that moment.

"He's alright, but sometimes he forgets where his life ends and your life begins."

"How is he going to get to heaven carrying such a heavy load?"

"John's a little strange, but I like a little strange once in a while." She smiled and gave me one of her big winks. "What about you?"

While I rubbed the front of her body from her throat down to her hips, Caren washed my back over my shoulders. She turned me around slowly, lathered the front of my body, then pushed me gently backward into the fall. The suds were washed from my skin and my bath was complete.

"Let's head to the beach and see what's going on," she said.

With two steps, Caren walked out of the pool. A trail cut through a gully and I followed Caren to the sand. Above the beach were the palis, those noses that give face to this magnificent piece of Earth. In their shadows, the noses showed their flawed complexion, the mottled skin of a million years of wind and rain.

In the distance, almost to the helipad, I could see Joe juggling his pins. Shannon and Judy sat watching him. The sun had fallen nearer to the horizon and the color of the sky had softened. Caren was stripped bare and the radiance of her smile glowed all the way to her feet. Perhaps I had arrived in heaven; if so, I hoped I'd made my bed before I left home.

the beach

With the tingle of Caren's touch still on my skin, I followed her across the sand. Walking nude along the beach felt comfortable but I knew that my pale skin announced my amateur status. On the other end of the spectrum was Caren, her skin bronze, her blonde hair bleached from exposure to the high tropical sun; she was the absolute portrait of a beachcomber. On her feet were sandals, around her neck was a string of whitish beads that were odd shaped and shiny although unpolished.

Halfway to our destination two women in bathing suits were sunning themselves. As we passed they scrutinized us closely and I became self-conscious.

"Hey, Caren?"

"Yeah, Peter."

She was walking several steps to my side.

"Is it alright to go nude on the beach?"

"Why not?"

"Isn't this a state park?"

"Peter, you need to loosen up. You have your permit." She laughed after this last statement.

Near the helipad, two men and a woman were sharing a blanket on the beach below a campsite. The men watched us through their dark glasses, pretending to be looking straight ahead.

One of the men leaned over to talk to the girl. She lifted herself up on her elbows and looked our way. The man spoke again and the girl smacked him on the shoulder before she lay back down. In a moment, the two men followed her lead and lay back on the blanket, their hands sifted sand deftly at the side of their blanket.

"Hey, guys."

Caren greeted Judy and Shannon as we approached. All of them including Joe were nude.

"Hi, Caren," Shannon said. Judy looked up and smiled. Without breaking his rhythm, Joe turned around gave us a big grin and continued juggling.

"I'm glad that's over," Shannon spoke again.

"Yeah, the famous Man Who Walked Backward Down the Na Pali Coast," said Judy. As usual, a smile filled her face but she seemed more relaxed here on the beach with her friends.

"John has really gotten out there." Caren spread a towel that was big enough for both of us. She gestured for me to lie down beside her.

"It's one thing to listen to him on Sunday at the heiau but this is ridiculous." Shannon declared.

"The way he runs Bill around is disgusting. Everyday he makes him get a goat. It's always the goat." This was Judy and she rolled her eyes as she spoke. I was surprised to hear power in her voice. In fact, I was listening dumbfounded to every traitorous word they were speaking.

"You guys better watch what you say in front of Peter." Joe walked over to the group while continuing to toss his pins in the air.

"Why should we, Joe?" Shannon demanded. "John is acting like an idiot and I am sick of his crap."

"You don't have to tell me, Shannon, but you should watch what you say. Marlie will get on us if he thinks we're picking on John." Joe moved back out on the sand.

"What about when Shannon came back from Thailand?" Judy asked.

"Yeah! He told me that if I left again I couldn't come back. Like he owns the place. Not the last time I checked," Shannon spat out.

"Rick was pissed after John told Marlie to sell Rick's surfboard to buy that kayak. Rick had that surfboard with him when he came to the islands." Judy had come alive.

In front of us, Joe kept right on juggling but I could see that the conversation was making him edgy.

I finally spoke.

"It doesn't sound like you girls are real happy with your guru."

Judy looked at me with only the glimmer of her eternally ecstatic smile on her face. "This happens every time."

"What happens, Judy?" I asked.

"Everyone who meets us thinks we're John's disciples or something. But that isn't true. He keeps us off balance with his visions and proclamations, but it's all nonsense."

"Most of the things he says I can't even understand. He talks too much." Shannon added her dollop.

Joe was beside us again, still juggling. It seemed he could take no more of the vitriol. He let the pins fly into the air, caught them one at a time and plopped down next to Shannon. "You guys shouldn't be so hard on John. He thinks he's helping us."

"That's fine for you, Joe. He never asks you to do anything. And he never threatens you with expulsion." Judy threw this statement out.

"Have you even noticed how weird John is acting lately?" Shannon asked Joe so forcefully that it demanded an answer.

"He's the same as he's always been. But he doesn't hurt anyone. So what's the big deal?" Joe replied.

"Maybe not, but he's taking the fun out of living here." Shannon was emphatic.

"What about the hike we just finished?" Joe asked, "Wasn't that fun?"

"Oh whoopee." Shannon's voice was full of spite. "What about this business with the goats? When we eat goat, we eat grass. Gawd! Then he disappears up valley, comes back and starts spouting some newfound bullshit. I think he's flipping out."

Joe looked down at the ground.

"That's right," Judy agreed. "If he keeps on like this he'll end up in an institution."

"Maybe he needs help." Caren rejoined the conversation.

Standing again, Joe walked around his blanket. He made a thoughtful circle and ended up back where he had started. "We shouldn't forget there were times we needed John and he was there for us. I don't have to remind you of that. You remember in the beginning."

The girls looked toward the ocean where a couple of tourist boys were walking close to the water. The boys wrestled together, looking in our direction, trying to catch the girls' attention. The girls looked past them and for some reason, I felt vindicated.

"Not the stories, Joe! Do not start with the stories," Shannon exclaimed sarcastically.

"We have to decide what to do, then. Do we walk out on John when he may need us the most or do we stand by him?" Joe was showing himself to be the compassionate type.

Judy started right back in. "Last night when we were at Honokoa, John started hassling me again. He told me that if I didn't start acting happier I was going to have to leave the valley. He said I was making everybody uptight."

"That's really mean," Caren stated.

Although Joe had been playing the devil's advocate, he finally decided to give his testimony. "A few days before we walked out to get Peter, he told me that he was getting tired of me juggling all of the time. He said that it showed a very basic flaw in my character. He told me that I couldn't juggle in the cave anymore. That it distracted him. He said that if I wanted to juggle, I had to go to the beach where he wouldn't have to watch me."

"That's harsh," Caren managed.

Joe hung his head as he spoke. "I thought so too. After all, I was the first one to give him the time of day. When I came out to Kalalau three years ago, John was living up-valley, in a blue hale, growing pot to earn his plane fare out of the islands. I remember the rangers came and tore up his crop, took down the hale, and told him he was going to have to leave. I helped him carry his stuff to the dry cave. He hung out at the heiau for a month watching the whales. He was a mess. And this is what I get for my trouble?"

"Something's got to be done," Caren said.

I was completely taken aback by what I was hearing. Here was a rift as wide as this valley, dividing The Man from his followers. When the conversation flattened, I butted in. "If John is causing you so much trouble, why don't you leave?"

They looked at me together, all at once. On their collective face was genuine confusion.

"Leave?" Joe asked.

"Leave?" Judy repeated the question.

"Yes, leave. The guy sounds like a dictator. Why would you want to be around someone like that?"

"Leave?" Joe asked again.

"Right," I answered firmly.

"The Valley?" Shannon asked dumbfounded. "We like it here, Peter. It's nice. No one bothers us. We can do whatever we want. Why should we leave?"

"But how can you enjoy the valley with all these threats hanging over you?"

"Like Shannon said, we like the valley. We don't want to leave," Judy insisted.

"Yeah. We can put up with John if it means we can stay here." Shannon was dead serious.

The response was daunting and I went silent. My face was immobile, my arched brows had made a point that no one was hearing. Shrugging my shoulders, I lowered my brows and frowned with rubber lips.

"Just a thought," I said, trying to extricate myself.

"Leave?" Shannon said again to ensure that the conversation had ended.

Lying back on the blanket, I closed my mouth tightly so no more big ideas would come out. As long as I lay with my eyes closed, not thinking of anything, I could retain my sanity. Underneath me, I felt the earth move or thought that I did. My mind was storming. This was no place for a logical man and for someone like me it was murder.

sunset

When the sun was well on its way toward the horizon, Caren poked me with one of her long thin fingers. I had fallen asleep and I was dreaming about a man in a long black car who was trying to grab my daughter as she and I walked on a road near the lodge at Yosemite Park.

"We didn't put any suntan lotion on you."

Looking across my body, I saw that my skin had turned a deep pink, the color of a wad of spit chewing gum.

"Oh shit."

"That's alright. We have some aloe up at the dry cave," Caren soothed me.

I stood and examined my burned body. Putting away his pins, Joe came over and turned me slowly using the tips of his fingers.

"It happens all the time, McDonald. Tourists come in, first day, they toast. We've treated hundreds of them," Joe said in a grave tone.

Walking up the beach we crossed over to the helipad. There was a huge, thick tree that Joe said was an ohi'a tree growing at the edge of the pad. It hung over the sand, dropping its red blossoms onto the beach. My skin was beginning to tighten and I moved gingerly. Joe walked off the helipad and into the forest with Shannon and Judy at his heels. Behind them, Caren walked with me, patient and concerned. The shade of the trees blocked the sun and gave me some relief. Up a rise we passed the abandoned johns full of garbage and entered the mouth of the dry cave.

Kneeling at the fire ring, the girl who had been in the boat with Rick was skinning and slicing some type of fruit into a pot of boiling water.

When I walked into the cave, she took one look at me and whistled. When she was finished slicing the fruit, she stood and walked over to me.

"We've got ourselves a casualty, Lynn," Caren said. Lynn smiled which revealed age-lines at the corners of her blue-green eyes.

"Uh-oh." She gave the diagnosis calmly. "What happened to you? You have a run in with the sun?" Apparently, Lynn was the resident doctor.

Off to one side Joe and Shannon were watching me. On a small cloth pad near the back wall and away from the fire, Rick was strumming a guitar and gazing into space. He was plucking some song that sounded familiar but I couldn't pick out the tune. He looked up at me long enough to catch my eye, nodded, and looked away.

"Someone tore up the aloe by the fall. They took all of the leaves off," Lynn said.

"Tourists," murmured Rick, in time with the chords he was strumming.

"Luckily, I kept some here at the cave." Walking to the edge of the shelter, Lynn reached down and broke two spears off a low plant that was growing there. She snapped one of the spears in half lengthwise and handed it to Judy. She opened the second spear and began to dig out the pale green pulp.

Lynn examined my red epidermis as she applied the cool balm.

"What kind of insurance do you carry?" Lynn figured she might as well have some fun while she treated me.

"Blue Cross."

"We don't accept Blue Cross or Blue Shield."

"Workman's Comp?"

"Were you working when this happened?"   .

"In a manner of speaking, yes."

"Let me get this straight. You were lying out on a beach in Hawaii with three naked women and a juggler."

"That's right."

Lynn shook her head.

"If you don't have insurance, I'm afraid it's cash only."

"I seem to have misplaced my wallet," I offered, going along with the joke.

"Alright girls, strip him and see if he's telling the truth."

"He's already stripped," Caren said trying not to laugh. "But I'll search him."

While this melodrama was being enacted, The Man walked in from the side of the cave. As usual he had his back to us so he could not see Lynn and Judy plastering me with aloe but the women saw him and fell silent. At the same time, Rick lightened the strum on his guitar.

"It's almost sunset," John exclaimed, taking for granted that everyone was paying attention.

A jubilant holler went up in the cave but after hearing the incriminations on the beach, I was astounded.

"Is everyone ready?"

Turning his back, John walked into the forest with his disciples in front of him. Grabbing a camera, I followed behind.

Walking through the forest, I became aware that there was one main trail with many smaller arteries, which connected the campsites. The trail we were on went from the dry cave, across the main trail, and toward the beach.

For the first time, I noticed that there were goats standing in the shadows of the forest. They watched us intently and when we got too close, they scampered up a hill where they congregated as a group in the talus of the broken cliffs which marked the back edge of the campground.

The trail cut down an embankment and we rambled onto the sand as the sun fell to touch the tops of the breakers. Against the cliffs at the end of the beach, huge waves crashed into the rocks and exploded in an orange sharing of the setting orb. The sun disappeared behind the swells, resurfaced as the waves cycled, was consumed, and regurgitated again. As we looked on, the pumpkin hue of the sun's rays grew deeper and rose higher in the sky. The sun fought its demise gallantly, bobbing like a child's bouncing ball on fire. As the sphere was drowned again, the crests of the waves were silhouetted by the flaming solar backdrop. The sun was full, then cut in half, then disappeared and then was full again, dissected imprecisely by the heaving ocean.

At the end of Kalalau Beach lay the wild southern palis. These headlands faced the moaning trade winds and were washed by a constant deluge of rain running off of their higher reaches and battered at their bases by the Pacific. After a million years of abuse, these pinnacles had been worn down to their black, rounded skeletons. The palis that stretched along this wind torn coast were an inaccessible wasteland of barren rock, virgin except for the constructions of the *Menehune* who live in their last stronghold, Waimei. Also buried in this region are the bones of the ancient Polynesian kings, protected forever by the spirits of their subjects.

John had stopped half way across the width of the beach and I stood beside him. Dispersed across the sand in small groups, the followers watched the sunset drama, but John, his back to the ocean, looked into the valley. The sun took its final plunge under the surface and the clouds above the ocean began to change color and shape. The sky was filled with an orange fire in all directions.

"The next valley over is the Valley of the Lost Tribe," John stated to me quietly.

With his back to the setting sun, John studied the dark sky to the south where a cape of blue velvet was falling over the valley. Standing next to him, I watched as the orange sun was quenched of fire, the dispersion of its daily life transformed from orange into a pink and purple sky.

"You can get there in the summer in a kayak," John continued. "The beaches there are beautiful and secluded. If you stay a while, I'll have Rick take you over."

"Must be something to see."

"It's beautiful in that valley—very precious. When you are there, you feel like the first human to ever step on shore. It's like Na'iaa, the forbidden island." John cocked his head toward a jutting of rock off to the west a few miles off Kauai. "The hands of man have not ruined those places."

Without another word, John turned and walked down the beach backward. In this way, he could see the sky where the sunset was blooming in death for the coming of the night. Forgetting the display of colors for the moment, I watched John receding into the distance. An unsought clarity struck me as I gazed along his path.

It occurred to me that as long as John was walking backward, he could see what was happening in the world by looking behind him. As long as he moved, his vision was alive, so it was imperative for him to plod along sullenly, contemplating, forever looking back. This was his existence.

Lifting a camera to my eye, I zoomed in and snapped several shots. Perhaps in the mood of his face, in these moments of repose, I could find the key to his madness but I wondered, as I shot, when I had started to care. After all, this was only a job.

Into the fog of mist that lay on the shore, into the residual spray of surf, The Man walked backward. For a moment, he was lost from sight at a small dune. He reappeared and then grew indefinable. Far out in the distance I could see his outline walking toward the river. The night grew darker and cooler and I watched him without blinking once.

Finally, it was impossible to determine his form and I suddenly remembered that I was standing in the twilight, naked, with the shredded pulp of aloe on my skin, my body shining with a green tint.

"So, how do you feel?"

I turned and found Rick standing beside me, smiling right into my face.

"Alright, I guess. A little cold."

"That's a good sign."

Lynn had joined us. "You better get some clothes on your white ass before you get a moonburn."

"What do you take for a moonburn?" I asked.

"Lilikoi tea." Lynn was the doctor.

"What about goat? Do you suppose we'll have goat for dinner tonight?" I asked.

"No doubt." Lynn laughed her reply.

"And lilikoi tea?" I asked.

"Just take care of that skin, honcho. There will be plenty of time for surfing tomorrow." Rick winked at me before he walked away.

The group made its way back toward the heliport pad and into the forest. Under the ohi'a tree, I stopped for a final look. The roots of the tree had been exposed in the crumbling bank by the nibbling of the goats. I stood on one of the thick roots and gazed into the waning sunset. Patches of dark silver and deep blue-grey lapped up the last of the day's color. Venus appeared as a bright pinpoint of light studding the western sky. As I watched, other stars broke through the backdrop of the night and twinkled proudly.

Standing alone for the first time since arriving in the valley, I felt the majesty that existed all around me. A thought sprang up from a fountain of emotion that nagged at me from outside of the beauty I was beholding.

One step ahead of me was my job and the reason I was here. A step behind was the softening patterns of memory. In between was life happening without my help. The feeling of belonging in the Valley was erratic yet unshakable. Tight within this nut of mystery were the followers and The Man. For one final moment, I searched the heavens for a sign. Then slowly, I turned and followed the followers back to the dry cave.

aloha kitchen

A fire was burning in the cave when I returned and the smell of seared meat filled the air. From the grill, which was manned by Marlie, billows of grey smoke lifted up into the night. The goat had been expertly skinned, its carcass lashed onto a papaya branch that was too green to catch fire. Ron assisted Marlie by playing his flute with no apparent melody. Bill watched from the alcove, his previous exuberance replaced by a mood of depressed lassitude.

"McDonald, the goat has arrived," John called to me as I entered the cave. John was walking in circles backward. He was as excited as I had ever seen him.

"Bill killed the damn thing with one bullet," Marlie cackled as he turned the meat on its skewer. "He had to grab it by the horns and drag it down. Put up one hell of a fight."

From his cubby, Bill smiled dully.

The fire was built high and the meat dripped goat grease into the flames as it was turned on its spit. The addition of this oily fuel made the flames sizzle and burn brightly, projecting dancing light across the rock. Marlie spun the goat slowly and with great purpose. Under his iron face, I could see the perverse joy of his task oozing through.

"God damn hot fire." The glow of the flames shone red on Marlie's cheek.

"You should have seen Bill," Ron said, lowering his flute from his lips to tell his story. "He wrestled with that goat until it bled to death."

Vacating the alcove, Bill reached into the fire to light a cigarette that had appeared out of nowhere. Bill sucked in and exhaled lethargically.

"You sound like it took all afternoon, Ron. I just pulled him down and held him."

"Anyway, I wished that you could have seen it. Peter should have taken pictures," Ron said.

Hovering over the fire, The Man assayed the trophy with rapt appreciation. John leaned over Marlie to ask him a question. In a subdued voice, the grizzled sea dog spoke into The Man's ear and made chopping motions with his hand. He pointed above the roof of the cave and made another motion with his hand that appeared to define the process in which the remains of the goat had been disposed.

Straightening himself, John walked to the front of the cave, turned, and looked out at the forest. I stepped away from the fire and went to where Rick sat on a mat playing his guitar.

As he played, Rick looked at me blankly; there was no smile of affirmation, just the plucking of chords and the squeak of his fingers sliding across the strings.

"So, how was the trip?" I asked.

"It was alright." He spoke quietly. "It took us four hours. I used to do it in three on my board."

"That's a long swim."

"It's not so bad. If you move fast, the sea doesn't get a chance to change its mind on you."

"It must be pretty rough in that kayak."

"Nah." He pronounced this negative in a convincing tone and looked to see where The Man was before he went on. "So John told you about the Valley of the Lost Tribe."

"You've been there?"

"Oh yeah. I used to go there on my board."

"How far is it?" I asked.

"About forty minutes. It's just right around there." He pointed to the barrier at the end of the beach, where we had watched the sunset. This was where the palis erupted from the water to become the shoreline. The coast here was cut off from all but ocean going passage. "I would take you over there tomorrow but the currents are pretty strong in the winter. If a storm hits, you're stuck. Can't get back until it clears. It's creepy over there."

"What do you mean?"

"It's hard to explain to someone who doesn't know Kauai. There's akua and stuff. You know. Spirits."

By raising my eyebrows I allowed him to elaborate.

"One time I was over there and I heard women singing these songs that sounded like tribal stuff. I didn't look for them that night. A person can get killed walking the palis in the dark. The next morning I couldn't find a trace."

"Is the Valley of the Lost Tribe sacred like John says that it is?"

"I don't know about that. But I do know that there are bones over there."

"Really?"

"That's right. There's a big dune in the valley that's steep enough to surf down with the keel fin off. But bones started popping out of the sand."

Once again, I lifted my brows.

"No shit, man. We found arm bones and leg bones. The only ones we didn't find were skulls. I guess they buried them somewhere else. They must have been small people though. Their shinbones were about this long."

Using his hands, Rick measured out a space that was eight inches between his palms. "Like Menehunes or something. It's an old place for sure. There must have been a village there. Some sort of lost civilization."

"Humph." This was all I could come up with at the moment.

"John thinks there used to be a land bridge from Kalalau to the next valley over. His theory is that some creature ate away the root system of the bridge and it collapsed into the ocean. That's why John says we have to eat the goats. He thinks there's some connection between the loss of that society and the way the goats are tearing apart our hills."

"I don't eat much red meat. Do you think I'll like goat?"

"It's more than meat, McDonald."

"It's grass."

"Exactly."

This brought the conversation to an end. I made my way over to John who was standing with his back turned to everyone. I had to step outside the cave to face him.

"Hey, McDonald. Am I getting to you yet? Look at this spread."

"It looks great."

"Wait until you taste that lilikoi tea that Lynn is brewing." John was almost giddy.

It was a good time to change the subject and I did.

"What's the score from here, John? You've got me for three more days, counting flying time back to L.A."

"You just got here, Peter. What's your hurry? There's still a lot for you to see."

"Such as?"

"What about a steam tomorrow? Something to ease your weariness."

"A steam?"

"Yes. A native steam. We have a sauna built into the rocks down at the river."

"True native steam?"

"That's right. We pour water over hot rocks. When you get too warm, you jump into the river. It's the genuine article."

This was an invitation that could not be passed up and I had to admire The Man's ingenuity.

"It sounds enticing."

"Just don't think that you're going to be snapping a bunch of pictures."

"Why no pictures?"

"Peter, when are you going to learn that there is no getting a picture of the spirit that lives within us? This is the real McCoy. No pictures in the spa."

It seemed obligatory to negotiate, although I did so half-heartedly.

"Look, John. I have job to do. If there are spooks, I not only have permission but I have a prerogative to search them out."

"Did you give your parents a lot of trouble as a kid, McDonald?"

Luckily, John gave me an escape route. He stood and spoke to his followers in a booming voice. "Everybody. People. Listen. We will do a steam tomorrow morning to cleanse us of anything that is clinging to us from the outside."

A subdued cheer went out from the followers.

Walking back over to Rick, I leaned down so I could talk in his ear. "Where is my bag?" I asked.

"It's with the boat at the river, by the heiau."

"There is something in there that I could use right now."

Rick looked up at me with a smooth grimace on his face.

I leaned in close. "I've got a quart of Wild Turkey in my clothes bag," I whispered.

"No kidding." This changed everything.

"Would you get it for me if I promise to share?"

"Jesus, McDonald. I can't remember the last time I had Wild Turkey."

"Bring the bottle tonight. We'll deal with the rest tomorrow."

"Not a problem."

Setting down the guitar, Rick stood and walked out of the cave. At the edge of the firelight, The Man sat on a rock looking toward the ocean. His back was to the kitchen.

Night had moved into the valley and the interior of the cave was quiet. Only the crackling of the fire and the sizzling of burning fat broke the silence. The light from the flames and the dark of the forest danced together soulfully, a tango of reflecting firelight, shadow, and pitch black.

Above the fire, the roof of the cave curved outwards and cantilevered into an overhang that kept out the elements. Here, the light could not catch a footing and it was dark up to the sky where an audience of stars hung brilliantly. From behind the cliff, an ambience of white moonlight was beginning to glow over the ridge of Kalalau. At Honokoa, I had seen the plate of the nearly full moon hanging in the sky by an invisible thread.

For the first time since our ill-fated meeting at the Red Hill trail, and my apology, Marlie approached me to talk. In his hand was a strip of well cooked goat meat.

"Here, champ. The first piece is always for the guest. Tonight that's you."

Taking the meat between my fingers, I lobbed it into my mouth and began to chew. "Not bad," I said through greasy teeth.

"If it were bad, would we eat it, hero?"

Although the initial taste of the goat was palatable, the gristle became tougher the longer I chewed it. My next idea was to swallow it all at once but this approach nearly choked me. Setting my teeth on edge, I dug into the scrap and ground the sinew down to a manageable lump.

The feast started at this point, although Shannon was missing and Rick had not returned. The ritual was less complex than I had imagined. There were no incantations and no blessings. Marlie handed out strips of meat and Caren served rice on plates.

Grabbing a couple of hunks, Marlie made his way to where I sat with John and he handed me the pieces. The flavors of citrus and pepper were heavy on the meat.

"The goat is soaked in papaya pulp. It's the best meat tenderizer in the world," The Man stated with great enthusiasm.

"That's a papaya tree there, isn't it?" I had noticed this tree at the edge of the cave earlier in the day.

"Yes, but that's a small one. There is a big one up-valley. And mangoes too."

Marlie leaned into my face as I chewed.

"You like it here, don't you, mug? I knew you would."

He straightened up and walked away.

"It looks like you and Marlie are going to be friends after all," John said without looking at me.

"We'll see."

John's observation did not deserve more than this answer.

"We'll have goat again tomorrow, McDonald. They'll kill it early in the morning before the steam. That way the meat can soak in papaya all day long."

"Well. It's not prime rib, but it beats freeze dried stroganoff."

"Besides, McDonald, since all flesh is grass, we are not eating meat, we are eating grass."

As I tried to make sense of what John was saying, I saw Rick signaling me from the shadows at the side of the cave.

"I think I'll take a walk. It's a beautiful night."

"It sure is." John looked over his shoulder as I stood up to take my leave. "While you are out there, don't forget, you ate the meat of the goat so you will now be able to traverse the path without any trouble."

I looked down at John. "You have got to be putting me on."

"Not at all, Peter. That is another reason we eat goat. It helps us to pick our way up the path into the higher regions where we could not go before."

"Well then, if I'm not back before morning, I went over the back wall for eggs and bacon," I kidded as I stepped out of the dry cave.

"Try it, Peter. You may find that you are able to do things that you never thought you could do."

Nodding in my retreat, I walked out of the firelight and into the shadows of the forest. At the edge of the darkness, Rick stood with the bottle of Wild Turkey in his hand. The seal was broken and I could smell the sweetness of whiskey on his breath.

"Here's the bottle."

"Thanks."

"It's a good thing Lynn and I didn't know that was in there."

"You've got a point. I've never met a boat captain who wasn't rummy." I took a sip from the bottle and offered it back.

"Precisely." He waved away the bottle. "I've had all I want. I should get back to the cave."

"I'll be back in a while."

"Go down to the helipad. It's the best place to watch the stars. "

Instinctively, I knew the direction, take another drink and walk into the forest toward the pounding surf. Stopping at the abandoned toilets, I stole another sip and wandered forward. I ended up under the ohi'a tree gazing out at the surf nipping at the shore while I nipped at the bottle.

Turning my head, I looked up at the walls of the Kalalau Valley rising as smooth, black cutters into the damp night air. Behind the valley and on the rise, the moon toed the line at the Tropic of Cancer.

On the grassy knoll, I sat and drank alone for an hour. Small sips reinforced the warmness of the first drink. Finally satiated, I leaned against the bark of the ancient, spreading tree, thinking about no one, staring into nothing.

kalalau

It was a warm night and falling asleep was easy. Close to midnight, Caren found me leaning against the tree, passed out with the bottle of Wild Turkey in my hand. Lifting me from the ground, she led me back to the cave where a tent was set up under the overhang. After putting me to bed, she stayed up talking to Lynn and Rick. Their muffled laughter came through the thin walls of the tent and I remember thinking they had the bottle of Wild Turkey with them. In the morning Caren was sleeping beside me.

Outside of the tent, the dawn was cool and beautiful. Grabbing my camera I stepped into the morning. At the edge of the dry cave I picked up a plastic water jug and drank in gulps to cool my hot whiskey ravaged tongue. The camp was silent. In the forest, birds went about their labor, breaking the morning quiet with high-pitched calls and drawn out whistles. Lifting the water jug above me, I dumped water onto my head.

Walking forward, I wound my way along the trail that led back to the helipad. The floor of the forest was wet with dew and glistened in the winnowed light that eased through the trees.

At the ohi'a, I sat where I had been so content the night before and relaxed into the soft dawn. A warm breeze blew off the ocean from a solar storm a hundred million miles away. I was so comfortable that I did not turn around when I heard somebody walk up behind me.

"Good morning, Peter."

Over my shoulder, I saw John standing above me. I was looking at his back.

"Turn around so that I can talk to you," I mumbled from within my comfort.

"Let's go for a walk," he said.

It was too early to argue, so I stood up and brushed the sand from my pants.

"Why not," I said. I was feeling that good.

There were no clouds over the ocean, only wisps of white air like scroll work in the deep blue background. The sun had not broken over the back wall of the valley and the dawn's coolness lay close to the earth in the shadow of Kalalau.

Taking two steps down an embankment we stepped onto the cool sand. At the waterline, waves crashed heavily, one on top of another. Each breaker rumbled like the clapping of thunder along the shoreline, echoing into the distant mists.

We took a trail at the end of the beach that went onto a bank and into the forest. Below us, where the waves hit shore, huge lead colored cobbles created a field of stone. At a fork in the trail we took the low route.

"Where are we going?" I finally spoke.

He raised his head and looked at me dreamlike. "The heiau."

"You aren't taking me to pray, are you? I was having a nice moment," I said, letting my cool flex a muscle.

"No, Peter. You made your feelings clear."

We came to a series of narrow rock steps that were bordered by white, waist high lilies. I followed John onto a thick pad of grass that was encircled by a black lava wall. This heiau was smaller than the one at Ke'e beach. Even in the past, Kalalau must have been secluded.

Stopping in the middle of the knoll, John backed up to a pile of rocks that was the altar. He knelt forward, away from the altar, and began to pray. Walking past him, I stood at the edge of the grass by the front wall of the heiau and looked out at the ocean.

Below me, waves crashed and swept over the stony shore. Crabs skittered across the rocks and disappeared into crevices. At the tide-line, moss was growing on the rocks. Below me, the Kalalau River, which here was no more than a thick ribbon of water, wound its way between several boulders before merging into the ocean.

"Did you see that?"

John had finished praying and his back was to the ocean. He was looking toward the valley, as if he had seen something in that direction.

"Where?" I followed his gaze and looked up at the back walls of Kalalau.

"Thar she blows," he yelled out.

This statement was made with Melvillian drama and I realized that John was commenting about something that he was aware of in the ocean. Whipping around, I caught a glimpse of a great eruption of water. A humongous object split the ocean surface, rose as a shiny black arch, and slipped back into the throbbing sea. As I watched, another of the animals thrust itself out of the water. At the apex of its flight, for one instant, the creature froze in vertical splendor. It balanced on its tail and cocked its head to the side before slipping silently back into the ocean.

"A whale," I yelled at the top of my lungs.

"A humpback." John sounded as excited as I did, although he probably had seen this many times before.

Another breach and the massive beast wiggled its way into the air. Balancing on its rigid tail, the great cetacean fought gravity for an instant and was dumped back into the water. An explosive circle of splashing water was all that remained of the event.

"Jesus. Look at that thing fly," I yelled. In my excitement I ran back and forth at the edge of the heiau.

"Those whales have been coming here every morning for a thousand years. Maybe a million years," John said, excitedly.

Again, not three hundred yards offshore, the surface of the ocean was wedged apart as the black fluted nose and neck of the monster burst out of the water. Halfway down its head, I saw its tiny black eyes staring toward shore, looking at John and me standing on the heiau.

"Unbelievable," I hollered.

"They come to the heiau to check on the people in the Valley."

Turning around, John stepped toward a cluster of violets growing on the river-wall side of the heiau. He broke off several sprigs and walked backward to the altar. Setting the flowers down, he looked into the sky.

A rush of adrenalin kept me staring at the ocean, hoping to catch another glimpse of the whales. Inside of a minute, I saw one of them rise out of the water. It made a vigorous plunge into the air where it was outlined by the blue horizon. Then another whale burst through the surface. I stood transfixed. When John walked in beside me, I lifted my camera to signal for a photo session.

"I want to get a picture of you on the heiau. Is that all right?"

John was silent for a moment before he nodded.

"Sure, why not."

"Walk to the edge of the grass," I directed.

John walked backward to the front wall of the heiau and turned around so his back was to me. The sun had broken over the valley and reflected diamonds sparkled on the surface of the water. I checked my light meter and reset the f-stop. As I peered through my viewfinder, I saw them coming out of the water, two great, humpback whales, lifting together for one final show. In slow motion, I pushed my finger down softly. The camera clicked, and the inside of the viewfinder went black.

When the mirror dropped back in place, the whales were gone. All that was left were two foamy reentry points, one on each side of The Man.

John did not turn around, but I knew that the session was over. The camera came down from my eye. My heart was beating so hard that I could barely hear the roar of the waves hitting the rocky shore behind me.

"Are you ready to go, Peter?" he asked causally, still looking at the ocean.

There was no need to answer. To me it was only a job. What did I care where we went? Turning, John began to walk backward. He looked at me as he passed and smiled.

It was a perfect picture.

the valley

Walking away from the heiau, we followed the river trail into a shallow gorge. The day was already warming in the bottoms by the time we reached the main trail. The Man halted at this junction where a small sign, painted Park Service brown was bolted to a four-foot length of inch and a half pipe. The pipe itself was anchored into the ground in a tangle of bushes at the edge of the path.

The routed letters of the sign had been white at one time but were now chipped and faded. The sign offered two destinations. The first choice was the main camp where the dry cave was, .4 miles ahead. Below that, barely visible in the remains of the white letters, the sign read: Kalalau Valley, 1.0.

"What's up there, John—in the valley?" I pointed with my chin.

"Paradise, my friend, and I am going to take you there."

"What is Paradise going to look like, John? So I'll know when we get there."

"Nothing special. More trees. Another waterfall. There's a great swimming hole up there."

The warmth of the day mingled with the wetness of the river bottom made the air feel sticky. I took my shirt off to ease the humidity that was already making me sweat. The trail followed the course of the river and we walked on flat ground with the sound of water to our left.

As we walked, I heard twigs snapping and brush rustling on the slopes that climbed away from the river gorge. The sound would stop and then a hundred feet up the trail I would hear it again. Sometimes the sound came closer and at other times it was farther away. When a particularly loud noise made me turn my head, I saw that John was listening with his head cocked to the side so that he could hear behind him.

"What in the hell is that?" I asked.

"It's the goats," he said finally.

Looking up, I saw two wire haired Billy goats standing where the ridge line melted in to the foliage. Their gnawing mouths, in leathered skulls, tore large servings of grass out of the ground. Craning their necks, they watched us with lazy interest. As they chewed, small clods of red dirt tumbled across the trail and down the slope.

Ahead of us, I could see a clearing where a dozen gnarled trees grew in dark soil. A broken down, black-lava wall surrounded the orchard. As we entered one end of the grove, I saw three goats with half a dozen kids scooting out the opposite end, their hooves rapping on the rocks as they vanished into the undergrowth.

At the base of one of the giant trees, John sat down to rest. Joining him, I stretched out my legs.

"It's hot up here."

"It's just the climb," replied John.

"What are these trees?" I asked looking into the branches above me. I picked up a hard, orange kidney-shaped fruit from the leaf-strewn ground.

"Mangoes," John answered.

Holding the fruit aloft, I studied it carefully.

"Last mango in Paradise," I said softly.

"Starring Marlon McDonald. You can't forget the illusion for a single minute, can you, McDonald?"

"Well, John. It's my illusion. I'll stick to what I know."

The animosity of our discussion was politely discarded. John tried another approach.

"Koolau planted this grove of mangoes a hundred years ago."

"Koolau?" I asked, glad that we were moving into a new dialogue.

"Koolau the leper. This is where his first camp was." John pointed to the wall that encircled the entire grove. "He built that wall with his followers. Some of them had no fingers. Koolau only had one thumb left on his right hand but he could still plant trees. And fire a rifle."

"There were lepers on Kauai?" Like the fool that I am, I stood, moved away from the tree, and brushed the dirt from the seat of my pants. "I thought the lepers were kept on Molokai."

"Very good, Peter. You know your history. That is precisely why Koolau came here. To escape the prison of Molokai. He grew up on Kauai. He was a Hawaiian cowboy. And a crack shot. When he came down with the disease, he resisted the law. They wanted to take him from Kauai, to live away from his people. So he brought other lepers to Kalalau. All they wanted was to disintegrate in peace."

"So what happened to this Koolau?"

"He hid out here for a year. When the authorities found out that he was in Kalalau, they sent a police force to take him. He fled deeper into the valley and retreated to the caves near the base of the big waterfall. They brought in the army." John pointed up valley. "That is where the soldiers attacked him. They brought cannons to the beach and they bombarded his followers in the caves."

"With cannons?"

"It seems stupid, to blow up a body that is already falling apart. There was a thousand-dollar bounty on the old kanaka. He killed a sheriff who came into the valley to take him to Molokai. The soldiers routed his followers but they never took Koolau. He hid out for another year with bounty hunters laying traps for him. He died alone. When they found his body, he was still clutching his Mauser to his chest."

"Incredible."

"An act of pointless courage but an act of courage nonetheless. He did what he knew he had to do for his belief that every man should live free."

"Is that why you walk backward, John? Will that make you free?"

"No, Peter. I told you that I walk backward because I do not want to forget."

"That's right. You keep your eye on the past so that nothing gets by you."

"Exactly."

From the bush came the sound of goats scampering as they flanked the grove.

"They come to eat the mangoes that fall from the trees. It's a constant battle to get to the fruit before they do. They take one bite out of each piece and move to the next one. It makes the mangoes rot."

"So when you eat goat, you not only eat grass, you also eat mangoes."

John became very thoughtful and I felt ashamed for mocking him. I walked toward the rock wall at the front of the grove.

On the ground the corpses of the goat-nibbled mangoes lay rotting where they had been discarded. A kukui forest encircled the grove but the dark green umbrella of the immense mango trees halted its advance, stealing the light that the forest needed to proliferate. The floor of the grove was bare except for leaves, mulch, and the once-bitten mangoes.

Outside of the grove and inside the tangle of kukui, I could hear the goats fidgeting, anxious for us to leave so they could get back to their foraging. Trying to synchronize my aural accounting with a visual exploration, I turned my head slowly in a panorama. There they were: three nannies and half a dozen kids staring through big black eyes down bony noses that ended in slit and puckered nostrils. Slowly, and only because goats had been doing this for years, they retreated farther into the brush, away from the humans.

"Maybe we should walk some more."

If John had heard me he made no motion to stand.

"Do the goats worry you, Peter? They should. They are demons. Eating the grass, tearing up the earth, destroying Paradise."

The Man had closed his eyes and left behind the thread of our conversation. When he spoke next it was as if in a trance.

"All the things they think I am, I am not. I am not their savior. I do these things because they need a leader. It's not for me that I walk backward, but for them. It's not for me that I search. I search because I have the ability to feel what they cannot."

I listened silently.

"They are like children. They need discipline. And they have placed that burden upon me."

His musing ended as quickly as it had begun. It was not clear whether John had been talking to me or to himself, or to someone not present.

Standing, John resumed his march down the trail that in the mango grove was only a thin line of trampled leaves leading deeper into the valley. With several long steps, I was able to catch up and keep pace. We continued into the lush mix of lehua, kulu' and hibiscus that made an impenetrable wall on each side of the path. Looking back, I saw that the goats had wasted no time returning to the grove. They stood with their heads lowered to the ground, chomping on the mangoes.

After a mild incline, we broke into the sun on top of a hill. The hill was nearly clean of grass and was starting to crumble in weak sections along its crest. From this hill, the destruction caused by the goats could be seen far up the slopes of the valley. The natural terraces had been denuded of turf. Red scars showed where rain was washing the earth away. Roots that kept the banks intact had been ripped up by greedy teeth.

We crossed the dirt-scarred summit and entered an opening in the forest. Walking through shoulder-high pampas, clouds of silky white seeds drifted through the air. At the next clearing, the long broad leaves of a haha tree stuck out at lazy right angles, giving shade to the seed pods shaped like purple worms that squirmed out if its straight round trunk.

The trail stayed on top of the hills and the river and its gorge were left behind in the thickets below. Off of the main up-valley trail, I noticed many spoors breaking away, dissecting the ridges, disappearing into thickets, leading across hills to other hills, and running parallel with the path that we followed. These spoors were narrow and crossed our path with regularity.

"Goat trails?" I asked John.

The top of the next hill was crisscrossed by a dozen of these spoors. This looked like a junction, the gathering together and the distribution of traffic in and out of the valley.

"Yes, goat trails."

The sharp-edged blades of the pampas cut at my ankles and left red itching welts on my skin. Above us were the towering palis cloaked in their fantastic drapery of vegetation. Snow-white Tropic Birds glided from perch to perch, their long, forked tails twisting in the shearing winds that rolled off the Alaki Swamp.

On our right, the steady sound of the river careening through the hidden gorge in the distance was a reassuring noise. On the hills, the bleating of the goats resounded as ethereal as an evil fog, their piercing croaks corrupting the magnificence of our surroundings.

Carefully, John felt his way backward down a shallow gully. Behind him, but in front of me, in the direction that we were walking, a set of stone stairs led out of the gully. Slowly and carefully, John began to negotiate the steps. I followed, listening closely to the water, which became more powerful and apparent. It was the sound of a fall or a series of falls. At the last step we climbed onto a flat rock outcropping.

In front of us was a circular pool of water about fifty feet across. The surface of the pool slid by as smoothly as a sheet of smoked glass. From a thousand feet up, behind the sliding pond, the cascades hurtled through thickets of hibiscus and ferns embedded in the soggy cliff wall. The streamers of water beat relentlessly against the tops of boulders, fell through the air the final thirty feet, and exploded as they hit the pool.

Sticky and raw from the heat of the trail, I set down my camera, removed my shoes, stripped off my pants, and plunged into the water. The pool was dark and cool and pulsing at the far end where a cataract fell over the edge. Bobbing to the surface I swam toward The Man who was sitting on a rock, rubbing his legs.

Gliding across the pool, I could feel the river running through it. As I swam toward the center, I suddenly felt the current grab my body. A gut wave of panic coursed through me as the stream took control and carried me toward the cataract at the end of the pool. My legs thrashed under water, my arms grabbed for a mooring below the surface, but there was nothing to hold onto. Helpless, I felt the river pulling me forward.

The front edge of the pool raced toward me at eye level. The current would throw me over the lip and crash me against the rocks below. As a last resort, I swung my head around to see if I could find John. Through my flailing, splashing hands, I saw The Man sitting calmly with his back to me. The current dunked me again and I lunged downward seeking something solid.

Kicking and stroking under the dark surface of the water, I felt my feet touching the rocky bottom. Pushing up with a burst of energy, I threw my arms out and came to the surface. This effort brought me to the bank and with all the strength that my body could call up, I threw my arms out and dug my fingers into the hard mud of the shore. The dirt packed under my fingernails as I dragged myself forward.

Just when I thought I had made it, I lost my grip, slipped back into the current and was again carried toward the cataract. My head submerged under the surface and I could feel the tingling buzz of liquid death flowing into my nasal passages. When I resurfaced, I was gargling water and drowning. Spitting out the suffocating draught, I choked out a pathetic cry to John who had not moved from his seat.

"John! Help me!"

When I heard his answer, I could not believe the words.

"Help yourself, McDonald. Do I look like a messiah?"

I would have heaved my guts if another wave had not smothered my words and pulled me down. Clutching a small root that hung into the water, I pulled myself above the surface again. As I pulled, I felt the root break from the bank. But in the effort it took to separate the root from its anchoring, I was able to raise my shoulders onto shore.

Throwing myself forward, I grabbed a tuft of grass and pulled. The grass ripped out of the ground and I tossed it into the stream with a flip of my wrist. The yank on the grass helped my progress and I was able to bring my chest onto the dirt of the shore and grab a small tree at the edge of the pool. With a firm grip on its thin trunk, I heaved my body out of the current. Leaping to my feet, my body mud-stained, my panic tasting like magnesium in my mouth and with canyons of rage opened up in my mind, I rushed at John.

Ten steps brought me looming over The Man who remained seated. Panting and shivering from fear, I stood over him, my face a mask of hideous temper.

"You son of a bitch. Why didn't you help me?" I yelled.

"I didn't think you needed my help, Peter." He was going to enjoy this.

"I could have drowned."

"You are acting like an idiot, Peter. Take a closer look at your doom."

Suddenly, another wave of panic overtook me. Although I was dripping water from the cool stream onto the damp ground, I could feel my forehead heating up. I turned an angry pirouette and stomped to the end of the pool where I had nearly been dragged to my death.

Over the rim, the cataract fell hissing through the channel but for all its roaring proclamation, the river fell only a few feet down into another pool, which looked deep enough to have caught my fall. Again, I flew into a blind fury, this time to save face.

Whipping my pride with the spurs of my ego, I stormed back to where John sat silently waiting for the remainder of my attack.

"You knew I wouldn't get hurt," I yelled into John's face.

"But you didn't, Peter, which proves my point."

"How can you play with someone's emotions like that, you asshole?"

"How can you play with your own emotions, McDonald? I thought that I wasn't responsible for you. I thought that you could take care of yourself. Are you suggesting that you need my intervention after all?"

"If someone is in danger, you help them out. It doesn't matter if they know it or not." I sounded like Marlie in one of his fits of anger. But The Man answered me calmly, ignoring my aggression.

"We are all in danger, Peter. That's what I've been telling you. No matter what degree the danger, people thrash about just as you did when you thought you were going to be killed by this lovely river. I tell you that all of this is an illusion. Just like your recent meeting with the ghost of doom, which as you can see was merely your mind reaching the limits of its experience."

I had to sit down as my strength left me. I rested my back against a rock and closed my eyes, trying to catch my breath.

John continued. "Here we are in a war with the unknown. And what do we do? We kick about and call for help. In the end, only our faith bridges the gap between fear and knowledge."

I lifted my head and opened my eyes. "God, I am so sick of your preaching. If you have so much faith, why do you have to keep talking about it all of the time?"

"Because death is all around us. It is growing stronger and it is advancing."

"Listen, John. If death is going to take this god forsaken planet, then bring it on."

"Like I have said, Peter. I don't do this for myself. There is a higher place and I will be there soon. But what of those who feel haunted and inhuman because they cannot buy into the illusion? It is for them that I teach."

"Jesus Christ, John. It is not. You preach because you don't believe yourself. You have to keep saying the words because it's the only way you can stay ahead of your own fear. I had you pegged from the beginning. Don't forget. I'm the photographer. I know why people hire me to take their pictures. You want to be remembered, that's why you walk backward—not because you don't want to forget."

"So if you know me, why did you come?"

"If you want the truth, I needed the money."

"But you were poor in more ways than you could understand. Everything that happens we bring upon ourselves."

"Exactly. And everything you say is meaningless."

"And there lies my case, Peter. You resist your own destiny and so your destiny never comes."

Overwhelmed by anger, I jumped up and went to where my clothes were lying on the ground. I yanked on my jeans and stuffed my shirt into the back of my pants. Grabbing my camera I got ready to leave. But I was not done with the conversation.

"Why does it matter to you what I think? Or if I'm happy?"

"I want you to be happy, Peter. You are one of us."

I took a step toward John and looked down at him menacingly.

"Listen to me. I will be happy when I decide to be happy and not a minute—"

"You're catching on."

Having been cut off in mid speech, I struggled to regain the initiative. I could feel the fire in my face smoldering red-hot.

"And I am not one of you!"

"Good, Peter. Get angry. Anger is energy."

"And so is walking, you son-of-a-bitch." I spun around to storm off but turned back for one more barrage. "My job is over, John. I'll turn the film over to a lab in Hanalei. I'll pay for the processing. If there is any money left I'll mail it to you general delivery."

"You can leave Paradise if you want to, Peter. You can come and go as you please; I won't stand in your way. But remember, all of this will follow you." He raised his arm and swept it through the air, presenting the walled valley to me as if he were making a present of it. "And you will never forget."

"Maybe if I walk backward, I'll remember it better, John. Do you think so? Do you think if I walk backward I will never forget?"

Facing him, I almost laughed, knowing what I was about to do. Taking a step backward, I looked down at John haughtily.

"There, how's that? You like that, you loser? Oh yeah. I can feel my memory getting bigger." I took two more steps backward and kicked dirt behind me with the soles of my feet like a rodeo clown. I had not felt this cruel since I had broken up with my wife. "I know this is going to do it. I'll never have to take another picture. The past will be remembered inside of me where I will never forget. Who needs film?"

I was screaming.

"It works for me, Peter."

"Go to hell, John. I'm done."

Spinning around, I stormed off the flat rock, into the trees, and down the steps into the gully. The valley walls were hidden from my sight and my mind was fuming.

Through the forest I stomped, viciously savoring my rage. Yet with every step, my victory eluded me. What had come over me? What did it matter? It was only a job. I had told myself that right from the beginning.

Over the hills I trudged with my thoughts as tangled as the forest around me. Past the goat trails, I made my way alone. Through the overgrowth, I stumbled on. Reaching the mango grove I finally gave up and collapsed. As my breathing subsided, I heard the first snort of my feral company.

From the cover of the forest, I could hear the goats yammering anxiously, trying to communicate with me. Their bleating tore at my mind. I stared into the trees but could not pick out the creatures that were making these crying moans. In terror, I got on my hands and knees and picked through the underbrush with my eyes looking for a shadow or a moving branch. The gnawing scream of the goats invaded my hearing and I threw my hands over my ears to stop the sound.

Pushing against the earth, I slid onto my butt, toward the trunk of the largest of the old gnarled mango trees. With my back against the trunk, I closed my eyes and immediately fell backward into a nightmare.

I did not realize that I had fallen asleep until I awoke. The Man was standing over me. I blinked into the light and gazed up at him. Standing slowly, I took my shirt from the waistband of my pants and pulled it on. Facing John, I knew what I had to do.

"I'm sorry, John. I lost my temper."

The sound of my own voice startled me.

"It's alright, Peter. Life is a hard path to follow. The cliffs are terrifying and when the trail narrows, we feel danger. But at the end of the path there is the Valley. And in the Valley everything becomes clear."

If I felt like arguing, I did not make the same mistake.

"Let's go back. The steam should be ready by now."

We walked out of the valley on the same trail that had brought us in, with the river rushing beside us, out of sight but beckoning with its clarion call. The voices of the goats were smeared across my brain but they were no longer advancing on me. I let John lead the way, walking backward. There was no use fighting him anymore. I was not certain if he had won or I had lost. As my mind settled, I felt myself coming back to life and what I wanted was to find the source of what had invaded me. And more importantly, I wanted to get back in step with my sole purpose in life, which is to chronicle everything that has gone behind me.

steam

We took the low path along the riverbank that led toward the beach. Approaching the knoll that is the heiau, I could see Judy, Shannon, and Caren sitting on the grass awaiting our arrival. John entered the stone circle with his back to them. The women stood and were careful not to get in his way. Stepping up to the altar backward, John laid several mangoes on the ground at the foot of the stone table.

"How was your hike?" Shannon was always first to ask. She spoke to John's back as he stood at the altar.

"Maybe you should ask Peter," John responded.

Shannon did not bother to ask but Caren broke ranks and came over. "It's beautiful up there, isn't it?"

Words did not form in my mouth, and my throat was not playing along either. I answered with as much enthusiasm as I could.

"It's a rare piece of earth," I said meekly. "But the goats are ruining the place."

"It's like Paradise, wouldn't you say, Peter?" Shannon asked without looking at me. Her voice was contrived. She watched John's back to gauge his response.

John gazed across the ocean with his back to everyone. The skin of his cheekbones tightened, which we knew was a smile. Satisfied that she had impressed The Man, Shannon took three prancing steps to the rock wall at the edge of the heiau. This wall bordered the riverbank and in three more steps, Shannon vanished over the lip of the barrier. It dawned on me as I watched her disappear, that I saw as much of her back as I did of John's. Shannon was always leaving, retreating to the location of the next situation. Except for Bill who seemed content to hang out in the cave all day, none of the followers stayed in one place for long.

Since Shannon was gone, I looked at Caren and answered the question, which seemed appropriate.

"Yeah, it was a lot like Paradise."

Caren smiled at me half-heartedly and I smiled back as best I could.

"So where are Rick and Lynn?" I asked, trying to fend off further inquiries.

From her position close to John, Judy answered.

"Lynn is back in the kitchen getting the food ready for tonight. I think Rick is swimming."

Walking a few steps closer to the ocean wall, John turned and with his back to the followers he faced the water. It struck me that two days into my commission it did not seem odd to see John approaching the world always with his back. Memory was slipping away from me and with it went all traces of reality. Culture changes within the human mind one experience at a time. The old falls within analysis of the new, that is the present just past. Thought moves without direction, creates the world, and is the output of time squared. I did not think of this at that moment but I think about it now when I realize how much my perspective was skewing.

"Is the steam ready?" John asked no one in particular.

"It's been ready for a while. Marlie didn't know when you were coming back so he started the fire early." Judy answered.

"We should go then. We wouldn't want to rile the old sea buzzard."

"He told me to bring you down as soon as you came in."

"Are you ready?" John asked Judy.

"I can't wait." A tinge of sarcasm colored her voice. If I heard it, The Man must have heard it as well.

With a loud sigh, John walked to the path where Shannon had disappeared. Judy followed, and as she walked past Caren and me, she looked at us and rolled her eyes but she still followed John obediently over the edge of the heiau. As Caren started forward, I snagged her arm and held her in place.

When we were alone, I spoke. "What's going on?" I asked.

"Why don't you tell me, Peter? For instance, how was your trip up-valley?"

This was a hard question to answer. I was not sure that I even knew. "Ah—" I stammered.

"You don't know, do you?"

"Well—"

"It's alright, Peter. It's the same thing we're all feeling." She looked over her shoulder in the direction The Man had gone. I could sense her discomfort. "We had better go. We don't want to keep them waiting. Just stay with me in case anything happens. You can trust me Peter, I promise."

This was a good place to end the conversation so I dropped her arm and followed her down the trail. The few hours Caren and I had spent together had me feeling a spark of passion. Her presence was beautiful, more beautiful than any woman I had ever known. My feelings for her were strong, but there was something standing between us. It was evident in her anxiety. This anxiety also showed in the movements of the followers, who never seemed to relax. I could feel the shadow they cast, a dark foreboding that went everywhere with them. Their fear had created a wall, like the kulu'i and hibiscus that encroached on the trails. And it was this fear that kept us apart.

We maneuvered down a torn dirt bank and into the bed of the river. The bank was raw dirt with river rocks protruding twelve feet above our heads. I realized that water must reach that depth when it rained hard enough up valley. In a storm, this stream would be transformed into a raging transport of flood and mud. The flow would be awesome, and beyond comprehension on a day like this, when the valley was drenched in sunshine. Now the water was only a few feet deep and only ten feet across. A blue sky rose over the ocean, a proscenium above a blue stage floor.

A solid wall of lava blocked our passage at a turn in the river. Without wasting time, Caren grabbed a handhold and pulled herself up and over the obstruction. Scaling the wall behind her, I shimmied to the top of the barrier and found myself standing above the rest of the followers who were waiting in a circle at the edge of the stream. The disciples were undressed but John was still wearing his grey robe.

"What took you two so long?" he asked.

"Oh, you know. Peter is a *malihini*. He doesn't have the trail down yet."

As we jumped the last few feet off the rock I felt compelled to say something in my defense. Instead, I looked around with a sheepish grin, cocked my head stupidly and remained silent.

"Well, come on. We've kept Marlie waiting long enough."

The followers walked forward but there was reluctance in their movement. Joe went ahead of John but his head was down. The women showed little fervor. Ron followed the others but he looked around him as if he were searching for an escape route. Bringing up the rear, Caren and I trailed behind Ron. John walked behind us backward toward a place in front of us where blue smoke hung over the gorge.

The steam house had been built against the side of the riverbank. Two giant boulders formed two of its outside walls. The bank made a third wall for the spa. Across the top of the rocks, thick tree limbs vaulted the span. The tree limbs acted as ceiling joists and large palm fronds were woven tightly into the grid of the limbs to create a roof. The front wall was built with more palm fronds and tree limbs. An old, red wool blanket covered a doorframe built from driftwood. The smell of a wood fire filled the air and a thread of grey smoke rose on one side of the structure and became a blue haze over the river.

As we approached the steam house, Marlie appeared and moved toward the front door, waddling with two buckets of water held in his hands, the muscles in his arms bulging from the weight. He pushed through the blanket and disappeared into the sweat lodge. Around the corner where the fire was built, Bill greeted us with a smile as he ambled past us. In his hands, he carried a large round rock wrapped in a broad banana leaf. As Bill entered the door, a billow of white steam exited and disintegrated in the heat of the air outside.

The procession came to a halt a few feet from the lodge. A commotion could be heard inside of the building, the sound of a solid object dropped on the ground, followed by a pause and then a steady hiss that lasted for thirty seconds. Through the blanket, Marlie stumbled out of the lodge; in his hands were two empty buckets. He approached The Man, his eyes red and teary.

"Took you long enough to get here," Marlie said in an irritable voice.

"This is an important day, Marlie." John immediately went into his act.

"I used up enough wood for a week keeping this fire stoked." Marlie wiped tears out of his eyes with a filthy sleeve.

"You will be rewarded."

"Right. Well, let's not waste any more time."

John had approached with his back to the lodge, so it was necessary for Shannon to part the curtain for him. Still garbed in the grey robe, John was allowed to enter the room first. Billows of steam roiled out of the opening.

The little man eyed the loss with frustration. "Come on. Let's get going. You're wasting my sweat and blood!"

I could see John's eyes, since he was walking backward, and I saw the look of resentment he cast at Marlie. The sea dog saw it also but it only seemed to make him more impatient. He pushed Joe through the open door and was going to push Shannon as well but she was having none of it.

"Get your hands off me, you creep."

Marlie hissed at her but he had his lesson and he touched no one else. When Caren and I stopped at the door, Marlie flung the blanket across the opening to halt the expulsion of steam. After Caren had shed her shorts and tank-top, she walked to the door, pushed aside the blanket, and entered. Stripping off my clothes, I laid my camera on the pile and was a few steps behind Caren, which allowed Marlie to stab at me with his tongue as I passed.

"So how did you like the valley, shutterbug? Get any famous pictures?"

I stopped. "As a matter of fact I got a picture of your wife sucking on a mango. Your kids look just like you." The patience I had been forced to show John came out as vitriol directed at the scrappy little man. There was no geniality left inside of me.

Bill rushed out of the lodge, coming between Marlie and me before the altercation could go any further.

"He says it isn't hot enough."

Marlie turned with a huff, and taking his buckets, he walked toward the river.

"Not hot enough, huh?" Marlie was grumbling under his breath but he certainly did not care who heard him. "I'll make it hot enough." He looked over his shoulder at me. "Screw you, chickenshit. I'll take care of your ass later." He shook his head as he stormed toward the river. "Not hot enough. We'll see about that."

I ducked into the lodge.

The heat inside of the place was overwhelming and the humidity seared my lungs and made me cough. Taking a seat, I kept my head as close to the floor as I could. It was cooler near the ground and this brought some comfort. As the seconds passed, sweat began to bead on my brow and roll down my chest.

It was dark inside the lodge. My eyesight was further obscured by thick steam rising off of hot rocks in a pit in the middle of the floor. The vapor cloud was so concentrated I thought that any minute the pressure would blow the roof right off the shack. I could not see anyone else in the dark and the steam.

Bill and Marlie returned with more rocks and water to enhance the heat. When the blanket was thrown off the door for a moment, I glanced around to see where everyone was sitting. Through the steam, I saw that the followers were lying on the floor with their faces pressed into the dirt. Caren was close to me, and before the blanket swung back and cut off the light, I crawled over and lay beside her.

"God, is it ever hot in here," I whispered into her ear.

"Don't talk, Peter. And keep your head down."

At that moment I heard Bill drop a rock into the pit, followed by the thin hissing of water being poured. The water was immediately vaporized into more steam. My face burst out in beads of sweat. I did not know how much more of the heat I could stand.

"How's that, John? Hot enough for you?"

Marlie's voice traveled through the dark looking for the ears of The Man. There was a pause, but I knew what everyone else knew.

"Not quite. Bring it on. Let's sweat the death right out of our pores. Let's just do it. We are ready."

The blanket was thrown back impatiently and I watched as Marlie and Bill hustled out of the lodge. Staring in the direction of John's voice, I spied him just as the curtain fell. He was sitting up, his legs crossed, his face staring at the wall of the bank. The grey fabric of his robe was clinging to his back. He was taking short quick breaths to keep from choking on the heat. Outside I heard the sound of the bucket crashing against the rocks as Marlie flung it into the river to get more water. The darkness had pervaded the room again and I lost sight of John.

"Today we sweat so that forever we will not burn in the eternal fire. Today we suffer so that tomorrow we will be whole. What shall we give to end our quest?"

There was no answer and I imagined that John could say anything inside of this room and never be questioned. It was too hot to open your mouth much less your mind. Through the door rushed Marlie and Bill again, Bill with his wrapped hot rock, Marlie with his water. Then came the sound of the rock plopping onto the ground and the hissing of steam like a snake on fire.

"What do you think, boss? Must be a hundred and seventy in here at least."

"Then make it two hundred and seventy. A demon has entered this room. It is stalking us in our own Valley. It is causing dissension. We must rid ourselves of all impure thoughts. Make it burn."

The curtain was thrown open. Marlie and Bill ran out of the lodge like a couple of coolies throttled by an invisible strap. We heard the sound of the bucket being flung across the rocks into the river. Someone giggled in the dark. It had to be Judy.

"Who is laughing at our trial? If we can exist in this heat, we can bear anything."

Although I wanted to yell out at John that this was crazy, I had learned my lesson. The more sense you try to make to a fanatic, the harder they hang onto their gospel.

"This is nothing compared to the smoking pits of hell."

Again, Marlie and Bill raced through the door. Again the steam engine was fueled and started. If the heat was unbearable a few minutes before, now it was hazardous.

"Is that going to do it?"

It was obvious that Marlie was doing his best to control his temper, as if his calmness would ostracize the demon from the depths of The Man's flaming evangelic soul.

"It is never hot enough. Never. But that will be all right for now, Marlie. Could you just bring me a bucket of cool water to douse my body?"

There was no answer.

"Marlie?"

Still no answer.

"Marlie? I know you're there."

"I'm here, boss."

"So bring me a bucket of water to kill this burning fire in my body."

There was a long interlude and I was sure that the demon had gotten Marlie and was moving into his soul like a cat burglar. I held my breath and waited for the answer.

"Hey, John?"

"Yes, Marlie."

Another long pause.

"What is it, Marlie?"

"Why don't you get your own god damn water? And while you're out there, why don't you go jump in the river?"

One final time the blanket was thrown back and I looked across the floor. Marlie was exiting the steam house. He dropped the bucket onto the ground as he let the blanket fall over the opening in the wall. Now, not only was the air tortuous with heat and humidity, but it was also filled with an anxiety that clung to the walls and infiltrated the deepest recesses of the room.

"Well, friends. It looks as if Marlie has gone over the edge again. What are we going to do about our lost lamb?"

There was a long silence that I could not translate but I knew that something was about to happen. As I listened, I heard the sound of movement as someone got to their feet.

"It's too hot in here for me, John. I'm going for a swim." It was Shannon's voice, always the first to stake her claim to humanity. Immediately, I heard another body rising up from the ground.

"Yeah, me too. We don't get nice weather like this too often in November." Joe went through the curtain right behind Shannon.

"It's too hot in here, John," Judy said.

Beside me, Caren stood. "I'm going with you, Judy. This is nuts. Do you want to come, Peter?"

Because of my recent experience at the pool, I was afraid to answer and did not.

"We'll be up in the valley if you want to join us for a swim."

"Alright," I managed.

Ron was not far behind, slinking out of the lodge without a word. The blanket was stuck open on the doorframe, and daylight filled the room. Bill stood looking at the pile of rocks near his feet, deciding whether he should stay and use the steam after he had put so much effort into creating it. Apparently he decided he wouldn't, because when Ron left, Bill was right behind him.

The steam was escaping into the outside air. I looked at John and saw that he had not moved a muscle throughout the mutiny. Sitting up, I leaned against a boulder and took deep breaths of the cool air that was being sucked into the room. The silence was unbearable.

"I think it was too hot for them, John."

"It's always too hot for them."

There was anger in John's voice but it was tempered by whatever patience he had left. It had been a terrible rout. I could not help but feel sorry for The Man as I sat there staring at his back through the receding clouds of steam.

"Maybe next time you should use smaller rocks."

"Maybe next time I will use fire and brimstone."

"That could get messy, John."

"All they want is to have fun. No one wants to make an effort anymore. That's the problem with the world, Peter. You offer people eternal life and they want to spend it at Club Med."

"I guess they figure there's no point in hanging around that long."

"They'll be back. They always come back. And next time I'll raise the roof off this joint. I'll make it so hot in here they'll beg to be saved."

"Well, you know what they say, John."

"What do they say, Peter?"

"Jesus saves but Moses invests."

"That's not very funny, Peter. You might as well go with them."

"Are you sure?"

"Yes, I want to be alone."

"Do you want me to build up the steam in here before I go? I don't mind."

"Nah. It gets too hot in here with all of that steam. Go ahead. I'll be alright."

As I got up to go, I tried to think of one more joke but nothing came to mind, so I left John sitting alone in the steam house. Once outside, I made my way quickly toward the heiau, hoping that I could catch up with Caren and Judy and take a swim before returning to the dry cave.

tourists

When I got to the junction of the trail, I was overwhelmed with nausea. My energy had been drained at the waterfall where I had almost drowned. The scene of revolt at the sweat lodge was an empty socket in my mind. I did not know what the mutiny would mean to the integrity of the group. The only thing that was clear was that I felt tired and hungry and confused all at the same time.

Since I did not know which direction the rest of the group had taken, I headed toward the campground. The trail rode a mound like a levee between the beach and the cliff face that harbored the dry cave. Past the two dilapidated privies with their cargoes of camper's trash, the trail led into the deep forest where the tourist campsites were located.

Inside this thicket, I walked until I came to where the backpackers had their tents set up. As I wandered through the camps, I saw that it was comprised of two different types of sites. The first type was the flat bivouacs under large trees that grew out of the bank where the soil of the forest became the sand of the beach. These sites had stunning views of the ocean and the sunset but no protection from the elements. In the afternoon, the tropic sun raged down on these sites and there was no shade to escape the heat. The other type of site was on the slopes among the low-lying kukui and oak. These encampments had been cleared of the talus that had collapsed from the cliff face and were protected from wind and sun by the trees of the forest.

At one of the choicest sites at the base of the back cliff, I came upon Dennis and Michelle, the couple I had met in Honokoa. When I approached the site, I saw Dennis pulling a cookie sheet with something that looked like biscuits out of a stone oven. The oven had a crude range on top, a flat stone counter above and a shelf at the side that held condiments and spices. There were pots and pans stowed in a niche beside the oven that were of a better quality than I had at home. Next to the stove was a large seat like a throne built out of rocks. On the boundary of his camp was a small stone altar.

Dennis greeted me as I approached, but when Michelle saw me she drew back into the tent and stuck her nose into a book. Dennis was obviously proud of the biscuits, and he was glad to have someone with whom he could share his accomplishment. Both Michelle and Dennis were completely naked.

"Hey, Peter McDonald. Do you have your camera? This should be recorded. Fresh baked buttermilk biscuits," he said, holding the pan up for my review.

As I greeted him, I scanned his campsite. Hanging from a web of nylon lines tied between the oak trees were two large tarps. These tarps covered the area around his tent, giving him a good twenty feet of cover. The tarp over the living area was designed to be raised and lowered on pulleys so he could let in as much sun as he needed according to the time of day. Inside the tent, where Michelle continued to evade my presence, there was a queen size blow-up mattress covered with a snow-white quilt.

Still feeling anxious, I entered the site trying to act normal. I felt used up from the morning's activities. I was thinking about the followers and wondering how they were dealing with the residue of their revolt. Probably swimming up-valley somewhere, enjoying the day. As for John, who knew what he was feeling beyond his need to control events at all cost and never to forget.

"I'm out of film. My reloads are up at the dry cave," I said as I looked at the biscuits lined up on a cookie sheet. My mouth began to water and I remembered that I was very hungry. "I can go and get some if you want."

Setting the biscuits on the stone counter beside the stove, Dennis dove into the tent and rummaged around. He came out triumphantly, holding a yellow waterproof Minolta.

"No need," he said handing me the camera.

Taking the unit, I tried to bring his secluded partner into the conversation. "Let's get Michelle in the picture too."

"Great idea," Dennis said popping his head back into the tent. "Hey, Michelle, come out and get your picture taken."

Lowering the book from her face, Michelle looked at me with a weak smile.

"Hi, Peter," she offered. She climbed out of the tent, nude, and walked to the oven. They were actually a very nice couple and I felt guilty that I had acted out so badly at our initial encounter. "I can't believe he did this, can you, Peter?"

"I want to tell you something, Peter. When I decided to get married, I chose a woman who would go camping with me on the first date," Dennis declared.

"Dennis is a connoisseur of fine camping. This is the third time we have been to Kalalau and every trip the gear gets more elaborate. Let's take the picture so we can try these biscuits," Michelle said eagerly.

"Do you guys want to put on some clothes?"

"Nah," said Dennis nonchalantly. "I show these pictures to clients. Let's face it, skin sells."

"I suppose you're right."

Holding the camera to my eye, I posed them with their tent frame left, and the trunk of the oak vertical in the background. I snapped a shot and took another as security. When I was done, Dennis walked over to hand me a biscuit and I took two.

"I should go get Juerg," Michelle said.

"Right-o. Get Juerg and I'll find the apple butter."

"Who's Juerg?" I asked.

"Another camper. He's from Switzerland."

Michelle strode away and I was left alone with Dennis. As he searched out the jar of apple butter that he knew "was around here somewhere" I ventured in behind him for a closer look at his setup.

"So how's the commission coming along?" Dennis asked over his shoulder as he went through a ditty bag filled with cans and jars. "Are you getting some good shots?"

"A few."

"That's a strange crowd you're working for. The famous squatters of the Kalalau Valley."

Digging into another nylon stuff sack, Dennis pulled out several bags of tea, a zip-lock baggie full of coffee, and a Tupperware container half full of sugar.

"You don't know the half of it. In fact, if you really want a show, you should come up to the dry cave for dinner tonight. "

"Sorry, won't work. I caught a big whitefish this morning that I'm cooking for dinner."

Considering how out of sorts I was feeling, I was surprised when I decided to raise the ante and see if I could get Dennis interested.

"The only thing I wonder is where in the hell did John get fifteen thousand dollars to hire me?"

As casually as he could, Dennis glanced up at me.

"You're a high priced guy, Peter."

He was giving the ball back to me but I knew I had gotten his attention.

"That's my rate for five days with expenses." I could play coy with the best of them.

"What do I owe you for the picture?"

"That's alright. I'm paid up."

We laughed together.

I went on. "You haven't heard of any bank robberies on Kauai, have you?"

"Do you think they're bank robbers?" Dennis eyed the gear that was lying around his campsite.

"Well, I don't know. Where does a person like John get fifteen thousand dollars?" Every time I mentioned the amount, I could feel Dennis's interest rising.

From the forest trail that led to the fall, Michelle walked back into camp with Juerg and a pretty lady who had charcoal black hair with dull silver threads running through it. She was introduced as Kate.

"So you made biscuits, Dennis?" Juerg asked in a think European accent.

"Aha." The presence of the others jarred Dennis back into the present.

"The apple butter," he exclaimed holding up the bottle. "Here, Michelle. You do the honors."

Dennis turned to me, trying to remain casual but too intrigued by the subject to keep away from it.

"You never know, Peter. A guy like that might have inherited money. Maybe he was an inventor or something. Maybe an author. I've seen all kinds. When I first got out of business school I worked for an investment firm where my sole occupation was separating people from their money. It didn't last long but I did learn one thing. Sometimes the dumpiest, most down and out looking person is the one with all of the dough. Some people are good at hiding their assets."

"What are you two talking about?"

Michelle had divvied up the biscuits and opened the apple butter.

"Peter was asking for some business advice."

"And what did you tell him?"

"I told him I was on vacation. Now, how are those biscuits?"

"Incredible."

It was unanimous.

Staying long enough to devour three more biscuits, I bade the group farewell. As I was leaving, Dennis sidled up to me.

"Maybe after we eat that fish we'll come over to the cave tonight."

"I would like to get your opinion on this, Dennis. As a professional," I added raising my eyebrows to increase my credibility.

"Of course."

Saying goodbye, I headed toward the waterfall where I could wash the taste of apple butter out of my mouth. The biscuits made me feel better and this spontaneous opportunity to cause mischief had brought back my energy, so I decided to follow my impulse.

The path wound through a garden of dark grey talus then dipped into a gully of black earth where several tents were standing in the shade of a stand of ancient kukui trees. At one of the campsites, a burly man was unloading gear from an old canvas backpack and setting up a tent.

The man looked liked a Hell's Angel. He wore blue jeans and a black Harley-Davidson tee shirt. His face was covered with an unkempt beard. When I passed he gave me a big grin. His woman, wife, or something-or-other was standing close by with no shirt on. She smiled at me as I approached. The woman was nearly as big as the man, with breasts that sagged down to her stomach like two great water balloons.

"Just get here?" I asked.

"Yeah, just got in," he replied. "I'm Bean." The man lumbered over to me. His big paw reached out and he squeezed my hand so hard that I almost winced.

"I'm McDonald." I pulled my hand away and it dropped like a wounded pigeon. "How long are you in for?" I asked.

"That sounds like somethin' they'd ask ya in prison. How long you in for?" He laughed out loud and bantered with himself. "Got ten years for whacking off on my chopper while I was hauling ass by a schoolyard." He laughed again.

An alarm went off in my head but I reconsidered when the woman took over the conversation.

"We're staying the night. We'll be walking out in the morning."

"Long hike for just one night," I mused.

"Yeah, it was Jinny's idea. Shit man, it was bad enough I had to leave my bike back in San Bernardino but I can't stand this walking through the jungle on a goddamn trail that ain't wide enough to catch a fart. Then we get out here and it's a dead end, so we have to walk back the same way we came."

The woman broke in with some good humor. As she turned to talk to me, her massive tits continued to swing; they ran out of slack and rocked back and forth just above her naval. "Don't fall for Bean's horse-shit. He loves it back here. Play macho, keep on top of things, that's his game. I don't know who he thinks he's going to impress out here."

As I listened, I began to formulate a plan. There was only one way to handle the situation. I could have patted myself on the back for this one.

"Say, Bean. Have you been to the beach yet?"

"I got no use for the beach. God damn sand gets in your sprocket. The beach is for faggots."

"Have you seen the crowd down on the beach?"

Although I was trying to divert his attention, he was fighting off dogs and devils that were jumping at him from the kennel inside his thick skull.

"Three thousand miles to sleep on the ground and nowhere to go but back."

"Bean! Have you seen the scenery down on the beach?" I insisted.

"Yeah, it's great. A big cat box for faggots and surf bums. Who the hell needs all that water? I'm air cooled."

"I don't know, Bean! The girls I saw down there didn't look like faggots."

"Girls?"

That caught his interest. I hoped that Jinny didn't mind and I figured it probably didn't matter even if she did.

"Yeah, Bean. There are definitely some girls down there. And most of them aren't wearing suits."

A handful of tent stakes hit the ground with a metallic sound. His woman laughed out loud.

"Boy, you called his number."

"Where?" Bean looked around as if there was Pirate treasure in the sand.

"Right over there, Bean." I pointed toward the beach in a general direction. He turned to Jinny.

"Listen, babe, I think I better go check this out. I mean, those girls might be in trouble."

"Yeah, you better go, Bean. Just get back here before dinner and don't bring home no dessert."

The poor man's feet were churning underneath him. Without another word, he bounded out of the campsite. Left alone with the woman, I felt a little guilty.

"I didn't mean to run him out of here like that," I apologized. "Do you want some help setting up camp?"

"Nah," she answered. "Don't feel bad. I'm happy to get him out of my hair for a while. In fact, I should thank you."

"What for?"

"I'm going to get it good tonight."

She went back to work, which was double duty now without her man to help her, but I caught her drift.

"You know, if you guys want, you could come up to the dry cave for dinner tonight."

"The dry cave?"

"Yeah, it's up there against the rocks." I waved my arm in the direction of the shelter. "We're having wild goat, tonight."

"I'll have to see what kind of mood Bean is in when he comes back from the beach. But thanks for the invite."

"No problem."

With a gallant smile, I resumed my hike to the waterfall as she resumed her domestic duties. When I looked back from the other side of the gully, she already had the tent raised.

The path made a bend and headed toward the beach. Walking onto a flat bank, I could see the fall spewing a mist like feathers as it dove into the pool. There were four camping spaces on this plain of brush and flowering shrubs. Each space harbored a tent.

The last tent in line was set up on the bank just above the basin at the foot of the waterfall. In spite of the sun shining on it, the tent was damp from the constant dousing of mist from the fall. As I walked past the site, I heard a familiar sound coming out of the tent. At the pool, I stopped for a moment to listen.

The sound of a woman moaning came through clearly while the grunting of a man's low, bass voice joined in harmony. The chorus crescendoed toward climax. The meter of the tempo quickened until it reached a maximum velocity of two grunts and one moan per second. The sound of sexual ecstasy pounded with the regularity of an atomic clock. And then— And then—

"Oh, baby, take me, I'm going to come— I'm going to—"

"Do it— do it— I want you— I'm coming too—"

Feeling embarrassed, I went to the edge of the pool and stripped off my clothes. Stepping into the water, I picked my way to the fall and dunked myself under the cascade. The stream hit me with great force, washing the heat from my body. When I reemerged from the fall I went to a rock and sat in the sun.

Through the rumbling of the fall, I heard a final scream just before the voices stopped altogether. Standing up from the rock, I dunked myself back under the vertical stream. I stayed under for several moments with my head against my chest so that I could breathe. Stepping out, I found myself face to face with a young man. He was tall and had thick, black hair. He was out of breath but his expression was full of joy.

"Hi," he greeted me. "I have to get some water for my wife."

Stepping from the pool, I went to my clothes and started dressing.

"Go ahead."

"Thanks." He stepped into the water and thrust his jug under the fall. It was filled in seconds. "Thanks again." He headed back up the steps, padding quickly along the slick trail toward his tent.

"Is that your camp up there?"

"Yeah," he said, turning around to speak.

"Isn't the mist getting you wet?"

"It's nice." He had a young face and his smile was disarming. "It keeps us cool."

"Baraka, honey, come back in here."

"Gotta go."

"OK. See you."

Like a servant bound, the man scurried up the bank, carrying the water in one hand and using his other to claw his way forward. When he got to the tent he ducked inside and zipped the fly.

Pulling on my shorts, I sat back on a rock and fantasized about the occasion inside their shelter. The performance had been stirring. Their aural emissions had a strange mechanical resonance but there had been pleasure also, pure and simple. I could not help what I did next. Scaling the steps out of the water hole, I went directly to the door of the tent.

"Anyone home?" I hollered.

"Who is it?" a woman's voice asked in a matter-of-fact tone.

"It's Peter McDonald. I've come to invite you for dinner tonight in the dry cave."

My greeting was answered quickly. The sound of a zipper and then a girl's beaming face poked out of the opening.

"Hi, I'm Maryjane."

"Peter McDonald."

Then the young man's face stuck out next to the girl's. He was also smiling. From my view they looked like a two-headed monster with a fat nylon body.

"Hi, I'm Baraka."

"Are you two interested in a goat dinner up at the dry cave tonight?"

They looked at each other and turned back to me.

"Where is the dry cave?" she asked.

"Who's cooking the goat?" he asked.

It was like having a conversation with Twiddle Dee and Twiddle Dum.

"The dry cave is up there under that shelf of rock." I pointed through the forest. "You'll see the smoke there after sunset. Are you vegetarians?"

"No. But I've never eaten goat before," the girl said.

"My mom used to make goat," Baraka added.

"Baraka is Egyptian."

"You're from Egypt?" I inquired.

"No. North Hollywood."

"So you like goat?"

"I guess so."

"Why don't you come to the dry cave tonight after the sunset? There are some great people staying up there. There's one guy who walks around backward so that he doesn't forget."

"Wild," said Baraka.

"I don't like people who live in the past," said Maryjane.

"Oh, John is different. You'll see. There's plenty of food, so come on up if you want to. It should be quite a night."

"Alright! Thanks, Peter."

"Sure. See you later."

"See you," they said simultaneously.

As I was retreating, I heard the zipper being secured again and the sound of cooing resumed inside of the tent.

The low trail wound through the campsites that overlooked the beach. All of these sites were occupied but deserted. The heat hovered around the tents, settling on everything as if the sunshine were dust.

Some of the campsites had rock seats similar to the throne that Dennis had built except smaller and cozier. Many of the sites had clothes hanging from clotheslines or draped across the branches of small trees. There were books lying on rocks and scratch pads shut against prying eyes. A pair of hiking boots was a standard feature at the mouths of the tents, exchanged for tennis shoes or sandals, which were better suited for the lifestyle of the valley.

As I walked past Dennis's campsite, he waved to me from inside his grove of trees and I waved back. Traveling along the sea bank, I gazed toward the beach. The waves continued to pound the shore. The sun had dipped past midday and it began its descent toward the waiting ocean.

Out on the sand I saw Bean sitting contentedly staring at two women who were sunbathing close to the water. Behind me, where the Na Pali coast recaptured the shoreline from the spit of sand, I saw Joe juggling, waiting for the sunset. Shannon was with him, watching from her seat on a cotton blanket. A young couple with very white skin was playing with a toddler by the run-off stream near the waterfall. As I watched, the child ran into the stream and fell face first in the water, laughing wildly. The water overcame its little body and the father ran over to rescue the child before it went under. The mother smiled. When the child saw the maternal appreciation, it ran back toward the stream and repeated the act.

At the end of the trail where the campsites ended, I came to the helipad. Strolling over the grass, I sat under the ohi'a with its bristling red flowers. Leaning against the tree, I gazed over the firmament of the valley and along the shoreline.

In all appearances, Kalalau was as close to Paradise as there was on earth. Although I had come here unwittingly, the place was having a huge impact on me. The wonder and grandeur of the valley was staggering. The vibration of magnificence sang through the trees in a euphoric scale.

It seemed to me that all of the people who had come to the valley were seeking escape from a menacing world. But what had chased them into the valley in the first place? The quickness of life, the fleeting passage of time into the void of forgetfulness, or the meager reward earned for manning the watchtowers of duty? What was it that caused people to seek out these bastions of hope? Why is there a word faith, if faith exists at all?

These thoughts crawled through my mind as I searched the beach for a cosmic conversation. Life was out there somewhere. The real life. The good life. Yet it was hard to let go and let the dream come to fruition. Although survival had long ago become a mundane chore for the vast number of humans, we continued to bolster our defenses and build our fortifications. There was nothing left to fear and yet fear held us always. The predators of the dark shunned the most deadly predator of all—Man. We had conquered the world. We had pushed back the jungle. The entire world was ours, yet we cowered and wasted blessings on ghosts in spires that were created in our own image. Our gods stared back at us dumbfounded because after all, we were their masters.

Across the sand, the sun inched toward the horizon. I watched as a caravan of hikers came from the direction of the valley trail. They walked over the sand with utter grace, their steps loose from a stupor evolved from the beauty and solitude they had encountered in the Valley. From the forests on the slopes and the camps on the bank, the inhabitants came forth. They moved forward as if in a religious procession. Peace filled my mind and was reinforced by the scene of repose in front of me.

As the sun moved to the horizon, the blue sky was washed out in an orange fire that licked the edges of the waning daylight with erotic pink tongues. The apron behind the valley walls dimmed to a hard dark blue. Above the cliffs, flickering points of light were stars, heaven's fireflies landed on the deep velvet glow of nighttime, twinkling to life in the twilight sky.

Against the fiery horizon, silhouettes of the seekers sat transfixed by the day's demise. Where I had seen Joe and Shannon earlier, the rest of the followers were now gathered. I knew that the conflict of the afternoon had to be hanging heavy within the group. There would be no going back. Choices needed to be made. Life was rolling ahead and Paradise was at stake.

Beyond the beach, on the heiau, John was standing alone, his back to the ocean. He was looking up into the dominion of Kalalau. The sound of the passing day blew by him in a lost wind. He was pitiful, yet righteous. His quest for immortality made him appear foolish, yet his very perseverance seemed to canonize him and give him power.

If this valley had not been within the great barricade of Na Pali, not a world unto itself, John would have frightened me with his psychosis. As it was, I knew that I could get away from his madness, simply by leaving this place. But what of the others, those who looked on the Valley as their final retreat from a chaotic world? How had they become so entangled with John? All they had wanted was a place to live freely, but now they were trapped, held by their desire for something larger. The earth is wicked. And sometimes I am certain that evil rules the world from pole to pole. Out of heaven walk the greatest sinners. They walk not into hell sadly, they simply walk away from heaven.

Lost in these ruminations, time had passed. The sun had dipped below the line of the horizon. Across the sand, the silhouettes made their way back to their camps to prepare evening meals. John was gone from the heiau and the sky was growing dark. Standing, I walked over the grass in the direction of the dry cave. As I strolled onto the trail that disappeared into the forest, I could not help but feel sad.

Images stop time, yet time moves forward, leaving us with a life that is nothing more than frozen pictures within our brain. Heaven beckons, but we are given this poor existence, this sad howling at the moon as it flies over the earth, full and high.

last supper

As I had expected, the mood inside the dry cave was solemn. There were two small goats on spits over the fire, but there was no celebration. Everyone was there except John, and his absence was conspicuous.

In the back of the cave, I discovered a couple of milk crates. Bringing one to the front of the overhang, I sat down and picked up a magazine that was lying there. It was a glossy fashion monthly. I flipped through an article on the proper application of make-up.

The followers sat quietly averting their eyes from one another. Against the back wall of the cave, Rick strummed a song on his guitar that I thought recognized. He played through the verse six or seven times before he sang half of the words of the chorus, *"Home is where I want to be, but I guess I'm already there."* Nothing more of the tune remained in his memory so he switched songs but continued strumming at the same tempo.

Inside the alcove, Bill lay on his sleeping bag reading a book by the light of a candle. Judy was standing at the back of the cave holding a calendar. She flipped the pages slowly and studied each picture.

Close to where I sat, Marlie braided a bight into a piece of old, black nylon rope. He was fashioning a snare. At the far end of the cave where the firelight dwindled into darkness, Joe was juggling three round rocks of similar shape and size. He appeared anxious and kept looking into the night. Sitting beside him, Shannon shared the vigil.

The tension inside the cave was excruciating. Lynn was sitting on a rock next to the fire stirring a pot of lilikoi tea. Beside her, Ron kept the goats turning over the flames. Grease was dripping from them and sputtering explosions fell onto the grill. The carcass of the goat had turned a dirty brown from the smoke and the flames. Looking at the others, Ron begged for reassurance but got none. Everyone was self absorbed and took no notice of him or each other. Taking the ends of the skewers in his hands he turned them faster.

From the darkness a form appeared and I could feel the anxiety rise up in the group. Into the light of the cave, Caren strode from out of the forest. Nine pair of eyes jerked in her direction. The attention made her uncomfortable. Avoiding their stares, she grabbed the other milk crate and sat next to me. Together we looked toward the ocean without speaking. She laid a hand on my thigh and sighed.

The moon was a sliver away from full. The quiet silver glow of the moonlight shimmered on the water. Above the horizon, opal stars twinkled across the black curtain of the night. Next to me, Caren awaited the interrogation. I gave her a few minutes to relax before I spoke.

"You didn't find him?"

"No," she answered looking into the sky.

"Did you try the heiau?"

"He wasn't there. I went back to the sweat lodge and looked there, too."

"I wonder where he is." I was feeling sedate and my question brought no inspiration to her.

"I don't know." Caren shifted on her seat. "He's out there somewhere." She looked at me and smiled uneasily, then rubbed the palm of her hand across my leg.

"He'll be back." Coming up behind us, Marlie gave this analysis while he twirled the snare between his fingers with an unconscious motion. "Ron is cooking it just the way he likes it."

From out of the dark forest, the first of the guests arrived. Walking in on the moonlit path, Dennis and Michelle entered the dry cave. With them were Juerg and Kate.

"Hi, everyone," Dennis said with his usual friendliness.

The return salutation was unexpectedly sparse. Dennis and Michelle walked to the fire. The followers were too lost in their thoughts to pay attention to the guests or question why they had come.

"So where's our Man?" Dennis wasted no time.

"He isn't here yet. There was some trouble today," I answered.

"What kind of trouble?"

"Mutiny," I said raising my eyebrows slightly.

"What are you talking about?"

"Ask one of them," I said pointing to the dejected followers.

It was obvious that Dennis did not like this idea. As he looked around, I saw his enthusiasm plummet.

It was not long before Maryjane and Baraka arrived for the feast. After their introductions, Baraka sat down next to Rick. After listening for a few minutes, Baraka asked to play the guitar. He began to play barre chords on the instrument. Bringing out his flute, Ron began to blow scales.

Having the guests in the dry cave made me feel less isolated. It did not seem to matter to the others that these outsiders had joined us. Marlie was back to working on the snare and he didn't say anything about the extra mouths to feed. After all, he had instigated the revolt and for the time being was just another follower, although shorter than the others.

When Bean and Jinny arrived, the party was complete. Looking around, Bean picked out Bill as a willing listener. He went to the alcove and began to describe the anatomy of each female body he had seen on the beach. This was uncomfortable because some of the bodies he was describing were sitting in the cave listening.

As Bean increased his pace, the descriptions became more precise and lewd. Bill was trapped inside the vestibule with Bean's loud voice pushing him back whenever he tried to move. Baraka played rhythm while Ron played melodies. At the foot of the musician's mat, Maryjane smiled and prodded her man to keep playing whenever the song seemed to be ending.

At the fire, Michelle was stirring a papaya stew that Lynn had been cooking. Keeping his head in the shadows, Dennis watched everything with a sharp eye. Near the fire ring, Juerg was comparing the scene in the dry cave to anything he had witnessed in Switzerland. The furrow in his brow told me he was not having much luck. Against the back wall of the cave, Kate stared into the fire with a Mona Lisa smile, not talking but apparently content.

Then, walking backward out of the darkness, The Man entered the cave and stood with his back to the gathering. The music stopped and the cave became still.

If the workings of the mind could be heard with the naked ear, there would have been a buzzing, humming, clicking cacophony of noise rising through the shelter, which was the sound of the group taking up their defensive postures against this grey robed invader. To me, it was only a job, so I looked on with seasoned disinterest.

"Is the feast prepared?" John demanded as if nothing had happened.

"Just the way you like it. I've got mango sauce and papaya—" Marlie started but was cut off.

"Who are all these people?" John asked gruffly.

Dennis stood and walked over to the holy man.

"Hi, John. It's Dennis Fitzpatrick. I met you at Honokoa."

"What are you doing here?"

It was clear that John was not in the mood for small talk. Even with his back to them, The Man was able to stare down the strangers.

"We came to try that goat meat, John. Heard the Aloha Kitchen has the best food in the valley." Dennis tried laughing but the sound fell hollowly onto the dirt floor of the cave.

"What is this, Marlie? I go away for a few hours and you invite tourists to take part in the ceremony?"

"Well, I sure didn't invite them, if that's what you are saying, boss."

"That's what I'm saying, Marlie. And I'll tell you I don't like the idea one bit. The ritual is for believers only."

"Hey, John. It's goat meat, isn't it? There's plenty to go around?" Bill exclaimed. "Tonight we all eat grass!" Bill chuckled and crawled out of the alcove. Glad to have escaped Bean's dialogue, he walked to the fire; the magic cigarette appeared and was lit.

"What do you mean it's just goat meat, Bill? It is grass. It is life. It is mangoes. It's our existence. Our key to survival. These people are unclean. They have not been initiated into the spirit."

"Hey now, just a minute. Who are you calling unclean? Turn around and let me have a look at you."

"Who is that?" John asked loudly.

"My name's Bean, if that makes any difference. We were just having a little get together before you came along. Why don't you pack up and find someplace else to have a bad trip?" He turned to Jinny who shook her head disgustedly. "What a dork," he said. "I told you the beach was nothing but faggots and surf bums."

"Weird dude, for sure," Jinny agreed.

"Who's that playing the guitar?" John hollered, ignoring Bean, as he attended to this new distraction.

Baraka had been unconsciously plunking on the instrument but he laid his fingers against the strings to stop their vibration and handed the guitar back to Rick. Standing up, Baraka walked toward John.

"Hey, you're the guy who walks around backward, aren't you? What a far out thing to do, man."

"Who are you calling man? I am the spirit. I am the earth. I am the four winds of tomorrow."

Baraka was stopped cold. "Wild."

"Who is that with Lynn? Why is she tending the meal?"

"It's me. Michelle. Dennis's wife." Michelle tried to sound courageous but her voice quivered around each syllable.

"How dare you touch the meal of sanctity. You are impure. You have not been tested."

"I've done a few dinner parties. You don't have to be one of the world's great chefs to roast a goat."

John's litany had Bean on his toes ready to throw The Man out of the cave and into the forest. Juerg and Kate were cowering at the back wall while Michelle stood over the fire glaring at The Man's back. Dennis was planted halfway between John and me. He was looking at the back of The Man's grey robe.

The followers remained surprisingly quiet. Watching closely, I knew that a decision was being made.

"Who brought you here? Who asked you to partake in our rites? This is a holy place."

"Maybe we should go," Dennis said.

"Maybe you should go! But who asked you here to begin with?" John demanded.

"Well, you picky-ass son-of-a-bitch. I'm going to kick your butt right out-a-here." Bean made his move, but Jinny held his arm.

"Let's just go, Bean. This guy's having a flashback or something."

"Michelle, I think that we should go now," Dennis tried again.

"To hell with that, Dennis. I'm eating some of this goat. I have suddenly come up with quite an appetite."

"No, Michelle. I think we should get going."

"You two aren't going anywhere. I'm going to throw this bum out and we're going to have ourselves a nice meal." Bean took a step toward John, but Jinny held on.

"What has become of you?" John's voice had grown sad and quiet. "Why have you betrayed me?"

"No one is betraying you, John," Joe said gently. "We just want to lighten up a little. It's Indian summer, you know. We won't have many more days like this."

"You of all people Joe. How can you speak against me after all I have done for you?"

"Joe is not speaking against you, John," Judy said from her position close to Juerg and Kate. "He's just telling you how he feels."

"He doesn't know how he feels unless I tell him. That's the way it is."

"John, you're looking for trouble," Shannon warned. "We have a right to our own feelings. We're human too. "

"Yes, that is the trouble with all of you. You are human. All too human."

"Is there something wrong with being human, John?" Shannon asked defiantly.

"Yes, as a matter of fact, there is. There's one very small problem with being human." Just for effect John paused long enough for everyone to lean forward to focus on his next words. They came out in a shout. "You'll never get to heaven if you are human."

"Who in the hell wants to go to heaven anyway, you peon? I'm going to kick your ass." Jinny held onto Bean with all of her strength.

"I want to know who brought these heathens into my temple."

"Oh relax, John. The goat is ready if anybody wants to eat." With these words, Lynn picked up a plate that she had sliced some meat onto. Walking through the gathering she began to hand out the meal.

"Stop! Now! Would you betray me?"

"You betray yourself, John. Have some food or leave us alone while we eat." Shannon took several strips of the goat flesh, stuck one in her mouth and started to chew, her eyes set.

"Who will betray me?"

Ignoring John, everyone started to take the meat as it was offered. The Man stood with his back to the crowd. His body began to tremble.

"Will you all betray me?"

Lynn continued to hand out the food. Not knowing what to do, Juerg and Kate each took their ration. On his mat, Rick accepted a piece and began to play his guitar as he chewed. Next to him, Ron took a piece and wolfed it down. With fingers slick with grease, Ron resumed playing.

From out of The Man's mouth came a shout so loud that it made me drop my goat meat on the ground in front of me. The pronouncement pierced the air with such intensity that sleeping birds could be heard batting their wings in the branches of the silent trees. Everyone was taken aback and the gathering fell silent.

"If you don't need me anymore, then I will leave this place tomorrow. Meet me at the pasture on Red Hill if you wish to see me one last time before my rapture. I will be there when the whales come in."

"Ah, John. Come on, man. It's just a little goat," Bill tried one last time.

"You have betrayed me."

With these words, The Man turned and strode into the night. Everyone watched him leave. When he was gone, they looked at each other and shrugged. The Man had finally crossed the line. Marlie disappeared a few minutes later but no one but me seemed to notice. The party resumed.

"Hey, can I have some more of that goat?" Bean asked, obviously glad that John was gone.

Walking over with the plate, Lynn let Bean help himself and then she offered some to Dennis who waved it off. Michelle chastised him with a glare and Dennis reluctantly grabbed a piece of the meat.

"Pretty wild guy," Baraka exclaimed taking several strips. "I can't believe he walks everywhere backward."

"I think I'll go back to my tent now," Kate said. She stood and slipped into the night in the direction of the waterfall.

Declining a second helping, Juerg left the cave not long after Kate. Satisfied that everyone was safe and filled with goat, Bean took Jinny's arm and dragged her out of the cave. After tea, Dennis and Michelle left without a word. Baraka and Maryjane were the only tourists left. Baraka played songs with Rick and Ron well past midnight.

Down by the ohi'a tree, I drank half of what was left of the Wild Turkey and sat with Caren until she fell asleep in my arms. Gazing at the sky, I saw the stars turn in the heavens until they began to spin. With a petting hand, I tried to wake Caren up without success. Eventually, I fell asleep with my back against the tree and the sound of the crashing waves in my ears. Tomorrow would be another day. Just another day in Paradise.

sermon at the summit

When I was younger, I had been a scoop photographer. If there was action anywhere in the world, I was the first one on the scene. Any hot spot would find me crawling in with my cameras around my neck and my heart in my throat. In those days I was running fast with the hottest correspondents in the business. Of course war was the only game in town for those of us who thought the thrill of the job was the measure of life itself. We thrived on the frenzy of battle and I lusted for that one elusive photo that would make me known. I had been to all the wars of my time, great and small, although I was too young to catch the Vietnam extravaganza.

Having missed Vietnam, I worked twice as hard to prove myself. Every day I labored in the company of the veteran photographers of that conflict and saw in their faces my own inexperience. Every night I plotted my strategy and every morning, I was up early scouring the countryside for a shot. My leads were wrestled from reluctant informants, but my perseverance paid off.

There had been the Khyber Pass where I photographed the mujahidin rebels laying waste to the Russian hordes who had invaded their homeland uninvited. When the U.S. Marine barracks in Beirut exploded along with the myth of American supremacy, I was standing on the rubble while corpsmen pulled dead soldiers from the debris. The shutter of my camera snapped automatically. A charge of electricity crackled in my head. And I got the picture.

When the Vincennes shot down an Iranian jumbo jet, one of my photos appeared in Time magazine showing civilian luggage floating languidly in a blood and oil stained Persian Gulf. A child's doll bobbed on the waves. My triumph was won by learning the morbid tastes of an irrational world.

Toward the end of their brutal territorial war with Iran, the Iraqis gassed their own citizens. With a bandana wrapped across my face, I tramped through the streets of that silent Kurdish village and I got the picture.

In time, I moved from those Asian locations. I began my exodus westward, toward home. Inside of myself, I did not realize that I was losing the thread of life that bound me to the earth. Looking back, I can say that as the days dragged on, I was losing my edge. Shot by shot, I was becoming dull. But I still got the picture.

When I look back at my work from that period, my style was actually becoming more precise, unique, and imbued with a clear moral vision. My eye was more attuned, revealing a picture that told not a thousand words, but a million or a billion words, all laid flat on a single frame. I had learned to expose people in the agony of their most tragic moments. Their screams were caught silent and in mid-air, the gruesome convulsions of flesh dying alone, away from any reason, the terminal pain of souls that could not stand to feel anymore, and so escaped into death instead. These were the easiest of subjects. They did not see my pressing lens where they lay in the pit of their eternal defeat. These losers in the game were gone, except for my witness to their futile struggle. Their will had become their fate; I was only there to chronicle their demise. And I had gotten the picture.

Closer to home, I moved like a spirit berthed in a fog. In Timisoara, Romania, I made my way through the four thousand who were strewn in the streets and the alleys. Migrating to Bucharest, I watched as the people shouted down their tyrant, and I wondered why I could not do the same. On Christmas Day, the dictator and his wife were executed with the fourth word of the song on their lips and the letter of the six in his pocket. Inside the palace, I filched a final portrait but I could not remember the carol or how it had once been sung. I had gotten the picture, but was the nightmare ever going to be over?

My sensitivity was changing. I could feel the heat of my own presence. Time was delivered to me in spasms. The end was held out to me like a layoff notice in the payroll line. The weather was telling me that it was time to quit.

Without warning one day, I could not find the energy to wake up in the morning. There was no longer the miserable drive to track down the blood and the tears. I had been used up by a grain of myself that could no longer bear the light of day. I was burnt out but my work and my perspective were as clear as ever. My eye was becoming the eye of God. It was beginning to scare the hell out of me. And I got the picture.

The end came from a blind side as it does almost without exception. To those that have accepted into their senses the shock of reality, each open door is a wall of truth and every revelation brings the other end of innocence. Slowly but surely, blindness wraps itself around the searcher to block the flood of awful emotion.

It was summer in Bosnia-Herzegovina and I had gotten up late with a feeling in my gut that I could not gauge anymore. The signs that had once guided me forward were now lost in a callousness that had scarred over my psyche to protect it from the blisters of reality that brought pain with every step. Before, my ambition had been enough to prod me forward. But now the battle between my aspirations and my subversion had raged to a standoff somewhere on the frontiers of my mind. The seconds of passing time were demons that shocked me with cattle prods.

There was a car waiting for me as usual in the square at Tuzla, so I took it. Steering the car was my Muslim assistant with his thick accent and his superficial optimism. He drove me into the countryside where a new assault was under way. The staging area was a small village in the mountains. The Bosnian army was allowing photographers to congregate there to follow the soldiers in their advance against the Serbs.

My colleagues had arrived early. With a daring I now found impossible to muster, they made their own deals. In the dawn hours, they worked their way to the front where the carnage was grisly enough to shock their subscribers into buying that day's edition to take one more peek at the wreckage. I was in the rear but I was not worried. My eye was a telescope. My mind was a tracking device that led me forward. Taking my time, I listened to the officers speak about their own destinies. In the late morning, I strolled into the surrounding hills.

A few miles outside of the village was an enclave. This had been Serbian held territory the day before but the Croatians had pushed them out that morning. In a field near the edge of town, on a hill, in a stone house, was a captured ammunition dump that was being guarded by irregular Bosnian soldiers. At the perimeter of the field, near the house and close to the road, was a huge and ancient beech tree. It stood unperturbed by the human struggle all around it. Its great branches held up the day with unabridged strength. It swayed slightly in the breeze, its leaves rustled on their boughs.

As I approached, I saw two small girls standing behind the massive trunk of the tree. From their hiding place, they watched curiously the comings and goings of the army vehicles that were taking inventory at the ammunition dump. When the vehicles passed, billows of dust rose into the air and the girls would run behind the tree to hide. They held the hems of their dresses down with small hands that would soon know labor. Their closed mouths would fill and then overflow with laughter. Their giggles mocked the roar of the military drama.

Their dresses were spotless and delicately stiff and seemed out of place in the chaos of poverty and war that clutched at the dark heart of this country. The folds of their skirts were layered in tiers of lace and crepe. The tiny upper bodies of the girls were hugged in embroidered linen with lace collars at their throats and lace armlets sewn onto the ends of the sleeves. One of the girls was wearing a white dress that looked like a tiny wedding gown.

My sensitivity had been transformed over the years and this was one of those occasions that made me realize how much. As I approached the tree, several trucks roared out of the front yard of the house loaded with the captured ammunition. As they raced down the road past them, the girls scurried away with their dresses sailing. It was not my job, but I had the overwhelming desire to take a picture of the two girls retreating from the blustering fury of the war.

The girls were hiding behind the tree again, laughing in their game, their legs turned at awkward angles that are sometimes confused with shyness but which are only the lack of experience in walking that a colt might have or a fawn. It would be the first picture that I had taken that day.

Even though my sensibilities had been corrupted by my own need to replace beauty with horror, I knew that no matter what picture I took it would be the right picture. I had fallen out of the flow of primal meaning but in so doing, I had entered a world that was my own. It was scary to be so alone and to hold the eye of God in my sockets. To press down the shutter button and allow twelve frames to click by as dust swirled around the girls giggling and the sound of fighting in the valleys above us. Without a word, I walked away because that was part of the bargain. I had gotten the picture.

Inside the enclave, there was not much to see, the usual peasants, some going about their work, others standing on sidewalks, no different from people in my own hometown.

Without raising my camera again, I walked away, satisfied that I had sufficient stock shots to fulfill my contract. My driver walked beside me making off-color comments about the enemy. I let the man lead me back down the road to our car, which would take us back to Tuzla.

As we approached the field near the house, I saw smoke rising into the air in white billows. I could smell the odor of explosives hanging inside of these clouds. As we reached the tree where the girls had been playing, I saw that it was shattered by the impact of an artillery shell that was meant for the ammunition dump. Looking at the remains of the ancient beech, I was shocked that only an hour before it had stood as a sentinel to the truth of this enclave's existence. Now it was a shattered trunk, smoking and dead.

At first I could find no trace of the two girls but as I walked around the wreckage of the tree I discovered the tattered remnants of their dresses caught in the dismembered branches and sticking out of the dirt like rags planted for cotton. There was other evidence of the girls' death but there is no sense in describing the slaughter. To those of us who have seen these things, it is so much litter. To those who receive the edited version of these conflicts, it would terrorize without cause.

At my side, the driver stood dumbly. The monstrosity of the loss had erased his smile. Two small girls who only a moment before had played a child's game were gone. Not for the day, or the summer, but for ever and ever, amen.

My driver looked on expecting me to take a shot to follow up my earlier work, but I could not. I could not get the picture.

I quit at that very moment and headed home, a place that did not exist anymore. My eyes were filled with tears as dry as sand. Darkness came through eyelids that could not close. Awake at night, I was dead during the day in the sunshine.

There was a time when I was a scoop photographer, when I would get up early to find the shot. That is why I was on Red Hill that morning, while goats dug up the earth and the whales played close to shore. When John arrived alone I held my ground. On the pasture, the goats raised their heads and watched him approach. When he was settled on the hill, they went back to eating.

"What are you doing here, McDonald?"

"I'm here to finish my job."

"I'm releasing you. Leave the film with Marlie. He'll take care of it."

"But I haven't finished my job, John."

"No job is ever complete, McDonald. I could talk to you for a hundred years and you would still not understand that simple fact."

"What are you going to tell the others this morning?"

"I'm going to tell them good-bye. They have forsaken my guidance."

"They still like you, John. They just want some room to live."

"I will give them all the room they need."

The triteness of the comment caught me off guard and I grew impatient.

"You know, that's what kills me about guys like you, John. You can't allow people to learn their own lessons. They seek answers and you throw them words. If they fall for it, you never let go. You hold them so tightly that it ends up holding you. It's the irony of prophecy."

"You are wrong, McDonald. You have no conception of these higher realms. You have deluded yourself. You are afraid to take the biggest step of your life. The step backward into the future."

"I may be wrong, John, but there's one eventuality that you should prepare for."

"And what's that, McDonald?"

"I may be right."

There was a pause.

"I want you to go, McDonald. I release you from your contract."

"You can release me from my contract, John, but you can't kick me out of the Valley. You were right, this is Paradise. But heaven is my decision, my responsibility, and my daydream if that's what it comes down to. "

"Suit yourself. There is nothing more for us to say to each other."

John walked backward toward the cliff and stopped just before the edge. He turned to face the ocean and looked out across the water, his back to me.

The followers came up the trail of Red Hill. Joe with Shannon, Judy, Bill and Ron. Caren walking slowly and Marlie far behind. Rick and Lynn came last. The followers straggled up the hill, plodding over the red earth. The goats parted for the followers. The group came slowly, but they had come, as sure as the day.

Toward the east, a veil of fog covered the sloping palis, blanketing the lush green slips of jungle in greyness. Over the ocean, clouds had begun to form in masses. Behind the walls of the valley, over the Alaki Swamp, dark clouds folded into the sky but could not reach the sun, which even this early was hanging high over Kalalau.

Standing to the side, away from John, I watched the followers enter the flat pasture and walk toward The Man. All around them, the goats bayed softly, apparently feeling safe in numbers here in the open. When the disciples were congregated in a half circle on the grassy slope, John began to speak with his back to them. He did not see them but he knew that they were there.

"I have always been a dreamer and for every dream, I have received a blessing. You know that I do not use big words but I have read many books and I know what was said in the past. The philosophers have spoken and yet the world remains a chaotic and confusing place. They have given us nothing of value and they have left nothing to work with. I searched for something to help us overcome this confusion. First, I came to the Valley. Then, you came to me. For a time everything was peaceful and we prospered in Kalalau.

"This has always been a sanctuary for explorers. This is where the Menehune tribes lived by the sea before they disappeared into the swamp. This is the place where the Polynesians chose to settle because the valley was protected. This is the resting place of Koolau the leper. Like all of them, we came here to escape the world because the world had let us down. Here, we could have any life we wanted. Everyone liked the way it felt to be in the Valley.

"From the beginning I knew that we were doing something special. So I tried to hang on to the feeling we had when things were going well for us. The times when we were high in the upper reaches. This is when I decided to never forget. I gave you roles I knew would make you feel comfortable, roles that allowed you to be yourselves. I learned when you were being untruthful and when you were being honest. I knew when the sun was shining on your path and when the tide was flooding your harbor. I knew because I cared enough to know. All you wanted was escape but I had other plans for you. I would help you to escape, not out of darkness but into purpose. I did this for you because I loved you. I vowed never to forget."

As the sermon continued I walked along the cliff and found that by climbing down a bank along the rim, I could get a good shot of John's face. He was speaking with his eyes closed so he did not see me. Behind him his followers looked on solemnly, trying to match his words with some emotion that they were feeling. Around the followers, the goats moved closer as if they wanted to hear the sermon. Their circle tightened as John continued his speech.

"To not forget was a tool for us. It was going to do no good to escape if we did not become something else in time. Would we be no better than the goats foraging everyday of their lives just to stay alive? I tried to make something positive out of our existence and create a world where others could feel safe. I looked behind us so that I could gauge what we would become. That is why I brought in the photographer, to get the word out that there was a place for people who needed relief. People who did not want to live with self-destructive behavior. People who did not want to sleep with the enemy. They could come here and be whole again."

A goat had moved in next to Ron and it nipped at the hem of his skirt. This distracted the followers for a moment and they looked down at the offending animal. Without disturbing the sermon, Ron swatted the goat trying to get it to go away. The other goats moved closer to the congregation, their heads to the ground, their mouths nibbling, their cloven hooves pacing forward.

"We have identified our enemy and we fight them with passion. The death cult does not want to accept people who think for themselves. They do not want us to be creative outside of their sphere, because we may reveal the truth about them. The truth is they want to see us dead while we are still alive. We don't have to compete in the Valley and they hate us for that. They want us at each other's throats so that we stay in line. They want us to be afraid so that we will not strike out for the higher places. What we needed was a clear approach to the problem. Like our solution to the problem of the goats. The goats are eating up the valley, so we eat the goats to keep the equilibrium of the earth intact. Is that senseless? No, that is perfection. We have to bring what we believe down to earth, so that everyone can use it. If I am to be faulted it is for caring too much. But I can live with that."

I was in a perfect position for a shot of The Man, with his followers gathered behind him. As John rambled I lifted my camera to take the shot. It is hard to describe what happened next. I was watching through my viewfinder. It occurred in slow motion.

As I checked the back focus, I noticed that the goat herd had infiltrated the place where the followers stood. The animals had their heads to the ground grazing but they seemed to be watching where they were going through the tops of their eyes. They were moving forward with precision, like a half-time show at a football game where the marching band moves in synchronized order across the field.

The next moment, I noticed that the goats had formed a grazing line between The Man and his followers. As I watched dumbfounded a big Billy lifted his head and took a long survey of The Man as if he were taking aim. He blinked his lids over his huge eyes. Bringing my camera around, I shot a picture of the animal. It looked that strange.

Suddenly, while the followers watched in horror, the Billy dug at the ground twice with his hoof, throwing tufts of grass and dirt behind him. Then he looked up again as if to orient himself. Again, he gouged the red ground with his cloven hoof. John continued to speak as I snapped pictures. Then all hell broke loose.

Snorting through his nose, the goat released himself from his stationary position. In a gallop, he charged The Man, picking up speed as he descended on him. At the last moment, the goat lowered his head and closed his eyes for the collision. John was in mid-sentence with his back to his followers when the goat slammed into him. This sent The Man flying forward, standing straight up, over the edge of the cliff and into the sky.

I had to swivel my head quickly to shoot The Man as he sailed into the air and flew right by me. Strangely, studying the pictures later, a look of total abandon was on The Man's face as if he had succumbed to the evil he had pitted himself against. A distant scream emanated from the clutch of followers as I continued to click the shutter. The disciples ran to the edge of the cliff as I snapped pictures. They watched as John sailed down a hundred and fifty feet to the surf below. In the last shot I have of him, John is going into the water feet first, like a statue facing the world backward. He did not somersault, did not flip or spin. He entered the water just as he had been standing in front of me only a moment before. And I got the picture.

Behind me, I heard the crack of the pistol. There was no reason to look back. Marlie had gunned down the Billy.

I quickly changed lenses and watched the crashing surf through my telephoto. I tried to focus at the place where I thought The Man would resurface. The waves blasted against the rocks where John had gone in. For one second I thought I saw him surface but then nothing.

"McDonald!?"

It was Marlie standing at my side looking down at the water.

"I don't see him."

"Why didn't you warn him?" he shouted at me.

"I didn't have time," I shouted back.

"We have to get down to him." Judy made the decision and the followers ran back to the trail and down Red Hill as quickly as they could without slipping in the slick red dirt.

I remained behind, standing at the spot where John had fallen. Putting my eye to the viewfinder, I scanned the surf looking for any sign, but my search was fruitless. The Man had disappeared under the churning water.

Panning my camera, I watched the others run as far as they could on the cobble beach before the cliffs cut off their advance. A small figure that was Marlie scrambled up and down looking for a route onto the face of the cliff. The rest of the followers, huddled in a group among the boulders, watched his frantic attempts. There was no way for him to get close to the location where John had plunged into the ocean but he continued to rush along the slippery piles of grey stones, searching the pounding surf for signs of life.

At that moment, I felt the first raindrop hit the top of my head. It drove its way through my hair and its chill spread onto my scalp. I looked into the sky. Clouds had gathered between the valley walls and the well of the ocean. A slow integration of grey boiled above the earth. Its movement was sluggish and could not be judged in degrees. It was a storm. Within a minute, a light shower was coming down. The sharp greens of the valley paled in the overcast. Within moments, my clothes were wet and sticking to my skin.

On the beach, Marlie was still trying to find some passage out to the tidal walls but his movements had slowed. A sense of resignation could be seen in the followers as they crowded together. They looked at Marlie and down at the surf that was growing more turbulent with the wind of the storm coming in at its back. The disciples stood in one place, frozen in their futile vigil.

Slowly, stepping over the body of the dead attacker, I pushed through the herd of goats that continued tearing chunks of grass up with their teeth. The dirt from the roots fell off the clumps of grass and scattered on the ground at the goat's feet. Their coats were slick from the rain. A wet, musty, animal smell pervaded the air within the herd. The last two Billys blocked my path with their bony hindquarters and I had to reach down and shove them aside. They looked at me indifferently as I passed.

At the bottom of Red Hill, I thought of joining the followers on the shore but it was raining harder now. Taking the high trail, I set off in the direction of camp. I would get Rick's boat and I would have Dennis bring his big fishing pole. We could use it to drag the bottom for John's body. I would think of something. On the other hand, if this rain stopped, I might just hike out of here this morning. It appeared that my job was over.

Little did I realize that this was only the beginning of the storm. The clouds would collide and the rain would fall from heaven in torrents. This was the price to be paid. This would be the reminder.

A Hard Rain

weather

In camp, the tourists were rushing about, bracing for the storm. Once they had weatherproofed, they crawled into their tents to escape the rain, which was coming down soft and warm. I ran through the campsites listening to the drops spatter on the canopy of the forest above me.

As I bore down on Dennis and Michelle's site, I saw their heads sticking out of the opening of their tent, watching the rain from the nest of their air mattress.

"Hey, Peter. You want to come in out of the rain?" Dennis greeted me as I approached.

Out of breath, I kneeled and peered into the shelter.

"Something happened."

"What is it?" Dennis asked without pause. I tried to catch my breath before I spoke again.

"John fell off a cliff and went into the water."

The couple stared at me but did not respond.

"Is he alright?" Michelle asked finally.

"I don't think so."

Dennis sat up and pulled on his pants.

"Where did he fall?" Dennis asked as he slipped his shirt on.

"The top of Red Hill. A goat butted him over the cliff."

Dennis came out of the tent. He finished buttoning his pants as he questioned me.

"What do you mean a goat butted him? It shoved him off the cliff?"

"It came right up behind him. Before any of us saw what was happening, John was over the edge. There was nothing we could do."

"Where are the others?"

"They're at the beach but they can't get to him."

"Let's get Juerg and go down there."

"Grab your fishing pole. Maybe we can fish his body out."

"His body?" Michelle looked terrified.

"Even if he survived the fall, the waves and the rocks would have killed him by now."

Underneath the tarps, their campsite was dry but at the edge of the site where the altar stood, the rain fell steadily onto the ground. Michelle looked at Dennis for reassurance but we were already walking away through the drizzle.

"You get Juerg," I yelled to Dennis above the din of the rain. "I'm going to the cave to get Rick's boat."

"I'll meet you at the other end of the camp."

"Two minutes."

"Check."

In the dry cave, I grabbed the rubber kayak that had been deflated and was stuffed into the sleeping alcove. I ran out from under the protective overhang and back into the rain.

At the entrance of the campground where all of the trails drew together, I joined Dennis and Juerg. It was faster to walk on the sand so we scooted down the bank to the beach and ran toward the river. The rain fell steadily but was still no more than a spring shower. A great, big, grey sky that was the color of a storm had filled the blue expanse. With the wind at their backs, the waves bucked onto shore and we had to walk high on the beach to keep from being washed by the rising swells.

Where the beach ended in a field of mossy, round stones, we jumped along carefully trying not to slip. Ahead of us was the heiau and from there it was a short distance to where the others were searching for The Man.

When we reached the heiau, we found that the followers had given up. They were sitting on the grass knoll, wet and looking defeated. I ran up to Marlie and grabbed him by the shoulders.

"Did you find him?"

With a violent slap of his arm, he pushed my hands away and stepped back to glare at me.

"No, we didn't find him. He's lost."

"Let's take the boat out. He could be trapped up against the cliffs."

"Why are you so interested, McDonald? You're the one who pushed John over the side," Marlie yelled out.

Rick turned to Marlie with panic in his face.

"What are you talking about?"

"McDonald saw the goat before it hit John. He could have stopped it."

I moved toward the old sailor but stopped. I turned back to Rick as I corralled my anger.

"Get the boat ready. The water's warm. We may be able to find him."

"Let's go."

On the beach, Rick unfolded the kayak and pulled the portable pump from its stowage in the craft. He had the vessel blown up in ten minutes but it seemed like forever as I thought of John being tossed about.

With help from Juerg and Dennis, we pushed the kayak into the battering waves and boarded it just in time to be engulfed by a surge. Grabbing a paddle I thrust it into the water and rowed. In the front of the craft, Rick plowed the surface of the ocean with furious strokes. We were submerged by another wave before we broke away from the shoreline and headed down wind. Above us rose the cliffs of black lava.

Dennis had agreed to go with Caren and watch from the point where John had fallen. As we bobbed on the waves, I looked up and saw them standing on the abutment above Red Hill. We still had a quarter mile to go before we reached their position.

Thrown about in the foam, we strained our eyes looking for some sign of the lost Man. The undulating flanks of the waves blocked everything from sight. The only clear view we got was when the kayak was catapulted to the top of a swell. There, for a brief instant, we could look out at the miserable soup before we were sucked back into the trough. Against the walls of the palis the waves blasted the rocks with horrifying force. We were thrown around for nearly an hour when Rick gave the order to turn back.

"He's gone," Rick shouted.

"What if he's not? We can't leave him behind."

"It's getting too rough to work out here."

"A little longer," I yelled out, but the wind blew the words back into my mouth.

Rick was already paddling to the left and turning us around. There was no choice except to heed his order. With the wind and the waves at our back, it was all we could do to keep ourselves from drifting into the cliffs. When we reached the place where the river entered the ocean, we were thrown forward on the curls of seven huge waves that thrust the kayak onto the shore. Juerg and Lynn were there to help us dock.

"There was no sign of him from the cliff." Dennis stood before me in his wet clothes and his boots covered in red mud.

"It was too rough out there. We had to come in."

Looking at the ocean, Rick paused for a moment and then directed Juerg and Lynn to help him drag the kayak into the safety of the river gorge and up onto the bank. He tied the craft to a thin hibiscus with an equally thin length of rope.

The rain continued to shower down on us while we decided our next step. After a short discussion that was devoid of expectation, we walked up to the heiau. It had been more than two hours since John had plunged into the waves. If he were alive he would have shown up by this time. There was nothing that we could do at this point to save him.

"What do we do now, Rick? Should we go for Search and Rescue?"

The followers were in shock: their faces were fixed; their eyes watched our mouths as we spoke.

"They won't get here in time to do anything."

"We should call them in anyway," Dennis said. "If we don't, they may think there was some kind of foul play."

"With this rain the rivers are going to flood and close the trail. There is no way to get out unless we go right now," Rick responded.

"What about the boat?" I asked.

"You were out there with me, McDonald. It's too rough to make a run. Besides, if this storm comes in hard, we'll have twenty foot seas in no time."

"Can I hike out before the rivers flood?"

For the first time since I arrived, I had no desire to return down the trail and out of the valley. Yet at that very moment it seemed as though it might be necessary to make that trek.

"If Marlie goes with you, you might make it. More than likely though, you'll only get as far as Hanakapei. That river can get twelve feet deep, quick."

I turned to Marlie who looked at me with no great love.

"What about it?" I asked.

"Forget it, McDonald. As much as I want you out of the valley, I wouldn't take one step down the trail with you. You're bad luck."

"Why don't you stow that crap, Marlie. You know I had nothing to do with John falling off the cliff. You saw what happened."

"You could have warned him, McDonald. You saw that goat coming."

"And I saw you standing there watching when the goat butted him. There was nothing that anyone cou—"

"Are you saying that I had something to do with John falling off the cliff?"

"This isn't getting us anywhere, Peter," said Dennis impatiently. "What are we going to do?"

"I don't know. It's up to Marlie. I don't think I could make that trail alone."

"I ain't taking him anywhere. Down that trail or where the light don't shine. He's on his own. John hired him, John's gone, so as far as I'm concerned, McDonald can take his stuff out of the cave and fend for himself."

"What in the hell is wrong with you?" Dennis pushed in close to Marlie. His quick movement made the little man nervous.

"Ain't nothing wrong with me, buddy. But McDonald ain't in my possession anymore, you got that? The pictures were John's idea."

"What pictures?" asked Dennis pushing his face into Marlie's mask. "What god damn pictures are you talking about?"

"The famous pictures of John walking backward down the Na Pali

Coast. He said that it would bring us fame and fortune. When I heard those two words I knew we were up shit creek."

"All we want to know is if you will take Peter out of the valley. Give me a straight answer." Dennis was visibly upset and in no mood for back talk.

"Straight answers? That's what you want?"

"That's it. Yes or no?"

"I ain't taking any of you lackeys anywhere. As for McDonald, he can get the hell out of the dry cave and set up with the tourists. He's been causing nothing but problems since he got here. There, is that straight enough for you?"

Dennis took one step toward Marlie and pushed him back so hard that Marlie almost lost his balance. In one quick movement that stunned everyone, Marlie jumped back and whipped the goat pistol out of his jacket pocket. He leveled it on Dennis.

"You're real close to following John, smart guy. You come within ten feet of me again and you're gonna get poked with lead. Got it?"

Dennis stood still, shaking his head.

"You little moron. Pulling a stunt like that in Kalalau. You're going to pay for that one, Marlie. And I don't have to be ten feet from you. You've had it."

Marlie pushed the pistol out in front of him, wielding it like a knife.

"Get the hell out of here. All of you tourists. We don't need you. We can take care of our own."

All the while the rain continued to fall. At a certain limit, I imagined the precipitation would soak my clothes and my skin to the point of saturation but the more it rained the wetter I felt. My body was like a human sponge standing solitary amidst an arrangement of other sponges absorbing the sky, which came down to be caught and held in reservoir. As tempers flared my own mood grew damp and doused.

"Let's get your stuff, Peter. I can't listen to this little jerk anymore."

"We'll see who's a jerk, college boy."

"We already know asshole."

Dennis marched away and Juerg and I followed. At the edge of the heiau, I tried to give Caren a hand signal but I was not sure that she had seen it. We walked off the grass mound where our feet sank into the boggy turf. The main trail back to the campground was quickly disappearing under the tide of the storm. Small sinks were spreading into pools. To our right, the ocean crashed onto shore, while from above us, the weather bore down without relief. It had begun to rain harder.

new camp

At the dry cave, I collected my belongings and with Dennis's help I moved to a site that was close to his camp. With only one spare set of clothes and no tent I was ill prepared for the growing storm.

What I did have was a camping hammock and two army surplus ponchos, items that I always carried when I was in the field. Stringing the hammock between two small trees, I rigged a poncho to cover my sleeping bag. When my camp was set up, I went back to Dennis and Michelle's tent to wait out the storm. As we drank coffee and watched the weather outside, Dennis grilled me on the morning's events.

Across the valley, the rain came down steadily but the storm grew in magnitude as the afternoon wore on. By dinnertime, the entire camp was awash and small streams were forming in the trail. That evening, the sun set behind a blanket of clouds and night fell on a day that had been destitute of light. The rain continued to spatter unmercifully on the forest cover as we listened with static nerves.

When the dark had consumed the last of the greyness, I slipped out of Dennis's site, promising to return in the morning. Swaddled in my spare poncho, I walked toward my new site, but at a fork in the trail I veered to my right and made my way to the dry cave. Creeping through the heavy cover outside the shelter, I pulled my hood around my face and snuck in for a closer look. Raindrops drummed the plastic of my poncho and were amplified by the hollow space inside the shell. From my hiding place, I spied on the followers.

The fire in the cave was well stoked. On the spit, a single large goat was cooking, which I assumed was the Billy that had gotten John. Fat from the beast dripped on the coals. It sizzled and smoked and sent flames licking up at the seared corpse. With a slow hand, Ron was turning the skewer.

At the side of the fire pit, Lynn stirred a pot of tea. From his mat, Rick was watching her work while he polished his surfboard. Across the fire from Lynn, Shannon stared into the flames with Judy at her side. Perched atop a milk crate, Caren was looking at Marlie.

To get a better view inside the cave, I had to move forward on my stomach. As I moved, I kicked a rock down the slope behind me. In the dark, I held my breath and put my head against the ground. The rock made a splash as it sank into a puddle at the bottom of the hill, but no one seemed to notice. Slowly, I let out my breath. Inside the shelter, Marlie was pacing nervously and talking in a gruff voice. Drawing in to listen, I heard his words echoing back to me from the cave walls.

"So tonight we eat goat for John. And tomorrow we eat goat so we don't forget John. Do you knot-heads understand?"

The disciples watched sullenly as their new leader pulled back on the cinch and let them have it.

"We are responsible for John's death. We let bad elements into the cave. We let them unclean tourists eat the flesh of the goats."

Through the corner of his eye Rick was watching Marlie. It was obvious that he was not happy with the performance.

"So why doesn't somebody say something?"

The followers looked down as Marlie scanned the inside of the cave. For no other reason than convenience, he picked out Rick to admonish.

"What are you doing there, surf bum? Do you think you can bring your board inside the cave just because John isn't here?"

"I'm waxing my board, Marlie. I'm going out in the morning."

"Oh no, you're not. You ain't going surfing until we have properly mourned."

Browsing through the gathering, Marlie was trying to gauge the response he was receiving. His gaze was met with silent faces. The only emotion betrayed in their expressions was a growing lack of patience.

Outside the cave, I stretched onto the ground and lay flat upon dead leaves that were sopping wet but which kept me out of the mud. Above me the rain continued to fall.

"You know, John told me this would happen. That the minute he was gone, we would forget everything he taught us. Well not me. I am not going to forget."

Marlie was talking to no one in particular. His words were bait but no one was biting. Between sentences, Marlie paused but he seemed unnerved by the silence so he continued his attack.

"Ain't I right? Didn't John forbid Rick from ever bringing his board into the cave? And look at you, Joe. You know that John would never let you juggle when the goat was cooking."

Joe let the rocks fly up into the air but he hauled them in self-consciously when Marlie picked him out of the crowd.

"It's raining too hard to go outside."

"Is that any reason to break the laws that John set down for us?"

"I don't really think of it as breaking any laws. I like to juggle when I'm nervous, that's all."

At this point, Marlie turned to Bill who was lying down inside of his bedroom alcove.

"What do you say, Bill? Should we follow the laws that were set down for us? I mean, John gave his life for us and here we are acting as if he never existed. Shouldn't we continue to eat the goat?"

"I don't have any problem with eating the goat, Marlie. But we're almost out of bullets."

"Listen, I can't help it if the store was out of .22s. You act as if it was my fault."

"I'm not saying that. All I said is that we're almost out of bullets. If we're going to keep eating the goats we've got to figure out a new way of killing the buggers. That's all I'm saying."

"What about all of this juggling and surfboard waxing that's going on inside the cave? What do you think of that?"

"To tell you the truth," Bill admitted, "I kind of like watching him juggle. It makes the time pass."

"What about Rick's surfboard?"

"It just doesn't bother me that much. But if it gets on your nerves I guess Rick should take it outside to work on it."

"I'm going to wax my board wherever and whenever I feel like it from now on. And in the morning I'm getting the hell out of here."

Everyone seemed surprised at Rick's outburst. It was unlike him to get angry.

"Where do you think you're going?" Marlie shouted.

"I'm not sure I would tell you even if I had my mind made up. You're putting out a lot of bad vibes. I don't think it's doing any good."

"Listen, local boy. All I'm trying to do is bring some order into this mess."

"What mess?" asked Rick. "It seems to me that everything is fine except that John fell off Red Hill this morning because he wouldn't turn around and face the world."

In a flash, Marlie lunged at Rick. Thinking quickly, Rick held up his surfboard so Marlie had to reach around the board with his short arms to grab him. This game only lasted a moment before Marlie ran out of energy and retreated.

"Rick, you're history. If you take that board out tomorrow, it is going to kill you. I've put a hex on that board. And as of right now I'm putting a hex on the entire ocean wherever you touch the water."

"The entire ocean wherever I touch the water?"

"That's right. Wherever you touch the water."

"Boy, now I'm worried."

"You better worry, alright." Turning to Bill, Marlie sought reinforcement. "Don't you think that I can put a hex on the ocean, Bill?"

"I suppose you can. I mean why not?" Bill turned to Rick and in a condescending tone, he backed Marlie up. "You better watch out next time you go into the water, Rick. There's a hex on the ocean wherever you touch it."

"Thanks for the warning, Bill."

"No problem, Rick." Bill turned back to Marlie. "There you go. I told him."

"He still doesn't believe me."

"He believes you, Marlie."

"I believe you, Marlie." Rick looked at the little man with an expression that would have unnerved the average man. "But I'm still leaving in the morning."

Ignoring Rick's last comment, Marlie turned to Joe to get a reading. Joe had resumed his juggling but he was tossing the rocks up just below his chin so that he wouldn't get attention. When Marlie spoke to him, Joe was startled and dropped two of the rocks.

"So what do you think about all of this, Joe?"

"What do I think?"

"Yeah, Joe. What do you think?"

"Well, what I think and what I know are two different topics."

"Let's hear it all."

"All of it?"

"Yes."

He glanced down at the two rocks that were lying between his feet. When he looked up he had a sheepish expression on his face. It was obvious that he wasn't comfortable sharing his opinions but he was too afraid of Marlie not to talk.

"First of all, I feel horrible about John falling off the cliff and everything. But if I think about it real hard, I think that if I went by John's way of looking at things, whatever happened to him is what was supposed to happen to him and so we shouldn't be sad. In fact, we should be happy that John is gone. I mean for his sake," Joe corrected himself.

"You know, he's got a point there," Bill said.

"Shut-up and let him finish!"

"Oh yeah, sure, Marlie. Sorry about that."

"Go on, Joe. So you're happy that John is dead."

"No. No. No. Not at all. It's just that by his own rules, whatever happens is meant to happen. So either he is happy that he is gone or he is out there somewhere breaking his own law. Either way, I don't feel bad about juggling in the cave."

"Is that all you have to say?"

"No, that's not all."

"O.K. Go on."

"Well, it's just that I want to be realistic and everything."

"Realistic?"

"Yeah. Because I was thinking."

"We are in trouble," Marlie spat out.

There was a smattering of laughter in the cave. Joe gazed through the firelight with an expression of genuine concern.

"I'm serious, you guys. It rained pretty hard today and it doesn't look like it is going to let up. By tomorrow afternoon the tourists are going to come up to the dry cave looking for shelter. If it rains for two more days, the tourists will be out of food and we're going to have to feed them. The only way to do that is to open up the Aloha Kitchen to everyone."

"Are you finished, Joe?"

"Well—"

"I think you're finished."

"Maybe I am."

Marlie stood up tall and rose to the challenge. He sucked in a deep breath and threw out his chest.

"Under no circumstances are the tourists to eat the goat. Until a sign has been given, we will remain in seclusion. No tourists in the cave!" he said with finality.

"That's pretty stupid." Shannon backed Joe up. "You know as well as I do that when it rains, the tourists come to the cave. They always have. It's going to be pretty hard for us to stay in seclusion unless we go up-valley to our other camp."

"The other camp is not prepared. You know that."

"Then we are going to have to allow the tourists into the cave and they are going to have to eat. If that means we're going to have to feed them goat then that's what we'll have to do."

"I would expect something like this out of you, Shannon."

"What in the hell does that mean, Marlie? I just think it's time to get real about our responsibilities in the Valley. All we do is take everything we want and we don't give anything back. Maybe it's time that we sacrifice a little to those in need."

"What do you think about this, Judy?"

"I don't know."

"What do you mean, you don't know?"

"I just mean that I don't know."

"Great analysis, babe. I'll make sure I get your opinion next time we get on a complex subject."

"You don't have to be rude, Marlie."

"Shut up, Shannon. I've heard all that I want to hear from you."

The discussion was being ground out by Marlie's irritability. He turned to Bill, from whom he believed he would gain support.

"So, do you think we should let the tourists into the cave, Bill?"

"I have to admit that Joe is right. The tourists are going to come up here whether we like it or not so we might as well prepare for it. But if you don't want them eating the goat, then they shouldn't eat the goat. Besides, we're almost out of bullets."

"So you agree with me?"

"Basically."

"And what about you, Ron?"

Outside the conversation, Ron had been turning the meat. When the question was flung in his direction, he looked at Marlie.

"Huh?"

"I said, what do you think about all of this, Ron?"

"Well, I think that we should do whatever John would have done."

"So you're with me then."

"I'm just saying that whatever John would have done is what we should do."

"I think that's clear enough. Go ahead and keep your eye on the meat."

Scanning the followers again, Marlie picked out Rick and Joe from among the eyes staring back at him. In the glow of the fire Rick continued to wax his surfboard. A few feet away from him, Joe tossed the small stones up in succession but with an underhand throw that kept them low and close to his body.

"What do you think about all this, Caren?" he said, still looking at Joe and Rick.

Pushing the hood back from my ears, I tried to hear what Caren would say to this new guru. Caren took a moment to answer and watched Marlie carefully as she picked out her words.

"I think that we should all stay as calm as possible until we know what our feelings are. This is not a good time to be breaking down the values that we have lived with, but it is a good time to look at what we need to get by without John's guidance. If you think you know how John wanted us to act after he was gone then I'll listen to you, Marlie. But you are going to have to relax and let us mourn in our own way if we are going to start over. Do you understand me?"

Marlie was barely listening. He read Caren's demeanor to mean that she was supporting him against the others.

"Yes, I understand you, Caren. You agree with me that this is not the time for changing our laws."

"That's close enough."

At the fire, Lynn stirred the tea. Beside her, Ron turned the meat with his head down. Shannon and Judy were staring into the fire as Marlie stalked the inside of the cave glaring at everyone.

As the rain blew harder, I slid down the slope and out of my hiding place. I had seen enough.

On the trail back to camp I looked through the trees behind me. There was an orange glow on the cliff above the dry cave, which stood concealed behind the low bushes and protected from the downpour by the overhang.

Returning to my new camp, I removed my poncho. My gear was stashed in the hollow of the oak to which my hammock was tied. Reaching into the cavity I could feel that my stuff was dry despite the saturation of everything around me.

With my clothes on, I slipped into my sleeping bag and slid onto my hammock. There was no place to put my shoes where they wouldn't get wet so I put them under the hammock hoping that it would keep off some of the water. But there was no escape from the rain. I was becoming resigned to that fact. Until it stopped, my feet would be soaked, so there was no use trying to keep my shoes dry. If it kept raining like this for another day, the campsite would be flooded.

As I lay waiting for sleep to come, I listened to the tapping of the raindrops against the poncho. For every drop that fell, my mind became more accustomed to the fact that in the morning there would be no comfort inside of this storm. Tomorrow there would only be weather and clouds and rain from the heavens. There was no hiding from this baptism. Fall back and the let your head go under.

I fell asleep on the offbeat.

forecast

Under the poncho, the smell of mildewed rubber was slightly stronger than the odor from my body. I had been lying awake for an hour in my sleeping bag listening to the rain dripping off the branches of the trees. Peeking out, I saw that the rain had let up. Grey clouds were floating high above the ocean.

While I wondered what I would do that day, retreat or remain, search out a dry camp where I could wait out the storm or just stay under the poncho and hope that nobody bothered me, I got an unexpected visit from someone I wanted to talk to in the worst way. At my feet the poncho was lifted. A miserable grey light flooded the interior of my dark cocoon. In the glow, I could see the silhouette of a woman's face peering through the tunnel. It took a second for me to recognize that it was Caren.

"Am I glad to see you."

"Did you stay warm last night?" she asked with a smile.

With one hand I flung the poncho away from my face. I remained in my sleeping bag gazing at Caren through sleep-swollen eyes.

"I was coming to see you last night but Marlie went kind of crazy at dinner. I had to stay to keep him calm."

Pretending that I hadn't seen the scene the night before, I looked at her with concern.

"What's going on with Marlie?" I asked.

"He's got it in his mind to take over where John left off. It seems that he wants to be the new leader."

"Pinch hitting for The Man, huh?"

"Exactly."

"How are the others getting on?"

"Everyone seems alright. If it wasn't for Marlie acting like an ass I guess we would have dealt with it and gone on about our business."

"What is your business, Caren?"

"My business is taking care of wayward photographers, wherever they may wander."

"That's awful nice of you, Caren."

"I'm racking up Brownie points."

"When I was a kid, I got kicked out of the Cub Scouts for eating Brownies."

"You're so simple, Peter."

"I can prove it to you if you like."

"I'll take a rain check."

"From the looks of it you may need one."

With my pass overthrown, I looked into the sky and motioned with my nose to the ceiling of grey that was swirling above us. Caren looked up and gave her forecast.

"It will be raining again by noon. We're socked in here for a while, I'm afraid."

"If you come down here with me I could shrug that news off easily."

"Someone has to stay with Marlie to keep him calm. The others are fed up."

"How many days do you think the storm will last?"

"I figure at least two more days, maybe three. It's that Indian summer that got us. We'd been setting up our winter camp before the weather cleared."

"Where is the winter camp, Caren?"

"It's hard to find unless you've been up there once."

"It's up-valley then?"

"It's up-valley near the base of the big fall, to the east along the cliffs. John said it was where Koolau made his final stand."

"Interesting."

"You've got to get up, Peter. Rick wants to talk to you. He and Lynn are leaving this morning."

"He was serious then." Caren looked at me with a quizzical expression. I had nearly given myself away. "Where is he going?" I tried to throw her off the trail.

"That's why he wants to talk to you. He says that he's going over to the Valley of the Lost Tribe."

"Isn't it a little rough to be navigating around the point?"

"Rick is amazing when it comes to sailing Na Pali. He's sailed all the way to Polihali before."

"Really?"

Polihali was at the end of Na Pali to the south and west. It was inaccessible from Kalalau except by boat.

Swinging my feet off the hammock, I crawled out of my sleeping bag. Picking up my boots I tried to wring the water out of them but it was no use.

"He's down on the beach," Caren said, while she watched me twist my boots. The water spilled from my hands into the puddles on the ground. "You can go barefoot if you want."

"This rain could wreck a person's vacation."

"Bring your boots to the dry cave after you talk to Rick. There's a fire going. Marlie is on Red Hill looking for John."

"I don't think he has a chance."

"Neither does he, but I guess he figures he owes it to him."

"What about the rest of you?"

"We put up with John for a long time. If there's nothing to be done, we won't do it, that's for sure."

"You sound bitter."

"That was my line."

"I guess it was."

Grabbing my cameras, we headed for the waterfall where I got a drink of water and washed the rain out of my hair. Beside the waterfall, Maryjane and Baraka's tent was sitting in three inches of water. Their wet clothes were hanging on a line that was sagging from the weight. From inside the tent I could hear the sound of their lovemaking. They had ridden out the weather, oblivious.

At the beach, Caren left me saying she had to get back to the cave. Promising to meet up with her later, I watched her go with a foreboding in my heart. She walked slowly across the sand and jumped up the bank at the helipad. At the ohi'a tree, she disappeared into the forest. When she was gone, I walked down to the ocean.

On the beach, I could see Rick scanning the horizon of grey weather and blue-grey water. As I approached, he turned to look at me and then motioned Lynn to prepare for departure. She took his orders gladly and as I approached, Lynn began to tie down the last of the bags. She checked each knot carefully. Finished, she stood up to greet me with a smile, although Rick remained stoic.

"Hey, McDonald."

"Hey, Rick. Caren told me that you're making your escape."

Lynn and Rick looked at each other as if they were confused.

"I wouldn't say that we're making our escape. We're just going to leave for awhile until things cool down," Rick answered for both of them.

"And you're going—?" I pointed with my chin to the east, past the last outcropping of symmetrical palis that swan-dived into the raucous ocean.

"We're going to the next valley over," Lynn said.

"The Valley of the Lost Tribe?"

"Yeah. It usually takes about an hour but with this sea I imagine it will take a little longer," Rick gave his estimate.

"Shouldn't you wait until after the storm?"

Behind Rick the swells of six thousand miles of open ocean lurched onto the shore with a shout of scorn for the land standing in its path. The faces of the cliffs where the orange sunset had cast its light were doused with dripping and foaming brine. Beyond the thundering surf the ocean heaved with heavy swells. It did not look like a good day to travel.

"We'll be alright. The boat is in good shape and if we have any problems I have my board. We could drift for days on that board."

Rick had fastened the surfboard onto the boat with the same line that had pulled the rubber pool. As long as they had the board, they would be safe. There is virtually no way to sink a surfboard.

"What did you want to see me about?"

"You may be gone when we get back and we have a favor to ask you."

"Do I get a favor in return?"

The question threw Rick off but it showed me how important his request was.

"Sure. If I can do something for you, I will."

"Alright then, you go first."

"This is going to be very easy for you, McDonald, but it will mean a lot to me and Lynn and to some others who haven't seen us for a while."

"You want me to take a picture of you and send it to your family."

It was too easy to guess, but Rick looked at me as if I had discovered a new planet.

"How did you know?" Lynn asked.

"Hey, I'm a photographer. I've taken pictures for a lot of people who thought they wouldn't make it back."

"Well?"

"That's simple." I lifted up both of my cameras and held them shoulder high. "Black and white or color?"

"Color, if you don't mind," Lynn answered the question.

"Color it is. But just because I take this picture and promise to deliver it doesn't mean that you don't have to come back."

"We'll be back," Rick stated flatly. "We were going to ask you before all of this other stuff came up. We want our folks to know that we're all right. Now tell us the favor you need."

"This one is easy too."

"O.K."

"I want you to bring me back some of those bones you told me about that are buried in the dunes over there."

Rick's eyes narrowed and he looked at Lynn. She spoke.

"I don't know if we can do that, Peter. That valley is very sacred. We might be disturbing the spirits."

I spread my nerve evenly throughout my body and went to work. There was a hunch that I had been playing with ever since I heard of the next valley over and the piles of bones that lay there.

"If my hunch is right, you won't be disturbing any spirits by bringing me those bones."

"And if we bring you those bones, you'll send the picture?" Rick asked.

"Either way, I'll send the picture. But I would like a sample of what's over there. To test a theory I have. You'll be back in two days?"

"No, but if it means a lot to you I could sneak back and get the bones to you."

"Only if it's safe. You got that?"

"I forgot what the meaning of safe is, McDonald."

After the pictures were taken, Rick gave me a piece of paper with an address on it and then went to the back of the boat. The paddles were strapped to the side of the craft but would be available when he needed them.

"Do you feel like getting wet?" he asked after he had rechecked the loads.

"Not really, but from the looks of this weather, I won't have much choice. You want me to help you launch."

"Yeah, could you?"

"No problem."

Depositing my cameras safely away from the water, I went to the opposite side of the boat from Rick. I grabbed the craft and lifted it to check the weight. It wasn't heavy even after Lynn had taken her seat. As we prepared to launch, she did some last minute arranging.

The surf was thrashing the shore where I stood and I could feel the eruptions shaking the beach underneath my feet. With all my strength, I pushed forward while Rick pulled. With a gritty squeal of sand against rubber, the boat slid forward. The flat keel hit the rushing water and then skidded forward with a lurch into the retreating tide. The rubber kayak picked up speed and glided forward, just as a huge wave hit the beach and submerged me up to my armpits. Holding on, I felt my feet leave the ground. I floated up on the wave and held on. Across from me, Rick jumped into the kayak. Grabbing a paddle he began to cut at the foamy water.

"Okay, McDonald," Rick shouted over the roar.

Still holding onto the craft, I tried to feel the sand below me. My head was above the gunwale and I looked at Rick. He paddled hard as the wave subsided. Suddenly the ground was under my feet. I backed out of the surf while facing the ocean.

The raft was kicked high onto the surge but Rick deftly turned his attention to the challenge. He paddled in hard strokes to get out of the path of the next tidal explosion.

Backing out of the surf, I watched Rick guide the kayak over the lurching waves beyond the cataclysm. Within a minute he was well out to sea. Standing on the shore I watched until the boat was buried in the troughs and no longer visible to my eye.

According to Caren, I only had an hour or two to dry off before the storm resumed. Wishing them luck under my breath, I walked quickly over the spit of sand. Up the bank, I returned to my campsite where my hammock hung and my shoes drained water into puddles.

bonsai

In their campsites, the tourists were wringing the storm out of their gear. Some of them were readying for more rain, tying up extra tarps to gain more cover, stowing dry goods in the crooks of trees and under rock shelves, drying wet goods over smoldering fires, working at these tasks with a soggy purpose. Other campers, those who lived on faith, were packing for the trip out. Apparently they didn't know or didn't care to know that the trail would be nothing more than mud floating across the treacherous palis. They would be stranded at Honokoa or Hanakapei, depending on when the storm resumed.

The rain had left everyone in mild shock. Walking through the camp, I received no greeting from any camper. They wandered through their sites and went about their tasks in a contemplative mood, insulted by nature that she could have the audacity to come forth so aggressively and ruin the fine time they had been having.

At my campsite, I retrieved my one change of clothes, stashed my color camera in the hollow of the oak tree and headed for the dry cave. A ribbon of smoke drifted into the forest from below the overhang. Pulling my courage together, I walked into the maw of the cave. On the dry earth inside the sanctuary, Caren was tending the fire.

"Is Marlie around?" I asked cautiously.

"No. He's still out. Come on in."

At the fire ring I set my boots on the rocks close to the flames. The rocks were covered with the residue of goat fat from the previous night's feast.

"Where is everybody?"

"We're in here." A voice came out of the bedroom alcove. Looking inside, I saw Bill lying on his bed of sleeping bags with Judy next to him. She was staring into space.

"Where have you been, McDonald? I want to talk to you."

"Don't tell me. You want me to take a picture to send home to your parents."

Bill looked at me with a questioning smirk on his face.

"That's not a bad idea, but no, it's about something else."

Bill rolled off the sleeping bags and crawled out of the alcove.

"What?"

"There's something that I want to show you. Actually, I have to show you. I mean I could tell you about it but it would be better if I showed you."

"Can you wait for me to dry my boots?"

"No hurry. Do you want some breakfast? There's plenty of goat left over from last night. I think we've all lost our appetite for cabra now that John isn't here to force the stuff down our throats. And into our souls," he added laughing. I was a little shocked at the casual attitude with which Bill was talking of the recent death of his guru.

"Is that the goat that knocked John over the cliff?" I asked.

"The very one," was Bill's answer.

"That goat could have been Hawaiian Magazine's, 'Animal Of The Year'."

"And you'd have the picture."

"Well, it wasn't my greatest shot, but yeah, I got the picture."

"What is the greatest action shot you ever took, McDonald?" Bill asked as he picked up an ember out of the fire and lit a cigarette.

"That's a hard one. I'll have to think about it for a minute."

"Take your time, McDonald. It's all we have until this storm breaks."

While my boots were drying, I stripped off my wet clothes and changed into a dry pair of jeans and a tee shirt. Hanging my wet clothes on a line that was strung over the fire, I retrieved my boots.

"So what do you want to show me?" I asked Bill as I put on my boots. He was well into his third cigarette. I had never seen him smoke so much.

"You ready to go?" Bill appeared surprised by my willingness.

"Is there some reason I should be afraid to go?"

"I just thought maybe you were getting tired of us already."

"As far as I'm concerned the party's just begun."

"This is where you really shine, isn't it, McDonald?"

I hesitated to answer because I knew he had identified my secret. In a pensive moment, I looked into the coals of the fire and took a deep breath. Turning my head to the side I glanced at Caren before I answered.

"Yeah, Bill, this is where I shine. Give me a disaster and I've got a reason to live. Give me a battle and I have a place to go. Give me a bloody body and I'll stop time and freeze it forever."

"You are far out, McDonald. I can see why John wanted you to join us."

"Is that what he wanted?"

Bill did not answer, which was probably better. Caren watched me closely as I finished lacing my boots. The beast was out of the cage and it was tamer than she had believed it would be.

"Let's go before it starts raining again," Bill said.

"Is it going to rain again?"

"You better believe it. You haven't seen anything, yet."

"Thanks for the warning. Are the girls going with us?"

"I can't, Peter," Caren said. "I have to wait here until Marlie gets back in case something comes up."

"Keep him occupied, would you? He already ran Rick and Lynn off. I'm afraid that Joe and Shannon will be next," Bill offered this advice.

"I'll try to keep him calm but it isn't easy."

"What about Judy?" I asked and glanced at the alcove where Judy was still staring into space.

Bill stepped up to me and spoke quietly to the side of my face.

"She's pretty broken up about what happened yesterday. She should stay here. It will relax Marlie a little to see someone mourning for John."

"So it's just you and me?"

"Right."

"I guess I'm ready then."

"You can bring your camera, too. I'm not like old John. See, I think you could take pictures of angels playing jazz at the pearly gates if you wanted."

"Are we going to some holy place, then?"

"You got it, baby. It's the holiest. But it's all free now. And it's all ours."

Bill looked over his shoulder at Judy who remained motionless. "John just couldn't relax and go with the flow. It caught up with him though. It got his ass good. You think that I should be sad. He had it coming. Those hills are going to fall down with or without the goats. It's evolutionary."

Walking out of the cave, we moved into the brooding grey day and hiked the main trail, staying on the high shoulder to keep out of the puddles. By now, the trail was no more than a muddy ditch. At a grove of fruit trees that looked like large overripe loquats, Bill followed a path into the forest. The leaves of the trees were saturated from the rain and drops of water fell onto our heads as we picked our way forward through the mud. Under the low canopy, some tourists had set up tents to try to keep out of the storm. They took no notice of us as we passed through their camp.

The grove ended in a thicket of pale red hibiscus. Our progress was halted by a wall of rock where the low cliffs rose off the floor of the valley. We pushed through the brush on a trail that was overgrown and little used. When we burst through the other side of the thicket, my clothes were damp and my boots were heavy with mud. Following the wall, we started up an incline and made our way upward until we were high above the arboreal roof of the forest. Off to our right I could see the ocean, big and grey and filling the horizon.

After a short distance, the ledge that we had been walking on widened and then disappeared. We stood at the mouth of a small valley that was broken by a dozen gentle ravines. A herd of goats grazed on a hill not far from us. They munched on wet mouthfuls of grass and ignored our presence. In the distance, the high walls of Kalalau rose like rounded skyscrapers, the tops of their spires hidden in the low clouds.

The trail we were on zigzagged through the forest. Taking first a right hand path and then a left hand path we ended up standing on an abutment, a quarter of the way up one of the grand palis and nearly five hundred feet above the campground. On a ledge that was no more than four feet wide I sat on a soggy patch of earth and dangled my feet over the edge. Beside me, Bill lit a cigarette and surveyed Kalalau. The valley twisted around us like a dragon sleeping in a fairy tale.

"Are we almost there?' I asked after I had caught my breath.

"We are there. It's just around the bend."

"So what we are going to see?"

"Don't you want to be surprised?"

"I'd rather be surprised right now."

"O.K. then." Bill licked his lips, took a drag off his cigarette and threw the butt into the ravine. "Have you ever seen bonsai trees, McDonald?"

I didn't have to think about the question. "Yeah, I've seen them."

"Well, here's the story. When John first came to the valley he had one hobby that he brought with him. He was an expert at pruning trees and turning them into bonsais."

"That's what you are going to show me? Bonsai trees? Up here? But why up here?"

"He didn't want anyone to know that he was still working with them."

"Why not?"

"Well, he wanted everyone to give up their worldly occupations. No more surfing for Rick, no more juggling for Joe. Caren used to make jewelry, he cut that out. Judy was a poet, he snuffed that out, too."

"What about Shannon?"

"Shannon liked to write in her diary but John burned her notebooks without even reading them."

"And you?"

"Me? I didn't have any hobbies. Except maybe women. I was an engineer before I came out here. I used to work at Hughes Aircraft building detonators for tactical nuclear warheads."

"You're kidding!"

"Strange, huh? I can hardly remember that world anymore."

"What about Ron?"

"Ron is a whole different story. When he came to Kalalau, he was looking for business opportunities. He was thinking about leading tours through the islands. He wanted to make a million bucks and buy a place on the Big Island."

"What was his hobby?"

"His hobby was buying and selling. He thought that he could lure John into one of his schemes, but it backfired on him. Ron ended up making flutes from valley bamboo but John wouldn't let him sell them to the tourists. All John would let him do was play for the feasts and other occasions. Outside the cave he was forbidden to play unless John was around."

"You know, Bill, the more I hear about all the crap that John laid on you guys, the more I wonder why you put up with him for so long."

My prodding was followed by a long pause. As I watched Bill, I knew he was looking for a good answer, for himself as well as for me. He stood above me scanning a distant place.

"That's a hard question," Bill offered finally. "You see, when we came up here this place was like Paradise compared to where we had come from. It was everything that we had been seeking but it was even more. In the Valley, we would never have to work again. Everything was available to us. Food was falling off the trees. The weather was always good. The ocean was perfect for swimming. The waterfall had the freshest water that any of us had ever drunk. People were friendly here. Everyone shared what they had and no one wanted much. All year round, the tourists flew thousands of miles to be where we were already." Bill looked down at me to emphasize his point. "It was as close to Paradise as a person could get."

"So what happened?"

"I guess you would say that we got confused. When we started to take root here, John would have talks with us. He was smart. He had been living up-valley for a couple of years and he knew the ropes. He knew how to scam food from the tourists when they were hiking out. He told us what to say to the rangers when they came in to check for permits. He showed us how to make the valley work for us.

"Once we were banded together, he started to have talks at the heiau on Sundays. He didn't really say much to begin with, he talked about living in the valley, really just thoughts we were already having. But he captured that energy and moved it forward. His spirituality filled a void we had been feeling. Somehow, along the way, we twisted it in our mind so that the Valley was something that John offered us, or at least we felt a debt of gratitude to him.

"The Valley had always been, we just didn't know about it until we got here. In a way we were tricked, but in a way we fooled ourselves. After we had acclimated, we realized that no one controlled the Valley. It just was. But by that time, we had settled into a pattern with John taking the lead. It was our fault. We let him get ahead of us. In the end, it was easier to go along than fight it.

"But then John started to catch on and he wanted to us. There was no reason to, he was just afraid that we would quit listening to him. He got insecure and he took it out on us, which started a cycle. The more he tested us the more we drew away and that made him feel even more insecure. It was the first time in John's life that he felt important and he didn't want to let it go. So he started getting tough. By the time we realized our mistake, John had us off balance. We couldn't just kick John out of our lives. Somewhere along the way, I guess, he figured out that he would have to ritualize what had started out as a gift. He began to make demands. And he started doing things to make us feel small."

"So heaven-on-earth became hell-in-a-hand-basket."

"That's why some of us aren't too sad about John being gone. When he fell yesterday it was as if the Evil Lord had dropped into the bottomless pit and we would be free forever. It's just too bad that it came to that."

"Because John was a good guy before he started getting paranoid?"

"John was a great guy. But you're right—he did get paranoid. He was so intoxicated by our initial enthusiasm that he was afraid to let us out of his grasp."

A long silence ensued. Bill and I both stared out at the surf crashing along the coastline.

"What about those bonsai trees?" I finally inserted into the silence.

Bill exhaled a big sigh and blinked his eyes. "Yeah, the trees. They're this way."

With that, Bill was off again. I got up feeling stiff and damp but satisfied with what I had just learned. Bill disappeared around a bend and I had to hurry to catch up. We ducked into a thicket of koa and I could hear my footsteps plodding over the wet earth. On the other side of the thicket, the sunlight blinded my eyes.

When I could see again I stopped dead in my tracks. There, in front of me was a forest of maybe a hundred tiny bonsais covering a ledge. Standing in place, I scanned the midgets that were rooted into the face of the rock. I lifted my camera and took a few shots.

"Pretty wild, huh?"

"Very."

"That's why I wanted to bring you here."

Treading lightly, I walked into the bonsais, careful not to step on any of them. The tiny trees were clustered on the ledge and on the slope behind the ledge.

"This is incredible."

"John used to come up here everyday to prune these trees."

"How did you find out about this place?"

"I followed him one day. He kept disappearing in the mornings and I wanted to find out where he was going."

"Did he know that you found this?"

"Never. I didn't want to hurt his feelings. He really had helped us in the beginning. I guess I felt sorry for him."

Stepping in beside me, Bill pointed to a miniature grove of trees that all looked similar.

"See those?"

"Yeah."

"Those are mangoes." Bill looked up at me to read my response. I raised my eyebrows for his benefit. "They're prunings from Koolau's grove."

"It's hard to believe."

"You see that cluster over there?"

"Yeah."

"Those are koa." He pointed to another group of midgets. "Those are Kukui. Candlenut trees."

"Do the mangoes bear fruit?"

"Oh yeah. Once a year. It's really funny. The mangoes are about the same size as regular mangoes but there are only one or two per tree. I never risked tasting them before, but now I guess I can."

"Are you the only person who knows about this?"

"I am."

"Who's going to take care of them now?"

"I know a little about trimming the trees to keep them small. There's a whole system. You have to leave each side with a branch except the back. That branch always gets hacked off."

"So you think that you can keep it up?"

"I think so. But I have an idea. There are different ways to trim bonsais and different sizes. I was thinking about experimenting on them."

"It couldn't hurt. What about the others? Are you going to show them?"

"I can't."

"Why not?"

"There's something else up here."

"What is it?"

"I'll have to show you."

I had trusted him this far and I saw no reason not to continue. Bill walked past the garden of bonsais and motioned me to follow. After he was gone, I took a final look at the grove.

The bonsais were clinging to their shallow pockets of earth on the side of the cliff. Tiny drops of water decorated their foliage. This dew sparkled crystalline in the grey light. There was something unusual about the trees. They were like stunted replicas of what they would have been had the hand of the pruner not kept them retarded. In their smallness, they looked determined beyond their stature. Following Bill along the ledge, I looked back one last time at that idyllic place.

We continued on through the rough. The brush was becoming thicker. Vines hung down a hundred feet from above. The tendrils of these vines caught my ankles and slowed my progress. The ledge that had harbored the bonsais wrapped around the cliff and narrowed until we were standing at a dead end. It appeared the only choice was to go back.

"Do you know where you're going?" I asked Bill as I surveyed the barrier.

"Of course I do. Just hang on for a minute."

There was no way forward, so my instincts turned me around involuntarily to look back from where we had come. If we had to return to the bonsais, I would have to go first, the trail was too narrow for Bill to move around me. A fit of vertigo gripped me and I felt an overwhelming urge to lunge back to the peacefulness of the bonsai grove.

"Bill, I'm going to go back."

Turning around to talk to my guide, I faced the dead-end wall. Bill had vanished.

"Bill?!" I shouted in a panic. "Bill!!"

Either Bill had fallen off the ledge or he had snuck away down some unseen path. My panic fueled, I shouted again but my voice reverberated off of the rock wall and dissipated into the air.

"Hey, McDonald. Come on down."

I would have spun around but my shoulders were already scraping the rock beside me.

"Where in the hell are you, Bill?"

"Down here. Grab the rope and let yourself down."

With my last ounce of courage I leaned forward and peered over the ledge. There, about thirty yards below me, Bill was standing on a outcropping that was as wide as the deck of an aircraft carrier compared to the slice of rock that I was standing on.

"How in the hell did you get down there, Bill?"

"There's a rope tied back into that brush. Do you see it?"

Full of fear, the vertigo stretched my heart into taffy. I inched forward with my hand in front of me. Digging through the vines, I found the neck of the wet rope buried in the undergrowth.

"Come on down, McDonald. This is what I wanted to show you."

Grabbing the rope with both hands, I swung my legs out and wrapped them around the cord. The wet rope set little resistance and I was standing beside Bill in seconds. He seemed impressed by my skill.

"Nice rope work." he said.

"I learned it in the navy," I replied.

"I didn't know you were in the navy."

"I wasn't."

"You are a stone cold wild man, McDonald."

"Thanks, Bill."

In reality I had learned about ropes in the photo corps. You never knew when you would have to get to an isolated position to get the picture. It was all part of the job, including the sweating, aching, sickening fear that I was feeling in my stomach at that very moment.

hello alii

"What did you want to show me?"

I looked around and saw nothing of great significance, just more of the clinging vines hanging down from the palis.

"We have to go down another level," Bill said looking over the ledge where we stood.

"What are we looking for?" I asked.

Bill walked to the far end of the ledge. He reached out and pulled the shank of another rope out of the overgrowth.

"Believe me, you'll know it when you see it."

"You're one hell of a guide," I quipped.

"Thanks, McDonald. Put in a good word with the tourist bureau, would you?"

Without waiting for my response, Bill stepped off the cliff. The rope went taut and I leaned over the lip to watch his progress. Twenty feet down the side of the cliff, Bill disappeared under an overhang and did not reappear. In another second the rope went slack. I would have shaken my head if anyone would have been there to see me do it.

"Come on, McDonald."

His voice was muffled but I had my cue. Grabbing the rope, I stepped off the ledge and followed his lead. Moving down the wall amid the tangle of vines, I used my feet to stabilize my descent. Suddenly the wall I was using to brace my feet gave way and I was dangling in mid-air. Losing my balance, I almost fell backward. As I spun in circles, I inched down the rope and tried to gauge when the floor would catch me. Looking over my shoulder, I caught my first glimpse of what Bill had brought me to see. Letting go of the rope, I jumped back a step to get away from the aberration that lay in front of me.

There, on a ledge two hundred feet up the face of the cliff, stuck into an alcove in the rock amid the litter of shattered plaster, was a Polynesian canoe. Immediately, I knew that it was an old thing. The wood was rotting through in several places. It was water stained and brown with age.

Lying prone in the bilge of the canoe, resting alone and with no great ambition, were the skeletal remains of a human. I stared at the cargo with intense interest that was tempered by mild hysteria.

"Good God. What is it?" I muttered to Bill.

"Alii."

"That's his name?"

"No, alii."

"I thought you said—"

"I said *alii*. Ancient Hawaiian noble person."

As I gaped, Bill looked directly at the thing and puffed on a cigarette. The sight didn't seem to affect him. Bill looked as though he were waiting for the skeleton to ask him for a smoke.

"This is too much. How did you find it?"

"One day John came up to the garden while I was up there and I had to go down the trail to hide. John must have known about this place because the rope was right there where it is now. This thing would be worth a fortune to the right people."

"I bet. But how did it get here?"

"Ancient custom. You see, when a minor chief died, he was wrapped in tapa and the kahuna would prepare a sepulcher in a cliff. The body would be lowered in its canoe, the kahuna would recite a burial prayer and close off the hole. The ropes would be cut and the place would be tapu."

Bill looked into the abyss below us and I looked down long enough to take my eyes off of the scene in front of me. When I looked back into the alcove the canoe was still there but I had had enough. There was an eerie presence in the cave and the only thing I wanted at that moment was to get the hell out of there as fast as I could.

"Let's get the hell out of here," I said.

"You aren't afraid are you, McDonald?" Bill looked at me and mocked a sinister smile.

"What if it starts raining while we're up here?"

"You've got a point there. But don't you want to take a picture? I mean this is a once in a lifetime opportunity."

My camera was dangling at my neck. Mechanically, I lifted it and snapped a few frames. Letting my camera down, I looked over the ledge again and saw that we were still several hundred feet from the floor of the valley.

"How do we get down from here?"

"Start down the rope and I'll cut it."

"That's not funny."

"Did you hear the one about the man who married a hooker?"

"Why don't you tell me when we get to the dry cave." I didn't feel right about telling jokes in front of the dead guy.

"It isn't very funny anyway. Oh well. Follow me. There's a ledge about fifty feet down that leads back into the valley."

"Great. I'll be right behind you."

"You know, Peter, you are the only person to ever see this burial besides John and me. I thought you would like it."

"I love it, Bill, but could we go down now? I think I've had my fill of holy places for one day."

Complying with my request, Bill latched onto the rope and stepped over the side.

"Alii ooop!" And he was gone.

When the rope went slack I turned to take one more look at the remains of the ancient chief. He stared back at me calmly, never letting on how he felt about our trespass. Taking the rope in my trembling hands, I got ready to depart.

There is something worthless about bones, but boy can they put fear into a person. I went over the ledge, keeping my own eyes locked on the skeleton's eye sockets until he passed from my sight. Fifty feet down, I landed on firm ground and let go of the rope. Looking up, there was no sign of the tomb hidden in the rocks above me.

"That was spooky."

"You don't seem the type to be squeamish, McDonald."

"Too many ghost stories when I was a kid, I suppose."

We walked back in silence. When we were on the main trail again, Bill headed up to Red Hill to see if he could find Marlie. On the trail back to the dry cave, all I could think about was the tomb and the bones and the ancient chief stuffed into the craw of the cliff with no one left to worship him. As I walked, I felt the first of many raindrops fall onto my back. Ducking my head, I ran for cover.

sighting

When I went out that morning, I had gone without my poncho and now I was running for shelter through the storm that had returned to the valley. It was no use trying to dodge puddles, the trail had become one long, brown lake stretching through the camp. As I ran, my feet made big splashing divots between the little raindrop craters that pocked the surface of this basin, while muddy water splattered up my legs. The rain was coming in at a slant from the direction of the cliffs and it stung my eyes as it hit my face. With my hand up to protect my vision, I slogged forward.

Back at my campsite, the hammock was swinging from side to side in the wind that was coming in from the ocean. The poncho that covered my sleeping bag had blown off on one side and the red bag was now maroon from the wetness. It was raining too hard to do anything more than fasten the poncho around my bag to cover it. With my eyes cast down, I put away anything that might blow away if the storm got worse. I stowed my camera in the hollow of the oak tree and grabbing my spare poncho, I slipped it over my head and left my camp behind.

There was a trail that ran in a direct course from my campsite to Dennis and Michelle's. This path was under the canopy of the trees, which blocked some of the rain and made it easier to see where I was going. Moving at a fast pace, I walked by the altar that marked the boundary of their site. Under the flapping tarp I stopped and shook the water off my poncho. Folding the hood back, I looked around but it appeared that no one was there. Standing alone, I called Dennis's name and then I called out for Michelle but there was no answer.

Now that I was out of the storm, I didn't feel like moving any farther. My clothes were soggy under my poncho, the legs of my pants were drenched and my shoes were filled with water. Wondering what to do next, I heard someone running up behind me. With all the commotion of the last two days, I had become anxious and spinning around, I looked to see who was approaching.

Down the path, a figure sprang from puddle to puddle, causing eruptions of water along its track. It was wrapped in a clear plastic raincoat and was hopping through the puddles, chased forward by the rain. As I watched, the figure ran right up to me. It might have plowed into me had I not moved aside. At the last possible moment it raised its head to see where it was going.

Stopping abruptly, it looked at me goggle-eyed. Its head was shaking and its mouth was breathing hard. The figure put its hand up and pushed its hood back. It was Juerg.

"Where is Michelle and Dennis?" he asked between breaths. He spoke with a European accent but I could understand his imperfect English, perfectly.

"I was going to ask you the same thing."

"I think they went to the valley today. They said they were going to look for freshwater shrimp."

"They better hurry and get back. This looks like the real thing."

"It's raining crazy," he said in his Swiss English.

"You can say that again."

"Maybe we should go to the dry cave with the others."

The thought of going up to the cave made me shiver in my wet clothes. Joe was right, the tourists were going to start congregating in the shelter if the rain kept up and it wouldn't be long before their food ran out. The squatters knew how to survive in the valley by foraging, so the tourists would be dependent on the squatters. With Marlie in command, there was great potential for a bad situation. Not wanting to go back to the cave, I tried to think of an alternative.

"We should go up the trail to see if we can find Dennis and Michelle."

"This rain will drown us, for sure."

"All the more reason we should go after them. They may be in trouble."

"Do you think so?" Juerg looked concerned.

"What if they got caught on the other side of the river?"

"I'll go if you think we should." Juerg was shivering. His blond hair was matted and his blue eyes were large under his thick blond eyebrows.

"Why did you come up here, Juerg?"

"My camp is flooding. My tent is already under the water. I have to find a place to stay tonight if the rain keeps coming."

"We'll grab your sleeping bag on the way back. You can set up in the dry cave," I promised him. "Right now, we have to find Dennis and Michelle."

"I'll go with you, Peter." He was a trooper and I was glad he had come along.

Walking past Juerg, I headed down the path. Raising the hood of my poncho, I nodded to the altar stones at the edge of the campsite and walked into the storm.

At the other end of the campground, we took the trail that led to the river. From time to time, I had to stop to give Juerg a chance to catch up. This gave me an opportunity to look at the swelling ocean and the falling sky. It was near the fork in the trail that led to the heiau that I first noticed the long tailed Tropic Bird. The *Bos'n Bird,* as Ron had called it, was flying against the wind just above the tops of the trees.

During my days in the valley, I had watched many of these birds flying along the walls of the big cliffs at the back of Kalalau, soaring from roost to roost like feathered angels. The birds were similar to those spirits because the Bos'n had no color in its plumage. It used its long tail for balance in its graceful dives in the drafts along the cliff walls. The Bos'n was white, which made it easy to spot against the green background of the palis.

To see a Bos'n so close to the beach was unusual. It was clear that this bird had been knocked out of the cliffs by the storm. Waiting for Juerg, I watched the bird's progress. The wind had picked up and the Bos'n was failing in its battle to move up into the safety of the high palis.

When Juerg caught up with me, I pointed the bird out to him. He tried to look up but the rain was blowing in his face. Blinking his eyes into the drops, he watched for a moment and then moved on.

The Bos'n was flapping its wings valiantly but even with this courageous effort it did not move forward more than a few feet as I continued to watch. When I turned to see where Juerg was, I realized that he had taken the wrong trail and was headed out toward the heiau. Glancing up, I wished the bird good luck and ran to catch Juerg.

By the time I was close enough to call out to him, we were already near the heiau. Without provocation, a strange feeling came over me. Instead of stopping, I followed him onto the ancient temple.

On the grassy knoll, I got in step with Juerg and we walked to the edge of the heiau where the ocean was smashing into the mouth of the river. The volume of the river had tripled, fed by the surge from up-valley. With its new strength, the engorged stream was giving the ocean a good fight at keeping the waves out of its course.

"Where are we?" Juerg hollered from inside the hood of his plastic jacket.

"We're on the heiau," I yelled back as loud as I could.

"Are we lost?"

"No. Haven't you been here before?"

"No, I haven't. What is this place?"

"It's an ancient Hawaiian altar."

Juerg glanced around at the stonework but he made no comment.

"Did you see that bird back there?"

Looking up, I tried to see if the bird was still in sight. To my amazement, directly above us the Bos'n was flying along the line of the shore, still beating its wings heroically, still arrested in its progress by the stiff wind.

"Look up there."

Looking up, Juerg picked out the bird but at that moment a slashing belt of rain bore down on us. Turning his face, he squinted and shook his head. As I continued to watch, the rain pelted me from behind but I was getting used to the rhythmic pounding of the rain on my poncho.

"It's a bad day to be flying," Juerg yelled out. "What kind of bird is that?"

"It's a Tropic Bird," I hollered back.

We were silent for a minute as the bird flew another few feet and then stopped in mid-air to find its bearings. It twisted its head about as it considered its course.

"It's a long way from home," I yelled over the wind.

"What do you mean?" Juerg looked up again but was struck by a gust of wind and rain. He turned his face from the onslaught but I was mesmerized and could not look away.

"It lives in the cliffs. That one must have been blown out by the storm."

"Where is it going?" Juerg asked.

"I don't think it's going anywhere," I answered truthfully.

There was a strong current of wind gusting up the river valley and the forward motion of the bird was halted. It was just off the heiau, flapping its wings without much result. As I watched, the bird began to slip from side to side, resting in flight to gather strength. It was flying as hard as it could but it was stuck in place. Its head swiveled back and forth to measure its progress.

As I watched amazed, with rain flying in my face and my poncho flapping in the wind, the bird finally ran out of energy. It could go no farther. A deep gust of wind sliced off the bank of the river gorge and the bird tilted to one side. The wind caught the bird full bodied and flipped it over. The Bos'n was thrown backward, like a kite whose string had broken. It disappeared into a thicket of high trees. I turned to Juerg.

"That bird is a goner."

Juerg looked up again but the Bos'n was out of sight.

"Where did it go?"

"It went into those trees. Jesus, it really gave it a go."

"Can we get to the valley from here?" Juerg changed the subject.

"No, we'll have to go back to the trail."

It was obvious to me that Juerg was trying his best to be a good sport but being in the storm was taxing him greatly. Standing on a rock, I turned my face away from the wind. Across from me, Juerg watched the surf pound the rocks below the heiau. In a puddle beside the altar lay the violets and the mangoes that John had placed there two days before. I gazed at the crashing waves and the tangled swells beyond. I tapped Juerg on the shoulder.

"That's where John went into the water yesterday."

His eyes half closed against the assaulting rain, Juerg looked out at the watery grave where Rick and I had searched for John in vain. Looking up, raindrops hit me in the face and obscured my vision as I tried to pick out the bluff where John had fallen. Through the rain, I made the sighting.

The bluff I had picked out was the top of Red Hill where John had given his final sermon. There was no doubt in my mind, but to this day no matter how hard I consider it, I can not tell if what I saw at that moment was real or if it was imagination mixed in and messed up by my eyesight, which was blurred by the pounding rain. For a moment, and only for a moment, I was sure I saw the form of a man on top of the hill, dressed in white.

At first, and without reason, I thought I was looking at the Tropic Bird back in flight, scudding along the rim of the cliff wall, close to the crest of the hill. The rain was picking up, the wind blew the storm into my eyes and I had to wipe my hand across my face to clear my vision. Blinking several times, I saw the form reappear facing the ocean, a snow-white ghost perched on the apex of the hill.

Trying to keep the form in sight, I reached for Juerg's arm but he was not there. Turning my head, I saw that he had moved several steps away. At the outer edge of the heiau he was looking down at the waves that were crashing across the grey boulders. Running to him, I grabbed his shoulder and forced him to look up at the bluff. But I should have known. The bluff was empty. All we could see was the onslaught of the storm coming in torrents. Dropping my pointing hand, I stared up to the top of the hill, dumbfounded. Under the poncho my skin was crawling.

"Did you see anything up there?" I asked in a holler. The sound of the waves crashed into my words and the wind blew into my mouth.

"See anything where?"

"Up there on the hill." I had to keep myself from raving.

"Up there?" Juerg looked at the bluff again but the rain knocked his face down.

"I thought I saw something up there."

"What did you see?" he asked, yelling above the roar of the storm.

"I don't know. It was white. It was on the cliff, there."

By now the rain was ripping into our faces and it took tremendous patience to keep our vigil for more than a moment. Finally Juerg couldn't take it anymore. He looked down at the ground and turned around.

"We should look for Michelle and Dennis."

But I couldn't take my eyes off the high place. There had been something up there. Maybe it was just the bird. But there had been something there.

"We better get going, Peter. It's getting worse."

As Juerg made a move to leave, I turned to watch him go. And there, in the corner of my eye was the form again, dancing white in the prison of the miserable day. When I turned to look, it was gone.

Then, far off the cliff I saw another white form moving through the squall, the image of an angel. It was the Bos'n Bird tracking backward toward the top of the hill. It had appeared out of nowhere from the forest, just off the ground. The bird was being tossed by the wind, fully out of control.

Watching in shock, I saw the Bos'n Bird thrown toward the edge of the cliff, as it lost its equilibrium. It dove, or rather was pushed over the palis. It tipped, erratically, from side to side as it tumbled and fell. In one critical instant, the bird sailed straight down along the face of the cliff and was cast into the swirling ocean with a final burst of fluttering wings. It did not have a chance once it hit the water and it disappeared under the waves. Looking one last time at the top of the hill, I saw that it was empty.

From the far edge of the heiau, Juerg called to me in a frantic voice. It was all that I could do to turn and follow him off the grassy knoll. Above me, the sky opened and a sheet of rain fell down with such force that I was afraid I might be knocked off my feet if I didn't move away quickly.

footprints

We walked along the trail that led across the edge of the sea wall. Now Juerg was in the lead, not wasting a second getting away from the heiau. Several times I had the tearing desire to look back at Red Hill, but I knew if I did I would stop and that stopping would give life to the illusion. Looking back would be to give up looking forward.

So I marched past the morning glories whose flowers were closed tight. As my legs brushed against the lauhala, their leaves deposited moisture onto my pants which were already soaked through. This new current drained into my shoes until they were sloshing audibly.

A peculiar osmosis was occurring in which the rain off the ocean merged into puddles, which soaked my feet and the runoff from the seams of my boots flowed into the ditch that had been the trail in and out of the valley. All of the moisture at once mixed together and a balance began to take effect so that the grey and the clouds and the misty, foggy air and the earth which contained it and the atmosphere which regulated it started to cave in upon itself until it could suck down no farther and so began to expand in a steamy reaction. And I was nothing more than all of the earth anchored inside of my soul as small as a raindrop. It was a dream of madness pulled intact, the weather of the ages falling from the sky in pieces.

And still the storm grew in intensity. The wind blew at our backs and pushed us forward. The trail was rocky here so it held our feet from slipping. The grass up the side of the bank was washed clean, wet and green.

At the fork of three trails, one path returned to the campground, another went out of Kalalau, and the third went up-valley. We stopped for a moment to determine our course.

As we stood trying to make a decision, Juerg looked at me for assurance, but as he looked my way a great smile came over his face. From the direction of the river, Dennis was running up to us. In his hand he carried a net that was made out of a clothes hanger and a funnel of cheesecloth. Michelle came in a few steps behind him.

"What a day to go shrimping."

Dennis had to yell to be heard over the wind and rain.

"Where have you guys been? We were worried." Juerg stepped past me and grabbed Dennis's hand.

"We hiked up valley to see if we could find a clear pool for freshwater shrimp. We ended up way past the falls. It started raining so hard I wasn't sure we were going to make it back."

At that moment, a gust of wind ripped through the brush at the side of the trail and a chunk of rain came down and hit the ground with a roar. Dennis raised his voice to make sure that I didn't miss his intention.

"Peter, we need to talk to you. There's something crazy going on." Dennis gave me a queer look and Michelle joined him.

"Yeah, I know there is, but I can't talk right now. I have to go up to Red Hill before it starts raining any harder."

"You'll never make it across the river."

"I have to go up there."

Even Juerg was alarmed by my statement. He looked at me and shook his head inside the clear plastic rain hood.

"There was nothing up there, Peter."

"What's going on, McDonald?" Dennis asked, but I didn't answer.

"I have to go before the river gets any higher. I'll come to see you when I get back."

"You can't go alone. I'll come with you."

"No, Dennis. I have to go alone. Go back to your camp."

"Peter, this rain is going to flood the valley. You might not get back over the river even if you make it across from this side."

"Don't worry. I'll be back. I've been in worse than this."

The only way to end the discussion was to turn and walk away.

"Listen, if I'm not back before morning, don't tell anyone where I went. Don't tell anyone, do you hear me?"

"I hear you, Peter. But I have to talk to you. It's important."

Once again Michelle was looking at me with a strange expression as if what they had to tell me would reconcile the madness of the weather, of The Man, of his followers, and of a world that was careening through the universe without destination.

"I have to go. We'll talk when I get back."

Throwing my face into the wind, I marched off, away from a fear that was gripping the very earth that we stood on. All I wanted was to follow Dennis back to camp. He had something important to say, but I knew it would only affirm my mission. There was nothing to fear but the word itself and the glamour of distress and the veil that creates the unknown, but my entire life had been spent keeping this fear in check, so I moved forward.

My friends looked at each other helplessly and watched me go. When I disappeared around the first bend, their minds would clear. The simple dread of the weather would settle into their souls like silt. The rain would drive them back to their shelters and I would walk alone knowing what I had to do.

Not far from the fork of the trail, I came to the river bank that would usually be twelve feet above the fair weather channel. Looking down, I saw six feet of bank scoured by the muddy deluge. Islands that had been prominent yesterday were submerged to their necks in chocolate milk. Trees stood in the middle of the flow, their lower branches twitching in the current. The rope that we had used to steady ourselves while crossing, now skimmed over the surface and was whipped forward by the torrent. If I stopped I would never go on so I grabbed the rope and stepped into the river.

Pulling myself forward, the current caught my legs and pushed my feet out from under me. With all of my energy, I focused on the other side and began to pull myself along. At the first island, I felt rocks under the surface. Latching onto the trunk of a tree I held on while thrusting my feet down into the water to gain a foothold. With a blind loyalty that seemed absurd, I slipped back into the current and pulled myself hand over hand toward the other shore. My fingers began to cramp but there was no rest without being swept away, so I continued forward. At the end of my own rope, in a rage of drained energy, I felt the bank of the far shore materialize below my feet. Pulling myself up onto this ground, I lay in a heap struggling to catch my breath. The sound of the thundering river filled my ears.

After some minutes, when I was able to stand, I rose and started up the trail. The valley was hidden under a blanket of weather. The camping area was out there somewhere but I could not see it through the clouds. After ten minutes of walking, I was at the foot of Red Hill. Streams of red water rushed across the green grass of the broken mount staining everything that it touched with its bloody color.

I sat on the ground exhausted. Wrapped in my dripping poncho, I looked up at my adversary, the steep red ridge I had to climb in order to face my delusion. It looked impossible to scale in this storm, worse than the river. The storm was ripping my sails, leaving me adrift in a sea of mud and rain and wind and self-doubt.

With the devotion of a dynamo, I forced myself to move. Slowly I began to climb up the bleeding hill, making the first switchback, my clothing drenched, my boots hissing at me as they expelled water. The tendons in my legs stretched unwillingly against the grade of the hill. The rain was flying down so hard that I had to turn my face away from its stinging blows. My shoulders drooped and I let my chin go down to my chest. Taking another tortuous step forward, I felt my right foot slip in the greasy red mud. My left leg caught the weight of my body but there was no foothold for me to secure myself.

In the mire of a pit that was dug into the switchback by the many boots that had come this way, I lost my balance and dropped heavily onto the ground. The red sewage that had accumulated on the trail filled the sleeves of my sweatshirt. I lay with my forehead against the wet dirt, breathing heavily. My head was screaming in mad, violent voices whose timber I could not recognize. There was somebody else inside of me, fighting against me, laughing at my weakness. All I could do to battle the thing was to listen closely. From my mouth came a spit of laughter. The earth filled my nostrils with its red, wet scent of life. Giving in, I raised myself to go on.

A crimson tide dripped from my clothing and fell back into the stream. My arms were stained blood red from finger to elbow. Lifting them, I stared at my hands. With hard strokes I wiped my palms across the chest of my poncho. Two red brands appeared there. As quick as they were created, the rain washed them away. Starting forward, I trudged up the hill with no doubts in my mind except that final doubt that makes all things equal.

At the summit, I sat with my back against a rock that broke the viscous wind. With my eyes closed, the day was locked out and I thought of nothing. When I felt that I could stand without fatigue, I got up and surveyed the bluff. This was the place where I had watched The Man fall.

In the soggy pasture stood the herd of goats and I walked in their direction. They were not going to move, so I braced myself and waded into the pack. They bleated in protest as I entered their ranks, insulted that I would show such courage.

When one of the large Billys blocked my way, I pushed it to one side with my knee. It stood its ground but I had had enough. With a swing of my leg I kicked the goat in the ribs. The bony animal bolted and hobbled to the outside of the herd. Only then did the goats make a path for me, allowing me to walk to the edge of the cliff.

Below me the ocean slammed against the rocks where John had met his fate. Staring into the water, I attempted to unravel the bickering of the tossing sea. Turning, I looked to see if there was any evidence of my delusion in the mud. The ground was washed with puddles. Dropping to my knees I searched for a sign. Slowly, I crawled to the exact location where John had been standing on the morning he offered his farewell to his followers. And there I saw what I was looking for.

In the mud, at the edge of the pasture were the footprints of a human being. The prints were filled with water and it was impossible to tell when they had been cast. It was more difficult because the goats had been walking all over the hillside. The human footprints were nearly obliterated by the smaller imprints of the stalking beasts. The herd watched me curiously. Standing up, I knew that I would never be certain who or what had been there or how long ago the footprints had been made. But there were two sets of prints of identical size cast in the red mud where John had stood and then fallen. One had its heels facing the ocean. One had its heels facing the Valley.

It had been a senseless quest but not altogether wasted. Standing at the edge of the cliff, I watched the rain fall.

The day moved forward and past me until I knew that it was getting late. If I didn't get off the hill, I would not be able to cross the river before night fell. Above the ocean, the greyness of the day began to fade to charcoal. My mission was being forced to completion by the running of the clock and the spinning of the planet. But I could go on now. It had been an illusion. Pushing back through the goats, I started down Red Hill.

The return crossing of the river was easier because I knew what to expect. When I exited the other side, the red stains of the hill had been washed off of me. Walking back to camp my mind became peaceful and calm.

It was dark when I made it to the campground and I decided not to go see Dennis and Michelle. There was no energy left inside of me so I went to my own site instead. Stripping off my clothes, I crawled into my sleeping bag, exhausted. Tomorrow morning I would pay my debt. Pulling the bag around me, I shivered myself to sleep.

up valley

In the morning, the rain was still coming down. My sleeping bag was soaked and my skin was clammy. When I peeked out from under the poncho, the grey dawn of another stormy day snuck in under the cover. In the murky glow it was hard to tell what time it was or how much time had passed since the sun had come up.

The rain was beginning to feel natural, falling steadily, drenching my body. From the tree where my gear was stowed, I grabbed the clothes I had dried at the cave the day before and slipped them on. Staying dry was an unrealistic goal, even under my poncho, but for a few minutes I felt arid and refreshed. The tourists were tucked into their shelters, and walking through the campground, I was alone with the rain.

Approaching Dennis and Michelle's site, I saw them lying inside their tent, on the blow-up mattress. The front fly was open but they were reading and did not see me coming. Leaning into the opening I said good morning. They were startled by my sudden appearance. Dennis laid his book aside and stuck his head out of the tent.

"Peter, where in the hell have you been?"

As usual, Michelle eyed me silently but without malice.

"I didn't get back until after dark. I was too tired to talk. I went right to sleep."

"We were worried about you," Michelle said.

"I should have told you I was back." I looked down at the ground for a moment and rubbed my finger in the dirt. "The river was hellacious. I just about didn't make it."

"We wanted to go after you last night but you told us not to tell anyone where you went. And I wasn't about to go alone," Dennis spoke next.

Looking into the trees, I viewed the sky through the foliage.

"This is some storm."

"We were supposed to walk out of here today, but there's no way," Dennis said.

"Not a chance."

"Did you find your ghost?" He studied me closely.

"What ghost?"

"Whatever frigging ghost you saw that dragged you into that hurricane."

"There's no such thing as ghosts." I changed the subject, which was the one thing I excelled at. "You said yesterday that there was something you wanted to talk about."

Dennis looked over at Michelle and then back at me. He moved away from the opening to allow me access.

"Come in here, Peter. There's some strange shit going on." When I didn't enter immediately, he waved me forward. "Come on, come on. Don't be shy."

Removing my poncho, I climbed into the tent. Unlacing my boots, I tugged them off and threw them outside the door. From the side of the mattress, Dennis pulled out a thermos and poured me a cup of coffee that was thick with cream and honey.

"I forgot to ask you if you like it sweet." His hand went back to the cranny and appeared with a thermos that was identical to the first. "We've got it black, too."

"This is fine. Thanks."

"I'm afraid you missed breakfast."

"That's alright. I only have a minute."

"What are you up to now, McDonald?"

"I don't want to say just yet."

"You're going back up that hill, aren't you?"

"No. I saw everything up there that I needed to see. Some Bos'n Bird got knocked off course, that's all. What did you want to tell me?"

"Come on, Dennis, tell him," Michelle urged.

Dennis ran his finger around the edge of his coffee cup.

"Come on," I persisted.

Finally, he took a deep breath, exhaled slowly and began to speak. "I don't know where to start."

"Start at the beginning," I suggested.

"You already know the beginning. We went up valley yesterday to catch some fresh water shrimp but the river got so high and muddy we didn't have any luck. I told you that we went past the small falls and the pool where everyone goes to swim."

"Right."

"We followed a goat trail through the forest and up to the cliffs. We were just walking to kill time and then it started to rain. We tried to find our way back to the main trail but it was coming down pretty hard and we got lost. We ended up in a small valley and there was a grove of liliquoi there that got us out of the rain for a while. We were sitting under the trees when we heard voices coming up the trail toward us. At first we were glad that someone else was there. We were hoping to get directions out. But for some reason, Michelle got a bad feeling. We decided to stay hidden in the grove to see who it was. I mean, a lot of strange things have been going on."

"Did you see who it was?" I asked.

"Yes and no," he paused. "We were looking through the trees. We couldn't see too well with the rain and all, but when the voices got closer I did see one person I recognized. It was Marlie."

"That's not surprising. That old coot knows the valley like the back of his hand."

"But that's not what was so strange, Peter. You see, what we were hearing were two voices talking to each other. But all we saw was Marlie walking alone. He was talking to someone, though. But we couldn't see anyone else."

"Did you recognize the other voice?"

"I told you we didn't see anyone."

"So whose was the other voice?" I demanded impatiently.

"McDonald, I'm going to tell you this but I don't want you telling another soul."

"I promise. Now who was it?"

Dennis looked at Michelle but he remained silent. He was going to make me answer my own question.

"It was John, wasn't it?"

They looked at me with wide eyes. They nodded their heads out of sync like opposite ends of a teeter-totter.

"It was John's voice, Peter. But we never saw him. Not a trace. We watched Marlie go by. But as sure as day, that second voice belonged to John. There is no doubt in my mind."

"What were they talking about, or do you want me to answer that question too?"

With a slight hesitation, they affirmed that I had the formula for that riddle as well, although this time Dennis spoke up.

"They were talking about killing goats."

"They were arguing about whether the tourists should be allowed to eat goat in the dry cave," Michelle added her voice. "They were arguing. Marlie was yelling at John."

"But you never saw John."

"No. I mean I guess it was John. He was telling Marlie it was all right to feed goat to the tourists when it was raining and there was no other food," Dennis exclaimed.

"But Marlie was yelling that it wasn't right. That the tourists shouldn't be allowed into the cave. That everything had changed. I mean he was angry, wasn't he, Dennis?"

"Yeah, Marlie was really upset. This other voice was telling him that nothing had changed and that was the way it had always been when he was alive. That when it rained, the tourists were allowed inside the cave."

"Let's stop there."

"I know, Peter. It sounds crazy but Michelle and I both heard him say it. That nothing had changed just because he was gone."

"Did you try to talk to Marlie?"

"No way. We were scared to death."

"So what happened?"

"Marlie walked away and I swear he was alone."

"Was he still talking to the other person?"

"No. When he walked away he wasn't saying anything. Once he was out of sight we figured out which direction he had come and we went that way until we found the river."

"Is that it?"

"What do you mean is that it?" Dennis was nearly hysterical. "Isn't that enough?"

With a flick of my wrist, I finished the coffee that was at the bottom of my cup and refused the offer of a refill. Reaching for the door I prepared to leave.

"I suggest you keep what you just told me to yourselves. Especially don't let Marlie know."

"We want to get out of here, McDonald. If it clears up tomorrow will you go with us?"

"If Bill thinks its safe, I'll go with you tomorrow. But I wouldn't count on it. This storm could last for a while."

"We'll be alright for a few more days but after that we'll be out of food."

"They'll feed you at the dry cave."

"I'm not eating any goat if that's what you mean."

"If you get hungry enough you'll go out and kill it yourself. Just relax. This is going to pass."

"You don't believe us then?"

"Of course I believe you. I just don't believe any of this is happening. It's an illusion."

"It's happening, Peter. I know it is and it's starting to freak me out." Dennis was scared and he looked it.

"Listen, Dennis, Michelle, I need you two to keep it together. If I'm right this is only the beginning. We're going to need each other before this is over. As soon as it clears I'll go out with you."

Throwing my feet outside the tent, I put on my boots.

"Where are you going, Peter?" Michelle asked with anxiety in her voice.

"I can't tell you, but I'll be back before dinner. If there's going to be trouble that's when it will start."

"What kind of trouble?"

"I don't know but if I were you I would stay away from the dry cave today. It's going to get crowded in there. "

"We'll take your advice, McDonald, but I want you to come back here when you're finished."

"I will. But I'm telling you again; don't talk to anyone about what you saw."

"Alright," they agreed in weak voices.

Their last reply was only a muffled sound coming out of the tent because I was already outside walking on the trail away from their campsite. The rain was coming down from buckets and I put my head down as I walked away. Back at my camp I went to my camera bag and took the exposed film and stuffed it into my pockets.

Slinging a camera around my neck and tucking it under my poncho I went directly to the bank that led to the beach. Sliding in the mud to the bottom of the seven-foot bluff, I skidded to a stop on the sand. Halfway to the water I cut to my right.

On the beach, where the sand ended and the boulders began, I saw someone facing the ocean. Slowing so that I didn't draw attention to myself, I tried to see who was there. It was important that certain people didn't see me going up-valley. As I got closer the figure in front of me began to take shape and I knew who it was without question.

It was Joe, juggling three large rocks that were almost too heavy for him to hold with his thin arms. From a distance, I watched him while the rain raged. I slowed my pace to give the appearance that I was taking a leisurely stroll, just a short walk through a rainstorm that ruled the world without challenge.

When I got closer, I noticed that Joe wasn't wearing a raincoat. His long hair was matted flat. His tee shirt was dripping wet and his trousers sagged. Although he saw me from the corner of his eye, he continued to throw the rocks into the air with great effort. Each one he caught caused a grimace to appear on his face.

When I was standing in front of him, Joe looked at me blankly and continued to juggle. I decided that I would have to start the conversation. To walk away without saying something could make him suspicious. My words broke through the rain that was dumping on us. From a far off place, his eyes focused on me as if he were meeting me for the first time.

"What are you doing out here, Joe?" I had to holler to be heard over the crashing waves and the falling rain.

Joe stared at me and continued his impossible labor.

"Joe, what are you doing here?" Stepping forward I forced my face into his dead gaze.

It was obvious he wasn't going to respond. I stood in place hoping to bring some order into the scene but my logic couldn't fill the gap. When it was clear that he wasn't going to answer, I started to move away. As I did, he muttered something under his breath. Facing him, I looked straight into his eyes.

"What did you say, Joe?"

He looked at me as if he were in pain.

"She doesn't love me." This time Joe's voice came out in a shriek.

"Who doesn't love you, Joe?"

"Shannon doesn't love me."

There was no reason to lie but I did it any way.

"Sure, Shannon loves you. She told me she did."

"You're lying, McDonald. She loved John but John was celibate. That's why she hung out with me. She used me."

"What in the hell are you talking about?"

"Tell me that you lied and I'll tell you what I'm talking about."

"Alright then, I lied. She didn't tell me that she loved you. But I could see it in her eyes."

Although he had forced the admission he conveniently ignored my explanation and answered a question that I did not ask.

"She didn't come back to the dry cave last night. She was out looking for him. She was waiting for the Ka huaka'i o ka Po."

"What in the hell is that?"

"She went to look for The Marchers of the Night."

"WHAT in the HELL is THAT?"

"Last night was the first night of Kaloa. Tonight is the full moon and there is going to be trouble."

"What kind of trouble?"

"She was looking for the procession of the dead when the chiefs and the warriors march together again. Tonight the gods will march into the valley."

"Snap out of it, Joe."

At that moment Joe's hand flinched and the rocks that he was juggling fell onto the sand. He looked at the rocks scattered at his feet and then he looked up at me with contempt.

Without a word, Joe walked to the boulders that were strewn at the edge of the beach. Very carefully he bent and picked up three new rocks of exactly equal proportion. These new rocks were larger than the ones that he had dropped. As he tested their weight, I watched in amazement. He flipped them up in the air one at a time with his right hand and held the other two against his chest with his left. When he was satisfied, he resumed his juggling. The anger was gone from his face and was replaced by a blank expression.

"She thinks that if she has sex with a Menehune that she will have a child that will rule the islands. She thinks that if she finds the Menehune before John passes out of the valley, the child she has will be John's child and she will have John in her body."

"What has gotten into you, Joe? This is a bunch of goat shit. There is no such thing as Menehunes."

Once again the rocks fell to the sand and lay in a disordered pile at Joe's feet. Once again, Joe looked at me angrily and went to the pile of boulders. He picked out three symmetrical stones that were larger than the last ones. I was stunned.

"Tonight there will be trouble. You have to get out of here, McDonald. You are in danger."

"What are you talking about?"

"Somebody has to stop Marlie."

"What is he going to do?"

"The goats are eating their way into our dreams. We have to get away."

It was impossible to speak with him anymore. Either the rain was driving him insane or he was in a hypothermic delirium. Either way, there was nothing I could do to help him. I had problems of my own.

"We're going to get away, Joe. Hang in there. Everything is going to be alright."

The third time the rocks hit the sand, I left. From a distance, I could see Joe struggling to juggle three new stones that were larger than the last. Their trajectory was shallow. Each time Joe caught one of the boulders his arm fell with the weight.

There was nothing to do but go on. At the end of the beach I climbed up the bank to the main trail. Going east I went in the direction that I had gone the day before. But this time I was aware.

The puddles that had been contained within the banks of the trail were overflowing. The path was now a stream. In the wide flat places, mud holes stretched seven feet across. I had to go into the brush to get around them. Cutting through a loquat grove, I slipped through slick mud mixed with rotten fruit and floating leaves.

At the end of the grove there was a wide grassy area where people congregated around bonfires on clear nights. I crossed this meadow while the rain battered me. After several stretches of trail that had turned to lake, I succumbed to the fact that there was no fighting the elements. Sloshing along, I watched the mud swirl beneath each step I took.

At some point in this trek I made it to the heiau and rested. I was looking at the ocean when I spied the new arrivals. It was a shock to see them striding through a puddle that was wide enough to fish in. They marched up the trail with mad grins on their faces. When they saw me they sped their pace and marched onto the heiau. As they approached me, their mad grins became madder.

"Did we make it?"

The young man closest to me had the radiance of a gypsy prince. His face showed no sign of fatigue. Returning his gaze, I tried to comprehend what in hell they were doing here in the middle of the storm, coming from the direction of the end of the road.

The man was twenty years old at the outside. His kinky black hair framed a face that was olive skinned Italian and chisel featured Irish. His blue eyes shone through the greyness of the downpour. There was something peculiar in his attitude but I could not put my finger on it. He was far too ecstatic to have just walked into the valley, apparently in the dead of night, in a rainstorm that would drown an alligator.

"I don't know," I answered. "Where are you going?"

At best it was a stupid question.

"Kalalau. We just came from a rave in San Diego, man. Hey, I'm Chick." Turning to his friend, the young man's voice got even more excited. "This is Jeff. He came all the way from Boston, man. Isn't that unbelievable? Two nights ago we were on Black's Beach raving and this morning we're in Na Pali."

The other boy didn't seem as grateful as his friend to be walking through the rain. His long blond hair was stuck to his cheeks. His face was red and puffy. On his back, he carried a guitar in a black nylon bag.

"I talked Jeff into coming with me. He's tripping, man. I told him how cool it was back here."

"Did you two just walk into the valley?" I was astonished.

"We walked all night man. We didn't have any sleeping bags, just the guitar. And a little surprise. Know what I mean?"

"So the trail is open?"

"I don't know, man. We were tripping hard. Know what I mean?"

"Not really."

"Bro', you never answered my question. Is this Kalalau? Is this the Valley?"

"This is Kalalau. If that's where you were going, you made it."

Without any support from his friend, the one called Chick let out a rebel yell. The greyness of the clouds, and the storm and the day took the edge off his holler. What started as a frenzied scream was folded back into the monotonous drone of the pounding rain.

"What a trip. Boy, is it raining."

"I'm surprised you noticed."

The young man continued to smile at me with his fairy eyes.

"You guys have to dry off. You could die of exposure," I said.

"Don't talk us down bro'. We are flying."

"You better fly over to the dry cave and get those clothes off. Someone there will help you out."

"How do we find the dry cave?"

"You haven't been here before?"

"No way, man. This is our first time."

"So how did you know that Kalalau was cool?"

"We heard. Everyone knows about Kalalau. Shit man, it is really raining."

"Take this trail into camp. When you get to the abandoned toilets go left and follow the path straight toward the low cliff. You'll see smoke there from a fire. You can't miss it."

"Far out. I can't believe we made it."

"You made it, alright." I was ready to go. "Listen, don't tell anyone that you saw me. Ask for Caren and she'll take care of you. Don't tell anyone except her that I sent you. No one else. Can you handle that?"

"No problem. But where are you going?"

"I'm going up-valley to look for spirits."

"No way!"

"It's just my thing."

"Can I come with you?"

"Not a chance. If you're here tomorrow I'll ask the spirits if it's cool for you to visit but first you've got to get dried off and warmed up."

"Tomorrow for sure then, bro'?"

"We'll see."

"Who'll see? You and the spirits?" The boy laughed out loud. It took him a minute to get himself back in control.

"No. Me and God. He lives in a cave by the waterfall. I'll tell you later what he had to say."

"Too much, man. I'm going up there with you tomorrow for sure."

"Alright. But remember, don't tell anyone except Caren that you saw me."

"Cool. Caren!"

Chick shrugged his shoulders as a signal to Jeff. He shook his head and shivered, a mad grin saturating his face. They sloshed through a broad mud hole in the direction of the camp, leaving a wake behind them. Watching them go, I nodded in respect to their madness and continued my journey.

At the fork where the trail headed up-valley, I veered to my right and walked on with a steady gait. There was no time to rest or hesitate. The rain was falling harder by the minute.

Passing through the mango grove, I saw fruit lying on the ground, knocked from the trees by the rain and wind. None of this fruit had been bitten by the goats. Apparently they had moved into the higher ravines when the storm came. Taking this as a sign, I moved as quickly as I could through the damp lowlands. The day was caving in on itself. The grey clouds were as thick as cement in the valley sky. Visibility was shrinking at the exact rate that the volume of the storm was increasing.

In a half hour, I made it to the pool where I had nearly drowned. It seemed so long ago that I had been in that place. I stopped and sat on a rock to catch my breath. Although I was soaked and exhausted, I knew I had to go on. There was something calling to me from the valley. Some secret, wild mystery was waiting to be unraveled. If there were spirits to be heard, I knew they would talk to me.

After a few minutes of rest, I stood feeling stiff and sleepy. The trail wrapped around the swollen pool, away from the river and into the heart of the valley. The by-ways of the goats ran straight up-valley so I followed their trail. In another hour, I had plunged deep into Kalalau. On a mesa, I was exposed to the wind and the rain as I surveyed the path forward. The day and everything in it was lost in the overcast. The world had vanished in the rain and the weather. There was no clear direction for me. Feeling defeated, I sat on a rock.

It's hard to say how long I stayed in that place thinking about nothing. The storm was swelling but it did not touch me anymore. When I finally rose, I headed deeper into the valley, although I had no idea how far I had to go. If I hadn't been walking so slowly, feeling lost, I wouldn't have noticed a narrow track into the dense brush on the side of the mesa. The trail veered back toward the river.

At the head of this trail was a spreading hibiscus that I had to duck under to enter the hidden path. The gut of the hibiscus was carved into an arch that was the size of a crouching person. Crawling on my hands and knees I made my way through the tunnel. After twenty feet of hunkering forward, I broke out onto the other side where I could stand again.

Looking around, I realized I had entered a small, hidden canyon. In the distance was the roar of the river, swollen and crashing through its course. I walked a few steps forward to get a better view. It was at this point that I saw the smoke rising through the trees and the downpour. The wind was calmer in this clearing and the smoke hung at tree top level where the rain forced it back to earth. Walking toward the smoke, I went to my knees again to see through the thick undergrowth. That is when I heard the voices.

Crawling, I made my way toward the sound. As I got closer, I lay on my stomach to get a view in front of me. There, in the clearing, a bright blue box was standing in the green and brown and grey of the forest and the storm. The blue swatch looked to be one of the blue plastic tarps that are tied over metal frames to keep out rain or sun. Shelters built from these tarps are so common in the islands that they are called *blue hales:* blue houses. Crawling in closer, I listened until I could hear the voices clearly. The voices were coming from the blue hale. They were discussing a topic with which I was now familiar.

"So what are we going to do about the tourists? They're starting to congregate in the dry cave."

"We can't keep them out. They have as much right to the Valley as we do."

"But they don't bring anything into the kitchen."

"That's not true. They have always given what they had."

"But we always give more."

"Like what?"

"Like goats."

"Why do you keep bringing up the goats? What do the goats cost us? Nothing. It's a sacrifice to keep the trail open. You know that."

"But we use our own bullets."

"You have got to drop this whole subject. If the tourists need our help, then we help them. That's it."

"We'll run out of room. Do you know how many people are looking for shelter?"

"Why does that bother you? Whose shelter is it anyway? Does it belong to us?"

"We run the kitchen and we clean the dry cave so it's our decision."

"Some decisions are out of our hands."

"When you talk like that, I can't help but think that you don't give a damn about anything anymore. Why should it matter to you anyway? You got what you wanted."

"How can you say that?"

"How can you say that the Valley doesn't belong to us? We protect it and keep it safe. You have really changed."

"No, I haven't changed. I was confused there at the end. That's all. We live in the Valley and we enjoy its beauty. That's the only rule."

"This is just crap. You had it right. You walked backward. You saw it all."

The conversation went on like this as I listened. What shocked me was that both of the voices sounded alike. And to my dismay, it was not Marlie speaking to Marlie or Marlie talking to John. As I listened, I realized that both of the voices were the voice of The Man. My head began to spin so I laid my face on the ground to stop the motion.

Then, with a will that was beyond my own, I stood from my hiding place. In a stupor I walked into the clearing in front of the blue hale. Tree limbs snagged my poncho and brush cut my face as I stumbled forward. Making sufficient noise to declare my presence, I descended upon the hale. The voices continued their debate. They argued as I walked into the middle of the clearing and around to the open wall of the shelter. I stood looking into the hale but the voices were now silent. All I could hear was the rain and the breeze blowing in my ears. The hale was empty.

In the interior of the blue hale a fire was smoldering. Smoke rose to the ceiling and drifted into the air. I stepped inside and looked around. It was obvious that someone had been there. The dirt floor was rubbed smooth around the fire ring. In the corner was a mat of palm fronds that was a bed. Walking out of the hale, I went behind the shelter. There was no escape route and there were no signs of life. I was alone.

Standing at the back of the hale I did not know what to do next. I had come here to find an answer, which I had found but which was of no use. It was now impractical for me to use my mind to make decisions. Every thought that entered my head was encased in nonsense and a soapy slime dripped from these bubbles.

Movement was my only hope. Without considering the direction, I walked into the forest. The sound of the river riffing in the undergrowth became a beacon to my inner compass. A hill rose steeply through the thickets. I went forward and stumbled up. The branches jabbed at me but I could not feel them. Numbness pervaded my being and grace erupted from my delirium. This small point of relief allowed me to feel the return of my sanity. Grabbing the trunks of trees, I plodded ahead. The call of the river became louder until I reached the top of a hill where a cataract sliced through the trees. On a goat trail, I walked upstream. Above me, the sky came from all sides, grey and foreboding.

If I had known where I was I would have known that I was deeper in the valley than a novice should wander. The river was coming down a steeper grade but my perceptions were untrue, so I did not notice. Walking forward, I swung my arms to balance my stride, drawn into the darkened heart of Kalalau, this paradise of attrition. Life was fading from my sight like the dead eyes of the alii when I had looked into its face. The alii had read my thoughts without judgment. It could identify dementia, a truth more nebulous than the line that exists between light and dark.

There are stories of Hawaii that may seem queer to people who never have gambled their reality against the sticky subjects of the unknown. There are tales of a race of small people who once inhabited these islands and who were destroyed by the Polynesian hordes a thousand years before the white man came.

Ascribed to the Menehune are teasing bouts of vandalism and glorious feats of accomplishment. Separated from the world by an expanse of ocean, these small people developed past the limitations of other humans. It is certain that every power they were known to possess was possible. The ancestors of these people are said to live in the swamps of Waimea. Kauai is their last stronghold.

On Kauai, the night belongs to the mystic as sure as the moon belongs to the night. Through these nights, the spirits of once-mighty Polynesian chiefs and warriors ply the ancient trails of their past victories. They proceed with the same regard for reason that the sea has for coming to shore. To witness these ghostly processions is fatal, although no doctor can diagnose the cause. The old people of the islands describe the torch-lit parades and they join in the songs of the marchers. The realm of the dead exists beside the districts of the living. But their processions go unheard by the deaf ears and unseen by the blind eyes of the moderns.

The religious soul of the ancient islands was conceived and formed in the hearts and minds of the *kahuna nui*. Those who were initiated were able to see spirits. These priests returned these wandering spirits into the bodies of the dead. In gratitude, the spirits served the Kahuna and a deep trust was established.

Under the covenant of this trust and under the guidance of the priests, the ancients were allowed to flourish in communion with nature. Their bonds to the earth were unbreakable and marked with holiness. They drew from the land everything that was needed and took from it only what was necessary. They fought battles and prolonged wars but they persisted with the blessing of eternity. They were a chosen people, delivered into Paradise.

If the bones of the past could reveal the tales of tomorrow, then the story of Hawaii would go on forever. For in the caves and lava tubes, in the crypts of the royal ancestors, lay the residue of laws that will not be broken. In this thighbone is the memory of a crime committed and justice dispensed. This arm bone held high the k hili and this collarbone raised the hand that drew a boundary line in the sand between the alii and the common people. There a sad truth was born. Somehow, something went wrong. The promise was broken. The white man came and brought down their houses. Like the Menehune, the alii could do nothing but hide and exist in the past.

Now, in these years after the fall, the ancestors of the spirits are heard in the forests of the night. Below the bulge of Waialeale, in the bogs and hollows of this uninhabited terrain, hikers tell stories of voices singing in the night. The sound of drums is heard through the silent darkness. The chorus of yesterday tattoos the crawling skin of those brave enough to listen, an awful fear that does nothing to stop the rituals of the past. The most courageous have hiked through the night and seen the fires. They return, their questions answered, their courage lost.

In the morning there is no evidence of ceremony. Only recollection remains and is described with excited clarity for years into the future. Whether the ancients still exist may never be determined, but the voices are there for those who have heard the climax of a native song in the wild places of Kauai, undaunted.

So when I heard a voice singing through the showering mists, over the roar of the raging river, I felt no apprehension. Stopping on the trail, I looked in several directions to see where the voice was coming from. Then I remembered that all that was required of me was to keep moving forward. There I would find the song and the singer.

Along the bank of the river, I walked slowly until I could feel the vaporous clouds of the collision of a waterfall against rocks. I had reached the palis at the back of Kalalau. Here the song was clear and certain. At the edge of the pool sat a woman. Her voice weaved a tune within the rhythm of the pounding water. Her hands worked slowly at some delicate hobby that I could not see.

"That's a beautiful song, Shannon."

She spun around and glared at me. "What are you doing here? Are you trying to scare me to death?"

"No, I'm not trying to scare anyone to death. But someone is sure having fun with me."

"Damn it, McDonald. Can't a person get a little peace?"

Pulling down the hood of my poncho, I took a seat on a rock next to Shannon.

"I've been thinking about that quite a bit lately."

"Leave me alone and I'll have my peace. Why are you here?"

I chose to ignore her suggestion and her question.

"You know what I wonder, Shannon?" She stared at me. "I wonder if there is such a thing as peace. When I think of all the places I've been and all of the things I've seen, it's hard for me to imagine human beings existing without the commotion. It's as if that is all that makes us feel alive. People are afraid to have a moment without conflict. They create it for themselves if someone's not creating it for them. We're unhappy if we are not sad. I'll leave you alone, Shannon, but do you think that will bring you peace? I doubt it."

"I want you to leave, Peter."

"There's something wrong here. But I can't put my finger on it."

"Please, Peter, I can't talk right now."

Shannon's expression changed to pleading and for a moment I felt sorry for her.

"Are you waiting for somebody?"

"Please, McDonald."

"You're waiting for John."

"God damn you."

"He's not coming, Shannon. Maybe that's what I am doing up here. To tell you that John is not coming back."

I must have believed what I had said because at the end of the statement I stood and looked down at Shannon as I prepared to leave.

"Come back to the dry cave with me."

"I can't, Peter."

"Joe is worried about you."

"I don't want to hurt Joe but I don't love him. I never did. "

"You should tell him that so he can go on with his life."

"I still need him."

"Then what are you doing here?"

"I'm waiting for The Marchers of the Night. Tonight is the second night of Kaloa. They'll come here tonight. I've seen them here before. This is where Koolau made his last stand. This is a holy place. I have to see John one last time."

"And then?"

"And then I am going to wait for the Menehune to come out. They'll be in the valley tonight fixing the paths that were destroyed by the floods."

"You're going to have sex with a Menehune so that you can have a child that will rule the islands."

With sufficient courage so that I was proud of her, she looked at me and nodded her head. "Yes, McDonald. You know my secret. Now will you leave?"

For a moment, I considered my responsibilities. If I left her in the storm she might chill and die from exposure. She was soaked and looked frail. But I knew that taking her from this place would break her spirit. I gave her one more opportunity in order to clear my conscience.

"You should come with me."

"But you know that I can't."

"Yes, I know."

Looking at her through the mist of the rain and the waterfall, I turned to leave. When I was several steps away she called out my name. With my back to her, I stopped to listen.

"Thank you, McDonald."

There was nothing for me to say so I remained silent. "And Peter, I want you to know that John liked you a lot. He had so much respect for you. But he thought you would join us once you came into the Valley. When he realized that you did not need him he began to doubt himself. He did not have your kind of strength and it confused him. He felt that he had to convince you to keep himself convinced. It broke him when you would not believe."

With my back to her, a single thought stepped forward and I turned to speak.

"If you talk to John, tell him that I have seen it all. I've been hurt and I will never heal. But my scars are my power. My wounds are my glory. That's what makes me human. And being human is a good thing to be while we are still alive. It wasn't him, Shannon, it was me. Tell him that, would you?"

It was almost dark when I got back to camp. There was no use in thinking about the blue hale or Red Hill or Shannon sitting by the river waiting for the march of the dead. There was no sense in doing anything but going on.

resurrection

The main campground was sinking under the storm. Where rain had concentrated from the day's weather, shallow lakes had formed. My own campsite was flooded and I stood up to my boot tops in a puddle looking at the mire. With night falling, I grabbed my sleeping bag and hustled up the rain-engorged trail that led to Dennis and Michelle's camp. When I got there, I knew they were no longer occupants at the site.

The tarp that had protected their site was hanging from the trees and flapping in the wind. Broken ropes blew about, frayed and limp. Their tent was soaked and sitting in a pool of water. The floor of the camp, which had been dry that morning, was a pond. Calling out, I received no answer. There was no doubt in my mind where Dennis and Michelle had gone. Past the stone altar that was drowned in mud, I ran back onto the inundated trails and headed for the dry cave.

As I approached the cave, I saw the light of a mighty fire glowing from inside the depths of the shelter. Holding my courage intact I walked up the slope and into the opening.

When I entered the sanctuary, I saw Dennis and Michelle sitting against the back wall. Juerg was there too along with Kate. When I emerged from the dark, everyone looked at me with a concerted gaze. Under other circumstances, I would have felt uncomfortable coming back into this church of my known enemy, but at this moment of necessity no such emotion came forward. Inside of myself, I felt clear and stable. If there was anything to fear I had seen it already and I was now ready for battle. Standing at the front of the cave I looked around to see where I should sit.

The fire was burning high inside of the fire ring. Red-hot embers overflowed the stone ring. The light of the fire illuminated everything inside the grotto so that it was easy to make my assessment.

At the edge of the cave sat Marlie with his back to the fire. He was staring silently into the darkness. The old sea dog was in a pensive mood and didn't look up as I studied him openly. On Rick's mat, Baraka sat crossed legged with his eyes closed, whamming out a song on Rick's guitar. Next to him sat one of the new arrivals, the one named Jeff, who was scaling notes on the instrument that he had brought into the valley on his back. Standing next to the two guitar players, Ron was blowing on his flute, a melody so loud and discordant that it was nearly impossible to listen to. The music blared angrily through the cave. The symphony echoed off the back wall so that the instruments could be heard at once playing and then a second later, replying. The noise would have been torturous except that it blocked out the drumming of the rain on the ground outside the cave.

In the alcove, where Bill kept his bedroom, Judy was sitting alone among the sleeping bags looking into the night, oblivious to the outside world. I searched for Bill but I didn't see him. Caren was sitting by the fire with Maryjane at her elbow, stirring something in a blackened pot. When I tried to signal to her, she looked away, ignoring my presence as she stared into the flames.

At the edge of the firelight sat Joe, looking more melancholy than when I had seen him that morning. At his feet were three very large rocks and he was looking at them as if he were figuring out the solution to a puzzle. As I watched, he picked up one of the large stones using two hands. He heaved it into the air as high as his strength would allow. As Joe concentrated on the arc of the rock, he caught sight of me. He froze and the rock passed through his hands and landed on the ground at his feet. He looked at me with a cowed expression. His head fell into his hands and he cradled it there, rolling his forehead in his palms.

Feeling that I had as good a fix on the situation as was needed, I walked directly to where Dennis and Michelle were sitting. Throwing my sleeping bag on the ground, I settled in next to Dennis.

"What's going on?" I asked. I nodded to Michelle to bring her into the conversation.

"Both my tarps broke. We went for a walk and we forgot to empty the water before we left." He seemed shaken.

"We're leaving tomorrow, Peter," Michelle said. Her face was thrust out at me but she spoke softly so that no one else would hear her. "Those guys walked the trail in the dark. If they can make it at night, we can make it during the day."

"I was thinking the same thing. Let's see what the weather does tonight."

"I don't know, but I think it's raining harder right now than it was this afternoon," Dennis stated.

"What are you going to do about your stuff?"

"It's a loss. We'll salvage what we can."

"Too bad."

"So where did you go today?" Michelle asked, poking her head in still closer.

Looking around, I watched to see if anybody was listening. I caught Caren looking at me but when I tried to catch her eye she looked down at her cooking. My attention returned to Dennis and Michelle.

"I went up-valley."

"Are you crazy? It was raining like mad down here."

"It wasn't a good day for a picnic up there either."

This time it was Dennis who eyed the rest of the inhabitants of the cave before asking his question.

"So, did you find John?"

"Jesus Christ, Dennis. John is as dead as Aramaic. Why in the hell did you think I was going to try to find John?"

"What did you find, then?"

"Nothing really. I met those newcomers on the trail. I came across a blue hale somewhere up there with a fire inside it and I ran into Shannon. We had a nice discussion about Menehunes and spirits and stuff like that. Then I came back."

"Is that it?"

"It was enough."

"No sign of John?"

"I just told you—"

"I know. It's just that—"

"John is dead. That's the end of the story. Has Marlie been here the whole day?"

"As far as we know."

"What about Bill? Have you seen him today?"

"We saw him on the beach earlier. But he hasn't been back since we came up. We've been here about an hour."

"I wonder where he is."

"No telling."

Our conversation dwindled and I looked at the other people who were gathered inside the sanctuary. Suddenly, Marlie stood and with his back to the inside of the cave he stomped his foot on the dirt floor.

"Where in the hell is Bill with that goat?"

For a moment, everyone looked at Marlie. The music stopped and the players gazed at the back of Marlie's head. When they decided that they had given the question sufficient attention, they began to play again as loudly as before. At the fire, Caren looked at Marlie with a troubled expression. She stood and walked to him. Leaning her head down, she laid her hand on his shoulder.

"He'll be back."

"What in the hell is taking him so long?"

"He might be having trouble getting a goat without the gun."

"That worthless bum. I could have killed every goat in the valley by now, with or without a gun."

"He'll be back. Don't worry."

Marlie sat down stiffly and continued his vigil of the stormy night. Over her shoulder, Caren glanced at me with tired eyes. She returned to her seat at the fire.

As it happened, Marlie didn't have long to wait. Sitting in our positions with the tension scratching our nerves, we heard the sound of feet running along the trail. As we listened to the approaching slosh, Bill and the new arrival named Chick ran in from the storm. They were both soaking wet but smiling from ear to ear. In the safety of the cave, they stripped off their dripping rain gear and went to the fire.

"Where in the hell have you been?"

On his feet again, Marlie glared at the returnees. Looking at Marlie, Bill smiled as if he were going to laugh.

"We've been searching for the sacred goat, your holiness."

"So where in the hell is it?"

Bill shook his body like a rag doll and smiled. At the fire, Chick began to giggle and not knowing any better, Maryjane put her head down and snickered.

"I'm sorry, Marlie, we could not kill the goat without the hallowed bullet." In his hand Bill was twirling the noose that Marlie had made the night before. "This rope just will not do the trick."

At his post, Marlie began to shake in an uncontrolled rage. I was sure he would lunge at Bill.

"Listen, you dumb-ass. If I send you out for a goat, you bring me back a goat. I don't want to hear any excuses, you got that?"

"No excuses! Yes sir. But I just want to say that it was very wet out there and the goats were moving up-valley and the river was too high to cross."

"You god damn idiot. Do I have to go out and get the goat myself?"

"They do say that if you want a job done right, then you will have to do it yourself. I di-i-i-i-i-d my-y-y-y-y-y be-e-e-e-est." Bill broke into his goat-speak and everybody smiled. Except Marlie.

"Are you refusing a direct order?"

"All I'm saying is that I did my best and I couldn't bring a goat down without a bullet."

Dennis tapped me on the shoulder but I was so engrossed in the spectacle that I ignored him, even when he tapped me a second time. Finally, Dennis grabbed my shirtsleeve and gave it a tug and signaled for me to look down at his lap. From underneath his leg he pulled his hand out. Opening his fingers he revealed a gun he was hiding there. After he was sure I had seen the piece, he closed his palm and stuffed his hand and its secret contents back into his lap. He looked at me, smiling.

"How did you get that thing?" I asked in a whisper.

"Shh. It must have slipped out of Marlie's pants. When I saw it, I grabbed it. And I grabbed the last three bullets too."

"What are you going to do with it?"

"Nothing. I just wanted to get it away from him."

"Good idea."

Outside the cave a gust of wind blew through the trees. The rain had gathered strength and it roared down with a groan. Even the music could not cover the increasing intensity of the weather.

"Alright then, you loser," Marlie continued his onslaught. "From now on I'm putting Ron in charge of the slaughter. You obviously can't handle the job anymore."

Still playing his flute, Ron raised his eyebrows in alarm but he did not say a word.

"Does this mean I won't be getting my Christmas bonus?" Bill continued to smile idiotically. It was hard to imagine why he continued to push back.

Everybody looked at Marlie sensing that something was about to break. Marlie was as still as a tombstone.

"I think I'll cancel Christmas this year."

"Alright, Marlie, but there are going to be a lot of disappointed children."

"You shit-head."

"I thought you said I was a dumb-ass."

"You're a shit-head and a dumb-ass and a worthless butt-wipe too."

"Did you forget anything?"

"I'm sure I did but by the time Ron brings the goat I'll remember all the best things."

"Thank you, Marlie. By the way, does that mean Chanukah is out, too?"

"Shut the hell up."

"Sorry."

Without changing his position, Marlie yelled out for Ron.

"Ron, get your ass over here."

The flute stopped playing, but Baraka continued to plunk on the guitar nervously. Ron ran over to Marlie.

"Yeah, Marlie?"

"Ron, you have the privilege of getting the goat for the sacrifice from now on."

Ron was silent and it was obvious that he was not thrilled by the news.

"I don't know, Marlie."

"What do you mean you don't know?"

"It's pretty wet out there and if Bill couldn't find any goats, I wouldn't stand a chance. I don't know the valley half as good as he does."

"I want you to go out and try, Ron. If you pull it off you could become the official goat slayer. I will personally teach you to use the gun."

"But Marlie. You know me. I hate blood and I can't shoot a gun worth a damn. The only people who used guns in Jersey were the crime boys. Besides, are you really going to cancel Chanukah?"

"Listen you jerk-off. If you don't go out there right now and get us a goat, I'm going to cancel your existence. Do you understand?"

"Not really. Would you run that by me again?"

"I said listen you jerk-off, if—"

"I got that part."

"Christ. I'm surrounded by imbeciles. Who is going to bring the goat?"

Everyone was silent. Not a sound was heard except for the immense howling of the storm. Marlie waited a little longer than I thought he should have before he slammed the gathering with his next threat.

"Alright, you chicken-shits. I'll go out and get the goat. But when I bring it back, Caren is going to cook it and you are all going to eat it. Is that clear?"

Marlie was smart enough not to wait for a reply. Turning up his pant cuffs, he waded forward, out of the cave and into the gloom and the fury of the storm. After he left, everyone let out a sigh of relief. Once he was out of ear-shot, Chick began to howl with laughter. At the cliff wall, Bill turned around and smiled.

"Boy, what a grouch," Bill joked. He ignored the light response his joke garnered. Miraculously, a cigarette appeared out of nowhere. "Wow. That was some good stuff." He was talking to Chick who had stopped laughing by now.

"Do you want some more?"

"No doubt. I could do that stuff all night."

"I haven't slept in three days behind it."

From his seat, Joe looked up for the first time since he had dropped the rock. He eyed Bill suspiciously.

"What do you have?" Joe asked.

"Chick brought something for us, Joe."

"What is it?"

"What is it, Chick?" Bill relayed the question.

"It's some new stuff that a chemist friend gave to me. It doesn't have a name yet, but I call it Lotus."

"Lotus, huh?"

"That's what I call it."

"Can I try some?" Joe was on his feet.

"Sure, no problem." Chick looked around the cave. "If anyone else wants some, come and get it. This stuff will keep your mind off the storm. It is the magic potion that got Jeff and me over Na Pali last night."

It was time to watch carefully and I did. Everybody was looking around to see who was going to volunteer. At first, only Joe stepped forward. Then, following Joe's example, Ron sauntered over to Chick.

"So what is this stuff?" Ron asked.

"It's a mild psychedelic. Something like mescaline. But it's synthetic."

"Is it clean?"

"As clean as a kitten."

"How long does it last?"

"About two hours, max. But the first twenty minutes will make you forget who you are. Seriously."

Ron looked at Joe and shrugged his shoulders.

"Why not? I'll try some."

"You will not regret it. Anybody else?"

Taking turns, Baraka and Maryjane joined the line and Bill decided that he would have some more. I was a little shocked when Judy came out of the alcove and joined the others. The rest of us didn't speak and thus provided our negative replies.

While we watched, Chick stuck his hand in his pants pocket and retrieved a small screw top vial that was filled with a clear liquid. He unscrewed the lid carefully and with Judy's help he dipped a pin into the top of the vial. One by one he dosed the willing with a single drop of the Lotus. In a moment the ritual was over. Chick placed the vial in a recess of the housekeeping wall as a sign of sharing what he had. Everyone looked the same but they were going to look different, at least they would look at things differently. They watched each other, waiting for the effects to kick in.

As I sat feeling uncomfortable with the fear that we would shortly be separated by the gulf of the narcotic, a huge flash of lightening lit the sky. It was followed by a resounding roll of thunder. We all walked to the mouth of the cave where the rain was falling like a curtain across the entrance. Standing in a line, we stared into the stormy night. The lightening must have been a freak occurrence because there was no follow-up and we settled back into our positions inside the cave.

We sat feeling strange, watching each other with a curious suspicion. Caren went back to the pot she had been tending and stirring it one last time, she had Maryjane hand cups to everyone, as she poured the tea.

"This is the first time that I've made liliquoi tea, so keep your suggestions brief. Unfortunately, Lynn didn't leave her recipe."

When Caren got to me, I tried to make eye contact but it was no use. She served me without a word and moved on. We sipped our tea in silence. Even the music had been quelled by Marlie's departure and the introduction of the narcotic.

The time passed quietly. No one spoke. Those who had been dosed waited for the effects of the dope. Those of us who had declined anticipated the change that would come over the others. We sat looking at each other wondering when the shining would occur. The firelight splintered the dark with its fibrillating light. The color of the fire was orangey and mellow. Everyone relaxed into the warmth and listened to the storm. The musicians were playing a dirge.

Outside, the storm grew in intensity. It was a full moon and a halo around the equatorial plenilune shone bravely through the thick grey clouds. In the moonlight, the clouds could be seen rolling heavily through the sky, folding in on each other, caressing themselves for their own pleasure. Below the sky, the surface of the ocean captured the moonlight and was illuminated in facets like a flat grey gemstone. The moon was so bright that it was impossible for the clouds to entirely blot out the radiance that reflected the sun from the other side of the world into the night on our side.

Beside me, Dennis and Michelle silently watched the others. As I got to know him, I had come to like Dennis a great deal. He was a solid character that I knew I could count on. The fact that he had ended up with the gun made me feel safer. His face had a look of confidence that made me feel secure.

The entire time I had been in the valley, I had kept one or the other of my cameras around my neck. Tonight I was carrying a Nikon F1 loaded with Tri-X, black and white. Staring into the sky I realized that I had been gazing straight ahead and that the clouds were swirling harder and faster than they had been when I had looked out a moment earlier. As I considered the time, I knew that what had seemed like a moment had actually been several minutes and I knew that I had been watching a witch's brew stirring above an ocean that was shimmering tough and beaded under the weather. My eyes began to itch and I wanted to take a picture but I realized too late that I could not move my hands.

Shaking my head, I tried to focus on the deep cloud cover, which was receding into a vortex. The light of the moon wavered and glowed with a frosty tinge that I knew was inside my head. The sky was reaching out for my eyebrows, all broken up into pieces and scouring the heavens between me and the horizon. With great effort I turned my head and tried to look into the cave. I got a taste of something sour under my tongue as I begged my head to stay on my shoulders. My neck felt like a gusher of flower oil and my sight slid into my throat where it gurgled. I had to wink my eyes to keep the fairy girls from smiling too far into my apartment.

Just beyond the shape of my body, grey-lined squares rolled in triple dimension past an asteroid storm that was snow falling inside the capsule of the geometry. It was no use to think. Flying was the only word that came to mind. It must have been in the tea. I tried to find Caren in the cataclysm of day-glo jet streams that blew a trumpet wind through the cave.

Next to me, Dennis and Michelle had slid to their elbows and were looking into each other's eyes with the soft euphoria that is virginity found among lost toys. I realized but could not tell myself that I was lying against the rocks of the back wall. My tongue crawled out of my mouth and smelled among the flowers and pollen of a springtime fall that was landing upon me as I rode my airplane into cotton clouds. The propeller snapped on the thread of a combine and I thrashed about unable to move past the vines of support and neglect, and god, was I coming apart.

Every act of justice was flipping past me in a second of dust. I had the pleasure of skipping stones over an ocean that was quenched with blood, its heart pumping an orgasm of pleasure. Trying to hold on was not enough. It was all that I could do to close my mouth and keep my teeth from chattering a Gregorian chant. Alice was there and the Scarecrow and Peter Rabbit and all of the days of questionable weather lay like a mask upon the corpse of paisley dragsters and neon judo. The initial rush had begun to fade but I held on with both hands and cupped the results of the worsening storm into the beginning of Easter. Jesus was there and another friend of mine on the veranda, waving.

My eyes itched. When I found sense enough left in the atmosphere to move my fingers I lifted my hands to my eyes and scraped them gently over the lines around my smile. Words were coming in backward and sentences taxied to the runway for take-off. I rubbed my eyes diligently but it was no use. Beside me Dennis and Michelle sighed as loud as the wind. They stared into each other's eyes for fun. I picked up my camera and attempted to look through the viewfinder. The damn box was filled with a garden of high rent daffodils and baby's breath and Texas highway medians, all springing for cover in their rainbow suite, me gazing down the tunnel of a lens, trying to pick out a subject. Tomorrow was scrubbed clean and dainty. Each shot I did not steal bit my membranes with psychedelia and I was falling.

Picking myself up, I stood long enough to introduce my mother to my shaking knees. My sleeping bag was handy so I made an excuse, threw in the towel and lay down just in time to witness the stroke of midnight on the lunch horn bell. Once again, I tried to look through the viewfinder and there I could see traces of our tribe but it was through a cistern of cartoon scriptures amid a musical hierarchy laced with single celled monoliths.

Looking for Chick, I finally found him up in a clear pyramid smiling back at Pluto, me sitting on a seat, and I saw Caren walking to the fire to stir a fusion of the multi-hued targets of a breeding buffoon. It was a dream of being awake. Beside me Dennis and Michelle sighed again as deep as philosophy. I turned the camera on them. They smiled. It was becoming easier not to exist. Snapping a shot cleared my eyes with a flash pot. Stopping this horse I needed to drink air. Dive into the silk. Lie inside the animator. Don't fall for fascination. Snap, snap. I found Joe cuddling his rocks. He looked at me and deserted. Out of the cave, he sauntered into the storm but I couldn't stop myself. It was definitely harder to speak than to rotate glycerin.

It went on like this for some time before Bill came to me. Sensing I could speak, I did not fight that feeling. He had something to tell me and I knew he had to tell me fast. I was rocking back and forth on my heels.

"McDonald, are you alright?"

"Never better."

"That's wild stuff."

"What stuff?"

He looked at me amazed.

"I put Lotus in the tea when everyone was watching the lightening. I knew that it was safe."

"I didn't have any tea."

"What?"

I thought Bill was going to come out of his clothes.

"I can't stand that liliquoi tea. It gives me diarrhea. What did you want to tell me?"

"I saw you drinking a cup of tea."

"It was just water. I didn't have any tea."

Bill's eyes were spilling out of his head in an expression like crime.

"I saw you," he mumbled.

"Sorry, Bill."

"I saw you."

"How could you have seen anything and been knowing enough to tell the story. Huh?"

"What—? You bastard, McDonald. I wish I could keep you as a pet. You sock my shoulder sometimes. Oh man."

"What did you want to tell me?"

He was laughing at my ruse and it took him a minute to gather himself together.

"Marlie sent us out for goat today and I took that new kid, Chick."

"Yeah, I saw him come back with you."

"Well, I wasn't in the mood for killing goats in the rain so we took a walk."

"Where did you go?"

"We went up to the bonsais."

"In this storm?"

"After Chick and I did the first dose of Lotus the rain wasn't falling on us."

"What Lotus?"

"Stop it!"

"OK. What did you see?"

"Somebody's been up there trimming the bonsais."

"How do you know? Did they leave a note?"

"Seriously, McDonald. The trees. They had been trimmed."

"How could you tell?"

"Remember I told you that there are different types of bonsais. Different sizes depending on how they are pruned?"

"Yeah, I remember."

"Every last tree on the ledge had been trimmed down. It's what they call *mame* in Japanese. It's a very sophisticated style of cutting. *Mame* means very small bonzai tree."

"I didn't know you spoke Japanese."

"I only know a few words."

"So who do you think was up there?"

"There's no telling. I thought I was the only one who knew about the garden."

"Obviously you aren't."

"Unless—"

"John is dead, Bill. Don't start that shit with me too."

"Who else?"

"Dennis and Michelle said they heard him talking to Marlie up-valley somewhere."

"What about you? You went up to the top of Red Hill. I saw you from this side. You thought you saw him up there."

"I thought I saw something up there. But it was just some bird lost in the storm."

"What about today? Where have you been all day?"

"I went for a hike."

"You went up-valley, didn't you?"

"As a matter of fact I did. But what great significance are you going to put on that?"

"You were looking for something."

"Yeah, I was looking for the meaning of life. But John is dead."

"Did you find the meaning?"

"Yeah."

"And what is it?"

"Listen close, Bill, because I got this straight from the big guy himself and I'm only going to tell you once."

"Shoot."

"There is definitely life before death."

"And—"

"And the world will be inherited by Homer Simpson and it will be fed at fast food stands by androids. That's the word I brought down from the mountain." My mouth felt bitter.

"You are rad, McDonald. When Rick comes back, I'm taking you surfin'."

"I forgot all about Rick. He's supposed to bring me something from the Valley of the Lost Tribe."

"You can count on him."

"I know. Besides I'm doing him a favor in return."

"A picture?"

"How did you know?"

"I can't tell you right now, McDonald. But before you leave, I have some things to explain to you about us."

"Who?"

"All of us. I can't tell you now though."

"By the way, the big guy told me one other thing."

"What is it?"

"We can't stay in Paradise if we want to get to heaven."

"I knew it."

"Don't kill the messenger."

"Thanks for the info."

"No problem."

Bill crossed over to the alcove that was his bedroom and sat on the sleeping bags. While I was still feeling intact, I took a few more pictures of the crew. At the same time, standing from his seat, Chick stepped forward and held up the vial.

"Anybody ready for another dose?"

This time everyone took up the offer and accepted a drip in their mouths. It didn't surprise me when I walked up to Chick and offered him the field of my tongue. The stuff was oily but it did not have a foul taste. If anything it had no taste at all. After their dose, people wandered back to their respective areas and sat waiting for the jolt. Depositing the vial in a recess of the cave wall, Chick went over and started playing Rick's guitar.

The entire time that we had been tripping, Jeff had been strumming his guitar lightly without a tune. In the heat of the battle of the colors, Baraka and Maryjane had disappeared into their tent, which they had moved into the dry cave. Everyone could hear them inside the nylon bedroom. She was moaning and he was grunting and the sound had gone on for some time but it was a good harmony for the restless storm that grew more ferocious by the minute and the music, which was dissonant.

As for Ron, he had not moved an inch since the initial reincarnation of his senses by the Lotus except to take a second dose. He returned to his seat and was holding his flute to his mouth with his head turned to the left, not blowing and with no sound coming out. He was frozen with one great symphony playing inside his head.

When Chick moved through the dream colors and started thrashing on Rick's guitar, Ron came back to life, as if he had been to some distant galaxy and had returned by molecular transporter. Slowly, with Jeff plucking out a meaningless series of notes and Ron attempting to find reality within his arpeggios, the musicians began to jam cautiously trying not to allow the airplane wind to debate their meaning. The result sounded like a trumped-up version of a Lonely Hearts Club Band with dope playing the brass.

As I waited, I looked into the alcove where Bill had retired and to my amazement, I saw that he was gone. What shocked me more though was that Judy was gone as well and that the last time I had seen her was just before my eyes had started to itch.

The storm was raging more fiercely than ever outside the sanctuary of the dry cave. The rain was coming down in sheets, literally. There is no other way to describe the downpour because when I looked into the moonlit night there was a transparent wall of water falling in front of the opening to the cave. The clouds were blowing in over the top of the cliffs behind the cave from the direction of the Akali Swamp. They had grown thicker and their race across the night sky could be gauged in the pale outline of the moon.

The second dose did not kick in as hard as the first. There was a cellophane slip and the color of mercy dragged my nerves along like a dozen clanking cans. But I was already on the other side and the added fuel only made words seem clearer and noises crack with drama. Sitting back against a rock at the edge of the cave, I looked out at the storm and prayed for beauty.

Once again my thoughts began to unravel, but this time I was ready for it. All of the color and sensation exploded inside of me with the force of a nuclear bomb. Holding on for dear life, I let the euphoria surround me. On the other side of the gulf, many strange things began to happen.

First of all, Bill came back into the cave and sat by the fire. He had been gone almost an hour in the worst part of the storm. His hair was wet and stringy and his clothes were drenched. Looking at him I knew that something was amiss. Without drawing attention to myself, I sat down beside him. With my hand on his shoulder I nudged him to life.

"What's wrong?"

When Bill looked up, I could see that he was scared solid. It took him a few seconds to answer.

"You won't believe what I just saw."

"You look scared half to death."

At that precise instant, Bill's eyes jumped in the direction of the cave opening. When I looked there, I saw Judy walking in from the storm, dripping wet. Without having to be told, I knew that Judy was the subject of Bill's fear.

In her wet clothes and with her curly hair soaked through to her scalp she went directly to the bedroom alcove. She sat on the blankets and looked up at the moon. A sinister smile was on her face. When I looked at her, the skin on my legs literally tingled. With her head cocked up at an angle on her shoulders she watched the moon with an expression that was so far away she might have been riding on the clouds rather than sitting in the alcove staring into them.

Suddenly, with a smile that made me shudder, her head dropped forward as if there was a weight on her chin. Her head rolled from side to side and then she was staring straight at me. Not at me, she was looking at Bill. When I looked over at Bill, he was frozen by her gaze. His mouth was wide open, his eyebrows were raised. The look of fear filled his face while she gazed in his direction but somewhat farther away. Then, with the same jerky motion her neck twitched twice, her shoulders swiveled, her eyes rolled back in their sockets, her eyelids closed, and her head fell onto her shoulders.

Her eyes popped open, her head slipped back as if she were dying, and the sinister smile left her face for a moment as she searched the swirling clouds for the moon. When she found it, her head twitched several more times, the smile returned to her mouth, and her shoulders drooped. With all the subtlety of a demon on a binge, Judy let out a bloodcurdling laugh that cut through my heart and left me holding onto the toes of my boots. She watched the moon from behind her distant gaze and continued to laugh until she was out of breath. When she gasped for more air, the smile left her face and her head began to rock back and forth spastically. Then she smiled and laughed bloody murder again, swung her shoulders, and let her head drop back so that she looked beyond the moon. Then she repeated the entire process.

Bill was staring at Judy in a fixed pose, which frightened me all over again. With a stern voice, I insisted that he snap out of his stupor. The narcotic joy was tickling me with emotion I could not control. With eyes wide, Bill pivoted his head on his shoulders and looked at me with the same expression he had been leveling at Judy. He was as close to being in shock as I had ever seen an unhurt man. Shaking him by the shoulders I brought him back.

"What is going on?" I hollered.

I was talking to a man whose eyes could not close enough to keep a fly from entering his head through his eye sockets.

"Bill, talk to me."

Once again, Bill glanced over at Judy, as if she controlled his speech. I looked at her too and saw that she was in the no smile head forward before it rolled back phase of her trance. When her head whipped back on her shoulders and her eyes opened, the moonlight filled her eyeballs with a ghoulish light that was unnerving. She laughed maniacally.

"Bill, talk to me!"

He shook his head and came out of the spell. He was still scared though and it took him a moment to speak. When he did, it was in a whisper. He glanced over at Judy to make sure that she was not watching him.

"You wouldn't believe what just happened."

"Tell me," I demanded. I glanced up at Judy whose head was now dropped down so that her chin was on her chest. It was obvious that she was not listening.

"I was sitting inside the alcove with the blankets around me when all of a sudden I realized that Judy had left. I was wondering where she had gone and I got the strangest feeling. There was no voice really but something inside of me was telling me to go out to the heiau. I couldn't resist it. It was like something was pulling me. I didn't have any shoes on but I got up like someone had a hold of me and was dragging me out of the cave."

"I didn't even see you go."

"I knew I was supposed to go without anyone knowing. The minute that I was out of range of the firelight and on the main trail, I started running. I mean I was really running barefoot down the trail. I wouldn't be able to run that trail in the daytime in this rain, McDonald. I wouldn't usually even walk it on a good day without shoes or sandals or something. But I'm telling you, it was like I was being pulled forward and I couldn't stop myself."

"And you knew you were going to the heiau?"

"Absolutely. And I mean I was running as fast as I could go. I was sprinting but my feet didn't hurt at all. The trail was flooded up to my ankles and I could barely see through the rain but I just kept running until I got to the heiau. That's when I saw her."

"Judy?"

"Yeah, Judy."

At this point he glanced at her again and I joined him. She was in the middle of another laughing shriek and her head was wobbling on her shoulders as if all of the tendons in her neck had been sliced.

"What was she doing?"

"God damn it, McDonald." I could tell he was reliving his vision and that it was scaring him as much now as it had before. "When I got to the heiau, the force that had been pulling me forward released me. I could feel it letting go. But then another force grabbed me and held me in place at the edge of the heiau. I was standing in the rain looking at Judy."

"And?" I prodded him.

"She was on her hands and knees in the middle of the heiau and she was scratching at the ground like some kind of god damn animal."

"Scratching?"

"I mean scratching right through the grass and into the dirt. After she had scratched and scraped for a while she stood up on her knees and kind of squatted like a dog and she started howling at the moon."

"Jesus Christ."

I glanced at the subject of our discussion and when I did my nerves crawled forward and ambushed me.

"She howled like that for a couple of minutes and I wanted to run away but I couldn't. I was rooted to the ground. And then while I stared at her she looked over her shoulder at me and she smiled like a lunatic. If I had been wearing shoes I would have jumped right out of them. She was laughing like an idiot and clawing the earth with her hands and feet."

"Then what?"

"Then she looked away from me and I could feel the restraint lifting and I knew I could leave. And when I was getting ready to turn and go, she fell onto her stomach and started groveling in the mud and rolling around on her back and rubbing herself between her legs and I got the hell out of there. I was scared out of my wits."

"Where did you go then?"

"I started back to the cave. I wanted to run like I did to get out there but I couldn't. There was no way. I could barely find my way through the dark, so I just walked as fast as I could. I kept looking over my shoulder because I was afraid Judy was going to come down the trail and rip my heart out or something."

"Are you alright now?"

At that moment, Judy let out an unusually loud shriek of laughter. When we looked over at her, her head had fallen forward and she was drooling on herself, her chin on her chest.

"I guess so. I'm still scared shitless though."

"It must have been the Lotus."

"I shouldn't have let her dose. The whole thing about John really got to her."

We sat silently for a time listening to the raging storm, which beyond all logic was getting worse by the minute. Above us only a donut of light showed where the moon hung. Finally, Bill stood up and walked to the alcove. Without hesitating he sat down next to Judy and put his arm around her shoulder just as her head fell back and her eyes blinked open and the laugh of madness spewed from her lips. When he had settled in, Bill looked at me, shrugged his shoulder, peered into the sky and picked out the moon.

Sitting near the fire, I watched the clouds going past. It was making me anxious sitting in the cave with madness all around me.

In their corner, Dennis and Michelle did not make a sound. They looked at each other lovingly, as if they had been slammed into static inertia by the chemical catalyst. At least they were smiling. The musicians were playing louder now and they had found a groove. For the first time the music did not jar me. The tunes were wild and the harmonies were distorted but I listened and became soothed by the melody.

In their tent, Baraka and Maryjane were still going for it. Sometimes their moaning and grunting would quicken and then it would slow to a crawl. It went on like this so long that I began to wonder who would get tired first, probably me.

In the alcove, Bill sat with Judy holding her up as she continued the journey to the far reaches of her trance. After some time, her affected laughter subsided. Still, when I looked at her, the hair on my arms stuck up on regimented goose bumps.

The entire time we had been tripping, Caren sat on her mat with her head propped on her knees and her arms wrapped around her legs. She stared straight ahead and didn't say a word. There was no use talking to her. She was in her own world where I would not be allowed until the Lotus wore off. Juerg was in much the same state. He looked around at the interior of the cave with a fat grin on his face. Every once in a while he would giggle at some joke that he had concocted out of his tangled thoughts. He was sitting close to Kate and they made a good pair. Neither one was coherent worth a damn.

Somewhere out in the storm I knew that Joe was juggling a burden that was too heavy for him. Shannon had not shown up. She must still be up-valley waiting for her Menehune lover to take her in the rain. As little as I cared for Marlie, I couldn't help but thinking about him, moving through the weather, searching for the sacrificial goat. Everything was crazy and I was starting to get hot.

Without bringing attention to myself I got up from my seat. Throwing my poncho over my head I walked out from under the overhang of the shelter and into the rain.

There was a broken series of intermittent waterfalls flowing over the lip of the cave that I had to pass through. Once outside, the rain hit me with such intensity that I became disoriented. Although I wanted to retreat, I continued on into the night.

On a path that was marked only by the flood of water along its course, I walked past the abandoned toilets and headed east on the main trail that led out of the campground. I was not sure where I was going but it was good to be out of the cave.

Walking through the rain, I felt like a ghost passing through a wall of water into another wall and another and another, which was the sky falling down from the heavens. The sound of the rain crashed all around me as if a tsunami were being wrung from the clouds. I had to walk with my head down to keep my eyes clear. Walking forward, unable to guess my speed, I stepped out of the trees and onto the open trail that led to the heiau. Before I could go too far, I had to make a decision. I knew that I could not go to that ancient altar after hearing the story that Bill had told. At the last junction to the beach I stopped and looked into the storm. The rain was unbearable. It was a thick curtain of water with no exit. I turned down the small trail that led to the beach. I slipped several times before I made it to the sand.

The place where I stepped onto the beach was at the point where the river and the sand ended in the field of boulders. I was shocked when I saw someone on the spit. With all of the madness of the rain and the Lotus and the belligerency of the dissent, I had little desire to confront anything new at this point. But my curiosity took charge and pushed me forward. Before I could make a positive identification of who it was out there bent under the storm, I was certain that it was Joe. This was the same place I had seen him that morning juggling rocks and taking on his burden with such guilt. Having reached him, I stood for a few seconds before he noticed me. He stood up and gave me an angry look that I let drain away with the rain.

"Leave me alone."

Shouting out, my voice barely carried over the screaming of the weather and the crashing sea that was only twenty feet from where we stood.

"What are you doing out here?"

"Leave me alone," he shouted again.

"You've got to get out of the rain. This storm will kill you."

"What difference does it make? Go away."

With this statement, Joe bent down. I took a step forward to see what he was doing. When I did, I saw that he had his arms wrapped around a boulder that was as big as he was. With a grimace on his face he tried with all of his might to loosen the stone from its bed of sand.

"Joe, you'll never do it."

He had to stand up again and this time there was a pathetic tone in his voice.

"I can do it. It's not too heavy. I just have to concentrate."

He leaned over again and gave it everything he had. The rock didn't move. Taking another step forward I leaned over and placed my hands on the boulder and together we tried to yank it from its mooring. The rock held firm and I stood up panting from the effort. Joe straightened from his crouched position and looked at me.

"It's my burden, McDonald. Let me alone and I'll do it."

"She's not worth it, Joe. She's out of her mind. You were right. Shannon is up-valley waiting for the Menehune. She doesn't love you. She told me so."

"But if I can prove myself I can make her love me."

He leaned over and strapped his arms around the rock. The muscles in his neck strained and the tendons of his shoulders stuck out from under his soaked shirt.

"What good will it do? She'll never forget John. She'll always think of him."

"I hate John. He held us like animals in a cage."

"So why are you doing this? It's only going to keep John's memory alive."

He didn't bother to answer. Although it was hopeless, he pulled on the rock with even more determination. The pounding echo of the rain on my poncho was becoming intolerable. With one more glance at Joe, I turned and left him in place, tugging at his impossible task in the weather that was beyond sense.

Breaking free, I began to run. Through my mouth, breath rushed in and then out of my lungs, amplified by the storm that had closed in around me.

On the helipad, I fell to the ground under the ohi'a tree and listened to my heart beating. Rolling over in the mud, I lay flat on my back. There was only a small trace of relief under the shelter of the ohi'a. Before me, the waves rolled in like angry tyrants at war with the beach. The moon that hung in the sky was no more than a spot of light directly overhead. At that moment I felt vacant and used up. My limbs were affected by a catatonic stillness. Even if I had wanted to, I could not have moved to save my life.

"McDonald, are you alright?"

Looking up through the rain and the dark I realized that my eyes were blurred from tears. Standing over me, Ron looked down with his cock-eyed face. Sitting up, I put my back against the trunk of the ohi'a and shook the rain off the hood of my poncho.

"I thought I would find you out here."

"What do you want, Ron?" I asked apathetically. My energy was tapped. The rain fell like bullets.

"We're leaving in the morning, McDonald. We've had it."

"Who's had it?"

"Only Bill and I so far, but we're going to try to take the others with us. Are you going to come?"

"If you think it's safe."

"If the rain stops even for two hours the rivers will fall enough to make a break."

"You can count me in then," I sighed.

"Good."

"What's going on in the dry cave?"

"Madness."

"I'll come back up in a little while," I said this as an invitation for Ron to leave. Apparently he wasn't through because he hemmed for a moment and then he hawed.

"Uh, listen, McDonald."

"What is it?" I asked impatiently but he didn't notice. He continued, distracted by his own thoughts.

"Ahem. Yeah, yeah, ah. Can I show you something?"

"Sure, Ron. But if you don't hurry up we're going to drown talking about it."

With the enthusiasm of a little kid, Ron stuck a hand underneath his yellow rain jacket. Feeling around for a moment he finally extracted a fist that was wrapped around something.

"What do you have there?" I asked. Little sparks flew from my mind as I watched his fingers open to reveal their cache.

In the dark, it was hard to see what Ron had in the palm of his hand. It was a small square of wood the size of a golf ball, with one end pointed and the other end wide. The object was rounded but its sides were flattened so it looked like a cube. On top of the cube was a small wooden rod sticking up an inch. Grabbing this rod with his fingers, Ron lifted the thing off his palm and held it up to my eyes. On each of its flat sides there was a strange character like the letter of an alphabet. The thing held no reference for me except that it looked a bit like a wooden top.

"What is it?" I asked trying to sound interested.

"Are you Jewish, McDonald?" The question was ludicrous.

"No, I'm afraid not. What about you?" I asked, certain of the answer.

"Oh yes. On both sides. My mother's people were Hasidic."

"The ones with the hair-dos."

"Right."

"So what is that?" I asked, doing my best to keep the conversation going. Ron had lost the thread of our discussion although he was holding it directly in my face.

"What is wha— . Oh, yeah. This— it's a *dreidel.*"

"A dreidel." I affirmed his response but Ron had drifted to some other thought. He was having trouble staying with me.

"Right, a dreidel." He rejoined the conversation.

"What's it for, Ron?"

"It's a game toy. We use it on Chanukah. It has these Hebrew letters on it, and each letter signifies something."

It was hard to see the letters and sensing my plight Ron pulled a flashlight out of his back pocket and shined it on the toy.

Sure enough, the round cube was a child's top. This type of toy was not very common anymore with kids. After all, a top didn't light up or scream a siren or have pictures of monsters or coquettish dolls on it. It was a simple plaything that did nothing but spin. And you had to spin it. Looking closer, I still could not make out the foreign letters.

"Where did you get it?" I asked finally after I had inspected it thoroughly.

"I made it," Ron answered, smiling proudly. "It's Koa wood. Very precious."

The top did appear hand made and with great care. The letters were painted finely and the toy shined with a lacquered finish. As I looked on, Ron placed the top in the palm of his outstretched hand. Holding it by the wooden rod, Ron gave it a flick. The dreidel spun with perfect balance. It came to a stop with one of the letters showing upwards.

"*Nun.* Now it's your turn."

Ron handed the dreidel to me. This did not seem like the right place to be playing the game but I thought that if I went along, Ron might be satisfied and leave me alone. Taking the top in my hand I set the pointed end on Ron's palm and gave it a spin. This time when the dreidel stopped it was on a different letter.

"*Gimmel,*" Ron said, shining the flashlight on his palm so that we could see.

"What do I get?"

"You win the whole pot."

"What are we playing for? Goat skins or matzo balls?"

"That's not funny, McDonald, considering what happened to John and everything." Ron was looking at me disconsolately.

"Sorry."

"That's alright. I understand, I guess." Ron offered his forgiveness. "So what do you think?"

"It's great, Ron. You should make a bunch of them and sell them." I must have said the right thing because Ron broke into a huge grin as he looked at me.

"Do you think so?"

"Sure, you could probably get five bucks apiece for them."

"I was thinking ten."

"Whatever the traffic will bear, I suppose."

"I think ten. I've made almost two thousand of them since I got to the valley, so I figure that I have twenty thousand dollars worth of dreidels to sell."

"What did you just say?" I had to have him repeat it although I knew that I had heard him right.

"I said that I made two thousand dreidels. At ten bucks a pop, that's twenty thousand dollars worth."

"That's great, Ron. But why did you make so many of them?"

As I asked him the question, Ron took the top and spun it in his hand and a new letter came up. Once again he spun it and another letter came up. He kept on spinning the toy as he answered my question.

"I was going to sell them to the tourists but John wouldn't let me. I also have a hundred and twelve bamboo flutes that sell for twenty dollars."

"Another two thousand dollars." I added it in my head.

"Two thousand, two hundred and forty dollars," Ron corrected me.

"Close enough."

"My only problem is that I can't sell the dreidels until Chanukah. That's a month away. I don't know what to do for money until then." Ron was eyeing me cunningly, watching every twitch of my face. When he thought that the time was right he sprung his pitch. "I was thinking you might want to invest some of your money in this. For five thousand dollars, I'll give you fifty percent of the dreidels and twenty-five percent of the flutes."

"I don't know, Ron," I almost laughed. He was adamant though and he went on quickly.

"Look at this."

Turning the top over in his hand he presented one of the flat sides to me and shined the light on the letters. On this particular side there were two letters, half the size of the ones on the other side in order to fit in the space. Between the two letters was a slash mark that delineated a boundary. Shrugging my shoulders I didn't respond.

"You don't get it, do you?"

"I guess I don't," I said, confirming his suspicion.

"Look. I forgot to explain something to you. These letters represent the first letters of the words of a Hebrew saying. Nun, Gimmel, Hei, Shin, the first letters of nes gadol hayah sham, which means 'a great miracle happened there'. Now do you see the two letters on the same side?"

"Yeah," I tried to follow closely.

"O.K. In Israel the dreidels there have the last letter Peh where Shin is on a regular dreidel. Peh is the first letter of Poh, which means here. You see? A great miracle happened here."

"Alright. I'm following you."

"So you see, by putting both of the letters on the dreidel they can be sold in Israel or anywhere else. I've invented the universal dreidel."

"A great miracle happened here and there?"

"Right. A great miracle happened here and there."

"Here and there."

"It's universal."

"Not quite."

"What do you mean?" Ron's hand closed around the top.

"Why don't you find the first letter of the word everywhere? That would be universal."

"Here, there and everywhere?"

"No Ron. Just everywhere. A great miracle happened everywhere."

"That means I would have to change every one of them."

"It's probably a bad idea. Forget it."

With glassy eyes, Ron looked at me and fumbled the dreidel back into his pocket.

"Really, forget it, Ron. They're fine just the way they are."

Standing, Ron backed into the rain and without a word, he turned and ran up the flooded trail and was gone.

Sitting under the ohi'a, I watched Ron disappear into the dark. The pain of awareness from the Lotus still ran a heat inside my stadium and all the cheering and the celebration stretched the skin on my forehead until my temples felt like native drums. There was no use waiting for salvation. A heartbroken man rode out ahead of me and called me back into the mix. Standing, I looked out from under the parasol of the ohi'a, took a reading, and dove back into the storm. The weight of the rain bore down on me as I ran across the soggy grass pad and into the forest.

The last steps on the inundated trail were traversed in darkness so black that I felt unborn. Then, in a single bounding leap I tore away from the hellish weather and was inside the sanctuary of the dry cave. The orange glow of the fire flowed liquidly onto the cliff walls. In the warmth of the shelter I stripped off my poncho and shook the water from my head.

Immediately, I knew that time had frayed since my departure. At first glance, everything looked the same but I could sense a change. Searching through the shelter I looked for a clue. In their tent, Maryjane and Baraka were still groaning and moaning like animals. Juerg and Kate were staring into the fire. The musicians continued to weave their music with closed eyes, rocking with the beat. Back from the storm, Ron sat on his own pad and ignored me conspicuously. In his hand, he cradled the wooden dreidel as if it were a small, dead sparrow. Down in the bedroom alcove, Bill was holding Judy in his arms as she laughed and drooled and searched the sky for the sodden moon.

By the fire, Caren was sitting alone on a milk crate. On her lap was a book opened in the middle. In her hands she was deftly working a length of thick cotton thread that had a needle on its end. With her eyes opened wide and unblinking, Caren was scanning sentences on the pages of the book. As she searched the words, she reached into a plastic bag that was filled with irregular shaped beads and chose one. The beads were tawny-white and shiny like some type of land pearl. As she read she would spear a bead with the needle and push it to the end of the string to join the beads that she was working.

Looking closer, I realized that Caren was making a necklace of Job's tears like the one that she wore around her neck. Although I wanted to speak with her, she appeared to be in deep speculation about the words she was reading. Her hands worked efficiently. On the string, the beads quickly added together.

Knowing that something was amiss inside the cave, I looked past the fire and saw that Michelle was sitting alone with a look of intense confusion etched into her face. Staring ahead, she gazed into the darkness of the night like an idiot with a problem. Going to her, I dropped to my knees and looked into her face.

"Where is Dennis?"

She stared ahead without answering. I tried again.

"Michelle, where is Dennis?"

She didn't seem to recognize me.

"He's gone."

Her answer came out of dumb lips.

"Where did he go?"

"He took some more of that Lotus. It spilled in his mouth. He took too much." Her words slurred together and were barely audible.

"Does he have the gun?" I asked.

"Yes."

If there was any chance of finding him, I would have gone out to look but it would never happen. There was no chance of locating him. Instead, I sat with Michelle, my arm around her shoulder comforting her.

As I considered my next move, the sullen quiet within the cave was broken by Caren's voice. Turning my head in her direction, I saw that her face was filled with a troubled expression. She apparently had found the passage she had been searching for. She furrowed her brow as she began to read out loud. The sentences that Caren spoke passed before my eyes like a shiny silver watch.

"If my troubles and grief were weighed on scales they would weigh more than the sands of the sea, so my wild words should not surprise you."

It was clear that the book on Caren's lap was a Bible and that she was reading Job. As I watched, she flipped several pages ahead and stared at the passage. In her hands, she added beads onto a necklace that was nearly complete. As she continued to read, her fingers arranged the beads with a quickness that was hard to focus on.

"Human life is like forced army service, like a life of hard manual labor. No! I can't be quiet! I am angry and bitter. I have to speak! I am tired of living. Listen to my bitter complaint. Don't condemn me, God. Tell me what is the charge against me? Is it right for you to be so cruel? Is your life as short as ours? Then why do you track down all my sins and hunt down every fault that I have? Won't you look away long enough for me to swallow my spit!?"

The words burst from her mouth with a hollow resonance. The fire-light swept in waves across Caren's face but her attitude remained steady. In her hands she had completed one of the necklaces. She tied a thick knot into the end of the string and without looking up she cast the necklace in the direction of the bedroom alcove.

On the pile of blankets, Bill held Judy to keep her from slumping over. It was a good toss on Caren's part, because the necklace struck Bill in the side of the face. Surprised, Bill looked up at Caren who already had another length of cord in her hand. The beads that Caren had thrown lay at Bill's side. Opening his eyes very wide, he looked down into the dark and found the necklace. He picked up the beads and placed them around Judy's neck. Judy's head fell back and she puffed up her chest. Her laugh came out hideous and diabolical but Bill had his arms around her and he pulled her in closer as Caren read on.

"Your hands formed and shaped me, now those same hands destroy me. Are you going to crush me back to dust? You gave my father strength to beget me; you made me grow in my mother's womb. You have given me life and constant love. But now I know that all that time you were secretly planning to harm me. You were watching to see if I would sin, so that you could refuse to forgive me. As soon as I sin, I'm in trouble with you, but when I do right, I get no credit. I am miserable and covered with shame."

Reaching into the plastic bag, Caren took a small handful of the beads and tossed them up in the air in the direction of the musicians. The beads struck the wooden faces of the guitars and the music stopped. On his mat, Ron was spinning the dreidel, looking down stupidly at some forlorn thought that had taken him prisoner. At the fire ring, Caren read on.

"If I have any success at all, you hunt me down like a lion; to hurt me you even work miracles. You always have some witness against me, your anger against me grows and grows; you always plan some new attack. Why, god, did you let me be born? To go from the womb straight to the grave would have been as good as never existing. Isn't my life almost over? Let me enjoy the time I have left. I am going soon and will never come back, going to a land that is dark and gloomy, a land of darkness, shadows and confusion, where the light itself is darkness."

Caren took another handful of beads and threw them at Ron. They scattered at his feet. He looked at them dumbly and then went back to spinning the dreidel as the sermon continued.

"I call to you, o god, but you never answer and when I pray, you pay no attention. You persecute me with all of your power. I know you are taking me off to my death, to the fate in store for everyone. Why do you attack a ruined man, one who can do nothing but beg for pity? Didn't I weep with people in trouble and feel sorry for those in need? I hoped for happiness and light but trouble and darkness came instead. My voice is sad and lonely. I am burning with fever. Where once I heard joyful music, now I hear only mourning and weeping."

Another handful of beads were cast into the air and they fell again onto the musicians where they sat listening obediently. In the bedroom alcove, Judy's laughter had subsided. Her head was on Bill's lap, her eyes open but unseeing. From her mouth came thick, phlegmatic breathing. On his mat, Ron had picked up some of the beads in one hand. With the other hand he held his dreidel. The story continued as Caren read on.

"I still rebel and complain against god. I cannot keep from groaning. How I wish I knew where to find him, and knew how to go where he is. I would state my case before him and present arguments in my favor. I want to know what he would say and how he would answer me. I am honest; I could reason with god; he would declare me innocent once and for all. Almighty god has destroyed my courage. It is god, not the dark that I fear—."

The sermon might have gone on indefinitely but Caren's words were interrupted. Out of the rain, two waterlogged bodies entered the cave from the east. It was Shannon and Joe holding onto each other as they stumbled into the shelter. They went to the fire and sat down in front of Caren. Looking up, Caren measured their close proximity. Her hands continued beading but her voice had fallen silent. Once she had accepted their presence, Caren looked back into the book and scanned the pages silently.

In shock, Joe and Shannon stuck their hands directly into the flames. They were drenched and shivering with the piss of the storm dripping off them. As they stood letting the warmth of the flames bring them back to life, I couldn't tell which of them was holding the other up. The casualties were mounting. Flipping past several pages, Caren searched for the appropriate passage. The madness of the gathering was once again beginning to gnaw at my sanity.

Shannon and Joe were leaning together and talking to each other in subdued tones. Shannon made an angry face at Joe and nudged him in the ribs. Reluctantly, Joe stood up and looked around the cave to find an audience.

"Where is Marlie?"

No one answered. No one even looked at him. Joe glanced around the cave again. He seemed to take courage from the silence.

"I'll ask you once again. Where is Marlie?"

Still silence. This seemed to make Joe mad and he pulled himself to his full height, using his thin hands to hoist his pants up from where they had fallen to the hump of his butt. His long wet hair hung from his head in clumps. Once again, Shannon nudged him.

"Alright, then. Since Marlie isn't here, I have something to tell the rest of you." Joe looked around severely and continued. "John is dead. Shannon saw him with the Marchers of the Night about an hour ago. Shannon has taken a Menehune lover and she will have a child that will live to be the King of the Islands. From this time out I will be in charge around here. Everything that John used to do I will do now. Do you understand? If you have questions, this is the time to ask. Shannon will be the Queen of Kalalau. When the child is born I will be its father and we will raise it in the custom of the ancient alii. Does all of this make sense to you?"

Joe looked around but no one was paying attention to him. Suddenly, Shannon stood up beside him and spoke into the silence.

"I talked to John tonight as he was going over to the other side. He told me that Joe would take his place as the spiritual leader of the valley. When Marlie comes back he will be driven from the cave and in the morning we will drive him from the valley." She paused. "Is that all clear to you?"

The music had resumed and it went on uninterrupted as Judy shrieked out once again from her cocoon of hysteria. Bill held onto her and scoured the sky for a sign. At the fire, Caren stared deep into the book but remained silent. Beside me, Michelle was sobbing and Juerg laughed at a joke that none of us heard. In their tent, Maryjane and Baraka continued to collide. When no one came forth to challenge his inauguration, Joe looked around him and spoke.

"It is time for the feast, then. Who will bring me the goat?"

Now this may seem strange, and believe me it was. But at that precise moment a gunshot rang out through the night. The noise caught everyone's attention. We all looked up at the top of the overhang from where the shot had come. Then, in what seemed like only a second, an object flew through the darkness and landed with a solid thunk at the opening of the cave. Lying in the mud was the body of a black goat with a bloodstain on the side of its head. As we watched, the thing twitched violently, its back arched in its death throes and then lay motionless.

At first Joe didn't know what to make of this miracle. He stood looking at the goat. Not wanting to appear foolish, Joe hustled into the rain and hauled the carcass into the cave. The goat had a single bullet wound to its head. Its body had been crushed by the fall. Once inside the cave, Joe backed away from the thing and looked at Shannon for support. She nodded her head as a signal for Joe to say something. Turning to the gathering, Joe spoke.

"Heaven has provided."

The goat lay there in a heap. Joe didn't know how to handle the situation and no one was coming to his rescue.

This might have turned into Joe's first crisis had not a more treacherous situation taken priority over the wonder of the raining goat. Up the path, into the dry cave, another waterlogged soul came trudging out of the dark with a burden loaded onto its back.

Into the light of the fire, Marlie returned. Packed across his shoulders was the carcass of a dead goat. When Marlie was in the cave the firelight illuminated him. I winced in disgust. From head to foot, Marlie was covered with the offal of the dead animal. His skin was smeared with blood and his clothes were stained red with the sap. It was obvious that Marlie had killed the thing with his bare hands.

The tattered remnants of his shirt hung from his shoulders as if it had been torn apart in the fight. Down the muscles of his exposed back, dark brown clots stuck to his skin where the goat had bled as he carried it. The animal had a gaping slash across its belly and its entrails were draped over Marlie's body.

I had to look away before the sight made me gag. When he had dropped the carcass onto the ground, Marlie stood gasping for breath. He did not see that there was already a goat lying close to the one that he had brought in.

"Okay, you derelicts, I've brought back the goat. Bill, you are in charge of cleaning the thing, Caren, you cook it. The feast will go on."

At that instant a second gunshot cut through the raging storm. A moment later another object heaved down through the atmosphere and landed face first at the mouth of the cave. This third goat lay right in front of Marlie's goat. Its neck had been broken in the fall and its head was twisted at a bad angle. Marlie looked at the thing lying in the rain that was gushing down. He was speechless. At his side, Joe knew exactly what to do.

Running out into the storm, Joe grabbed the goat and dragged it into the cave. He laid it next to the first goat. Then Joe turned around and approached Marlie. Joe stood toe to toe with the soiled sailor, but a head taller.

"I'm glad you're back. But we don't need your goat. I have brought the sacrifice without having to leave the cave. God is great and from now on I am in control here. We don't need you pushing us around. And from now on we will always remember even when we forget."

Marlie stood silently for a moment. Finally he spoke.

"What are you talking about, Joe? Where in the hell did that goat come from? Are you the one who stole my gun?"

"I don't need a gun to bring forth the sacrifice. Heaven provides."

"Someone took my gun. Was it you, Joe?"

"God giveth and God taketh away."

"Listen here, you corn sucking son-of-a-bitch. John left me in charge after he died. Now get to work skinning that goat I brought in and I'll pretend that nothing was said." Marlie's face took on a menacing expression. "And from here on out, we will never forget even when we can't remember."

"You're through around here, Marlie. Tomorrow I want you out of the valley. Do you understand me?"

"Joe, I'm going to give you one more chance. Skin that goat or I'll take you outside and drown you."

Standing firm, Joe faced Marlie but neither of them was giving in. At any second the two adversaries were going to go to work on each other and it wasn't clear who would come out on top. Standing, I made ready to stop the fight if it got out of hand. Joe and Marlie began to circle each other, looking for an opportunity to jump their opponent.

"Imposter," Marlie yelled at Joe as he wiped smeared blood off his face and stared straight ahead. "John said that we should never forget."

"Deceiver," Joe leveled his charge as he circled his foe. "That was the past. From now on we remember."

"Pretender," Marlie prodded. "Never forget."

"False prophet," Joe countered as Shannon goaded him on. "Always remember."

At the edge of the firelight, the musicians played on with sad grace. From the bedroom alcove, Judy's head rose up from Bill's lap, a sick demonic gurgling emanated from her throat. Beside her, Bill held on tight. Against the back wall of the cave, Juerg laughed at a silly joke inside his head that was told in German, then French and then Italian. At the fire ring, Caren stared into the book, trying to find a message.

"Never forget."

"Always remember."

What happened next is beyond my power of reasoning so I will tell the details and hope someday logic will sort it out.

At that exact moment, out of the sky, there was an eruption of rain that was greater than the previous onslaught by a quantum magnitude. It would have seemed impossible for the weather to worsen but with this monstrous burst of rain came a gale of wind that swooped into the cave with such force that everyone including the musicians stopped what they were doing. The collection of books and papers that were on the ledges of the back wall fluttered in the wind and the sound of their rustling became louder than the storm that was blowing them about. For once, the overhang couldn't hold back the rain as the wind pushed the storm into the sanctuary.

The rain that had fallen in sheets now gathered its hems and unloaded. It was as if whoever was throwing the goats over the rim of the cave had picked up a quenchless bucket of rain and was pouring it onto the ground at the front of the cave. A waterfall fell from the sky.

Looking into the night with rain slashing our faces, we watched as a new bank of clouds flowed swiftly over the ridge behind the valley. Like a blanket of cold ink, the clouds spilled forth and blotted out the sky. In a moment, what was left of the moon quickly disappeared into the murk of this terrible new front.

Even the sounds of sex in the tent that housed Maryjane and Baraka's carnal circus were quelled. In a moment the two marathoners came out pulling on their clothes. They scrambled forward with their eyes cast upward. The music was hushed. The dead goats were forgotten. The only sound that pierced the gushing storm was the convulsive mirth of Judy possessed. Even Bill had stood from his post next to her and joined the rest of us where we stood at the mouth of the cave. What happened next is neither clear nor easily described.

The full moon night had become as black as a bottomless hole. The trees were whipping in the wind and danced dervish-like at the edge of the cave.

Slowly, from a space a dozen steps out of the mouth of the cave and three feet off the ground, an eerie and mysterious glow began to form. The scene was so startling that I could not move. We were all stranded in a state of rigor mortis as we faced the night and the storm and the sound and fury of creation unleashed.

As we watched, mesmerized by the accumulating vision, the glowing ghost slowly began to take shape. Through my eyes, it was like watching an embryo passing through the phases of gestation in rapid succession. The form gently elongated, it divided its thin torso into sprouting limbs, and then a head appeared on top. At that point, it was obvious to me that what I was looking at was a reflection in a pool of light of a human being devoid of all distinguishing features. As I watched, horrified, the features of that human began to float to the surface. In seconds the features were pronounced and our poltergeist could be named.

Above the muddy ground, in a white gown, freshly groomed and for all appearances untouched by the squall that was coming from all sides, stood The Man. He was facing us squarely. The shock grabbed my abdomen and twisted my gut. Slowly, the now solid entity floated downward until his bare and pale feet touched the ground lightly. On his shoulders rode a Bos'n Bird, snow white and majestic.

For a moment, neither the ghost of the lost Man nor those of us in the cave moved. Outside, the thunder of the storm continued but at that instant all sound dried up and a high whining hum filled the gulf between what we saw and where we were.

Then, with all the grace of a drag queen on dope, John took a light step forward. All together we took a heavy step backward. As John approached us, we retreated. Finally The Man was standing under the shelter of the overhang and within our sanctuary. We were backed against the wall of the cave. My head would not turn so I could not judge how anyone else was taking the unannounced visit. As for me, I could feel my veins constricting the blood inside my body as my heart beat in gulps and my breath stilled to a whisper. The Man began to speak.

"What's going on here, Marlie? Joe?" The figure that was The Man shook his head sadly as he continued. "What is the meaning of this? I can't leave you alone for one minute. Is it already brother against brother?"

If you expected there to be an answer you were wrong. Not a sound came out of their chastised mouths. Not a word of explanation or excuse. John continued.

"I have crossed over to the other side and I see everything now. But what I have seen does not make me happy."

Everyone stood humbled in the presence of The Man without a hope in the world of ever changing his mind about anything that he may have seen if he had been watching. The one thing I noticed, and it made me rejoice, was that The Man was facing us straight away. Wherever he had gone to spy on his flock, he no longer felt the need to talk with his back to the congregation. Somehow he had been freed of his burden.

This realization loosened the hold on my existence. Blinking my eyes, I felt life coming back to me. Remaining as still and quiet as before, I knew I could now fight or flee, whichever was needed.

"Well. Goat got your tongues?" John asked and chuckled.

"We were deciding who is in charge now that you weren't here to guide us." Of course it was Shannon who took the offensive.

"Is someone supposed to reign in my place? What gave you that idea?"

"We needed someone to lead the sacrifice." Joe was braced by Shannon's confidence but he spoke in a halting voice.

Marlie was quick to jump in and present his case. "Yeah and that twit thought that he could pull it off. I was your second in command, wasn't I? If the president dies then the vice-president takes over, right? Besides, Joe says that from now on we should always remember and I say that we should never forget, just like you always said, boss."

"What do you imagine we're running here, Marlie, a student body government?" The Man hesitated for a moment before he went on. "These things take great thought. Do you want to know what I think? I think you should look forward and move ahead. All things must pass. Times change. People grow. The new order cannot be defined by the old."

"Where does that leave us, John? Who is going to take charge of the sacrifice?" asked Shannon bravely. "And should we always remember or should we never forget?"

"In my opinion, the goats have suffered enough. Let them be. Besides, I don't understand the question. Should we always remember or should we never forget? It's the same thing."

"But what about the hills? The goats will eat the grass and we'll lose the valley," demanded Joe.

"That's nonsense, Joe. Can't you see what has happened to you? The goats have become more important to you than your own lives."

Silence overtook the gathering and John looked at each person in turn and then back at Marlie and Joe.

"Well?"

"We were just doing what we thought you would have done." Joe said in a sullen voice.

"You can't live your life for me. You have to live for yourselves. What if everybody felt like you did? There would be no change for the better. I've thought about this a lot since I left you."

It was my turn to speak and I stepped forward with all the courage I could bridle.

"I don't know if they can think for themselves anymore, John. You were too strong. You took away their power of reason."

"Good old, McDonald."

"We thought we'd seen the last of you, John."

With an expression of great joy on his face, John looked at me and smiled.

"I miss you all, but I especially miss you, Peter. You really made me think." He paused and then went on. "You know something, McDonald, you were right. It doesn't do any good to talk about god. Every person has their own god and each one is different. Of course that doesn't make sense if there is only one god, right? So it's obvious, God should never be spoken of between people. That's the one thing that I learned from all of this. God should only be spoken to alone. Two people speaking of God, two gods. Not one."

"Careful, John. Don't try to describe it," I said and John laughed.

"Whoops, there I go again. Back to the wilderness with me. I still have a lot to learn."

"We all do, John. But that's life."

"You know, I don't worry anymore, Peter. Everything has become so easy."

"Don't believe in anything?"

"And don't believe in that!"

It was my turn to laugh.

"Do you miss the valley, John?"

"Yes. I miss the sunsets the most. But it's nice here, too."

"Incredible."

"You wouldn't believe it."

"Really incredible."

"You know, McDonald, I never thought it would be you who would save me."

"Religion acquaints us with strange bedfellows, John."

"You are a card, McDonald. I will always remember you."

"I hope so. And I hope you never forget."

"Now, Peter."

"Just kidding. Listen, do you have an address where I can drop you a line?"

"You kill me, McDonald. I wish you were here. It would sure make the time go by quicker."

"Pretty slow, huh?"

"Like an eternity."

At this point John turned to Marlie and Joe. With a steady gaze he made this proclamation.

"If you want my opinion, McDonald should be the new leader. There are a lot of things you need to lead, but there's one thing you need to be a good leader and that's a sense of humor."

Looking down at the floor of the cave, John saw the three dead goats lying there and he shook his head.

"If you keep killing goats there won't be any grass left in heaven when you get there."

With this proclamation, the glow that was John began to fade into the darkness of the surrounding night. As he began to disintegrate, I thought I heard him chuckling.

Before anyone could say goodbye, John was gone.

When the ghost that was The Man had disappeared, we stood silently for a moment absorbed in our thoughts. In a daze, we looked at each other, shyly. The Lotus had definitely worn off. As we regained our senses, we heard the wind dying down outside of the dry cave.

Above us, the moon poked its full and shining face out from behind the clouds. The sky and the sound of the rain began to decrease as the moonlight broke onto the floor of the cave. Within minutes, all that remained of the storm was a light spattering of rain on the leaves of the trees. A gentle breeze blew from the beach. The ocean once again shone with the facets of the grey moon glow. Slowly, the clouds began to back away and the swirling mass of the sky began to calm.

And then we heard the third shot. And off the cliff came the body of a goat sailing down to earth. It hit with such force that the belly of the beast split open and its insides spread evenly upon the muddy ground. Everyone looked down at the hideous sight. In a panic Maryjane grabbed Baraka and let out a squeal.

The body of the goat had split across the abdomen and there in the guts of the animal laid the fully formed body of a kid. The little creature was kicking through the placenta, attempting to birth itself. Unwilling to watch it struggle any longer, I walked over to the carcass of its mother and sticking my hands into the warm entrails, I picked up the kid and felt for a pulse. Deep inside of its chest I could feel the beating of its heart.

"Someone get a knife and cut the umbilical cord," I ordered. "I think we can save this one." Since I was giving out orders, I didn't stop there. "Bill, you and Ron go up and get Dennis down from the cliff. I think that was his last bullet. Be careful though, he may think you are gargoyle warriors coming to spit on his euthanasia, so take it easy. Tell him that Michelle is waiting for him in the cave. Shannon, see if you can drain those tits before the milk goes bad. Caren, you better put that book away and get some tea going."

I could sense that everyone was watching me closely so I turned around to see what they were doing. They were watching me closely.

"Listen, I know what you're all thinking but it was just some sort of hallucination. Let's forget about it and get this kid some milk before it dies."

The group broke ranks and relieved to have something to do they went to work, all except Marlie. He stared at me from under his bushy eyebrows, his eyes dilated, the wretch of his kill hanging from his body. Inside the bedroom alcove, Judy had fallen asleep on the blankets and I imagine she was dreaming of another life in which she was sleeping and dreaming of another life. I held the kid in the palms of my hands as Joe came forward with a knife.

"You got a problem, skipper?" I said to Marlie.

He glared at me with the moon in his face. "You'll never get out of here alive, McDonald. All of this happened because of you. If you wouldn't have come here, everything would have stayed the same."

With a skill learned on the farm in Ohio, Joe cut clean through the umbilical cord and tied it off as I held the bleating kid firmly in my hands.

"Marlie, Marlie. When are you going to learn to relax?"

"Go to hell, McDonald."

"I did once, Marlie, but the food was lousy and the service sucked."

"I'll get you, McDonald. The next feast we have we'll put your ass over the fire."

"Marlie, your threats are getting old. Take your bad attitude and go somewhere else."

Just before Marlie ran into the night, he looked at me and made a menacing sign with one of his hands. "You'll burn in hell for this, McDonald."

"Thanks for telling me, Marlie. I'll make sure I bring sun block."

Stomping out of the cave, Marlie ran into the night. I figured he was heading to the blue hale to sleep away his scorn.

At that moment I felt liquid warmth running through my fingers. Looking up I saw that Caren was pouring the last of the liliquoi tea over the quivering body of the tiny kid. This brought life to the creature and the scrawny animal lifted its head and for the first time it looked around at all of us who were looking at it.

"Looks like this one will live," Caren said, as she took the kid from my hands. She walked away with the tiny newborn and I saw her slip a half finished necklace of Job's tears around its neck. Smiling to herself, she carried the animal into the dry cave.

Standing alone for a moment, I saw my chance to get away from the chaos that had wrested control of the night but was now subsiding along with the storm. As my companions went about their chores I stepped into the darkness beyond the firelight that illuminated the dry cave. Without another word, order, or command, I was gone. Inside the dark forest, a brush of cool air hit my cheeks. My eyes opened in reflex to the refreshing surge of humid atmosphere.

A hundred feet outside the cave, I turned and looked back. The top of the overhang glowed with a flush of orange light. Inside I knew that everyone was working to keep themselves from falling into reflection on what had just occurred. From this distance I could not estimate what thoughts were occupying my companions. Only the glow of the campfire let me know that they were there. With the last mists of the storm in my face I hiked through the night.

Making my way down the trail that was draining the last of the run-off into the ocean, I walked past the abandoned toilets that stood like sentinels on the forest floor. From the trees, drops of water fell onto my shoulders and my head. Breaking out of the forest I stepped onto the wet grass of the helipad and walked to the ohi'a where I sat down with my back against the trunk of the ancient tree.

There was no feeling left in my body except exhaustion from all that had happened in the last three days. But now the madness was gone and there was nothing to do but try to find relaxation, knowing that I would go home soon. The memories of this trip would mix with all my other memories so that one day in the future, I could look back and find the meaning in all that had gone behind me. There was only one thing I knew for sure, I had gotten the picture. It was only a job but it was my job and I had done it well.

Leaning my head against the bark of the tree, I looked into the sky and watched the clouds breaking up and falling away from the moon. Although the effects of the Lotus had worn off, there was still an edge left inside of me that kept me from recognizing common objects. The effect of the experiences that lay behind me would not let me focus on the light breaking through the sky as the full moon once again took command of the night.

Reaching into the burlish roots of the ohi'a, I retrieved the bottle of Wild Turkey from its hiding place. Holding the bottle up to the light of the moon, I measured what remained inside the vessel. With a motion that surprised me, I twisted the cap open and turning the bottle upside down, I dumped the contents onto the ground. When it was drained I laid the empty bottle on the dirt at my hip and closed my eyes. An involuntary sigh erupted from my lips and I slid down farther so that my shoulders were leaning against the massive tree. At that moment, I fell into a light sleep and was awakened from a deep forgotten dream by a familiar voice.

"McDonald, are you alright?"

It was Bill smiling down at me. I sat up and took a breath.

"Yeah, Bill, it looks like I'm going to live. What time is it?"

"What time?" Bill seemed surprised by my question and I laughed at myself and the habits that were still scratching at me.

"I mean, has it stopped raining?"

This new question relieved Bill. His smile broadened and he sat on the ground beside me. He eyed the empty bottle.

"Yeah, its all clear. Man, I hope that's the last of it. That was the worst storm I have ever seen in the valley."

I noticed that Bill had a pained look in his eyes and I knew there was a question biting at him.

"What do you want to ask me, Bill? Go ahead. I'll give you a full account of everything I know."

My rambling did not ease the pressure of Bill's dilemma and I had to be quiet for some seconds waiting for him to speak although I already knew the question.

"So—" He began. I became more certain of my prediction and then it was out. "What was it?"

"What do I think it was?" I clarified the question without changing it.

"Yeah, what do you think, McDonald?" Bill prodded me with my own revision. But I had the answer and I knew that when it was spoken I would be freed to go forward beyond this night.

"What I think is that I have spent too much time looking back."

It was the most honest thing I could say.

"That's heavy, McDonald, but what do you think about what we just saw?" Bill paused for a second before he asked his next futile question. "Was it John?"

"Was what John? I never saw anything back there, and if anyone asks me that's what I am going to tell them."

"Was it an illusion?"

"Of course it was an illusion, Bill. What else could it be? The Lotus, the rain, the pain of losing a friend. It made us crazy. Too crazy to ever know if what we saw was real. It's been a long three days. It's time to rest.

I think tomorrow we should walk out of here together and have a nice meal and get some sleep. I'll treat as long as it's not sushi."

The moment between us might have become uncomfortable if we had not been joined by Joe and Shannon who walked out of the night forest and sat close to us on the heliport pad. They were both silent but I could tell that our presence was calming to them. In a few moments, Ron came out of the forest leading Judy and holding her up in his arms. The sleep had separated her from her trance and she was smiling like a child. Behind them came Dennis and Michelle, followed by Maryjane and Baraka. The group was complete when Caren arrived holding the crying kid in the crook of her arms. When she sat down, Maryjane brought out a soda bottle with a piece of plastic ballooned over its mouth. The bottle was filled with the milk of the dead mother. As Maryjane coaxed the kid with the bottle, Caren pointed its mouth in the right direction until the tiny creature began to suck hungrily.

If anyone wanted to speak, their need for quiet was stronger because we sat in silence staring out at the ocean and the calming storm and at the kid who was sucking for its life.

My breathing had become regular and I could feel the edginess leaving my body as I leaned back against the tree. Suddenly, I realized that we were missing someone and I turned to Caren.

"Where did Chick and Jeff go?" I asked.

Caren looked at me with an expression of warmth that could melt the ice caps. She stared at me for a moment before she answered.

"They're gone. They said they had to make a scene in Tulsa."

That was all I needed to know to be able to sit back and relax again. I watched Caren holding the kid and felt as if my life were landing right there on the heliport pad. A band was playing in my head and I reveled in the accuracy of the moment.

As we enjoyed the luxury of our companionship, I heard whispering coming from the front of the group.

"Check that out," Bill said in a dreamy voice as we gazed forward.

Above the ocean where the clouds had lifted, the moon was bright grey. There in the night, forming above the counter of the water, several bands of color began to stretch into an arc. What we were looking at was a rainbow of dark colors, a perfect half circle that stood upon the ocean with thick, bowed legs. Silence once again overtook us as we watched the spectacle grow brighter.

A moonbow was a seldom seen phenomenon on the islands but we were due for a treat. This beautiful impression lasted for ten minutes and then it was gone. Slowly, the others began to stand and make ready to leave. I stood with Caren and in one group we formed a procession and walked back to the dry cave.

Nothing more was said about The Man or about whether what we had seen was real or a figment of imagination created by the storm. Back at the cave we found places to lie down and watch the fire die away until we were asleep.

My job was over. In the morning I would head for home. It was no use speculating whether I would miss this place. How can you go to heaven and ever hope to live on earth, so far away from the light of the Valley?

Exodus

morning

Morning came and I awoke in a tent in the dry cave. The sounds of the forest filtered through the nylon window, a quiet resurgence of life after the storm. In the distance I could hear the waterfall. Closer to the tent were the sounds of small birds, chirping as they flitted through the canopy. The morning was peaceful and clean. Beside me, Caren lay sleeping, her blond hair falling around her shoulders.

At my feet, the tent door was open. Looking over the tips of my toes, I could see a clutter of bodies and blankets on the floor of the shelter. On their grass mat, Joe and Shannon were lying together, face to face, their heads on stuff sack pillows that were filled with clothes. Ron was sleeping alone, his arms wrapped around the backpack that held his dreidels. Surveying further, I saw that the bedroom alcove was empty, Judy and Bill were missing.

Climbing out of the tent, I walked to the edge of the cave, grabbed the water jug, and took a long drink. The sky had cleared and all that was left of the storm was a whitewash of lacey clouds cast against an azure sky. It was a beautiful morning and it would be a perfect day to hike out of Kalalau.

Walking into the forest, I made my way toward Dennis and Michelle's camp. Puddles remained on the trails but the tropic sun and the morning breeze were quickly drying the campground. When I arrived at Dennis's site, I saw Bill and Judy standing, listening to Dennis talk. What had once been the most elaborate camp in the valley was now a shambles. The tarps were flapping in the breeze. Dennis had spread much of his gear on the ground. It covered a large space under the oak tree.

"Good morning, McDonald!" Dennis saw me coming and greeted me in his usual affable manner. "We're going through this gear to see what is salvageable."

"Hey, Peter," Bill said as he picked through the remnants of Dennis's shattered kingdom. Judy smiled at me as I joined the circle and looked on.

"I'm taking the tent with me. It has sentimental value and I can use it again," Dennis said. "But the down comforter has to stay. It'll take too long to dry. Do you want it, Judy?"

"Sure," she said, holding it in her hands as if it were a treasure.

"What about these spices? Look, saffron." Dennis held up a small bottle.

"We can use them in the dry cave," Judy said.

Bill walked to one side of the site and picked up the fishing pole. He looked at the instrument with a deep longing. Dennis stepped in before Bill's desire became ingrained.

"Sorry, Bill, I'm taking the pole. It's brand new and I only used it once. But I'll tell you what. I'll give you these two spinners. It's what I used to catch the whitefish. You can use them with a hand line."

Bill's eyes lit up. "The rangers don't like us to use poles anyway. But I'll definitely take the spinners."

As I watched, it dawned on me that the myriad knickknacks and food-stuffs lining the rock shelves of the dry cave were donations made by tourists, lightening their load for the trip out. On one side of Dennis's site was a set of pots and pans, the blow-up mattress, the comforter, spices, rope, rice, freeze dried soup, coffee, sugar, and some extra rope. All of these things would stay with the tenants of the dry cave. Still in negotiation but destined to land on the pile were a heap of wet clothes, a headlamp used for reading, two thermoses, three coffee mugs, two stainless steel plates, and a brand-new first aid kit.

There was another pile near the upper edge of the site comprised of three books whose pages had been soaked through, a sheet for the air mattress that was stained with mud, a torn windbreaker, cardboard food boxes melted by the rain, and other sundry objects that had been ruined by the storm. These items would end up in the two abandoned privies to rot with the rest of the garbage, until the park service decided it was a health hazard and hauled it away.

"Are we hiking out today?" I asked.

"I should think so." Dennis made a face that got Judy and Michelle giggling.

"I'm going down to the beach for a while." I stood as I said this.

"Two hours, on the heiau." Dennis set the schedule and the place of our meeting.

As I walked away, the bazaar continued with each available item being held up to Bill and Judy for inspection. The item was accepted or rejected and then put on the appropriate pile.

Walking to the helipad, I slid down the bank and onto the sand. The ocean had calmed and the waves came onto the shore delicately. Taking off my shoes, I walked to where the surf pushed as high as it could onto the beach. When it could reach no farther, the wave slithered to a halt, buckled slightly as it struggled to hang onto its progress and then slid backward into the sea. With the remnants of the previous wave wilting into the sand, I took my clothes off and walked forward until I was up to my knees in the surf. When the next wave came in, it swelled around me until I was in waist high water.

In front of me, the ocean throbbed in a mass. Where the sea and the sky merged, there was a line of demarcation that was the horizon. There was no separation between the sky and the water except the water was a slightly darker, thicker blue. To the west and halfway to the horizon, a black dot bobbed on the ocean.

When we were children, my father took my brother and me to a cold water beach on the far north coast of California. When we were finally worn out from running on the sand and collecting shells and throwing rocks into the surf, we would stand and stare at the horizon. As we looked out, we talked about a place that we could almost see. It was a land that lay somewhere in the ocean. We called this place Japan. We had no other concept of Japan and never talked about it or thought about it if we were not standing on the beach looking west. It was just the name of a place our father had told us about.

We knew that the people in Japan looked different from us but we knew nothing more about this distant land. We thought that Japan must be right there, just beyond the horizon. We could almost see it. We could swim there if our arms were stronger. Our father could swim there if he wanted. We said that someday a bridge would be built to Japan. Hawaii was there too. The bridge would go to Hawaii first and then to Japan. It would be easy to build. In fact we didn't know why there was not a bridge to Japan already. We had no conception of how far away this place might be. But it was right there; where the sky and the sea meet.

That is the way the ocean made me feel even after I grew up. The water was immense but it was not empty. There was a mysterious place somewhere out there at the horizon where the color between the sea and the sky shifted slightly in blues. It might be a place that no one had found. But there was something out there. My father would take me if he were here now. That was how certain I was that this place existed.

As I contemplated this belief that I had carried throughout my life, I walked farther into the surf. The next wave came in larger than I had expected and I was submerged to my chest in water. The undercurrent pulled at my legs as the wave receded. Digging in with my toes, I felt the sand swirling around my heels as it raced away with the dragging wave. Instinctively, I began to walk backward out of the water. I continued backing away until I was standing on dry sand.

For a long time, I stood looking at the ocean with its mystery left intact. The sky rode the water bareback and the universe whispered into the sky's ear. With my back to the valley and my face to these open spaces I sat on the sand. Three days on a rock and now I was leaving. I would fly across this same ocean on my way home. I would go back to checking my mail for letters and waiting for work. All that was left was counting my days until they were all numbered.

parting

Two hours later, I stood with the others on the heiau. In a puddle of muddy water lay the purple violets that John had placed at the altar two days before. Beside the flowers, in their own puddle, were three orange mangoes rotting in the sun. On the ocean, the black bobbing dot was getting closer and gaining color.

After leaving the beach, I had gone up to the dry cave and grabbed my camera bags. There was not much left of my clothes so I hung them over a line to dry. I imagined they would be given to whoever needed them. Since I was leaving I went through the items in my shaving kit. Toothpaste, dental floss, aspirin, and nail clippers were placed in nooks on the back wall. No one else was in the cave, so I stood for a moment looking around.

The shelter seemed vacant that morning. Without the rituals and the faithful, the dry cave was nothing but a small patch of dirt littered with odds and ends. A calendar was leaning against the back wall of the cave, a Buddha was laughing through its bronze mouth and a book of verses with its red cover closed, all of this, litter. In time, someone else would look into the cave and find new meanings. For me, these were memories and that was all that was left. They would remain in the past where they belonged. Throwing my bags over my shoulder, I walked out of the cave for the last time.

Standing on the heiau, I studied the gathering. These were the squatters, the former followers of The Man. Bill sat on a rock with Judy, smoking a cigarette. Judy was oblivious to the gouged turf in the middle of the heiau even though there was still dirt from this place under her fingernails. On the shore side bank, Joe and Shannon were looking at the ocean, surprisingly, Joe was not juggling. Caren stared at the altar in quiet contemplation while Ron stood on the other side of the altar, looking into the sky, blowing a soft tune through his flute.

As for the tourists, Dennis and Michelle were all that remained of that group. I had seen Baraka and Maryjane earlier, their packs on their backs, walking toward the river to begin their return trip back to civilization. They had not seen me, but I waved goodbye to them anyway. I was not sure what had happened to Juerg and Kate. Apparently they decided to walk out together, without us. As for me, my job was over. Officially I was just another tourist.

It was apparent that some of the group had changed their minds about leaving. Only Ron had his belongings, the large leather pack filled with dreidels. He had another longer cloth stow bag, which I guessed was filled with flutes. It was time to take a survey. I glanced at the ocean and walked forward.

"Looks like Ron has his things. What about the rest of you?"

The others looked around at each other. Finally Bill spoke.

"Well, Peter," Bill stammered. He took a breath, which seemed to give him confidence. "While you were at the beach we were talking. We don't think we're ready to leave, yet."

Bill focused his eyes on me to gauge my reaction.

"That's right," Judy agreed, stepping forward. "We like it here."

There was not a lot I could say. I scanned this line of people, all of whom had become my friends.

"Fair enough. What about you, Joe? Shannon?" I asked, although I knew what their response would be.

"We're going to stay for a while, Peter." Shannon spoke in an even tone. "We like Kalalau. We never got to experience it the way we wanted. And now that John is gone—" She did not finish her sentence. Beside her, Joe stared at the ocean and did not offer any comment.

I turned toward the altar.

"Ron?"

"I have business on the mainland. I'm going with you. "

"Sounds good." I took a moment before I asked the last one. "Caren?"

"I'm with you."

My heart settled when I heard her answer. I turned to the beach and looked at the waves. There was a single tourist playing in the surf.

"I think I figured something out this morning."

Everyone turned and followed my gaze toward the beach.

"What is it, Peter?" Caren asked.

"The first time I went to the beach, my father told me something. He said, 'never turn your back on the ocean.' When you walk out of the ocean, you always keep your eyes on the waves so a big one doesn't come out of nowhere and crash on you."

"I remember that, Peter," Bill said. "My big brother told me."

"I remember that too," Shannon said.

"I grew up in Ohio," Joe said and he shrugged his shoulders.

"South Dakota, no beaches," Caren offered.

"Right." I smiled and went on. "Watch that tourist," I said, nodding my chin in the direction of the beach.

Everyone focused their eyes on the shore where the tourist was playing in the waves. The tourist ran into the water and went up to his chest in the surf. When the next wave hit shore, it came up high and the tourist was swimming as he rose on the swell. His body disappeared in the wave so that only his head was showing. As the wave receded, his body began to reemerge. We could tell when his feet touched ground. We could see the tourist brace himself as the wave tried to drag him away. His eyes were on the ocean, and he was leaning against the force of the retreating wave. Once the water had receded it was only up to his knees. Slowly, he began to back out of the surf. He took several steps backward until he was on dry land. With the inertia built up from balancing against the wave, the tourist walked backward slowly toward a towel that lay on the sand, his eyes gazing across the surface of the ocean.

"Oh my God." It was Shannon who saw it first.

"You see what I see?" I asked.

"Jesus." Bill was next, but now everyone had caught on.

As we watched, the tourist pushed his hair out of his face with his hand. He took one last backward step and sat on his towel. His eyes were on the horizon.

"So it was all a mistake'" Shannon said and she shook her head in amazement.

"I'm not sure if it was a mistake as much as it was a notion," I offered.

"A whim," Caren said quietly.

Joe walked to the edge of the heiau and then turned to the group.

"I always wondered where John got the idea to walk backward. I thought he had gone up-valley and had one of his revelations."

Shannon followed with the full thesis.

"So he walked backward out of the surf one day, watching the waves, and he just kept going."

"So it would seem."

Joe had been looking at the ocean ever since we had arrived at the heiau. He had seen the black bobbing object coming closer. I had been watching it, too.

"Speaking of walking out of the water, look who's coming," Joe said.

"Is it Rick?" I asked.

"Rick and Lynn," Joe stated.

The kayak with its two passengers was coming toward shore. Slowly, the group started single file down the trail that led to the beach. This was the trail that the followers had taken to the heiau after their fruitless search for John after the fall. It was where we stood when the storm began. That was three days ago but it seemed like an eternity.

By the time we got to the water, Rick was bringing the kayak into the surf at the front of the river. With expert navigation, he caught the crest of a wave, cut his paddle into the water and launched himself forward. As the boat slid toward the shore, Bill and Joe went into the surf and dragged it onto the beach. Jumping from the boat, Rick helped drag the craft up to the boulders where it would not be swept back into the ocean. From the gullet of the boat Rick removed a knapsack and walked directly toward me.

"Hey, McDonald. I figured you'd be leaving today. I wanted to keep my end of the bargain." Rick didn't smile but I knew he was satisfied with himself.

"Let's go up to the heiau."

The mood of the group was so subdued that everyone followed Rick and me without comment.

Back on the grass of the heiau, Rick loosened the string that tied the top of the pack. When it was open, he held the bottom and dumped its contents onto the ground. The bones tumbled out of the sack in a pile and everyone looked at them, silently. Kneeling, I picked up a bone that was the length of a butter knife. Rick kneeled beside me.

"It's like I told you, whatever they were, they were small. Looks like Menehune bones to me," Rick said seriously.

Shannon looked at Rick and then glanced at Joe.

"Menehune bones, huh? That's not what they look like to me," I said.

"What do you think they are, McDonald?" Shannon asked.

Standing, I walked to my camera bag. When I had returned to where Rick was still kneeling, I unzipped the bag and reached inside. From its depths I retrieved a parcel wrapped in a piece of an old tee shirt. When it was unwrapped, I held its contents out for the others to see.

"Do you know what these are?" I asked as I looked at each of them.

For a moment there was silence. But I could tell by Rick's expression that he was following my thoughts. When no one else spoke, he did it for them.

"I think I do."

Everyone looked at Rick and then looked back at the contents of the parcel.

"Who wants to say it?" I asked.

"It's bones from the goats we ate in the dry cave." Of course, Shannon spoke first.

"Exactly." I said as I picked up one of the bleached bones that had come from The Valley of The Lost Tribe. I held the bones together. "Do you notice something?"

"They're the same size."

"Right. Those aren't Menehune bones. Those are goat bones. That dune is full of goat bones. Someone over there was killing goats and dumping the bones in the sand."

"What does this mean?" Ron asked.

"I have no idea," I answered. "And you know something. I am really tired of thinking about all of this. When Rick told me about these bones I knew that something was up. I watched the way Marlie got rid of the carcasses and this just seemed logical. But now that I know, it doesn't make any more sense than it did before. Who was in that valley? Who is the Lost Tribe?"

The group looked down at the pile of bones. Then, all at once they stepped away conspicuously.

Everyone was silent. Another piece of the puzzle had fallen into place. Now, only one part of the mystery remained to be answered.

"There's only one part of the mystery that needs to be answered," I said.

The interlude was brief.

"Why we brought you here." This time it was Caren who jumped ahead.

"Yes," I answered. "Why am I here? What were the photos for? Where did John get fifteen thousand dollars? And why me?"

The others looked at each other to see who would represent them in this discussion. Bill stepped out in front of the group.

"It isn't like a big secret. I was going to tell you last night. Remember?"

"OK. So let's start with the simple stuff. Like whose idea was it to take the pictures of John walking down the Na Pali Coast backward?"

It surprised me that it was Ron who stepped forward. For the first time his eyes were not cocked and crazy. They focused on me with perfect confidence. He raised his eyebrows and spoke.

"To tell you the truth, it wasn't John who wanted the pictures, at first."

"Then who was it? And where did the money come from?"

"Who is going to tell Peter what is going on?" It always surprised me when Judy spoke out because her lucid attitude when speaking contrasted with her usually shy demeanor. She looked at the others but she was getting no takers. "Alright, then I'll tell him." She turned to Ron. "It was Ron's idea."

Caren was now ready to take her turn.

"Ron wanted to get a photographer out here to take some pictures of us together. He convinced John that with photos he could get into magazines and stuff. People would see the pictures and they would come to Kalalau to join us. Ron thought it was comical that John was going along with the idea. Ron explained to us how a man walking down the Na Pali Coast backward was going to look like a man walking frontward down the Na Pali Coast. That it would just look like a man walking. But we didn't tell John that."

"Hold on there a second," Bill interjected. "You're not telling the story right. That came later."

"Well yeah," Caren conceded. "So you tell it."

Bill turned to me.

"All of us wanted to get pictures to send home. Ron came up with the idea of hiring a photographer. We wanted pictures of the trail, and the camp, and the valley, so we couldn't just ask a tourist to do it."

"That's why I wanted you to take the pictures of Lynn and me before we left," Rick jumped in.

"We were going to tell you," Shannon said with emphasis.

"Then John fell off the cliff," Judy added to keep up the momentum.

"O.K. But where did the money come from?"

Looking around, they smiled at each other.

"It was Ron's idea so he came up with the first share," Caren said.

"What do you mean?" I asked.

"Let me explain," Ron said.

"No. Let me explain," Shannon butted in.

"Ron came up with the idea and then he talked to us about it. He said that we could hire a photographer to take pictures to send to our people. He didn't think John would like the idea, so Ron told John that the pictures would be of him walking backward down the trail."

"That really got John going," Judy pitched in.

"But then John insisted on getting a professional photographer. Someone with a name," Shannon continued.

"But that raised the ante," Ron clarified the situation. "Originally, I was just thinking about some local photographer coming out for a day."

Shannon had been on a roll and she was getting antsy. Ron noticed and turned the conversation back to her.

"Go ahead, Shannon. You can tell it better than I can."

"No you tell him, Ron," Shannon said realizing that they had come Ron's part of the story. Slowly the scattered details were coming together.

"I had five thousand dollars in a savings account. I was going to pay for the photographer with that money. Initially I thought a local would cost a thousand bucks at most," Ron said and Shannon came in right behind him.

"John sent us into town to look in books and stuff."

"We came up with some photographers. We gave John their bios and he chose three that he liked. We went to Hanalei and bought their books for him." Judy placed her two cents into the kitty.

"So John looked at the books and he liked my work the best?" I asked.

I looked at the circle of faces and waited for an answer. The group was silent.

"Not exactly," Caren said.

"So?"

"Actually, John liked this other photographer better. He was a fashion photographer." Shannon kicked it forward.

"Then why me? Wasn't the other photographer available?"

"Not exactly," Caren repeated. "This is embarrassing. Judy, you tell him."

The insane asylum smile appeared. For a second I thought Judy was going to start laughing. It was all she could do to hold it in.

"You'll never guess." Judy looked at the others and smiled broadly.

"No," I said. "I'm sure I won't."

Looking at Caren I saw that her face had turned beet red. Even her deep tropic tan could not hide her new complexion. Judy wrinkled her nose.

"Your picture was on the jacket of your book." She paused and smiled. "Caren thought you were cute."

"You have got to be kidding me."

"No. And she told Ron. And he talked John into it. He convinced John that you were a photographer of gravity. That you were more worldly."

Ron spoke up.

"I sat with John and we looked through your book. After reading about you, he decided that you were the best. In fact, in the end, he swore that you were the only one that he had even seriously considered."

"So, the reason I am out here taking pictures of a man walking backward down the Kalalau Trail is that Caren thought I was cute." I looked over at Caren and smiled, my face now as red as hers.

She winked at me and laughed out loud.

"But how did you get my address?" I asked.

"Caren was the one who thought you were cute, so we made her do the work," Shannon explained.

"Caren went into town and called your agent. His name is in one of your books," Judy chimed in. "He told Caren that he wouldn't touch you with a ten foot pole."

"That's nice," I said mockingly.

"When your agent told us that, we knew you were our man," Shannon laughed.

"He told us your rate and gave us your address. He said you could use the work."

"Wonderful. But you are still ten thousand short of a bushel."

"We were in too deep to back out," Bill came back into the conversation. "John was adamant about getting you to be his photographer."

It was Ron's turn.

"So I found some partners."

"Let's quit teasing him," Shannon stated flatly and looked at Ron.

"Well, unless my partners want to remain anonymous?"

"I'll tell him. I don't care." Bill looked at me and smiled broadly. "I put in five thousand from my 401K. I told you, I used to be corporate."

"You're still five thousand short of a stack."

Caren stepped forward.

"I put in the other five."

"Great. And where did your five thousand dollars come from? The pockets of your swimming suit?"

"I have a trust fund. My family had moved to South Dakota, but my grandfather was a water baron in Southern California. He made a fortune drilling wells in the San Joaquin Valley. He was a wild-catter. He used to drink whiskey in his office."

"That solves that part of the story. But I have another question."

They all looked at me.

"Did Marlie know anything about this?"

They continued to look at me. Then they turned and looked at each other.

"No," Bill said finally.

"Because Marlie was too close to John?"

"Marlie was John's shadow. He was waiting in the wings thinking that once John was famous, he would leave the Valley. Then Marlie could take over at the dry cave." It was Shannon who revealed this.

"Why? What did he want to take over?"

"That's a good question. I think the answer is that Marlie didn't have a unique thought in his head. He was the type that looked to others for ideas. He saw us listening to John and to Marlie that meant John had power. He wanted some of it for himself," Bill said.

"The problem is that Marlie didn't understand that we followed John because we owed him something for showing us how to live in the valley."

"Marlie? We didn't owe him anything."

"So the end was in sight either way?"

"That's right. We were going to get the pictures and move on. It was getting too tedious living with John," Judy said.

"Let me guess. The end came when John started walking backward."

"That was the final straw. It was just too strange."

"But you wanted to get the pictures so you hung in for a while longer."

"That's right."

"One more question. Why didn't you just buy a camera and take some pictures?"

Ron fielded this question. "I wanted a professional. After all, anything worth doing is worth doing right."

"Then let me ask you something, Ron. Why did you decide to put your money into this venture?"

Ron smiled and looked at me thoughtfully before he answered. "I had this uncle and he told me 'it's better having money in a risky business than having money in the bank." He continued in his own words. "After all, money in the bank brings interest but money in a risky business, there's no telling what it will bring."

Reaching into my gear I extracted a weatherproof stuff bag. Inside this bag was most of the film from the six days I had spent with the group.

"So who ends up with the film?" I asked.

Bill, Caren, and Ron looked at each other but it was not going to be a big decision.

"I'm staying in Kalalau, so I can't take it," Bill said.

"If I get a few pictures for my photo album, I'm fine," Caren said.

"So the film goes to Ron?"

Everyone agreed and I handed the bag over to Ron, who then put it into his own leather backpack. He was becoming so weighted down with cargo that he was taking on the dimension of a Venetian.

"Well, that's that, then. My job is officially over."

"I have something for you, Peter." For the first time since the conversation started, Ron's eyes went cocked. A crazy grin stretched across his face. From the top of his leather backpack, Ron brought out an object wrapped in a paper napkin. Holding his hands out to me he unfolded the package. The others leaned in to follow the action.

When the object was uncovered, I could see that Ron held a dreidel in his hand. I thought that this was a nice gesture considering my suggestion the night before.

"Do you like it?' he asked. "I finished it this morning."

"I love it, Ron. Thanks for thinking of me." I reached out for the top but Ron held onto it.

"You don't get it, do you?" Once again I seemed to be on the short end of the conversation.

"It's a dreidel," I said.

"But look." He was mildly irritated.

I stared at the square piece of wood.

"It looks like the one you showed me last night."

"Look again."

Putting my face as close as I could to the top, I scanned it for clues. And then I saw it.

"It doesn't have a line between here and there?"

"Oh, Peter. You are such a *shagitz.*" Ron was clearly frustrated with my ignorance. "That's not here and there. Those aren't Peh and Shin. That's Bet and Mem."

He could tell I was puzzled but I did not feel bad because everyone else in the group was looking at Ron with distinctly perplexed expressions as well.

"You told me that 'here' and 'there' were not universal. There is no word in Hebrew for everywhere, so I put in 'every place' on the dreidel. 'A great miracle happened in every place.' Bechol Mechom. In every place. It's a universal dreidel."

"That's great, Ron." I laughed.

He cut me off before I could ask the obvious question.

"And no I am not going to change them all. But, I have to tell you. I think you're on to something."

I smiled.

In his hand, Ron took the rod end of the dreidel and put the pointed bottom of the top on his palm. With a flick of his fingers he spun it. The dreidel came to a stop.

"*Gimmel!*" he shouted, and for no particular reason, everyone cheered.

red hill redux

On the other side of the river we stopped to rest. We had crossed the stream on the tops of the largest rocks. The water had receded but it was still high. Using the yellow nylon rope we were able to make it across.

At the bottom of Red Hill, I stopped to look back at Kalalau. It was a beautiful day. The sun sparkled onto the earth. It was as if there had been no storm and no rain. The back walls were dark green and the sky above the walls was cobalt blue. Along the cliffs, the snow white Tropic Birds sailed. They came out of the thick vegetation and rode high into the air currents. The lofty circles they made hypnotized me and I stood for several minutes watching their ascent.

We moved as a group up the switchback trail of Red Hill. Behind us was the campground. The fire in the dry cave had gone out and for the first time since arriving at the bottom of this red dirt hill five days earlier, there was no haze hanging over the forest. Only the crystalline day, the ohi'a and oak, the sand of the beach, and the ocean stretching as far as the eye could see.

The dirt of the trail was damp but not wet. It was slippery but the corners of the switchbacks gave us a place to stand and rest as we moved farther up the winding trail. It did not take us long to reach the plateau where John had fallen off the cliff. At this point we stopped to get our bearings. This is where we would leave behind those who were staying. This plateau had become the place of goodbyes.

Having carried the kid, who someone had named Maggie, the last hundred yards, Caren set her down. The little goat, still wearing the necklace of Job's tears, scampered around the pasture, her nose in the air. Grazing on the hill was the endemic herd of goats. They did not look at us as we approached. They did look at Maggie though as she marched clumsily in circles. When one of the goats made a call, Maggie looked in that direction and traipsed over to the group. It took no time at all for her to attach herself to the herd.

"That was easy," Judy exclaimed.

Everyone was feeling relaxed. We watched as Maggie found a mother with another kid. Maggie immediately started suckling. Joe walked over to shake my hand.

"We may not see you any time soon," he said.

Shannon walked in beside him.

"I don't know whether to hug you or kick you, McDonald," she laughed. "You sure brought the house down."

"We never got to go surfing," Rick said casually.

"I'll come back and we'll go out."

"It's a deal."

And so, we had reached the end of the road or the end of the trail, which led back to the end of the road.

"Aren't you going to take a picture of us?" Bill stood with his always willing smile.

"I guess I should. Stand there." I pointed toward the edge of the pasture. It was the place where John had stood and given his final sermon.

The group hesitated and I shrugged.

"It's just the best place for a picture."

Reluctantly, they walked over to the spot and stood in a line. The goats looked at the group, amused by the herd of humans that had come into their territory. Maggie sucked at a black teat. Her adopted mother glanced at us and went back to grazing. I raised the camera to my eye to focus.

As I was studying the shot through my viewfinder I noticed a sound on the uphill slope like someone was approaching with heavy boots. I looked over the top of my camera. The rest of the group followed my gaze.

To our surprise, Marlie stormed from behind a black lava boulder where he had been hiding. Within the feeling of calm and security that had immersed us, my senses were shocked to see him alive on such a beautiful day. But I was not surprised to see that he was walking backward. He stopped in the middle of the pasture. Since he was between me and the group, his back was to the others but he looked right at me, his eyes glaring red under a mound of wrinkles on his forehead.

"So what is this, photo man? You come to recreate the scene of the crime?"

Honestly, I was so blanketed in comfort that I did not feel any need to answer. His little body stood straight up as if he had a wire running through his back.

"I told you that you weren't going to get out of here alive, you jerk. And what are the rest of you doing with him?" he shouted.

Everyone was silent while Marlie waited for the answer to his question. The goats had also become interested in the stupid little sailor. They stopped their foraging and looked at him, thirty sets of black eyes staring at his back. Taking a step backward, I felt my butt touch a large black boulder that was behind me. It was the same rock I had rested against during the storm on the day of the sighting. Little by little, I began to slide down the rough face of the rock, my camera in my hand, my eyes on Marlie. Then I was sitting, my body leaning against the rock.

Believing he had me beaten, Marlie turned his angry attack on the others.

"Where do you think you're going? We are not done around here. We have not properly mourned. We are going down to the dry cave to start a fire and then we are going to have a steam in John's memory. Ron, you are going to haul the rocks and Bill, you are going to fetch the water. Is that clear to you mutineers?"

No one said a word. But the goats were watching and they began to move closer to the action to get a better look. The others glanced at the goats and then they looked at Marlie. The goats moved in closer but Marlie did not see them approaching.

"Well, aren't you idiots going to say something?" Marlie wailed. "You don't think this is over, do you?" he asked. "John is coming back. I saw Him in Koolau's stronghold last night. And when he gets here we better have everything ready. And that means goats over the fire. And no tourists!" Marlie screamed this last order.

Not a sound came from the group. They stared at Marlie's back.

"Did you hear me? John is coming back!" Marlie was hollering although there was no need since he was standing only a half dozen steps from the former followers of The Man.

Suddenly, from the back of the pack of goats, a tiny but brave creature broke through. It was Maggie and she stepped to the front of the herd. Her newborn legs were wobbly. Her eyes, which were seeing their first day of life, gazed at the back of the scruffy screaming human that stood before her. With the naivety that only a being without a past can honestly have, the kid planted its cloven but untested hooves into the ground and made her remark.

"Bah," stated Maggie.

"What?" screamed Marlie spinning around in a circle. "What did you say to me? Are you questioning my authority? I'm telling you, he's coming. Who was that?"

Maggie enjoyed her first declaration so much she went ahead with a follow-up.

"Bah!"

The rest of the goats appeared to be in agreement. One by one, they began to bleat in staccato voices that filled the air. Spinning around again, Marlie looked at the herd of offending animals and picked out the kid who was in front and appeared to be leading the rebellion.

"Listen here you little bone headed, weak kneed, blabbering, leather bound shish kabob. I have had about enough of your backtalk. If you're not careful, I'm going to come over there and wring your neck. You'll have an advance ticket to the front of the line for the sacrifice."

Considering the odds, this was the wrong thing for Marlie to say. The goats had learned their lesson. They not only stood firm, they looked at each other and quickly made a decision. Lowering their noses to the ground, the herd snorted in unison, dug their hooves into the red dirt, and began to charge. All except Maggie, who stood in place taking it all in. At the very last moment, she made her final commentary.

"Bah!"

The goats chased Marlie to the exact spot where his mentor had spent his final moments preaching the gospel of always looking back and never, ever forgetting. The others had to split into two groups to let Marlie run backward through their ranks while their heads rotated on their shoulders. They watched the chase but it didn't last long. In ten leaping steps, Marlie was over the edge and sailing through the air, head first toward the water.

The group ran to the rim of the cliff and looked down to where the ocean crashed against the rocks. They got there just in time to see Marlie hit the water at the top of a huge wave. They watched as he came to the surface and began to swim for his life. They watched as Marlie made it to the boulder-strewn beach near the river where he stood on the rocks waving his fist at the black cliff where the others looked down at him amazed. It was at this point, I was told later, that the group noticed I was not with them.

"Where is Peter?" Bill asked.

They looked over to where I had last been seen. There, at the base of the rock where I had slid for convenience, I was lying in an unconscious heap. They ran over to me, and Bill, who got there first, shook me by my shoulders. Caren leaned down and peered into my eyes, which were now open.

"Peter?"

"What happened?" I asked.

My question confused them because they did not know if I meant it.

"Are you alright?" Caren took my hand.

"I think I fell asleep."

There was a brief pause.

"I was dreaming," I added.

Silence dropped on the group like a curtain at the end of a play. It was several seconds before anyone else spoke.

"You were dreaming?" Judy asked.

"Yes, I was dreaming."

The others moved back to allow Caren to move in closer to me. She was holding both of my hands now. Her nose was only a few inches from mine.

"What were you dreaming about, Peter?" Caren asked quietly in a nurturing and concerned voice.

Her eyes were like two still pools of quiet water and were so close to mine that I could have fallen into them. My own eyes began to fill with tears and the answer choked in my throat as I spoke one perfect word.

"Peace."

There was only silence. Caren squinted and looked deep into my soul. Her eyes began to fill with tears of their own. We would have both started sobbing except at that very moment, the sound of footsteps on the trail made us all look up.

"Did we make it?" It was a familiar voice and as we turned to see who it was, the voice cackled with laughter.

Walking up the trail were Chick and Jeff, their faces splashed with the all too familiar grin.

"I told you we went the wrong way." Jeff was laughing hard. They were both enjoying a comedy routine to which none of us were privy.

Standing slowly, I wiped off the butt of my jeans and walked over to the two pranksters. I stood in front of them without saying a word, which prompted the story from their wandering minds.

"Hey, we made it to some river last night and we got halfway across. We decided to rest and do a little more Lotus to get us through." It was Chick doing the talking.

"We couldn't remember which direction we had come from. The moon had gone down." Jeff looked at Chick and shook his head. "I told you it was the other way."

"You did!" Chick laughed and looked at me. "But we were flying! Know what I mean?"

How could I answer? I looked at the ground and then I looked up at the blue sky, and the valley and the vertical shore in both directions. The palis were lined up against the wide blue water, like black-scaled fish hung in the market. Shaking my head I gave my reply.

"Holy shit."

And for no apparent reason, we all began to laugh.

Afterward

We walked out of Kalalau that day and made it to Hanalei in time for a very decent meal. Michelle and Dennis treated, which I thought was damn kind of them. At the end of the evening they invited Caren and me to come to Berkeley to visit. When we went there a few weeks later, Dennis put me to work taking product shots for their grocery store. Within a month, I was handling all of the graphic work for their marketing department. It was an easy job, something good for a worn out photographer.

Caren and I stayed a couple of weeks on Kauai seeing the island and getting to know each other. We went up to Waimea and over to Polihali but we never saw the Menehune. Still, I am sure they are there, in the forest, waiting to do some good deed.

Those are my recollections. Looking back, I know that something changed inside me, traveling with The Man Who Walked Backward Down The Na Pali Coast.

In the future, I will spend my time, looking forward.